THE DEADLINE

A Cora Baxter Mystery

Jackie Kabler

ACKNOWLEDGEMENTS

When I wrote the acknowledgements for the first novel in the Cora Baxter series, *The Dead Dog Day*, I thanked everyone who'd inspired characters in the book. Consider yourselves all thanked again. Virtually every silly, embarrassing thing that happens to Cora and her friends in my books is drawn from real life and has happened to me or, in some cases, to friends of mine. Thank you for the inspiration, and the giggles. You know who you are.

Since I first – very, very nervously – entered the world of novel writing, I have had the most incredible support from so many wonderful, passionate, talented book bloggers and reviewers. I started to write a full list, but it became ridiculously long and I was also scared of leaving one of you out! But I do want to name just a few: Ana Tomova, who gives me so much time, advice and encouragement; Kim Nash, who has always been so supportive and who organised my first, fabulous blog tour; and Laura Holdsworth, Kirsty Sibley and Joseph Calleja, all of whom to my great astonishment and utter delight mentioned *The Dead Dog Day* in their lists of top reads of 2015. And to all of you who have hosted me on your blogs, been part of my blog tour or reviewed my book, thank you so much. Your kindness and support means more than you will ever know.

Thank you also to all of my followers on Twitter and Facebook – your support is so important to me. A huge thank you too to my scientist friend and former colleague Karen Dillamore who checked my DNA facts in this book. And it's been a while since I covered a murder as a TV reporter, so many thanks also to former police DCI Stuart Gibbon for his advice on current police and court procedures.

And, as always, a massive thank you to my agent Robin Wade and to everyone at Accent Press, in particular my fabulous editor Greg, brilliant Bethan in marketing and Queen Hazel who steers the ship. You rock.

1

Monday 6th May

'You stuck your what to your WHAT?'

Incredulity in her voice, senior producer Samantha Tindall stared at Cora Baxter, who had her jacket on, ready to leave the newsroom after her early morning shift in the studio.

'Errr … my finger. To my handbag.' Cora looked sheepish.

Sam plonked herself down in her chair and ran her fingers through her wavy, caramel-coloured bob, a frown creasing her pretty face.

'OK, you're going to have to explain further. You left the studio between the seven thirty and eight o'clock bulletins and, instead of grabbing a cup of tea and a make-up touch-up like you normally do, you … you glued your finger to your own handbag?'

Cora sat down too. 'Yes, Sam, I did. Accidentally, obviously. That's why I had to keep my right hand out of shot during the eight o'clock news. Because it had a handbag dangling from it. It was quite uncomfortable, as you can imagine …'

'Yes, I bloody well can imagine!' Sam exploded, her exasperation making her sound even more Scottish than usual. 'But *why*? How? What on *earth* were you doing?'

She sounded infuriated, but a grin was creeping across her face. There were sniggers coming from nearby desks

1

now too, as researchers and producers within earshot took a break from working on tomorrow's *Morning Live* show to enjoy the bizarre conversation between their senior producer and newsreader.

Cora grinned too, relieved that Sam was seeing the funny side – that wasn't always the case when it came to Cora's occasional on-air blunders. At work, the breakfast show producer was technically above her in the pecking order, but outside work they were the closest of friends, and it seemed that Sam was in a lenient mood today.

'I was trying to repair my earring. A stone fell out of it when I was putting it on this morning, and I had some of that super-strong glue in my drawer. It fixed the earring brilliantly, but I must have got a bit on my hand without noticing because when I picked up my bag, well ...'

She rubbed ruefully at a red mark on her finger.

'Got it off then, I see.' Sam rolled her eyes.

'Yeah. Sherry in make-up had some solvent stuff. All is well. Sorry.'

'You're such a numpty. Don't worry, I don't think anyone at home would have noticed. Don't think Betsy did either, so I reckon you're safe.'

Cora's pale green eyes followed Sam's towards the glass-walled corner office at the end of the long newsroom, but the door was closed and the blinds down.

'Phew.' Cora smiled. She got on well with Betsy, their relatively new boss, but she was even more passionate than Sam was about the show being perfect – a newsreader going on air with a bag glued to her hand might not go down terribly well.

'Anyway, why haven't you gone home yet? Isn't your shift over?'

'Wanted to see your latest delivery.' Cora leaned across the desk. 'You've got a secret admirer, you've got

2

a secret admirer!' she chanted, then ducked as Sam threw a bread roll at her.

'How old are you, five?'

But Sam was smiling broadly too. She buried her nose in the exquisite bouquet of pink peonies and white roses that had been delivered earlier to the *Morning Live* news desk, then looked again at the typewritten card nestling amongst the fragrant blooms.

'Because you're wonderful.'

'Well, whoever it is, they need a psych test,' she said wryly, then sneezed violently. She pushed the posy aside, fumbled in her pocket for a tissue and blew her nose loudly.

'Hay fever or the newsroom cold?' asked Cora.

Sam shrugged. 'Bit of both probably. Whoever bought these obviously doesn't know that flowers and me don't really go together. Although they are very pretty.'

'Well, if your lovely boyfriend is still insisting it's not him, I think it's rather fabulous to have a mystery man sending you things. Chocolates last week and now flowers. I wouldn't be complaining! And it'll keep Marcus on his toes.'

'True. Although as I told you, I honestly think he's about to propose anyway, keeps hinting ...'

Sam was interrupted by her phone trilling. She grabbed it.

'Sam Tindall. Oh, Greg, finally!'

She gave the thumbs up sign to Cora, who nodded in acknowledgement and stood up. Sam had been trying to get hold of Europe correspondent Greg Winters for the past hour to assign him to a complicated German political story and, knowing how many questions he usually asked, Cora knew it was unlikely to be a brief chat.

She yawned and started gathering her things together,

then picked up the bread roll Sam had tossed at her and lobbed it back across the desk, hitting her friend squarely in the chest. The producer didn't even pause her conversation, simply grimacing and shaking her spare fist at Cora, who laughed and turned away. Then she jumped as Betsy Allan's voice carried across the newsroom.

'If only the public could see the antics of our esteemed newsreader, Miss Baxter. A food fight? With our top producer? What *would* our viewers think?'

Cora blushed, but Betsy was beaming. Relieved, Cora smiled back, and crossed the room to where the programme editor had just emerged from her office, hoping fervently that there'd be no questions about glue or handbags when she got there. Tall and elegant, with an impossibly bouncy, curly, blonde bob, Betsy had been the TV breakfast show's editor for just over nine months, but had been an instant hit with the staff, partly on her own merits and partly because of the stark contrast between her and the show's previous editor, Jeanette Kendrick. The deeply unpopular Jeanette had been murdered about a year and a half ago, and it had taken *Morning Live*'s executive team a while to replace her. In the interim, Sam had stood in as temporary editor, and was now very much Betsy's right-hand woman. The new editor had even introduced serial dater Sam to Marcus, a move which had proved so successful that Sam had finally taken herself off the numerous dating websites she'd frequented for years. Now, just eight months after they'd first met, the couple were in loved-up bliss with Sam convinced a proposal was imminent.

'Sorry, Betsy – just teasing her about another delivery from her mysterious suitor. Flowers today!'

Betsy looked across at the news desk, where Sam was still engrossed in her phone call, and raised her eyebrows.

4

'Popular girl, isn't she! Wonder who's sending them? Poor Marcus is absolutely besotted, you know. I've known him for years, but I've never seen him like this before. It's very sweet.'

Cora nodded. 'She's crazy about him too. I'm delighted for them, I really am.'

'Everything all right with you? Still dating that hunky policeman?'

Cora nodded again, unable to suppress a big grin. 'Yep. And now that I'm in London three days a week on a regular basis, I'm staying at his place instead of in hotels like I used to. It's nice.'

'I bet it is. See you tomorrow Cora, have a nice afternoon – enjoy what's left of the Bank Holiday.'

'You too, Betsy.'

Cora shifted her heavy leather bag onto her shoulder and headed for the door, then stopped as she spotted the fiery red Irish curls of Wendy Heggerty at a desk in the far corner of the room. Along with Sam, the graphics designer was one of her closest friends at work, and the three of them were long overdue a proper night out.

'Oi, Wend!'

Wendy looked up and waved. 'Come over!'

Cora weaved her way between the tightly crammed desks where producers, runners and forward planners were industriously putting together the rest of the week's shows, smirked as she overheard a snippet of conversation about "the new trend for vagina facials" and reached the corner where Wendy was talking through some graphics ideas with the programme's new on-air medical expert, Dr Miranda Evans.

'Women do get nervous about how the menopause will affect them, and I don't want to frighten them, just educate them,' Miranda was saying thoughtfully. 'So I

5

think that's perfect. Thanks, Wendy.'

'That's what I'm here for,' said Wendy, then turned to Cora. 'Hey, you!'

'Hi. Hi, Miranda!'

'Nice to see you, Cora. Got to love working a Bank Holiday, eh! Look – I have another meeting now, but let's have a coffee sometime. Soon?'

'No such thing as a Bank Holiday in breakfast telly land, sadly! But as for that coffee – definitely.'

Cora smiled as the TV doctor marched off. 'She's nice, isn't she?' Cora said, perching on the edge of the doctor's vacated chair.

Wendy nodded. 'She is. I'm still getting to know her, but I like her, and Sam's really pally with her. You OK?'

'Very. But we need a girlie night out, it's been ages. Will you and Sam put some dates together, see if we can organise something in the next couple of weeks? Maybe we should invite Miranda too, if Sam likes her so much?'

'Sounds like a plan. You finished for the day, part-timer?'

Cora punched her friend gently on the arm and stood up again.

'Cheek. It's nearly two o'clock and I've been in since before 4 a.m. And Alice is coming round at four, so I need to run. See you tomorrow, dwarfy.'

'See you, lanky. And give Alice my love. Get her to come out with us too, give her a break from the baby?'

'Good idea. I'll ask her. See ya!'

She headed for the door again and entered the lift lobby, ready to play her usual game of lift lottery, which involved pressing the central call button and then quickly moving to stand in front of one of the three big elevators, crossing her fingers that she'd chosen the right one. It was a silly game she played with herself, but it kept her amused, and now she whooped quietly as the green light came on above the double doors of the left-hand lift, the one she'd chosen to position herself next to today. Her glee was short-lived however, as the doors slid open and she recoiled in fright.

'What the …?'

Instead of a person, emerging from the shiny, mirrored interior of the lift was an enormous polar bear, black eyes gleaming, front paws with long claws held aloft as if about to pounce.

'Only me, don't panic.'

The weathered face of Bob, one of the front-of-house security guards, suddenly appeared under the bear's armpit.

'Bob! You nearly gave me a heart attack! What on earth is that?'

Bob shoved the giant cuddly toy out of the lift and leaned on it, breathing heavily.

'It's bloody heavy, that's what it is. Is it your friend Sam's birthday or something? Second delivery of the day for her, this is.'

Cora stared at the bear, now noticing that a card decorated with small red glittery hearts hung from a pink ribbon around its neck.

'No, it's not her birthday,' she said slowly, reaching out to steady the swinging card and read the single line of text typed on it.

'For somebody bear-y special.'

'Well, someone's very fond of the lass then. Killing my back, this is,' Bob said grumpily, and he grabbed the bear under the armpits again and staggered off towards the newsroom, muttering under his breath about lazy delivery boys who dumped things in reception for him to deal with, even though he was nearly sixty-three and suffering from lumbago.

Cora watched him go, not sure whether to be amused or a little concerned. Not about Bob – he was probably in better health than half of the cigarette-smoking, junk-food-eating, hard-drinking-staff in the newsroom. But all the gifts Sam was getting – that was a bit weird. Flowers *and* a huge and clearly very expensive cuddly toy, on the same day?

Oh well, I'm sure whoever it is will reveal themselves, eventually, she thought, and pressed the lift button again, wishing she had time to hang around to see Sam's face when the latest present appeared at her desk. Anyone who was close to Sam knew she hated soft toys – what on earth would she do with that one?

2

Alice Lomas was laughing so hard that a tiny gobbet of spit had just exploded from her pink, glossy lips and landed on her five-month-old baby's nose.

'Oh Claudia, darling, I'm sorry! What a terrible mummy I am,' she cooed, leaning down to the child's pink designer floor recliner and wiping the offending blob away with the sleeve of her white silk shirt. Claudia gazed up at her mother with enormous, serious, cornflower blue eyes and then smiled a huge, toothless smile. Cora, who was refilling their mugs with Earl Grey, shook her head in amazement.

'Honestly, Alice, I have never known the mother of such a young baby to look so glamorous. You're going to absolutely ruin that shirt, you know that, don't you?'

'Standards, Cora, standards. And I'd be less likely to ruin it if you didn't keep telling me such ridiculous stories! I mean – a giant polar bear? For *Sam*? She will *hate* it!'

Alice snorted again, and Claudia, who was now chewing contentedly on a plastic monkey, looked up at her mother and then at Cora with a resigned expression.

'Even your daughter despairs of you,' Cora said, but there was affection in her voice. She still found it surprising that she and Alice were such good friends – once sworn enemies, their relationship had taken a dramatic turn after Jeanette was murdered. The trauma they had shared during the investigation had brought Cora and Alice together most unexpectedly, and now they even shared a job. Alice, once *Morning Live*'s main newsreader, and now a single mum, was doing just two days a week for now so she could concentrate on motherhood, with Cora covering the remaining three. She loved being in the studio Monday to Wednesday, but also adored the other two days of her working week, which she spent on the road as a roving reporter with her beloved camera crew. She and the three boys had been through a lot together over the years, but no matter how tough things were, they had never stopped laughing, and she knew the four of them would be friends for life. I'm so lucky, thought Cora, as she nibbled on a shortbread biscuit, watching with amusement as Alice dabbed dribble from her baby's chin, this time with an immaculate white muslin cloth embroidered with a large, silver letter C. Claudia's father was a taboo subject, but fortunately the little girl didn't resemble him at all – she was a perfect miniature of her beautiful mother.

'Any idea who Sam's mystery man might be? Bet Marcus isn't very happy about it,' Alice said, leaning back in her chair and tossing her perfectly styled, long blonde hair back over her shoulders.

'I bet.' Cora touched her own straight, brown shoulder-length bob self-consciously. She never felt as well-groomed as Alice. How on earth did the girl manage it? 'He's so in love with Sam. You know she's convinced he's about to pop the question?'

Alice nodded, her vivid blue eyes bright. 'Yes, she said when we caught up last week. So – mystery man? Any ideas?'

Cora shrugged and took another sip of tea.

'Maybe. Remember that guy David, the one she had just started seeing a few weeks before she met Marcus?'

'Vaguely. Worked in IT?'

'That's the one. Well, he was very, very keen on her, a bit over-keen really, considering they'd only had a few dates. She finished with him as soon as Betsy fixed her and Marcus up, and apparently he was quite upset. Rang and texted her repeatedly for a couple of weeks, telling her he was still available if it didn't work out with Marcus. He stopped pretty quickly when she made it clear she wasn't interested, but when I was chatting with her about the mystery gift-sender, he was the only possible she could think of.'

Alice frowned. 'Suppose it could be. Bit odd to start sending her anonymous gifts months later, though. What would be the point?'

'Dunno. Yes, definitely very peculiar. But hopefully if Marcus *does* propose, and they announce it publicly, whoever it is will get the message and stop sending her stuff.'

She grinned suddenly. 'Ooh, Alice, I wonder when he might do it? I haven't been to a wedding in ages, wouldn't it be exciting!'

Alice bounced up and down on her chair. 'Soooo exciting! Hope he hurries up. I could get Claudia the most divine Baby Dior dress, saw it online last night, pale pink jacquard with the cutest butterfly print – ooh, Cora, do you think Sam might ask Claudia to be a bridesmaid?'

'She's five months old! What use would she be as a bridesmaid, you nutter?'

They both laughed, and Claudia, who'd been watching them both closely, suddenly joined in, her deliciously infectious little baby giggles making Cora and Alice hoot even louder. It was with some surprise, a minute later, that Cora realised that her boyfriend Adam had materialised beside them, watching their mild hysteria with an amused expression in his deep green eyes.

'Adam! I didn't hear you come in! You're early.'

'Finally brought charges in that serious assault case, so we wrapped up early, seeing as it's a Bank Holiday. Thought we could celebrate.' He smiled and pulled a bottle of champagne out of the supermarket carrier bag he was holding.

'Definitely! Better pop it in the fridge for a bit though.'

'Will do.' Adam bent down and kissed Cora's lips gently, then leaned over to peck Alice on the cheek.

'Hello, Alice. Looking gorgeous as always.'

Alice smiled demurely. 'Why thank you, officer. And on that note, I shall depart. Madam will need feeding soon. Speak to you later in the week, Cora. Thanks for the tea, and the giggles!'

Cora saw her friend and her baby to the door and waved them off, then returned to the kitchen where Adam had turned on Classic FM and was already chopping vegetables for tonight's stir fry. He winked at her, and she grinned happily back, admiring his skill with the knife. Thank goodness she'd found a man who could cook, she thought for the hundredth time. Cora detested cooking, and was truly dreadful at it when she occasionally attempted anything more complicated than toast, a fact that Adam had quickly learned, but didn't really mind. He found cooking relaxing, an escape from the stresses of his job, and was more than happy to take control of the kitchen. Looking forward to the evening ahead, short though it would have to be due to her 3 a.m. start, Cora stifled a yawn and perched on one of the four swivel stools at the breakfast bar, lazily flicking through her emails on her BlackBerry, enjoying the companionable silence.

She'd met Detective Chief Inspector Adam Bradberry

when he was investigating Jeanette's murder and Cora had been assigned to cover the story for the breakfast show. Their relationship was now almost a year old and blossoming, with Cora now spending Mondays to Wednesdays with Adam in his Shepherd's Bush home while she worked her breakfast news shifts, before returning to her own flat in Gloucestershire for the rest of her working week on the road. Their weekends off were divided between their two places, and Cora couldn't remember a time when she'd been happier. All her friends had said it – Adam was good for her. Always a bit of a party girl, she had calmed down a lot in the past year. Although she still enjoyed a drink, she was now equally happy to stay in with Adam on a Saturday night, nursing a mug of tea and snuggling up in front of the television. She'd even taken up running, finding it cleared her head after a long stressful day at work – stress that she'd formerly handled by collapsing on the sofa with a large Sauvignon Blanc.

Yes, Adam Bradberry was very good for her indeed, she thought now, as she slipped off her stool and moved towards him, wrapping her arms around his broad chest from behind and rubbing her nose on his neck, enjoying his musky scent. Adam paused halfway through chopping a red onion, turned and kissed her forehead.

'Can I help you, Miss Baxter?' he asked softly.

Cora snuggled her face into his neck, her voice muffled.

'I was just wondering – after the yummy meal, and the champagne … do you fancy celebrating your latest crime fighting success story with an early night, perchance?'

'Perchance,' said Adam, 'that sounds like a very excellent idea.'

3

Several hours later, in her flat on a leafy Chiswick street, Sam Tindall was feeling far from contented. The giant polar bear, which she'd grumpily crammed into her car and driven home, was standing in a corner of the living room, its little black eyes glinting in the light from the stainless steel chandelier overhead. She'd been pretty horrified when it had arrived at her desk, but Betsy had refused to let her leave it in the newsroom, and Bob had erupted when she'd suggested she might put the creature in the skip at the side of the building.

'Samantha Tindall, that thing's worth hundreds – I saw similar ones in Harrods at Christmas when I took the grandchildren shopping. Give it to charity if you don't want it. The kids' hospital or something. It's not going in my skip!'

Feeling a little shamefaced, Sam had spent several minutes forcing the enormous toy into the rear of her red Ford Fiesta, and had driven home with one of its paws protruding annoyingly over the back of the passenger seat. Punching said paw every time she stopped at traffic lights meant a little of her exasperation had eased by the time she got to Chiswick, but now, with the usually calm and gentle Marcus standing there glaring at the giant bear, she was feeling increasingly stressed.

'Sam, you *must* have some idea who's sending you all this stuff. He's spending a fortune on you. Nobody does that for a perfect stranger.'

He ran his fingers impatiently through his cropped dark hair, brown eyes narrowed in rare annoyance.

'Marcus, why would I lie to you? I love you. You know that. There is nobody else, I wish it would stop too, it's getting ridiculous now. I don't even like soft toys.'

Marcus shook his head. 'I love you too, Sam. I'm crazy about you. But you need to get to the bottom of this. If we're going to make this, well, more permanent …'

He paused for a moment, and Sam's spirits lifted.

'Then I need to be sure there's no one else, no unfinished business. You understand, don't you?'

'Of course. But I don't know what I can do, I honestly have no idea who's sending it all. You need to trust me, Marcus. Or this is never going to work.'

They stared at each other for a moment, then Marcus turned around abruptly and reached for the jacket he'd slung onto the sofa when he'd arrived fifteen minutes earlier.

'I'm going for a quick walk. Need to clear my head. Can't think properly with that stupid thing looking at me.' He looked at Sam and managed a small smile.

She smiled back, but as the door closed behind him she felt a flash of irritation. She loved the man desperately, but he really was being unfair about this. She genuinely had no idea who was sending the gifts, and she didn't really see why he was making such a big deal about it. It wasn't her fault some saddo had become a bit obsessed with her, and if it didn't bother her, why did it bother him so much?

Cross now, she stomped around the small apartment for a while, tidying away newspapers, opening her post and crossing the room every now and again to kick the polar bear hard. When it was lying on its back on the carpet, paws pathetically clawing the air, she looked at the wall clock and decided she could wait no longer. She picked up her mobile and dialled Marcus's number. Straight to voicemail. Damn it. Was he ignoring her, screening his calls? Sam paused in her pacing, unsure what to do. It was after ten o'clock and he'd been gone for nearly an hour. He was probably either in the park down the road or walking along the river, she reasoned, two of their favourite local spots for a wander. She'd go out, find him, and have it out with him once and for all. This silly argument needed to be settled, and settled tonight. Pulling on one of the several old black hooded fleeces that always hung on the coat stand by the door, Sam grabbed her keys and headed out into the night.

4

Tuesday 7th May

An insistent ringing sound jolted Cora out of a deep sleep. Groaning, she reached out and bashed the big shut-off button on the top of her alarm clock, but the ringing continued unabated.

BRRRING. BRRRING.

She rolled over and nudged Adam in the back.

'Adam! Your phone,' she hissed.

Adam grunted and, eyes still closed, groped around on his bedside table until he located his mobile.

'DCI Bradberry.' His voice was thick with sleep. Cora glanced at the clock. Just before 2 a.m. Whatever this call was about, it was unlikely to be good news. Wide awake now, she listened to Adam's end of the conversation, which consisted largely of 'When?', 'Where?' and then 'On my way.'

He put the phone down and rolled across the bed towards her. 'Sorry, darling. Body's been found in a park. Got to get straight over there.'

Cora made her decision quickly.

'I'll come with you. My alarm will be going off soon anyway and I might as well be the first reporter on the scene – it'll be a good top story for the six o'clock news. I'll call the desk, get the overnight crew to meet me there, then he can drop me back at the studio. OK with you?'

'Fine.' Adam was already up and pulling on his

clothes. 'You've got five minutes.'

Cora leapt out of bed, threw on a light cashmere jumper and jeans and ran to the bathroom to wash her face. Everything else could wait until she got to work, she thought, and she was already at the front door, jacket and bag in hand, when Adam appeared, jangling his car keys.

As they sped through the dark, quiet streets, Cora rang the news desk and gave the night editor the location and few details she had gleaned from Adam – a body, clearly the victim of a violent attack, found in a wooded area of a small park, and reported by a homeless man who often sought shelter there but who tonight had found his sleeping area already occupied. Reassured that the overnight cameraman, Ted, was on his way, Cora sat back and enjoyed the ride, blue lights flashing on Adam's unmarked car.

'Sam lives near here,' she remarked, as they reached the familiar streets of Chiswick.

Adam nodded, intent on reaching his destination, and a minute later he turned the car sharply left, manoeuvring it expertly through a narrow gateway, and cutting the engine. A black sign with white lettering welcomed them to Pope's Meadow and politely requested that dogs be kept on their leads. Two Metropolitan Police cars were already parked on the grass to the right, and just beyond them a long strip of blue and white tape had been tied between two trees, marking the no-go area for civilians.

'Right – duty calls.'

Adam leaned across and pecked Cora on the cheek. 'See you tonight. Have a good day. And stay behind the tape!'

'I know, I know! I have covered a murder once or twice before, you know!'

But he was already out of earshot, marching across the

grass to flash his ID at the police constable guarding the tape, and then disappearing into the darkness towards a clump of trees about a hundred metres away where a spotlight had been erected, bathing the area in an eerie yellow-green light. Nearby, the swing in a small children's play area creaked softly as it moved back and forth in the light breeze, and even in the semi-darkness Cora could see that the hedges around the edges of the park were neatly clipped, the flower beds well maintained. A park which by day, no doubt, was full of Chiswick's well-heeled parents and their happily shrieking children, with lunching office workers, joggers and dog walkers, was now a murder scene.

Grim, thought Cora, and then spotting Ted already setting up his camera next to one of the marked cars, she pulled on her jacket and went over to brief him as fully as she could. Then, leaving him to shoot his pictures, she looked around for someone to interview. In a little huddle of police officers to her left, she spotted a bedraggled man of around fifty, in a filthy duffel coat, grimy-looking jeans and tatty trainers. The homeless man, who had called in the murder? Cora edged closer until she could hear the conversation, the man's voice urgent and guttural.

'Head stoved in, stoved right in. So much blood. Blood everywhere. Right there, where I usually sleep. Nice and dry it is, in there. Good shelter. Can't ever go back there now, can I? 'Orrible, it was. Gonna give me nightmares for ever. Been on these streets for years and never saw nothin' like that. It's a nice area, round 'ere. 'Orrible. Bleedin' 'orrible, mate.'

The man sounded genuinely horrified, and Cora shivered slightly, despite the mildness of the early morning. She stood quietly, listening to the soothing voice of the female officer asking the scared man more

21

questions – had he seen anyone else in the area, anyone acting strangely, had he touched anything at the scene? The man answered no to everything and, sensing the interview was winding up, Cora gestured to Ted, hoping they might be able to get a few words on tape before the police released the witness and he vanished.

But as her cameraman approached, tripod on his shoulder and camera in hand, Cora turned to see Adam striding towards her. Even in the pre-dawn light she could see that his face was white and tense, and her stomach suddenly flipped. Something was wrong.

He grabbed her arm, moving her away from the group of officers.

'Cora … I don't know how to tell you this, so I'm just going to have to say it.'

She stared at him with frightened eyes. 'What? Say what?'

'Cora, it's – it's Marcus.'

She carried on staring, unable to quite grasp what he meant.

'What is? What's Marcus?'

'The body, Cora. The victim. The murder victim. It's Sam's boyfriend, Marcus.'

5

'Adam ... look at this. Murder weapon?'

Adam turned to see Ray, one of the white-suited
scenes of crime officers, approaching, a long object
grasped carefully between gloved fingers.

'It was in the bushes, just over there, a few metres
from the trees. Stuffed in pretty deep, so we didn't see it
on the first sweep this morning.' Ray gestured with his
head as Adam moved closer to inspect the find.

'What is it?'

'A bit of park railing. There's a broken section just
along there ...' he gestured with his head again, 'and
there's a few bits scattered around in the grass. Look –
clearly blood, and hair, on this end. I'll bet on my
grandmother's life that this is what killed the poor
bugger ...' He paused. 'Well, my grandmother's dead, but
if she weren't, I would, if you get my drift.'

Adam patted the SOCO on the shoulder. 'I get your
drift, Ray. And yes, good work, that's probably it.
Excellent. Bag it and let's get it in as soon as possible.'

Ray bobbed his head and headed off towards the police
van parked on the grass just inside the cordon, and Adam
shivered, pulling his collar up around his ears and wishing
he'd worn a warmer jacket. The relatively warm early
morning had been followed by a damp and increasingly
grey afternoon and now, as evening drew near, a biting
wind had sprung up, as if to remind those getting
complacent about the recent unseasonably balmy May

23

weather that this was actually still Britain.

Feeling in need of coffee, and confident that the SOCOs were now close to having gathered everything they could from the scene, Adam squelched across the grass, mud sucking at his shoes, to where he could see two of his colleagues standing next to the open boot of one of the cars and pouring something from a large silver thermos flask.

'Enough for me?' he asked, and the two young detective constables smiled and nodded. Gary Gilbert and Karen Lloyd had both worked with Adam on the Jeanette Kendrick investigation, and he was pleased to have them on his team again. Both were likely to pass their sergeant's exams soon, they were both savvy detectives with an excellent work ethic – and with a murder as close to home as this, he needed good people around him, Adam thought grimly. He wondered, not for the first time, if he really should be senior investigating officer on this one. But there were so many murder investigations running on his patch at the moment that his bosses had asked him to stay on the case for now, arguing that although he knew the victim they hadn't been particularly close, and that there was simply nobody else with his experience available.

'Looks like we might have the murder weapon then, boss?' said Gary, handing Adam a mug and then reaching into a cardboard box in the boot for a plastic-wrapped sandwich. He offered it to Adam, who shook his head.

'I hope so.'

'How was the girlfriend, when you saw her? Somebody said you know her?' Karen took a sip of her steaming coffee, and grimaced.

'That's revolting. So – do you? Know her?'

Adam took a mouthful of coffee from his own chipped

white mug and swallowed with a shudder. Karen was right, it was foul.

'I do. Pretty well, actually – she's one of my girlfriend's best friends. I knew him too – the victim – not as well though. But we'd been out to dinner a couple of times, the four of us. He was a nice bloke.'

Karen sighed. 'Well, somebody didn't think so. Or didn't care. Pretty brutal attack to cause a head injury like that.'

Adam nodded. The post-mortem examination had yet to be carried out, but there had been little doubt about what had killed poor Marcus. His skull had been virtually cracked in half. It had been a fact Adam had avoided telling Sam when he'd gone round to her flat this morning to break the terrible news. Telling people about the death of a loved one truly was one of the very worst parts of his job, but when it was somebody you knew …

Adam rubbed his eyes and shivered again. At least Cora was with her now. Poor Sam.

'Somebody tell me this isn't real. Please, please tell me it isn't real. Please …'

Sam, her eyes red and swollen, looked desperately around the room, then sank her head into the cushion she was gripping between white-knuckled hands and sobbed. Wanting to bawl herself, Cora put an arm around her friend's shaking shoulders and hugged her close, feeling utterly helpless. She looked with anguished eyes at Alice and Wendy, who were sitting on the sofa opposite, both with tears rolling down their cheeks. Sam was right – this just couldn't be real, could it? Marcus, the man with whom their friend had finally found happiness, brutally murdered in a park? It made no sense. He had been such a nice, sweet man. Who on earth would want to kill him?

25

'Oh Sam, darling. We're so sorry. So, so sorry. Can we do anything? Have you eaten? What about some tea?'

Sam lifted her face from the cushion, pushed her hair back off her forehead and smiled a tiny, crooked, tear-stained smile.

'If I have another cup of tea today, my internal organs will start floating,' she said. 'I'd already had a cuppa in bed, as it was my day off, and then after Adam came to … to tell me …'

Her voice shook, but she took a deep breath and continued. 'There were just so many people. Every few minutes, new people. My mum's away in Scotland, but she was on the phone every ten minutes seeing if I was OK. And then police, family liaison, even a vicar at one point I think … I don't even know who they all were. But they all made tea. Endless, non-stop, tea. My FLO offered me tea eleven times, I counted. So, no more tea. Thank you, though.'

She reached out an unsteady hand and squeezed Cora's knee, and Cora put her own hand on top of her friend's reassuringly, unable to suppress a smile. Sam was right – family liaison officer Detective Sergeant Anna Watkinson, a gentle woman in her early forties with long, already greying hair swept into a severe bun, had indeed seemed almost comically obsessed by tea.

'In fact,' Sam continued, 'What I actually need right now is a wee. Can you imagine, the queue for my single solitary loo, with all those people drinking all that tea?' She stood up. 'I nearly did a Peter Ryan, I got so desperate at one point.'

She gestured at the wastepaper bin under the coffee table as she headed out of the room, and they all smiled, relieved by the brief moment of levity. The Peter Ryan story was legendary among the *Morning Live* camera crews. A big problem with broadcasting live on location at antisocial hours was that there was never anywhere to go to the toilet. Little wonder then that Peter, a satellite engineer, had once been caught using the little swing bin in his van, out of sheer desperation – 'and not just for a wee', Scott Edson, Cora's own regular satellite engineer, had told her darkly.

There was the sound of flushing from down the hallway and moments later Sam reappeared, wiping damp hands on her jumper. She sat back down next to Cora with a sigh. The girls had been at her flat for several hours, but the interminable stream of visitors had meant this was the first chance they'd had to actually sit down with her, just the four of them. Betsy, shocked and clearly very upset at the news about her friend Marcus, had let Cora and Wendy leave the newsroom before lunch, and they'd phoned Alice on the way to Sam's to tell her what was going on, with the result that an hour later she too was on the doorstep, brandishing a box of raspberry macaroons and a tin of lemon biscuits from the artisan food shop on the corner.

'I didn't know what to bring!' she'd hissed in a despairing voice. 'What's appropriate, when somebody's been murdered?' The confused expression on her face had raised another of the day's few smiles among Sam and the others. They had grown very fond of Alice indeed, but she really did have some ditsy moments.

Now, they all sat in the living room, the giant polar bear still languishing on his back on the carpet in the corner, Sam and Cora together on one of the blue suede sofas with its colourful stripy scatter cushions, Alice and Wendy on the matching sofa opposite. On the floor, in her recliner, baby Claudia cooed and chatted to herself and the little pink teddy she was clutching in her plump fingers, oblivious to the shock and sadness that hung like a thick haze over the usually cheerful room.

'So – do you want to talk about it, Sam? Tell us what happened last night?' Cora's voice was gentle.

Sam nodded slowly.

'I don't know. I mean, nothing happened really, not here. We had a row, nothing major, just a silly row about the stupid bloody polar bear and the other presents. Marcus was really pissed off. I don't think he believed me, that I don't know who's sending them. But I don't, honestly. I haven't a clue.'

Wendy leaned forwards, red curls swinging, her face earnest. 'Well, we believe you.'

Sam pulled a tissue from the box on the coffee table and blew her nose. 'Thanks. Anyway, he went out. Said he needed to clear his head, go for a walk. This was about nine o'clock. I didn't think he'd be long, so I just banged about a bit – I was quite cross too, to be honest, and I half expected him back any minute, really. But then it got to around ten and there was still no sign of him, and he didn't reply when I tried calling, so I went out after him. I figured he'd go along the river, or to the park, so I had a quick look, in the bits we usually go to. But it was dark, and he wasn't there that I could see. So I just came back here. I thought – well, I hoped – that he might be here, waiting for me ...'

Her voice cracked and tears sprang once more from her puffy eyes. Cora put her arm round her friend's slim shoulders again, stroking her wavy bob, as her body shook with huge, gasping sobs. Alice and Wendy sat tense and stiff, the crying paralysing them, the room otherwise totally silent except for the rhythmic ticking of the big metal clock over the fireplace and Claudia's soft babbling. Finally, Sam calmed herself enough to speak again.

'But he didn't come back. So I assumed he'd gone home in a huff. He still wasn't answering his mobile or anything, and after a few more tries I just gave up. I was really angry by then … I mean, what an overreaction to something so silly, a few mystery presents! That's what I thought. I thought he'd be round here today, apologising. But he won't, will he? He'll never be here again. Oh Cora, I can't bear it! How can I bear it?'

A howl like a distressed animal's escaped her, and the tears came again, her weeping loud and agonised. Feeling powerless to ease her friend's pain, Cora simply rubbed Sam's back as she doubled over, face buried in her cushion. Claudia, her attention finally drawn away from her soft toy, turned anxious eyes towards Sam and started to whimper, and Alice, wiping fresh tears from her own eyes, picked her baby up and held her close. Wendy, head bowed and eyes closed, was crying too. What an absolutely horrific day, Cora thought.

It was several minutes before Sam slowly sat up straight again, pushing her damp hair back off her face and reaching for yet another tissue.

'I'm sorry,' she said softly. 'I'll get myself together in a minute. I must look a wreck.'

'Don't be silly, you're fine.' Alice smiled a watery smile, and then they all jumped as the doorbell rang.

'I'll get it.' Glad of something to do, Cora ran out to the narrow hallway off the open-plan living area and opened the front door. Two people stood there, one a tall, handsome black man in a new-looking brown leather jacket, the other a small, blonde white woman, both holding up police ID cards. Cora gave the warrant cards a cursory glance and nodded, sighing inwardly. Here we go again, she thought. Poor Sam.

'Detective Inspector Glenn Arnold and Detective

Constable Helen Jones. Just wondering if we could have a quick word with Miss Tindall?' the male officer said. His voice was warm and friendly.

'Of course. Come through.' Cora, who had recognised his name and realised that he was Adam's number two in this investigation, led the pair into the living room, where Wendy had switched seats and was now sitting next to Sam, stroking her arm.

'Sam – two police officers to see you.'

Sam wiped her eyes fiercely with both fists, like a small child, then stood up slowly, as if she was aching all over.

'Hello,' she said quietly. 'Any – any news? Do you know what happened yet? To – to Marcus?'

Glenn Arnold shook his head. 'Not yet, I'm afraid. We're looking at every possibility – maybe a mugging that went too far, maybe some crazy off his head on drugs – it's going to take us a while to sort through the evidence, look at any CCTV footage and so on. But as soon as we can tell you something, anything, we will. Your FLO will be back in the morning.'

He paused, and looked down at his colleague. There was at least a foot of height difference between them. She nodded, a sympathetic look on her freckled face, then turned to Sam.

'I know this has been a terrible day for you, and we promise to leave you alone for the evening after this, but ...'

She stopped, as if unwilling to complete the sentence, then sighed gently and continued.

'Look, this is obviously just routine, but we need to get a sample of your fingerprints and DNA, if that's OK? Just for elimination purposes.'

She spoke in a strong Welsh accent, the syllables of

'elimination' rising and falling like music.

'The DNA's just a cheek scraping. It'll only take a few seconds.' She pulled a notebook and a plastic bag out of the pocket of her dark, masculine-looking overcoat and waved them vaguely in the air. 'Just because – well, you're his girlfriend, so clearly there may well be traces of your DNA on his body, or his clothes …'

Her voice tailed off, and Cora felt a pang of sympathy. This couldn't be easy for the police officers involved either. She glanced at Sam, afraid that the request might reduce her to tears once more, but to her relief her friend was crossing the room, nodding.

'Of course, I understand,' she said. 'What do I have to do?'

'It's easy. If you could just sign here first?' She held out the notebook and a pen, and Sam obliged. Helen Jones smiled and put the plastic bag on the small oak dining table to her left, then shook the contents out onto the polished wood. She pulled on a pair of cream latex gloves, then picked up a long, clear packet and ripped it open, removing a swab with a small, bulbous cotton end.

'I just need to rub this – well, two of them actually – on the inside of your mouth. Your cheek, under your tongue and behind your lips. Is that all right?'

In reply, Sam simply opened her mouth wide and, with a deeply grateful expression on her face, the policewoman deftly wiped each side with a separate swab, then quickly inserted both into individual test-tube shaped containers and pressed lids onto them.

'Thank you. Really appreciate it.' She smiled at Sam warmly, then bent to scribble some notes on a white form.

'And now, some quick fingerprints?' That job too swiftly completed, the two police officers nodded their gratitude.

31

'Thanks for your co-operation,' Glenn Arnold said, looking around the room at each of them in turn, an even-toothed white smile lighting up his face as he spotted the baby, who was now back in her recliner on the floor, clutching her favourite plastic monkey and cooing softly.

'Beautiful baby. Got one about the same age myself – six months?' He looked questioningly at both Wendy and Alice, clearly unsure about who the mother was.

'Five months – but she's quite big for her age.' Alice caressed Claudia's soft hair proudly.

'Beautiful,' the officer said again, then turned to where the constable was tidying her kit back into the plastic bag. 'Ready?'

'Ready. Thanks again – somebody will be in touch soon.'

'Thank you. I'll see you out.' Sam headed for the door, the two officers in her wake, and Cora sank down onto the sofa next to Alice, suddenly exhausted.

'What a hideous, horrible, vile day.' She closed her eyes, feeling a desperate need to be cuddled up on Adam's sofa, his arms around her. Unlikely tonight though, she knew. She had no idea when he'd be home, but it would probably be long after she'd succumbed to sleep.

'Horrendous,' Alice agreed sadly. She patted Cora's hand briefly, then stood up.

'Do you know what we need? Wine. Wine, and pizza. What do you think? Or would that be, I don't know, inappropriate?' She frowned, uncertainty in her blue eyes.

Wendy, who'd been slouched in a depressed-looking heap on the sofa opposite, eyes closed, suddenly sat up straight.

'I don't think wine is ever inappropriate. And we still have to eat, no matter what's happened. Sounds good to

32

me. But only if Sam's up for it, obviously.'

'Wine and pizza? Did I hear that properly?' Sam was back in the room, pale and somehow looking thinner than yesterday, but wearing an interested expression on her face.

'Could you?' Alice sounded wary.

'I could, actually – I don't think I've eaten a thing all day. Plus that swab tasted foul. Wine would be medicinal, right? I'll get the glasses. Cora – wine, fridge. Alice – pizza delivery company number on the corkboard by the front door. Wendy – mind the baby.'

And duly assigned by their senior producer, and suddenly all feeling a tiny bit better, they did as they were told.

6

Thursday 9th May

'The DNA results should be here in a few minutes. It's taking anything from three days upwards at the moment normally but they got a wiggle on for us. Told me we'd have them by ten.'

DC Gary Gilbert straightened his slightly bobbly navy sweater with a satisfied tug and turned to the whiteboard where, at Adam's request, he was about to sum up what was known so far about Marcus Williams' murder. He picked up the paper cup of coffee that was perched precariously on the ledge where the marker pens lived, took a long swallow and then looked around for somewhere safer to sit it, settling on a towering pile of green files on the closest desk. Then he turned to the room.

'Everyone ready?' he said.

'Should be in about one minute, Gary.' Adam finished the email he was writing and hit send, then looked around the room in the west London police station that was his base for this case, taking in the faded pale grey paint, stained blue carpet and battered chairs and desks, about two-thirds of them occupied by members of his team. The usual occupants of the empty desks were already out of the office, assigned to various tasks including checking CCTV and further house-to-house enquiries along Marcus's likely route, as well as at homes around the park itself. Through the row of windows along one wall, shabby cream blinds all hanging at different levels, the morning looked as grey as the walls inside, and as Adam's mood. Once the lab report was in though, things might speed up significantly, and he hoped fervently that this would be the case and that the DNA they already knew had been found at the scene would be a match to some low-life thug already on the National DNA Database. Comprising millions of DNA profiles, it was one of the largest of its kind in the world, and a powerful asset for those trying to solve crimes.

As well as holding daily briefings himself, Adam often asked members of his murder investigation team to summarise 'what we know' for him – he found it helped him to think, to clarify the case in his head. He also knew it helped to build the confidence of the less-experienced detectives, many of whom dreaded speaking in front of a room full of hard-nosed older cops. It had certainly worked on Gary, who was markedly more self-assured now than he had been even a few months ago. Adam stood up and leaned against the edge of his desk, nursing his own coffee cup, and turned to the whiteboard, grimacing slightly as he saw yet again the bloodied, distorted face of poor Marcus, this time in half a dozen colour photos spread across the top of the board. Below them were rows of neatly written notes, Gary adding something with a red pen before turning back to the group and clearing his throat loudly. The twenty or so officers in the room slowly stopped typing, scribbling notes and discussing ideas with their colleagues and turned to face him, with the exception of two who were on the phone. Both gestured to him that they'd only be a minute and continued their calls in hushed voices. Gary cleared his throat again and began.

'Right.' He pointed to one of the crime scene photos. 'Marcus Williams, thirty-two years old, project manager for a marketing agency located just off Regent Street. On Monday night, that's the Bank Holiday, the sixth of May, he was visiting his girlfriend Samantha Tindall at her flat in Chiswick. She's thirty, and they'd been dating for about eight months. She's a TV news producer, bit of a hot-shot. All going well, by all accounts ... in fact, marriage had already been hinted at, according to Miss Tindall, and that's backed up by comments from some of his friends and family, and their work colleagues. Sounds like they were pretty smitten with each other. In fact, everyone we've spoken to so far says he was very happy – relationship and job going well, no money problems, no drug or alcohol issues, not known to the police, just a normal, nice guy. Popular. Friendly. Had it together.'

He paused. 'So – the night he died, there's a bit of an argument with the girlfriend. Nothing major, she says. She'd had a few mystery presents – flowers, chocolates and a huge stuffed polar bear. She said it was possible they were coming from an ex-boyfriend but she really wasn't sure. We've tried to trace who sent those, in case they ended up being relevant – they all came via a small florist shop called *Blooming Lovely*, near Waterloo, not far from TV Centre. Well, we hit a major snag there. On Tuesday night they had a fire in the back room, where all the sales records were kept, and everything from the past three years was destroyed. It's an independent, so no centralised records anywhere. Hence, boss, we can't find out who sent those gifts.'

'That's a bit of a coincidence,' said Adam. 'How did the fire start?'

'Chip shop next door – something blew. Seems genuine, just bad luck for us. I spoke to the florist – he remembered the bear, being so recent and so … well, so *big*. But he said he was pretty sure it was a telephone order, he never met the sender, and he couldn't remember a thing about them.'

'Great. OK, never mind. Go on.' Adam took a sip of coffee.

'Right. Anyway, Marcus wasn't too happy about the gifts that night – it was the day the bear arrived. They had a few cross words, and he went out for a walk to clear his head. This was at approximately 9 p.m. Around 10 o'clock, the girlfriend got concerned. He wasn't answering his phone, so she goes out to look for him, guesses he's probably in the park or walking by the river. She wanders around for a while, but it's dark and she feels a bit unsafe out there on her own, so she gives up and comes home. Tries his mobile a few more times, nothing. Presumes he's gone home in a huff, gives up and goes to bed. Hears nothing more until you arrive on her doorstep the next morning, boss.'

Adam nodded slowly, remembering the horror on Sam's face as he'd gently broken the news. Gary reached for his coffee, took another gulp and replaced it on the pile of files, which swayed perilously. He turned back to the board.

'The body was called in by a rough sleeper, Andrew Lane. He's fifty-four, and an alcoholic, but seemingly harmless – no previous, not even a parking ticket. Used to be a painter and decorator but the booze got in the way. His wife left him, he couldn't make the rent, the usual story. Uses hostels around west London but quite enjoys sleeping out when the weather's good, and had made this little patch of trees in Pope's Meadow park his own …'

He pointed at another of the crime scene pictures.

'He's been drinking with his friends down by the river, decides to bed down, gets back to the park around midnight and stumbles right into the body. It's just at the edge of the little copse of trees, not far in at all but if you were just walking through the park with a dog or something you probably wouldn't have seen it in the dark, those few trees would have blocked your view.' He tapped the picture again.

'He's shocked, runs straight out on to the road, flags down a car and asks them to call the police – he doesn't have a phone of his own. He waits there until we arrive, tells us all he knows which isn't much. We'll see when we get the lab results, but he says he didn't touch the body and we're not really looking at him as a suspect right now.'

Gary moved to his right, pointing to another photo, this one a gruesome close-up.

'Post-mortem indicates time of death to be between 10 and 11 p.m. The pathologist says she can be fairly certain of that – he was pretty sheltered where he was lying, and it wasn't a cold night so she was able to judge it pretty accurately from his liver temperature. I'll talk about CCTV footage in a moment, but first, the murder weapon.'

He tapped a photo showing the bloodied section of park railing. 'As suspected, looks like this is it. The head injury on the victim is consistent with the shape and size of this, and his blood and hair is all over it. Looks like he was only struck once, but it was either a skilled attacker or a lucky blow, because it killed him pretty much straight away.'

'Hence, possibly not a pre-planned killing,' Adam interrupted. 'The killer just grabbed whatever was to

39

hand – in this case a lump of metal lying in the grass?'

'Looks like it, yes.' Gary stared at the board again. 'OK, forensics. The holy grail – the lab's initial report says there were traces of somebody else's DNA on the murder weapon. No decent fingerprints sadly, any on the weapon were messed up by all that blood. But still, the DNA is all we need. We're just waiting for the full analysis, which we should get shortly … say your prayers.' There was a murmur of heartfelt agreement from the room.

'As for motive, we're struggling. As I said, nice guy, no issues that we can find at this stage. Not a mugging – his wallet, phone, everything was still on him. So maybe a crackhead taking a swing at him for no reason, or something else we don't know about yet.'

He rubbed his nose. 'House-to-house hasn't turned up anything of any use … there are houses nearby, but nobody saw or heard anything out of the ordinary. Would have been a quick killing though, with very little noise, so that's maybe not that surprising. There are one or two persons of interest on the CCTV footage though, and I'll show you that in a minute, just trying to get this file to load …'

PING. Adam jumped as the email alert on his computer sounded. He really needed to find out how to lower the volume on the stupid thing, he thought, as he returned to his chair and opened the message. It was from the forensics lab.

'Guys! DNA results are in.' Every head turned.

'Give it to us, boss. Is there a match?' Gary looked up from his monitor, eyes bright.

'Hang on.' Adam flicked his eyes down the screen, looking for the single line of information that would either elicit a resigned groan from the team or send them into a frenzy of activity. And then he read it, and froze. What? That couldn't be right, could it? He read it again.

'Holy shit,' he said.

7

'I can't believe you've come in. Honestly Sam, you should be at home, resting or something.'

Cora looked at her friend with an expression which was a cross between affection and exasperation.

'I'm not tired. And if I'm at home, I'm just sitting there *thinking* about it all, Cora.' Sam paused and frowned. 'Why are you here on a Thursday anyway? Shouldn't you be on the road?'

'Alice is off all week, remember? I'll be back to my usual pattern from Monday. And stop trying to change the subject. You shouldn't be here!'

Sam sighed. 'Oh come on, give me a break. You understand, don't you, Betsy? Please, I need to be doing something.'

Betsy, who had just joined the huddle around Sam at the news desk with Cora, Wendy, Dr Miranda, three producers and a couple of runners, sighed. The senior producer had arrived unannounced in the newsroom ten minutes ago, despite officially being on compassionate leave, and nobody was particularly surprised. It would take a lot more than the mere murder of a loved one to keep Sam away from her post for long.

'OK, if you really want to. But not until Monday, all right? At least take the rest of this week off for goodness sake. Deal?'

'Deal.' Sam smiled a satisfied smile, but she looked dreadful, Cora thought. Her usually shiny hair was lank,

43

her pretty face marred by dark shadows under her still puffy eyes.

'Good decision. Grief is hard on the body. You need to rest,' said Miranda.

'Yes, doc.'

Sam grinned, and Cora turned to Miranda and smiled too, then noticed that the TV doctor looked pretty tired herself, her long brown hair tied back in a messy pony tail, striking grey eyes bleary. *Morning Live* newbie syndrome, Cora diagnosed. The hours were a killer even when you'd been here for years, but those new to the lifestyle often looked dead on their feet for the first few months. Miranda should be coping better than most though, really – having been a medical student was surely about as good a grounding for breakfast television shifts as it was possible to get.

Recruiting the young doctor had been one of the first changes Betsy had made when she had taken over as editor, letting the show's long-serving, sixty-year-old resident male doctor go and taking on thirty-year-old pretty brunette Miranda as health correspondent instead. There'd been a lot of unease about the move at the time, but several months on everyone agreed the new boss had been right. Dr Rob had been a grumpy old sod, dispensing vaguely decent medical advice from the *Morning Live* sofa but with very little charm. The six million viewers had quickly taken his replacement to their hearts, and while Cora still hadn't spent enough time with Miranda to get to know her properly, she seemed like a sweet girl who hadn't let her sudden transformation from West London GP to media personality go to her head. Plus, Sam and Miranda had hit it off from day one, which was a good sign. If Sam liked her, Cora knew she would too.

'Right, well if I'm being sent home, I'll need

sustenance for the journey. Fancy a cuppa, Cora? Wendy? Have you got time?'

Sam looked hopefully from one to the other.

Cora and Wendy both feigned indecision for a moment, then smiled.

'Of course. Only if you eat something too though. They had some divine raspberry brownies earlier,' said Cora.

'OK. You've twisted my arm.'

Sam stood up and reached out to give Betsy a hug.

'See you on Monday. And thanks,' she said quietly. Betsy nodded, eyes full of compassion. 'And thank you, to all of you, for all the messages and phone calls. I really appreciate it.'

There was a chorus of 'don't mention it' and 'the least we can do' from the group, and Sam spent another minute squeezing sympathetic hands and accepting further hugs before finally turning to Cora and Wendy, her eyes suddenly shiny with tears.

'Everyone's being so nice. I'm not sure I can cope. Can you two insult me for half an hour over this cuppa? Make me feel normal?'

Her friends laughed. 'No problem whatsoever, Sam!' said Wendy, grabbing her blue leather backpack from where she'd dumped it on the desk.

Cora fumbled in her own bag for her purse. 'Let's go.'

They were almost at the door that led downstairs to the canteen when a sudden commotion at the other end of the newsroom made all three turn around simultaneously. To Cora's surprise, Adam was striding towards them, flanked by two other men she vaguely recognised as detective constables he regularly worked with.

'Adam! What are you doing here?' Her smile faded as she saw the serious expression on his face. He glanced at her, but then turned and fixed his gaze on Sam.

'Sam – this is very difficult.' He stopped, ran a hand across his blond cropped hair, something he often did when he was nervous, then looked at Cora again and back at Sam.

'What is? Have you found out what … what happened?' Sam's voice was barely a whisper.

Adam took a deep breath. 'Samantha Tindall, I am arresting you for the murder of Marcus Williams. You do not have to say anything …'

'WHAT?' Cora and Wendy shouted the word as one. Sam looked stunned.

'… but it may harm your defence if you do not mention when questioned something which you later rely on in court. Anything you do say may be given in evidence. Do you understand?'

Sam, white-faced, stared at him. Cora grabbed his arm, turning him to look at her.

'Adam – what the hell? What are you doing? Have you gone stark raving mad?'

Adam shook her off gently. He was almost as pale as Sam.

'Not now, Cora. I'll talk to you later, OK? Sam – do you understand?'

Sam, seemingly struck mute, nodded bleakly. Adam turned to the officer on his left.

'OK,' he said. Stepping forward, the two detectives each took one of Sam's arms and began to guide her towards the door, across a newsroom which had suddenly fallen eerily silent. One of the producers who moments ago had been hugging Sam was standing literally open-mouthed, gaping as she was led past him. Another, incongruously wearing a T-shirt emblazoned with the logo 'Happy Day', had her hands clasped over her mouth as if to stop herself crying out. Miranda stood stock still, staring, a dumbfounded expression on her face. At every desk appalled eyes followed the three police officers, unable to comprehend what they were seeing, exchanging horrified glances. As the group reached Betsy's office, where she stood wide-eyed in the doorway, Adam paused and said something to her, and she nodded. Moments later, the three men and their charge disappeared out of the door. As it swung shut behind them, the silence became a torrent of noise.

'What the HELL?'

'What's happening? What do they think they're doing?'

'Sam? Not Sam! That is LUDICROUS!'

Cora and Wendy looked at each other, bewildered and dismayed.

'Cora – what on earth?'

Cora shook her head. 'I don't know, Wendy. I really don't. But believe me, I'm going to find out.'

8

Betsy, her knees suddenly feeling weak, stepped into her office, shut the door and sank down onto the black leather sofa she'd recently had installed along the side wall so staff meetings could be conducted in a little more comfort. DCI Adam Bradberry had just told her, in their brief exchange as Sam was led away, that he would need to carry out interviews with her and a number of other staff members who were close to the senior producer, and she'd nodded her agreement. Now, a sudden wave of nausea swept over her, and she lay back and shut her eyes, willing the feeling to go away, breathing deeply, aware that her hands were shaking and her skin was clammy. She was still trying to shake off the cold that had been sweeping the newsroom in recent weeks, that was all, she told herself. She was fine. After a few moments she opened her eyes again, her gaze taking in the bright room with its big windows on two sides, the fresh flowers she always kept on her desk, the 1970s newspaper front pages she'd had framed for her wall. One was about the Watergate scandal; another showed a harrowing photo from the genocide in Cambodia; and yet another announced the death of Elvis Presley. It was headlines like these which, as a child, had sparked in her a desire to be a journalist, to have a front row seat as these events unfolded, and she had achieved her dreams, travelling the world as a reporter for the BBC and CNN, winning awards and loving every minute.

And now, her latest challenge, editing what was now Europe's highest-rated morning news show, had brought her fresh joy, a new sense of fulfilment as she strove to drive the ratings even higher and mentor the young reporters in whom she saw so much of herself. She had changed the show too, made it her own, no longer covering so many of the silly, frivolous stories the programme had previously been known for, giving it a harder edge. It had been a tricky change to make at first, resisted by some of the staff, but now everyone was starting to see how much better the show was, how successful. This job was made for her, perfect for this stage of her life. A sudden wave of fear rolled over her. Could she be about to lose it, lose it all? No. NO. Stop this. Her breathing steadied. No. She was *not* going to lose this job. She could handle this. There was nothing to worry about. The police wouldn't cause any problems for her. Nothing at all to get stressed about.

Betsy looked at her watch and stood up. She was due in a planning meeting in two minutes. She walked to her desk, swallowed the last of a now tepid cup of camomile tea, straightened her navy pencil skirt and marched out into the newsroom.

'We've reserved interview room one. The doc gave her the all clear, no issues there, no need for a formal psych assessment. And her solicitor is on his way so we should be able to start questioning her in about an hour, boss.'

Adam looked up at the genial face of DI Glenn Arnold. He still felt slightly shaky after the deeply unpleasant experience of having to arrest somebody he knew and liked very much, and wished for the hundredth time that he could pass the senior investigating officer role in this particular case to somebody else. He had at least managed to hand over the job of questioning Sam to two colleagues, DI Arnold and DC Helen Jones, two detectives he trusted and who he knew would do a good job. But, right at this moment, he would have been quite happy to be just about anywhere else in the world. The next few days were *not* going to be easy.

'Great. Want to do a quick recap on what we've got on her?'

'Please.' Glenn sat down heavily in the empty chair next to Adam's and wheeled it a little closer to his boss's. Then he pulled a blue hard-backed notebook from his jacket pocket.

'Shoot,' he said.

Adam turned to his own notes. 'Right, well the DNA evidence you know about.'

He hesitated, still unable to quite believe what he had read on the report from the lab. He'd called them immediately when he'd received the email, asking if they were sure, if there could be any mistake, but the three members of staff he'd spoken to were all adamant. There was no mistake. Their findings were correct, and the DNA was a perfect match.

'So – a DNA match to Samantha Tindall's on the murder weapon, and on the victim's body.' He paused again. This was horrendous. He dreaded the conversation he'd have to have with Cora later. How on earth was she going to deal with this?

He dragged his thoughts back to the matter in hand. 'OK, so the body element doesn't mean much because obviously she was his girlfriend, so that could have been transferred at any time. But on the weapon? Fairly conclusive really. Looks bad for her, I'm afraid. CPS will probably give us the go-ahead to charge her on that piece of evidence alone.'

Glenn nodded slowly. 'She's on the CCTV footage too. Right place, right time.'

Adam turned to his computer monitor and clicked his mouse a few times, trying to locate the video file Gary had forwarded to him after the morning briefing.

'Want to see it again?'

Glenn nodded. Adam hit play and they both leaned forward as the grainy images filled the screen. There weren't any cameras in the park itself, but they had a good shot of the road that ran alongside it, and of the entrance gate. Adam fast-forwarded the footage until the clock on the top right hand corner showed 9.47 p.m., and then pressed play again.

'Right. That is Marcus Williams. Enters the park now. Doesn't come out again, sadly, for obvious reasons. Between then and 10.16 p.m., only three other people go in – all a few minutes apart, all dog walkers. One clearly a man, coming from the direction facing this camera. Has a big dog, possibly a Labrador. He's only in there for about two minutes. The other two, sex indeterminate, as they're both in trousers and we can't see their faces because they're walking in the other direction. The first spends about five minutes in the park before emerging, the second a bit longer, about fifteen minutes. They both have smaller dogs – the first one looks like a miniature poodle, the second is even tinier, probably one of those irritating ratty little things.'

Glenn grinned. He shared Adam's dislike of small, yappy dogs.

'Appeal gone out to trace them yet?' he asked.

'Yes, the press office are sending the footage to all the news channels as we speak. Should make the evening news programmes and the papers tomorrow. We urgently need to find these three, see if they saw anything, because

Marcus was definitely in the park at the same time they were. But I'm not really thinking of them as suspects, Glenn. They had all left by the time Sam arrived in the park, and as she's now chief suspect ...'

Adam sighed heavily. He felt slightly sick. How could it be that Sam, Cora's lovely, clever, fun friend, was currently in one of his cells awaiting questioning for this horrific murder? A woman whose previous record comprised one parking ticket, and a single speeding fine more than ten years ago? It felt impossible, but the evidence didn't lie. He fast-forwarded again, watching as all three dog walkers emerged one by one from the park. Then, at 10.18 p.m., she appeared – Sam, in what looked like a dark hooded jacket, walking briskly down the street in the direction facing the CCTV camera and turning into the park entrance.

'Definitely her?' asked Glenn.

Adam nodded. 'Yes. Clear image of her face. Definitely her. And to be fair, she *did* tell us on day one that she had gone to the park to look for Marcus sometime after ten.'

He zoomed the footage forwards again. 'She wasn't in there long – about four minutes, look. But that's plenty long enough to bash someone over the head. And when she re-emerges, she's walking quickly. Very quickly. Almost running.'

Glenn watched closely as Sam, hood still up, moved swiftly down the road and disappeared out of sight of the camera.

'She said in her initial statement that she'd felt nervous, looking for Marcus on her own in the dark, so decided to go home. Her brief will say that's all we're seeing in that footage – a woman who's just had a quick scoot round a park looking for somebody, and is now rushing to get home to safety.'

'Yes, and her brief will also say that somebody else, some potential killer, could easily have got into the park another way – that's the only gate, but someone could easily scale the fence or hop over a hedge if they wanted to. So yes, all this footage does is place her in the park at the right time. But that, plus the DNA ...'

His voice tailed off. Glenn gave him a sympathetic glance. 'Know it's not easy for you, this one. Sorry.'

Adam managed a small smile. 'No, not easy.'

He turned back to the screen. 'Anyway, for what it's worth, not another soul enters the park by the main gate until 11.57 p.m. when Andrew Lane, the rough sleeper, arrives. He comes running out a couple of minutes later, flags down a car and, well, we know the rest.'

'What about earlier?'

'We've gone back through the footage as far as three hours before Marcus arrived. Everyone who went in via the main gate came out again.'

Glenn flicked over a page in his notebook. 'Still waiting for the phone records?'

'Yes. Should have both the victim's and suspect's by mid-morning tomorrow.'

'Good.' Glenn snapped his book shut. 'Let's do this then.'

Adam watched him leave and then, suddenly overcome with a feeling close to despair, sank his head into his hands. Moments later he jumped as his mobile phone rang loudly. He pulled it out of his pocket and looked at the display. It was Cora.

9

Friday 10th May

'So – how does it work then, Cora? Come over and show us – looks quite simple?'

Cora slipped from her newsreader's chair and crossed the studio, treading carefully to avoid the thick camera cables which snaked along the shiny cream floor. Reaching the big red sofa, on which were perched *Morning Live*'s two main presenters, Jane and Jeremy, she squatted down next to the glass coffee table and turned to camera two.

'It's really simple, yes,' she said, and reached out to angle the 3D printer that was sitting on the table, helping the camera to get a clearer shot. Betsy's new, more serious show policy was relaxed somewhat on a Friday, when the 8 a.m. news always ended with a story about the latest, wacky gadget, and this printer which could easily and cheaply print three-dimensional objects for you in your own home was today's choice. If the programme planners could manage it, they always got a sample of the item for Cora to do a quick demonstration of at the end of the news, a task which always filled her with dread. She could just about handle her laptop, BlackBerry and Twitter account, but she really wasn't terribly talented when it came to technology.

She took a deep breath. 'So – it's quite a retro design really, for something so high-tech. It's quite a nice combination. There's an easy on-off switch here, look …'

She pointed. 'And then, there's a big knob here in the middle, and you just turn it to the relevant …'

'BIG KNOB? COULDN'T YOU FIND AN ALTERNATIVE TO BIG KNOB? DID YOU REALLY JUST SAY THAT? ON LIVE TV? AT 8 O'CLOCK IN THE FRIGGING MORNING?'

Cora froze, horrified, as the incredulous voice of Anthony, that morning's senior show producer, bellowed out of her earpiece. Oh, shit. Shit, shit, shit. But it *was* a knob. What was another word for knob, for goodness' sake? Feeling utterly panicked, she wracked her exhausted brain, and came up with nothing.

'So, you er … you twist the, erm, the …'

'BLOODY HELL. PLEASE DO *NOT* SAY KNOB AGAIN,' Anthony hollered even more loudly, almost deafening her. She winced.

'Well, you just, er, turn it to the setting you want and then press go and, well, that's it really …' Cora stuttered to a halt and turned back to Jane and Jeremy.

His kind face creased with barely suppressed mirth, Jeremy cleared his throat and nodded, seemingly unable to speak. Jane, who was biting her lower lip and staring fixedly at her notes on the table, swallowed hard and looked up.

'So – really easy then. Just switch it on, turn the *dial* to whatever you want to print, and hey presto. Fabulous, thanks as always, Cora.' She turned to camera three. 'Right – coming up in ten minutes, just why did this French couple have a horse called Derek as bridesmaid at their wedding? But first, a quick look through the morning papers …'

Cora sat motionless for a moment, waiting for the giggling floor manager to indicate that she was clear to leave, then crept back to the news desk, wishing the floor would open up and swallow her. Dial, she thought. *Dial.* Yep, that would have been a more appropriate word. A *lot* more appropriate. Twitching her computer mouse to wake up the screen and check the running order for her next bulletin, Cora hoped fervently that Betsy had not been watching the programme on the monitor in her office at that particular moment, then sighed and decided not to get stressed about it. There were, after all, so many other, more important things to worry about right now. No wonder her brain was scrambled and spewing out double entendres this morning. She'd probably only snatched about an hour's sleep last night, and even that was disturbed and restless.

She stared at her screen, not really seeing it, her thoughts filled with Sam. The idea of her friend spending last night in a police cell was just too horrible to contemplate, and Cora desperately wanted to go and see her, bring her some fresh clothes, tell her everything was going to be all right. But was it? Adam and Cora had always been careful to keep their relationship separate from their work – as a reporter and police officer, it was almost inevitable that their professional paths would cross, and Cora was very aware that there were rules about what Adam could and could not tell her about his cases, and tried to behave accordingly. But this was different – it was *Sam*, for goodness' sake – and last night her usual restraint had gone out the window, and she had begged and badgered Adam until he had finally cracked and divulged just enough to make it clear that things were not looking good at all. Looking absolutely terrible, in fact.

'I shouldn't be telling you this, Cora, and you're not to breathe a word to anyone else, OK?' he'd said, and she'd nodded impatiently, desperate to find out what was going on.

'Right, well – actually, the truth is that Sam already knows this, so when you do eventually get to talk to her I'm sure she'll tell you anyway ... the reason it's looking so bad for her, why there seems so little doubt that anyone else could be responsible, is that we found her DNA at the scene. Including on the murder weapon, which was a bit of broken park railing.'

Stunned, Cora had simply stared at him. He sat down heavily on the sofa next to her and, face grey with exhaustion, sunk his head into his hands.

'DNA? Sam's DNA? That's not possible, Adam. It just can't be right! They've made a mistake.'

He looked up again, dark green eyes bloodshot. 'Trust me, I checked and double-checked. No mistake. It's hers all right.'

'But ... but *why*? Why on earth would she kill Marcus? She *loved* him, Adam. She wanted to marry him! It makes no sense, there's no motive. Surely you can see that? I mean, maybe ... maybe she picked up that bit of park railing another time, when she was walking in the park or something, and her DNA got on it that way? Maybe ... '

Adam shook his head slowly. 'All the evidence was fresh, Cora. It all ties in with the time of death. Look, I know it seems impossible and unbelievable and all of those things. But if this job has taught me one thing, it's that sometimes good people do bad things – inexplicable, spur of the moment, totally out of character bad things. I don't want this to be true any more than you do, but at the moment, it's looking like it might be. I'm going to do everything I can, and I love you, and I'm so sorry, but ...'

He'd held out his arms, and Cora, tears suddenly

running down her cheeks, had willingly accepted his embrace. But after they'd gone to bed, she'd lain awake for hours, thoughts racing. This couldn't be real – there would be some explanation, there had to be. There was no way Sam was a killer, no matter what the DNA evidence said. The two of them had bonded instantly when Cora had started working at *Morning Live*, finding in each other the same ambition, the same sense of humour and the same wry way of looking at life. In the past four years they had become incredibly close friends, and Sam could no more murder somebody than Cora herself could, she was convinced of that. No, it wasn't possible. She had covered enough crime stories in her career to know a bit about DNA, and she was very aware that the chances of two unrelated people having identical DNA profiles was something like less than one in a billion. So there *must* be a mistake, a mix-up. Adam would sort it out. He had to. Clinging on to that belief, she'd finally dozed off. And now, cheeks still burning from her studio faux pas, she told herself the same thing.

'Adam will sort it out. Keep strong, Sam. We'll get to the bottom of this. Adam will fix it.'

'Her clothes are clean. But we only have her word that that's what she was wearing on the night of the murder. She had plenty of time to dispose of the outfit she was really wearing. She's a clever girl – if there was blood on her clothes, she'd know to get rid.'

Detective Constable Gary Gilbert pushed the sheet of paper with the latest report from the forensics laboratory across the table. Adam nodded. Sam's flat had been searched yesterday and her clothes seized, but no blood or anything else incriminating had been found. She'd told officers that when she'd gone out to look for Marcus she'd been wearing black leggings, which were now in her wash basket, and a black fleece she'd grabbed from the coat stand next to the front door. The CCTV footage appeared to back up her statement, and they had found three pairs of black leggings in the dirty washing, and four black fleeces on the coat stand, all of which had gone straight to the lab. Forensics had come up with nothing significant on any of the garments but, as Gary had pointed out, that meant nothing. Sam wasn't necessarily telling the truth, and could indeed have easily thrown out the actual clothes she was wearing – there had been plenty of time for her to do that between the night of the murder and her arrest a few days later.

'Phone calls?' Adam asked the question with a heavy heart. He really did not want to be involved in this investigation for a minute longer.

'They all tally with what she told us. One call to the victim's mobile just after 10 p.m., when she says she was trying to get hold of him to see where he was. Then a further four calls between 10.50 and 11.15, when she says she was back at home and still trying to track him down. Those calls are a bit of a problem for us, possibly. Why was she still calling him if she'd just bopped him over the head in the park and left him for dead?'

It was true, Adam thought. One little piece of evidence that actually went in Sam's favour.

'Agreed,' he said. 'But she *could* have made those calls to throw us off track. That's what the prosecution will say. She's clever, as we've said. She comes home in a panic after murdering her boyfriend and thinks that if she makes a few calls to his phone, that will make it look as if she thinks he's still alive. It's the only bit that doesn't fit, and when you stack that up against all the evidence that she *did* do it, it's not a lot.'

Adam sighed. Sam had looked him straight in the eyes after her arrest, and told him she hadn't killed Marcus. But the evidence ... he was trying so hard to be totally impartial, but it was so difficult. He had to get off this case, and soon, he thought, picking up his lukewarm mug of coffee and taking a deep gulp.

'Yep, I reckon we have enough, boss. Shame those dog walkers didn't have much to add though – has the third come forward yet?'

'Not yet. Pretty impressed that the first two got in touch so quickly actually. The power of the media, eh?'

The first of the three people seen entering the park with dogs had contacted the incident room last night, minutes after the footage had appeared on *News at Ten*. The forty-year-old man had explained that he'd made a two-minute circuit with his chocolate Labrador – which he said was slightly obsessed with squirrels and which 'wouldn't listen' when told they would all be asleep at that time of night – and then left again, once he'd proved the doubting dog wrong. He'd told the officer who took his call that he vaguely recalled seeing a man who might fit Marcus's description sitting on a bench, but saw nothing untoward.

The second, a nurse in her twenties, had called in this morning, after seeing the CCTV picture featuring herself and her poodle in the morning paper. She apologetically said that she'd taken a call from her boyfriend on her mobile phone just as she'd entered the park, and had been so engrossed in conversation for the five minutes she was there that she hadn't actually noticed anybody or anything.

The third person, who'd spent around fifteen minutes in the park with his or her small 'rat' dog, had not yet come forward, but Adam wasn't overly concerned, suspecting whoever it was would have little to add to the investigation either. He leaned back in his chair and stared at the ceiling for a long moment, then rocked forwards again and slapped both hands firmly onto the desk in front of him.

'I can't put it off any longer, can I, Gary?'

Gary shook his head. 'Don't think so, boss. Sorry.'

Adam nodded. 'Right. Let's see what the CPS make of it. Maybe they'll make a decision today.'

If the Crown Prosecution Service reviewed the evidence today and decided there was enough to charge Sam with murder, she'd appear in magistrates' court in the morning. He shuddered slightly at the thought. Cora was not going to like this one little bit.

10

Saturday 11th May

'I can't stand it. Look at her, Wendy. How can this be happening?'

On the press bench of London's Barwick magistrates' court, Cora grasped Wendy's hand as Sam appeared in the dock. Dressed in a faded blue sweatshirt, her hair unkempt and with no visible make-up, she was barely recognisable as the slick, stylish, pulled-together producer they knew so well and loved so much. As she sat down, Sam looked across the packed courtroom to the press area, and the expression of despair and fear in her dark eyes was almost too much for Cora to bear. She let out a tiny sob, and Wendy squeezed her hand even more tightly.

'This is a nightmare. How could the CPS decide there was enough evidence to charge her? It's insane. We're going to get her out of this, Cora. We have to. She *didn't* do it,' hissed Wendy.

'Court rise.' There was a sudden rustling and shuffling as everyone stood. The public gallery was full of curious onlookers, some who used courtrooms as a regular source of entertainment and gossip, others possibly just sheltering from the rain on this damp May day. And, unsurprisingly, despite it being a Saturday morning, the press bench was packed, with another half dozen or so reporters who had arrived too late to get seats standing near the door, notebooks and pens poised. At national

63

level reporters, whether TV, radio or print, got to know each other well over the years, meeting often as they covered the same stories, and Cora knew almost everyone here. She'd spoken briefly to several as they'd waited outside before the hearing, and most had seemed genuinely upset that one of their own was appearing in court on such a serious charge. But even so, a story was a story, and despite her grief, Cora knew this was a big one. A senior producer on a top-rated show like *Morning Live*, charged with battering her boyfriend to death in a park? It would be front page news. Cora knew it, and Sam would know it too, and the prospect of those front pages tomorrow must be compounding her friend's agony, she thought, as everyone sat down again and she glanced back at the dock.

'Will the defendant please rise?'

Sam stood, haunted gaze crossing the courtroom again and pausing for a long moment on the public gallery before she fixed her eyes on the three magistrates on the bench. Cora stared at the crammed seats, wondering who her friend had been looking at. Then she spotted her, in the middle of the second row – a short, dumpy woman in a yellow coat, dark hair plastered to her head as if she'd been caught in a shower just before entering the courtroom, and clutching a handkerchief to her mouth. It was Ellen Tindall, Sam's mother. Cora had met her a couple of times over the years, just very briefly, once when the woman had been visiting Sam's flat and again when she had popped in to meet her daughter after work one evening. Sam was an only child and her dad had died when she was in her early teens – she and her mum were close, and Cora could only imagine the anguish poor Ellen was now going through.

Sam was speaking now, confirming her name and

address, her voice uncharacteristically quiet. Now the prosecution lawyer, briefly outlining the case and recommending that the defendant be remanded in custody, and the defence lawyer announcing that an application for bail would be made. It was then the turn of the lead magistrate, a man in his sixties with a sharp pointy chin and heavy spectacles, who told Sam that her case was too serious to be dealt with at magistrate level, and that it would be passed to the Crown Court for trial. Sam nodded, bowing her head. Nothing unexpected here – they all knew the procedure.

Minutes later, it was all over, Cora and Wendy desperately trying to signal their support as Sam looked at them again before being led back down the stairs and vanishing. Her first Crown Court hearing, when her application for bail would be heard, would be on Tuesday, followed by the plea and case management hearing which had been fixed for just under seven weeks' time, on the twenty-eighth of June. Cora knew she had already indicated that that plea would be not guilty, of course.

'Then they'll set a trial date, which will probably be a few months after that – maybe around September,' she explained to Wendy as they made their way slowly out of the courtroom, jostled by the other reporters who were eager to file their copy or do their live radio and TV broadcasts as soon as possible. *Morning Live* had sent a cameraman to get a few shots, with Betsy acknowledging that the story would have to be covered by the breakfast show whether a staff member was involved or not. But by Monday, it would merit just a twenty-second piece in the round-up of the weekend's news. Even so, Cora was already dreading having to read it out on air.

'What about bail? Will she get it, when she goes to the Crown Court on Tuesday? They can't keep her in prison, surely? It's all just so … so scary and horrible.'

Wendy, who as a TV graphics designer wasn't used to attending court cases, looked pale and shocked. She stopped walking suddenly, sinking down onto one of the hard plastic benches that lined the corridor. Cora sat down next to her, eyes scanning the faces walking past them. She wanted to catch Sam's mother, but she'd lost sight of her in the crush at the courtroom door.

'I don't think she will get bail, not in a case like this. Adam says she's already been told by her solicitor that the application's unlikely to succeed. But I'm going to try and speak to her as soon as possible, Wendy. See how she's doing, and see if there's anything, anything at all we can do to get her out of this. There must be something, something she hasn't told the police. Adam says he can't believe she's guilty either, but that DNA evidence …'

'I know. But it has to be a mistake, doesn't it Cora?' Wendy's pale blue eyes fixed pleadingly on Cora's, begging for reassurance.

'Of course it does.' Cora wished she felt as confident as she sounded. Only identical twins had the same DNA – although in fact, even *they* had very minor differences on extremely detailed analysis, as she had learned recently while interviewing a fertility expert for a story on multiple births. With Sam being an only child though, the chances of her DNA profile matching somebody else's were zero. So how on earth did her DNA end up at the crime scene? Cora wasn't remotely surprised that the Crown Prosecution Service was happy to proceed with the case, given the evidence, but surely, *surely* there was some mistake?

'Ellen!' Wendy suddenly jumped up, pointing down the corridor. Ellen Tindall was shuffling down the hall towards them, her yellow coat flapping open, a large red

66

shopping bag clutched in one hand. She still held her
tissue in the other, and was now dabbing her eyes. She
looked dreadful, eyes sunken and swollen as if she'd been
crying non-stop for days. She probably had, poor woman,
thought Cora.

'Mrs Tindall! Are you OK? We are so, so sorry.'
Wendy, who had known her for much longer and who had
even spent a weekend away in Scotland with her and Sam
last year, had reached her first, and enveloped her in a
hug. Ellen let out a huge sob.

'Oh, Wendy. My darling Sam. What's going to happen
to her?'

She buried her face in Wendy's shoulder for a
moment, her damp, matted dark hair mingling with
Wendy's fiery red curls. Then she released herself,
noticing Cora standing awkwardly nearby.

'And Cora, how lovely to see you, dear.'

Cora reached out and touched the older woman's arm.
'Hello, Mrs Tindall. I wish we were meeting in better
circumstances ...' Her voice tailed off.

Ellen wiped her eyes again and nodded. 'This is a right
sorry mess, isn't it? But my Sam isn't a murderer. You
both know that, don't you? Her lawyer will sort this out,
won't he?'

Cora and Wendy looked at each other and back at
Ellen. 'I'm sure he'll do everything he can, Mrs Tindall,'
Cora said.

'Of course he will. She'll be out in no time, and back
to causing havoc with you two.' Ellen smiled a watery
smile. 'And now, I have to rush. My bus is in five
minutes. Lovely to see you, girls. Keep ... keep in touch,
won't you? In case you hear anything I don't? I know you
often get information first, in that newsroom of yours ...'

She fumbled in her bag and pulled out a small printed

card, thrusting it into Cora's hand. 'My address, and phone number. And when Sam gets out, you must both come round for tea. To celebrate? I'll make a cake. Sam loves my Victoria sponge.'

Cora slipped the card into her handbag and smiled. 'Of course, that would be lovely.'

Wendy grabbed the older woman again, planting a kiss on her tear-stained cheek. 'You take care, Mrs T.'

Ellen nodded, and then she was gone, swallowed up in a fresh wave of bodies which had just emerged from the courtroom down the hallway.

'That poor, poor woman.' Wendy's eyes had filled with tears.

'I know. Come on, let's get out of here.' Cora took her friend's arm and they walked as quickly as they could towards the exit, weaving through the crowded corridors, both lost in thought.

11

Thursday 16th May

Cora sighed heavily and aimed a petulant kick at the massive trunk of the fallen oak tree which was blocking the main road into the Berkshire village of Little Hook. Nathan Nesbit, her on-the-road cameraman since she'd started reporting for *Morning Live*, pushed his dark floppy hair out of his eyes and grinned.

'Cora, kicking it isn't going to help. It's at least six feet thick. Do as the nice producer told you and start climbing. Rodney's dressed as a lumberjack today so he might give you a leg up, if you ask him nicely.'

Soundman Rodney Woodhall, who was crouched on the road nearby fiddling with his mixer, sniggered. He was indeed wearing trousers that closely resembled the red and black check shirt of a Canadian lumberjack, and Cora wondered for the millionth time where on earth he found some of his clothes. Notorious within the company for his unique fashion sense, he had today chosen to team the vividly hued pants with a bright blue fleece jacket with pink trim, underneath which was visible a lime green T-shirt.

'Actually, correction,' Nathan added, 'He's dressed as a parrot, *glued* to a lumberjack. Excellent look, Rodders.'

'Shut up.' Rodney straightened up and walked over to the fallen tree.

'Want a leg up then, Cora?' Cora glared at him, then at

Nathan, and then at the tree. They'd been called out in the early hours after reports had reached the overnight news desk that a Berkshire village had been completely cut off by an unexpectedly violent storm overnight. Now, at just after 5 a.m., the sun was slowly rising on a beautifully calm day – but the reports had been correct. There were only two roads in to the tiny village, which had a population of just two hundred and ten people, and this one was entirely blocked. The other, they'd been reliably informed by a grumpy on-call Environment Agency press officer half an hour ago, was currently flooded, so there was no access from that end either.

'This is ridiculous.' Cora gazed at the enormous tree lying on its side across the narrow roadway, branches soaring above her into the air, roots baldly exposed. The high walls of a country estate along both sides of the road meant trying to get round the obstruction wasn't an option either, but a call to the *Morning Live* newsroom to explain that they couldn't get into the village and therefore wouldn't be able to get any residents to interview for the 6 a.m. news had been greeted with derision.

'Cora, it's simple,' Anthony the stand-in senior producer had snapped. 'Climb over the tree, walk into the village, knock on some doors, get some people out of bed, bring them back over to the tree and interview them. It's hardly brain surgery. And do it yourself. The crew need to be setting up for the broadcast. If you don't get back in time, at least they can feed us some live pictures from the scene.'

'Bring back Sam,' Cora had muttered as she'd ended the call. Now she sighed again, gritted her teeth, put a tentative foot on a branch and looked over her shoulder at Rodney. 'Right, I'm going in. Come on, give me that leg-up.'

70

The soundman pushed his little, round glasses higher on his nose and obliged. Swearing under her breath and wishing she hadn't worn her favourite Hobbs red wool pea coat, which no doubt would be snagged to bits on the jagged branches, she started to climb.

'Good luck, Cora! We'll be having a nice cuppa in the truck if we're not here when you get back!' Nathan and Rodney's giggles followed her as she disappeared over the top of the trunk, cursing again as a twig poked her in the ear. She loved her camera crew, but bloody hell, they were irritating at times.

Two hours later, she was snug in the satellite truck, mug of steaming Earl Grey in hand. She'd struck lucky when she'd arrived in the village, grumpily picking pieces of stick and bark out of her hair – even at that early hour, there had already been a little cluster of worried locals outside on the village green, discussing their predicament and pondering how they were going to get to work that morning. Three hardy souls had been happy to scale the fallen tree with her and had provided excellent live interviews for both the six and seven o'clock bulletins, fortified during the hour in-between by coffee and Jaffa cakes from satellite engineer Scott Edson's seemingly bottomless supply in the truck. Now, with just a quick live piece from Cora alone scheduled for the eight o'clock news, and nearly an hour to kill before that, the thoughts of her and the boys had inevitably turned to Sam. As predicted, her application for bail made at the Crown Court earlier that week had been denied, and she would now remain in custody until her plea and case management hearing at the end of June.

'It was nasty, seeing her on the front page of every paper on Sunday,' Scott pronounced morosely in his broad Bolton brogue. 'Her little face …'

He rubbed his shiny shaved head, and Cora nodded, shifting uncomfortably in her seat. She was fairly certain there was a bit of twig in her bra.

'It was just awful. At least now that she's been charged, reporting restrictions have kicked in. There won't be any more coverage until her next court appearance.'

'That's a relief.' Rodney unzipped his jacket, revealing more of the lime green T-shirt, on the front of which they could now see a pink and blue owl, its outline picked out with delicate embroidery. Nathan raised an eyebrow, but for once refrained from commenting. He took a loud slurp of his tea and turned to Cora.

'So, what do you think, Cora? Did she do it?'

Rodney and Scott turned to look at her too.

'Yes, did she? I mean, I can't imagine Sam hurting anyone, but ...' Rodney's brow crinkled with apprehension.

Cora shrugged. 'They'd argued earlier that evening, she was in the park where he was found at the right time, and her DNA was on the murder weapon, all of which is hard to argue with. I know that as well as you do, and I totally understand why she's been charged, and I totally get why people might think the police must have the right suspect in custody. But she says she didn't do it, and I believe her, guys. It's as simple as that.'

Cora had finally managed to speak to Sam on the phone on Tuesday night, after a couple of days of waiting to get her phone number approved by the prison. Her friend had been devastated by her failure to be released on bail and desperate to talk, the words spilling out of her in such a breathless jumble that Cora had several times been forced to gently tell her to slow down and breathe.

'I denied it, over and over and over again, all through

72

the police questioning. I kept asking *them* questions too, which they didn't like very much, mainly about what possible motive they thought I had for killing a man I loved so much and was hoping to marry,' Sam had said, her voice cracking with emotion.

'They seem to think it was a sort of crime of passion – they kept trying to get me to say that we had an argument that got out of hand, that I just flipped and attacked him. My solicitor was brilliant, pointed out all sorts of stuff in my defence – that anyone could have got into that park out of sight of the CCTV cameras, and killed him, and then hopped out again over a hedge or something, unseen by anyone. And he asked them why on earth I would carry on phoning Marcus when I got home if it had been me that had just murdered him. *And* pointed out that there was no sign of any blood or anything in the flat, and that I willingly gave a DNA and fingerprint sample, with no hesitation, which I'd have been unlikely to do if I'd killed someone. If I was about to be unmasked as a murderer, would I really behave like that? But it made no difference, Cora. They believe I did it, and that's that.'

'Well, I don't think you did. None of us do, Sam, OK? But it's the DNA evidence that's so damning. It *has* to be a mix-up, a mistake, of course, but ...'

'No, not a mix-up. Not necessarily. I've been thinking about this, Cora, thinking about this non-stop, and we both know how unlikely a lab mix-up is. Maybe it *was* my DNA.'

Cora had been stunned. 'What? What do you mean? On his clothes or body, yes, probably. But on the murder weapon ...?'

Sam's voice was matter of fact. 'You may think I'm crazy, and heaven knows this *sounds* crazy, even to me. But what if I was framed, Cora? Come on, there's enough

73

stuff on TV now about DNA, shows like CSI and all that. People know you can get DNA from hair, from saliva, from all sorts of things. It can be done easily enough …'

'But – who? Who would want to frame you? I don't mean to sound dubious Sam, but surely a forensics mix-up is a lot more plausible? Framing someone for murder only happens in books and on telly, surely? Not in real life?'

Sam had sighed down the phone. 'I know, I know. But it's *possible*, Cora. And if Adam and everyone else is insisting the DNA evidence is accurate, and it really is mine, then it's the only answer, isn't it? And it *could* be done …'

'How? How could anyone get hold of your DNA?'

'Well, from a tissue for example. I've been sneezing for weeks, haven't I – anyone in the newsroom could have grabbed one of my used tissues from the bin and stashed it away to help frame me. Not that I'm blaming anyone at work, but I'm just saying. And I've been thinking – David, maybe? My ex, the IT guy, the one who I suspect might be behind the mystery gifts? If he *has* been sending me all that stuff, and is therefore clearly a little deranged, he could be mad enough to kill Marcus and frame me, couldn't he? And I had a cold at around the time I was seeing him, I clearly remember snuffling all over him one night and him commenting and asking me if I needed a hot toddy or anything. I mean, I know that was months ago, and I don't know how long DNA lasts on a tissue, but you hear stories about police using DNA evidence from years and years ago, don't you …?'

She stopped, breathless again. On the other end of the line, Cora was silent for a long moment, thinking. Sam sounded quite manic, and was clearly clutching at straws, but could there be something in her theory?

'OK, so let's consider this for a minute. Wouldn't *their*

DNA be at the scene too – the person who killed Marcus and then framed you for it, assuming someone did?'

'Not if they were careful. Gloves and all that.'

Cora nodded, unseen. It was feasible, she supposed. Not every murder scene had DNA evidence, after all. But seriously, somebody *framing* Sam – surely not?

'OK.' She tried to keep the scepticism out of her voice. 'But it's just that someone would have to really hate you, Sam, to do that. Surely not even your jilted ex hates you that much?'

'Cora, I don't know. All I know is that I didn't do it, therefore somebody else did. And if my DNA was at the scene, then I can't think of any other explanation. Can you? Am I crazy, seriously?'

Cora took a deep breath. It sounded crazy, yes. But on the other hand, she had absolute faith in her friend's innocence. So …

'OK. OK, Sam, leave it with me. I'll talk to Adam, see if he'll look into it.'

Even as she reassured her friend, Cora felt she already knew what her boyfriend's reaction might be. But true to her word, she *had* spoken to Adam, just half an hour later. He was in Cambridge, working on another case for a few days, and his reaction to Sam's 'I was framed' theory was predictably incredulous.

'Cora, I know she's your friend, and you want to help her, and I'm pretty horrified by the way this has turned out too. But the investigation was over before it begun – it was one of those very rare open and shut cases. It's not *just* the DNA evidence, it's everything else too – she was there in the park at the right time, she had been arguing with the deceased an hour or so earlier, it just all fits, Cora. It's about proof beyond reasonable doubt, and there's zero evidence against anyone else other than Sam.

If you only knew how many convicted killers insist they've been framed ... and think about it. If she's pointing the finger at that ex-boyfriend of hers, why would he on one hand be sending her nice presents with notes telling her how fabulous she is, and then on the other be setting her up for life in prison? It doesn't make any sense. I just don't think those mystery gifts have any connection with this case, Cora, and I don't think anyone has framed Sam. I'm sorry.'

Upset, Cora had ended the call. Adam was making sense, she knew. The evidence against Sam was frighteningly solid. With her reporter's head on, it did indeed seem that Sam had to be guilty. But, and it was a huge but, this was her friend, a woman she knew inside out, and the Sam she knew was simply not capable of murder.

As she recounted all this now to her camera crew, it was Nathan who was first to respond. He carefully placed his now empty mug on the truck floor then held up four fingers, thumb tucked into his palm.

'Well, as far as I can see it, we have this many possibilities here.'

'Four?' Cora frowned.

'Four. First, someone framed her, as she seems to think. Fairly unlikely, but can't be ruled out, I suppose.' He folded his little finger down.

'The police *are* ruling that out though, sadly,' said Cora. 'OK. Go on.'

'Second, a lab mix-up. Adam has dismissed that too, hasn't he?' Another finger vanished.

'Yes. He says he checked and double-checked.'

'OK. Third, by some miracle there is somebody else out there with DNA that matches Sam's.' He folded a third finger down into his palm.

'Not possible. Next?'

'Right.' Only Nathan's index finger remained, held up in front of him. 'So, there's only one possibility left. Sam *did* kill Marcus. Not intentionally, maybe killed him in some sort of crazy moment of madness. She might not even remember doing it, might have had some sort of mental meltdown or something, but she did it. If we've dismissed all the other possibilities, Cora ... well, isn't that the only one left?'

There was silence in the truck. Cora's eyes were glued to Nathan's, a wave of nausea suddenly sweeping over her. Was he right? Was it, if she was being really honest with herself, the only possible explanation? She could see the pain in her cameraman's eyes, and she knew he hated saying this to her. They had always been straight with each other, and he was just trying to get her to face the facts, brutal though they were. But it was Sam. *Sam*. It wasn't possible – was it? Cora took a deep breath.

'No. No, it isn't. She says she didn't do it. She doesn't know who did, or how. But I believe her, Nathan. I believe her.'

Nathan nodded slowly, then reached across and gripped Cora's hand.

'OK,' he said simply.

Rodney, who'd been looking from one to the other with a deeply anxious expression, exhaled suddenly.

'Well, what do we do then?' he asked.

Scott leaned forward in his seat, eyes burning.

'Well, if we think she's innocent, we bloody do *something*,' he said. 'I know what it's like to be accused of something you didn't do. If you truly believe in her, we've got to help her Cora, and that's the end of it.'

Cora nodded slowly, then looked across at Rodney and Nathan. They were nodding too. Scott had, for a brief time last year, been considered a suspect in the murder of Jeanette Kendrick. It had been a horrible, tense time for all of them, but because Scott hadn't confided in them about what was really going on, they had been unable to help him through it. This was different, Cora thought. This time, I *can* help, even if Adam can't. Or won't.

'You're right, Scott. We have to do something. And I think I know where to start too. The mystery gift sender is an obvious suspect, right? So tomorrow, after work, I'm going to go and see this David bloke, Sam's ex, see what he has to say.'

'Get all your ducks in the road first. And take someone with you, in case he did somehow frame Sam and he tries to bump you off too …'

Scott paused as he noticed grins breaking out on all three of his colleagues' faces. 'What have I said?'

'Ducks in a *row*. Not in the road. Oh, Scott, I do love your malapropisms.' Cora reached over and grabbed the engineer awkwardly round the neck, pulling him in for a hug. He hugged her back, blushing, and then his face grew serious again.

'When's Sam's next court appearance, to enter her plea? End of June, did you say?'

'Twenty-eighth.'

Scott did a quick calculation on his fingers. 'Just over six weeks. You've always been good at meeting the deadlines Sam gives you for filing stories, Cora. So that's your deadline. That's *our* deadline. Six weeks, to prove her innocence.'

They all stared at each other. In all their time working together, they had never, ever missed a deadline.

'Challenge accepted,' said Cora.

12

43 days until the deadline

'Say that again – a fashion collection made entirely from *what*?'

Nicole Latimer plonked herself down on one of the two vast brown suede sofas in Cora's lounge, sank back and sighed blissfully, her long dark hair splaying out over the teal cushions like a mermaid's in the ocean.

'Ahhh. Love these new cushions of yours. My back's killing me. Thirteen spayings today. *Thirteen*. And one of them was a St Bernard. Weighed over seven stone. I'm going to have to get a hoist for the surgery or something, if these monster dogs keep appearing. Took three of us to get him on the table … anyway, *what* did you say?'

Cora, who was pouring the wine, grinned. It was good to be home. A night of inane chit-chat with her two oldest friends was exactly what she needed right now, she thought, as she passed Nicole a glass of the crisp Sauvignon Blanc and then filled another for herself.

'Ironing boards. Apparently she uses the covers and foam bits to make the bulk of the outfits and then hammers the metal bits flat to add detail. Or something. Not sure, really …'

Rosie Gregg, who was already curled up on the sofa opposite and cradling her own drink, snorted.

'That is *mental*! I can't even bear to *look* at my ironing board most of the time. Certainly don't want to wear it.

Young people today, honestly …'

Cora laughed, sat down next to Nicole, and took a glug from her glass. It was indeed a rather bonkers concept, but a Friday morning trip to Bristol to cover a story about a fashion student who was being tipped as a rising star for her innovative designs was absolutely perfect. With just one live hit scheduled for 8 a.m., Cora and the boys wouldn't need to be on location until seven, and the fashion college was less than an hour's drive from her Cheltenham flat. On call twenty-four hours a day when she was on reporting duty – and always expecting the phone to ring in the early hours with a breaking story – nowadays Cora rarely allowed herself the luxury of drinking alcohol on a week night, just in case; Adam had scared her with stories of 'morning after' drink driving arrests, and Cora knew her licence was too important to her job to put it in jeopardy. But with her assignment for tomorrow already fixed, she thought she'd risk a couple of small glasses tonight. She needed it, after the traumas of the past week. Pushing the bowl of smoked cheese and caramelised onion crisps across the coffee table so that Rosie could reach it, she suddenly felt a little of the weight she'd been carrying for days floating off her shoulders.

'So – tell us some more about Sam. You're really going to go and see her possibly crazy, possibly murderous ex?'

Nicole, straight to the point as always. Cora and Rosie had known each other since they were twelve years old, and had met Nicole at a party about seven years ago. They'd instantly liked the tall, clever vet, whose abrupt, no-nonsense manner belied her kind and caring nature. Married to Will, a sweet, studious science teacher, and now with an adorable three-year-old son, Nicole had quickly made their Cheltenham twosome into an inseparable three. They were all so different – Rosie was a mum of three with a successful furniture designer husband and her own booming floristry business – but somehow, it worked. Cora missed them when she was in London, and these weekly catch-ups always made her feel that all was right with the world, no matter how difficult things were outside the walls of her beloved apartment.

Now, she put her glass carefully down on the little Perspex side table next to the sofa and nodded.

'Yep. As soon as the Bristol shoot is over in the morning, I'm heading back to London. Sam gave me his address, so I'm just going to knock on his door and hope he's in. And I'm not telling Adam I'm doing it. He's away until tomorrow night anyway. Don't worry, Wendy's coming with me,' she added, noticing a sudden look of alarm on Rosie's freckled face.

'Well, thank goodness for that.' Rosie pushed her soft, lightly highlighted red fringe out of her eyes and frowned.

'I am a bit worried about you doing stuff like this though, Cora. Surely it's a police job? And … well, I hate to bring it up again, I know we've talked about this, but … are you absolutely sure? Sure Sam is innocent? I mean, if the evidence …'

'Yep. If all the evidence points to Sam … Rosie's right. Are you sure, Cora? I mean, we obviously don't know her as well as you do, and you know we'll support you in anything you do, but if you're doing something stupid …' Nicole stretched her long limbs, clad as always in black jeans and a dark top, with a groan, and turned to look at her friend.

Cora sighed. 'Look, I get why you're both sceptical, I do. But the boys and Wendy and I know Sam inside out, and we've all agreed. *We* believe her, despite what the police think and yes, despite what all the evidence says. And we're going to try and help her clear her name. I know it seems mad, and pointless, I do, honestly. But I can't just wait, and see her go down, and not try to do something. I'll go mad. I need to do something, anything. And what harm can it do, just talking to a few people? I'm a reporter, I do that for a living. It'll be all right. I promise.'

Rosie was still frowning, Nicole's expression a mix of concern and cynicism. They looked at each other, and then both shrugged.

'OK. Just be careful.' Nicole said, then added: 'And I hope this secret detective work of yours isn't going to come between you and Adam, Cora. He's so good for you. Please don't screw it all up.'

'I know. I won't. He's doing his job and I'm doing mine, as usual. It'll be fine.'

But even as she said the words, Cora felt a little frisson of fear. Would it be OK, really, if one of her closest friends ended up in prison for life, thanks to Adam? Would Cora be able to get past it? She pushed the thought from her mind. Deal with it when it happens, she told herself. *If* it happens.

'Heard from Justin recently?' said Rosie suddenly, clearly wanting to change the subject.

'Yes, a few weeks ago. He's great, really happy,' said Cora.

Cora and her ex-boyfriend Justin had split up a year and a half ago because she was adamant that she would never want children, a view he had initially said he shared, but then had changed his mind about. It had been a difficult time, but they had finally managed to part as friends. Justin was now living in Spain, having met Annie, a mother of three who ran a nursery for the children of ex-

82

pats in Valencia. Little Alexandra, Hannah and Lyra were keeping him busy and very happy, he had told Cora in their occasional email exchanges, and she was genuinely pleased for him.

'That's good. And as far as Sam goes – good luck. Let us know if we can help.' Nicole patted Cora's arm. 'But be careful, Cora.'

'I am being. Look – nobody except us, the boys and Wendy know about this. The information about the DNA and the murder weapon hasn't been made public yet, obviously, and won't be until the trial. I only know because Sam, and Adam of course, told me. So we need to keep it as quiet as possible, OK? We're not even going to tell Alice – I love the girl, but she can have a bit of a big mouth at times, and if somebody *has* framed Sam, we don't want them to know we're on to them. So don't breathe a word, OK?'

'Of course not.' Nicole and Rosie both nodded solemnly.

Cora smiled, trying to quell the ever-present feeling that what she was taking on was an impossible task. If the police had such solid evidence, how on earth was she, a mere TV reporter, going to convince them they were wrong? But she just had to try, for Sam's sake …

'Uh oh.' She suddenly sniffed the air anxiously as the faint aroma of burning pizza assailed her nostrils.

'Damn it. Oh well, we can scrape the burnt bits off.' And she jumped up and scampered out of the room, leaving Rosie and Nicole rolling their eyes and sighing.

'Can't cook won't cook Cora strikes again,' said Nicole. 'Got that takeaway menu, Rosie?'

Rosie reached down into her handbag and pulled out a sheaf of leaflets.

'I brought four,' she grinned.

13

Friday 17th May
42 days until the deadline

David Cash's house was in a quiet residential road in Richmond, just a few streets away from the River Thames footbridge that linked the district to its neighbour St Margarets. It was one of London's wealthiest areas, and the street was one of elegant Georgian townhouses, their owners' Range Rover Evoques, Porsches and Mercedes parked nose to tail along the kerb.

Cora and Wendy sat in Cora's BMW, which she'd miraculously managed to find a space for up the street from number sixteen, and looked at each other nervously. The *Morning Live* team's week always finished at lunchtime on a Friday, a perk which everyone was deeply grateful for – and had meant this visit could be made in the early evening, which they'd gambled would be a good time to catch Sam's ex, as long as he hadn't gone out straight after work. They'd been parked up for a good ten minutes, urgently discussing the best plan of action, both suddenly unsure about whether this was really such a great idea.

'I mean, we can't just barge in there, into the home of a complete stranger, and ask him if he murdered Marcus and framed Sam for it, can we?' Wendy said. Although Sam had showed them some photos of David at the time they were dating, neither of her friends had ever actually met him.

'No, we can't. And he's bound to have seen all the press coverage anyway, isn't he? So if we tell him we're friends of Sam's he'll instantly be on his guard, if he's got anything to do with it. I really don't know how to play this one, Wend.'

Wendy leaned back in her seat, adjusting her V-necked blue sweater so it showed slightly less of her ample cleavage.

'Well, honesty is usually the best policy, Cora. Maybe we just tell him we believe Sam is innocent and are trying to help clear her name by talking to everyone she's been involved with over the past year, and in particular trying to find out who's been sending her mystery gifts. Then just see how he reacts. If he starts behaving suspiciously, we pull out and just call the police.'

That sounded like a good idea to Cora. 'OK. Let's do it.' She pulled down the driver's mirror, wiped a stray fleck of mascara away from under her left eye, ran her fingers through her dark bob and flicked the mirror back into place.

'And let's hope he's *not* a killer. I'd quite like to be alive to greet Harry when he arrives this evening. I've missed that little bundle of trouble.'

Harry was Adam's six-year-old son. He lived with Adam's ex-wife Laura in Swindon, but spent regular weekends with his dad, police work permitting. Although Cora had no desire for her own children, she had grown extremely fond of the cheeky little boy, who shared his father's sharp intelligence and stunning green eyes.

'We'll be fine. There's two of us and only one of him.' Wendy opened her door and clambered out, and Cora followed suit. As they approached the red-painted door, she wondered again what on earth they were doing, her nerves suddenly mixed with a little anger now. Why was it she and Wendy who were having to do this? Yes, the police had compelling evidence that Sam was guilty. But Adam *knew* her, had known her for over a year, knew that Cora thought the world of her. Surely *he* could see that she couldn't possibly be a murderer? Couldn't he look past the evidence, just for a little while, and investigate the case further?

Well, if he can't, or won't, I suppose it's up to us, she thought, and pushing all nerves aside, she pressed firmly on the traditional cast iron door bell.

Wendy looked at her. 'No going back now. Hope he's in,' she hissed. He was. Moments later they heard footsteps approaching from inside the hallway and the door opened. Standing there was a tall, lightly tanned man in a stripy cobalt and white shirt. He had a neatly trimmed beard and looked to be in his mid-thirties. From the pictures Cora had seen, this was definitely their man, although he was decidedly better looking in the flesh.

'Er – David Cash?' she asked.

'That's me. Can I help you?' He looked puzzled, but smiled.

'It's a bit complicated. We're friends of Sam Tindall – remember, you dated her briefly last year? I don't know if you've seen the news …'

A look of surprise flashed across David's face, and he looked from Cora to Wendy and then back again. Then he nodded.

'Yes! I was absolutely horrified. I couldn't believe she was capable … but what has this got to do with me?' He frowned and ran his fingers through his short brown hair, the temples flecked with grey. 'I mean, I only dated her very briefly, as you said. Then she met that guy, Marcus, poor bugger, and told me she didn't want to see me any more. We exchanged a few texts and emails, but I never saw her again after that. That was months ago now.'

'Look – is there any way we could come in, explain properly? It's just that we don't think she's guilty either, and we're trying to prove that. If you could spare us just five minutes, we'd really appreciate it.'

He looked unsure, then took a step back and waved a hand down the hallway behind him.

'I suppose so. Come in.'

He let them walk past him and then shut the door. 'Second on the right,' he said. 'Can I get you some tea or anything?'

'No, no, we're fine, thank you,' Wendy said, as they entered a cosy sitting room at the back of the house. French doors led out on to a long, sweeping garden, its beds bursting with purple alliums, splashes of colourful begonias and tall delphiniums. A small dog was scrabbling under a bush, soil flying out behind him, some sort of terrier, Cora thought, and she instantly remembered the third dog walker on the CCTV footage, the one who hadn't come forward after the press appeals. Could this be the dog in the pictures?

'Wow, what a gorgeous garden!' She turned to David and smiled.

He smiled back. 'It is lovely mostly, except when the damn dog decides to start digging.' He tapped loudly on the glass of the French window, and the dog turned abruptly and slunk away. It stretched out on the grass a few feet from its digging spot, keeping a wary eye on the window.

'He'll be back at it in a minute, when he thinks I'm not looking. His name is Doug, and for a very good reason – he's a Cairn terrier, digging seems to be their life.' David smiled again, and Wendy and Cora both laughed.

'Anyway – the garden. It's my way of relaxing. I work in IT and it can all get a bit stuffy. I love getting out there, getting my hands dirty. It's a work in progress, but yes, it's not looking too bad at the moment.'

His face grew serious again. 'But you're not here to talk about gardening. Please, take a seat.'

He gestured towards a small, cream sofa, and Cora and Wendy sat down, while he perched on an antique-looking leather wing armchair opposite them, looking uncomfortable again.

'So? How can I help?'

Cora looked at Wendy, then back at David. She took a deep breath and began. 'OK, so this is a long shot, but we're desperate. As you've probably seen in the papers, Sam has been charged with murdering her boyfriend and is currently on remand in prison. It's a nightmare, David. We've known her for years, and we know she could never do anything like that. But the police have evidence, and have stopped looking for anyone else in the case.'

She wondered if she should mention that it was her own boyfriend who had led the investigation, then decided against it.

'There's been something a bit weird happening recently. In the weeks before the murder, Sam had been getting presents from a secret admirer – chocolates, flowers, a giant cuddly toy, things like that. She had no idea who they were coming from –'

'And you think it might have been me?' David laughed, disbelievingly. 'Why on earth? I told you, I haven't seen or heard from her in months!'

Wendy cleared her throat. 'It's just that – well, when Sam told you that she'd met someone else, she said that you seemed, well, quite upset? And kept emailing and texting her for a couple of weeks. We just thought that, maybe ...'

David stood up, his face flushing. 'That maybe I was still obsessed with her, all these months later? And suddenly decided anonymous presents were the way forward? Seriously? And then what – I murder her boyfriend? Are you crazy?'

'No, no, of course not.' Cora tried to keep her voice calm despite her rising anxiety. 'We're just trying to understand what happened, and the mystery gifts may or may not be related. Of *course* we're not accusing you of anything. I'm sorry if it came across like that.'

'Yes, I'm sorry too,' said Wendy. 'It's just that we are *so* worried, about Sam ...'

David sat down in his armchair again. 'OK, OK. I'm sorry too. It's just such a strange thing to come here and ask me, but I understand it must be a difficult time.'

He sighed and rubbed his eyes. 'OK, so yes, I was upset when Sam told me she didn't want to see me again, had met someone else. We'd only had a few dates, admittedly, but I really liked her. And yes, to my shame, I did pester her a bit for a couple of weeks. But when she made it clear she wasn't interested, I stopped. And that's that. I've never made contact with her again and I certainly haven't been sending her presents. My girlfriend would kill me, for a start.'

He pointed at a framed photograph on a side table, and Cora and Wendy both shifted in their seats to get a better look. It was a picture of David, smiling in sunglasses and a white T-shirt, arm draped over the shoulders of a petite brunette in a red floral dress, also grinning at the camera.

'That's Sue. We met about six months ago – at Richmond garden centre, coincidentally. We literally bumped into each at the bulb display and got talking, and the rest is history. She's wonderful, and I haven't given Sam a second thought since I met her. Well, not until I saw the story about the murder on the news. I was gobsmacked. Told Sue I used to date her, and she was gobsmacked too.'

He walked over to the table and picked up the photograph, wiping a small smear from the glass. 'This was taken in Rhodes a couple of weeks ago. I have a very busy summer ahead, workwise, so we thought we'd get some early sunshine. We'd just flown back actually, when I saw the story about Sam. Might even have been the same day, now I come to think about it.'

He turned back to Cora and Wendy. 'What date was it, the murder?'

'The sixth of May, Bank Holiday Monday, late at night. The body wasn't found 'til the early hours of Tuesday morning, the seventh. Sam was arrested a few days later, on the ninth, and her first court appearance was on Saturday the eleventh.' Cora reeled the dates off effortlessly.

David nodded. 'Yes, that makes sense. We were away all that week of the Bank Holiday and flew home on the Saturday, so I would have seen it on the news that night, after her court appearance.'

Wendy nudged Cora, and they gave each other a sidelong glance, knowing they were both thinking the same thing. If David had been abroad on the night of the murder, he couldn't possibly have been involved. Coming here had been a complete waste of time. Sighing inwardly, Cora stood up.

'We're so sorry to have come here like this. It's obvious you didn't have anything to do with what happened, David. We'll leave you in peace.'

He nodded solemnly, then beamed. 'It's really not a

problem. Sam is a lovely girl, and I'd probably be doing exactly the same if I were in your shoes. And it was nice to meet a fellow gardening fan.'

Cora grinned back. 'One day, I'd love to have a garden like yours. For now, it's just a few pots on my balcony, but hey ...'

David reached out and shook her hand, then did the same to Wendy, before showing them out.

'Good luck. I hope it all works out the way you want it to,' he said, as he closed the door. Cora and Wendy walked in silence back to the car. Once inside, Wendy groaned.

'What a total dead end. Now what?'

Cora shook her head. 'No idea. I had high hopes for a few minutes when I saw that he had a small dog – remember that CCTV footage the police released to the media? But that's clearly just a coincidence, damn it. Look, I'm going to arrange a visit with Sam as soon as I can. If we put our heads together, I'm sure we can come up with something. You should come too.'

'Of course, I'd like that. Right – quick drink somewhere before we go home? There are some great little bars in Richmond.'

'Can't – driving,' said Cora morosely. 'Quick coffee instead?'

Wendy sighed. 'Oh, all right. Come on, let's get out of here.'

In the hallway of number sixteen, David Cash was still standing by the front door, forehead resting on the cool wood, trying to steady his breathing. Things were so good in his life right now. He'd met Sue, they were in love, everything was perfect. Why did those two have to come along, suggesting he might still be infatuated with Sam? If

Sue had been here …

He shook his head violently to dispel the thought. It was fine. The two women had seemed content with the thought that he was abroad, had gone away happy that he had had nothing to do with the murder. He wouldn't see them again. Buoyed by the thought, he straightened up and headed upstairs to change. He was taking Sue out for dinner later. Wouldn't do to be late.

14

Saturday 18th May
41 days until the deadline

'Harrison Bradberry! I've called you three times. If you don't put that game down RIGHT NOW, I'm eating your toast as well as my own – you have been warned!'

Cora smiled as Harry quickly dumped his iPad on the sofa and scampered over to the breakfast bar where she was sitting, mug of tea in hand and a plateful of only slightly burned wholemeal toast in front of her. The little boy who at the age of four had informed his amused father that he wanted to be the tooth fairy when he grew up, now suddenly seemed well on his way to being a teenager, with the appetite to match.

'Don't you dare!' he said, clambering onto a stool and grabbing three slices of toast, one of which he took an immediate large bite out of before starting to smother the rest with butter and honey.

'OK, you saved it. But only just.' Cora ruffled his already messy, slightly too long hair and he squirmed, but he was grinning. They had liked each other from the moment Adam had first introduced them, and her fondness for Harry had led to Cora finally breaking her long-held rule of never dating men who had children. The fact that she only saw him on random weekends, depending on Adam's work schedule, plus the odd weeknight and special occasion visit, meant that she could play her role as honorary stepmother with pleasure, getting all the nice, fun bits of having a child without too much of what Cora considered to be the tricky stuff. She had met Harry's mum Laura a couple of times too, during visit handovers, and she had always been perfectly pleasant. It was, Cora thought now, as she sipped her tea with a happy Harry munching contentedly beside her, about as perfect as it could be, considering.

It was something many people in her life had taken a long time to understand – why Cora, who clearly liked children and got on so well with them, had no desire whatsoever to procreate. She had known, for as long as she could remember, that she didn't want children of her own, and that had never changed. Friends had fallen pregnant and given birth, and tried to persuade her that it was the most wonderful experience in the world, one that she would one day regret missing out on. People less close to her had even, over the years, accused her of being strange, self-centred, career-obsessed or a child-hater because of her decision. Now, thankfully, most of her friends and family had come to terms with it, and the gentle, well-meaning nagging had subsided. Cora herself was utterly content with her lifestyle choice, knowing that she simply wasn't cut out to be a mother with just as much certainty as her "mummy friends" knew that motherhood was their destiny. She didn't even get irritated by the occasional jibe nowadays, apart from when she was referred to as "childless".

'Child*free*, not child*less*,' she would point out. 'Childless implies a lack of something that I want – I'm lacking nothing. I'm childfree, and very happy.'

Now, she hopped off her stool and wandered to the window. She'd opened it earlier, partly to let the smell of burning toast escape and partly so she could enjoy the gentle rustling of the leaves on the sturdy plane trees which lined the street outside. The trees were a common sight on London streets, with their dappled bark which seemed to change colour with the seasons, and their striking branch pattern which meant they looked beautiful even in winter. Today, a gentle breeze nudged the foliage, and the sky above was clear and blue.

'A perfect May day,' Cora announced. 'Daddy said he's only going to be a couple of hours at work and then we'll head out with your skateboard, and maybe grab some lunch – sound OK to you?'

'Wicked! Can I go back to my game for a bit now then? I've cleared my plate, look.' Harry waved the plate at her, scattering crumbs across the breakfast bar.

'Go on then, messy pup.'

'Thank yooooooo.'

He jumped off his seat and returned to his spot on the sofa, within moments becoming absorbed in his game of Minecraft again. Cora gave the counter top a wipe, stacked the crockery and cutlery in the dishwasher and picked up her phone. She desperately wanted to see Sam, tomorrow if possible. Unlike convicted prisoners, who could only have a visit every fortnight or so, prisoners on remand were usually allowed up to three visits a week, and a visiting order wasn't necessary. Sam was being held in Henworthy, which in the past had housed some notorious female prisoners. The thought chilled Cora as she dialled the number to book her visit. How could it be real, that her lovely friend Sam was in a place like that?

'We have to get her out, we *have* to,' she murmured, as she waited in a queue to speak to the relevant person. It took nearly fifteen minutes, but finally she ended the call, a visit for herself and Wendy booked for three o'clock tomorrow afternoon. Between them, they'd come up with something, some other avenue to pursue, Cora promised herself as she checked on Harry and then headed into the bedroom to put on some make-up.

She'd decided to come clean to Adam last night about the meeting with David Cash, and he'd listened with a resigned look on his face, warned her that while this time she'd been lucky, acting like a police officer could get her in trouble, then confessed that he'd managed to get *himself* in quite a lot of trouble earlier that day on Sam's behalf too.

Back from his trip to Cambridge unexpectedly early yesterday lunchtime, he'd made what in retrospect was a rather unwise decision, and taken a detour to visit the forensic lab which had analysed the evidence from Marcus's murder scene. The force had used the lab for years, and there had never, ever been an issue with a mix-up, but Cora's insistence that Sam was innocent, and indeed his own knowledge of the accused's personality, had been enough to plant a seed of doubt in his mind. He had, therefore, asked for a meeting with the most senior forensic scientist available; this turned out to be a severe-looking woman in her fifties, who immediately took great offence to his suggestion that the DNA sample Sam gave in her flat might have somehow ended up contaminating the murder weapon, and entered into a prolonged and irate explanation about lab protocol and how this could never, *ever* occur, and never would, not while *she* was working there.

A suitably chastened Adam had returned to his car, only to have his drive home interrupted fifteen minutes later by a furious call from his superior, Chief Superintendent Brian McKay, who had just received an official complaint about him from the lab. Adam's drive home became a drive to the station and a deeply unpleasant dressing-down in McKay's office.

'Now I've got to write a formal apology to the lab staff. But I'm totally convinced, Cora – there was no mix-up,' he had said firmly, and then changed the subject.

Grateful that he had gone so far to check the possibility out, Cora had not mentioned the case again last night, but this morning she was feeling fired up again. OK, maybe there'd been no lab mix-up, but she wasn't giving up yet. She knew Adam thought what she was doing was a waste of time, but surely if she found something, some real evidence in Sam's favour, he'd have to take it seriously?

'You'd better, DCI Bradberry,' she muttered as she applied eyeliner with a steady hand. 'Because if you don't, I'm not sure what will happen to us …'

Could it, in the end, come down to a choice between her friend and her boyfriend? A shiver ran down Cora's spine. Bloody hell, I hope not, she thought.

'We still haven't heard from that third dog walker, have we? The final one to go in and out on the night of the murder, the one with the little rat dog who spent about fifteen minutes in the park?'

Adam pushed a pile of papers across his desk and looked up at Gary Gilbert who was hovering nearby, chomping on an apple and answering the random questions his SIO kept throwing at him.

'Nope. Although I thought you didn't think it was that important?'

'I don't, not really. But it's just a loose end that hasn't been tied up yet. It bugs me that they never came forward, and disappeared out of sight of the CCTV cameras so we can't trace them. I'm not keen on loose ends, Gary, as you know. And I've already got myself into trouble on this case ... I don't want any screw-ups.'

Gary raised his eyebrows and nodded vigorously, then took another bite of his Golden Delicious.

'And what about Sam Tindall's mystery gifts? Have we totally given up on tracing the sender of those now?'

Gary held his hand up in the air, chomped his mouthful of apple, and swallowed.

'Sorry, boss. Missed breakfast. Yep. Nothing we can do, after that fire. Everything's gone, all the records destroyed. And the sender never actually touched the gifts, just ordered them to be delivered via the shop, so no point in trying to get any fingerprints or anything off that polar bear.'

'OK. Again, probably not really relevant, I suppose. I'd like to know who sent them though. Another bloody loose end I can't tie up.'

Adam sighed and ran his fingers through his blond crop, several shades lighter than his son's but no less unruly if he ever let it get any longer than a barber's number two. After yesterday, he'd decided it might be prudent to pop in to the incident room briefly on his day off, knowing there was still work to do to complete the file of evidence for the murder. Now, more than ever, he couldn't afford any slip-ups in this case – and he knew the media interest in the trial would be intense, just as it was last year when Jeanette Kendrick was murdered. Adam wasn't comfortable being in the spotlight, but in recent times he'd reluctantly come to accept it as part of his job. And this case *was* pretty water-tight, he was sure, despite his feeling of disbelief that Sam Tindall had turned killer. He understood why Cora was finding it impossible to believe, and why she was desperate to prove him wrong, but she'd have to accept it, sooner or later. The evidence didn't lie, and Sam's DNA was all over it, quite literally.

He stood up suddenly, tired of thinking about it. 'OK, let's leave it for today. I'm off to watch my son try and break his leg on a skateboard. I'll see you bright and early on Monday, Gary. Thanks for the updates.'

Gary waved the apple at him. 'Any time, boss. Have a great weekend.'

In her flat in Waterloo, not far from Television Centre which housed the *Morning Live* studios, Betsy Allan was struggling to have a great weekend. True to his word, Adam Bradberry had sent officers to interview every member of staff in recent days, herself included. She'd felt nervous and twitchy ever since, paranoid that her perfectly constructed world was starting to crumble at the edges. As far as she had been able to gather, nobody in the newsroom had had a bad word to say about Sam, although a few had mentioned in their statements that she showed occasional flashes of temper when reporters missed deadlines, satellite trucks failed to work or guests cancelled at the last minute. But that was normal behaviour really, for a producer of a national news show, especially a producer like Sam who had worked so hard to get where she was. At thirty, she was young to be in such a senior role, and she guarded her position fiercely. But there was nothing that would ever lead any of her colleagues to suspect her of being capable of murder. And yet there she was, in prison, awaiting trial.

Betsy shuddered, pulling her cashmere wrap a little more tightly round her shoulders. She'd turned the central heating off in the recent mild weather. Maybe she should put it back on again. She leaned back in her chair for a moment, wondering if the police would be returning with more questions, or whether that would be it. But it was too late now – she simply didn't feel safe any more.

She forced herself to take several deep breaths. It was OK, she reasoned. All attention was on Sam. Nobody was looking at her, despite the fact that she'd been Marcus's friend. She'd been asked a lot about him, of course – about his background, his financial affairs, his love life – and she'd answered as honestly as she could, telling the police that as far as she was aware, he was happy and all was well in his life. And that she missed him. Because she did. Marcus had been a good friend to her in the past, and she missed him terribly.

She felt the tears welling and wiped her eyes fiercely. Sitting here brooding was pointless. It was a beautiful day, and a little stroll to the park and then to the deli to pick up some cheese and wine for later would do her good.

'Toby! Fancy a walk?'

From the faded tartan cushion he'd dragged into a patch of sunlight on the wooden floor earlier, Toby the Chihuahua perked up his long, pointed ears and gazed at her for a moment with luminous eyes before scurrying joyfully towards her.

Betsy smiled. 'Come on, then, trouble.'

15

Sunday 19th May
40 days until the deadline

Cora stood in WHSmith, staring at the rack of magazines. What would Sam like? She didn't think prisons allowed visitors to bring food, but reading material was OK, wasn't it? And Sam would definitely want to be keeping up with the news while she was inside, so she could get straight back to work if she got out. *When* she got out, Cora corrected herself. So – a mix of magazines then. She selected *Private Eye*, the *New Statesman* and *The Economist* from the news section, then added *Hello*, *Red* and *Heat* to her pile. *Morning Live* staff needed to have eclectic reading tastes, that was for sure, she thought as she paid and headed back out to her car. She was juggling magazines, car keys and handbag when a voice behind her made her jump.

'Cora! Fancy seeing you here.'

She turned to see Miranda Evans smiling at her. The TV doctor was wearing a pretty floral tea dress and red cardigan, her long brunette locks swept up into a messy bun, pale skin free of make-up.

'Oh, hello, Miranda! Not my usual haunt, no – I'm on my way to see Sam, and suddenly thought I didn't want to arrive empty-handed, so I pulled over to get her something to read. Do you live near here, then?'

Miranda shook her head. 'No, I live in west London.

But I'm having afternoon tea with a couple of friends from medical school in a minute – they both live around here so it was just easier.'

She gestured towards a tea shop on the other side of the road, then turned back, her smile fading.

'So – Sam? I still don't understand what's going on, Cora. I mean – how on earth can the police think she's guilty? Everyone's been talking about it in the newsroom. It just seems … well, it just seems all wrong. I don't get it.'

Cora sighed heavily, finally managing to open her car door and throwing her bags across onto the passenger seat. 'They say they have evidence, Miranda, but none of us can believe it either. It's horrific. We're still hoping something will come up, you know, before the trial. But in the meantime, we're just trying to keep her spirits up.'

Miranda nodded, and they both stood in silence for a moment.

'Well … give her my best, won't you? It's not the same at work without her. We'd become quite close, and I miss her. And she's such a fantastic producer. Anthony isn't … well, he's not Sam,' Miranda said, diplomatically.

Cora smiled. 'Agreed,' she said. 'I'd better go – have to pick up Wendy, she's shopping down the road. And yes, of course I'll give your regards to Sam. Thanks, Miranda. I'll probably see you during the week. Enjoy your tea.'

'Bye, Cora.'

Ten minutes later, Wendy on board, Cora set the satnav for the nearest public car park to Henworthy Prison. She was feeling horribly nervous. Although she'd been inside prisons a handful of times for work, usually to interview the governor, she'd never actually visited a prisoner before.

'I'm scared to see what she looks like,' she said. 'She looked so dreadful, didn't she, in court?'

Wendy leaned over and briefly squeezed Cora's hand on the steering wheel.

'I know, but we're going to have to be strong, just like she's being. Don't react, even if she looks terrible. We have to concentrate on finding a way of getting her out of there, just focus on that.'

Cora nodded and gave her friend a reassuring smile, but as she manoeuvred her BMW through the traffic-thronged streets, anxiety twisted her stomach. Finally, she couldn't contain the thoughts churning around her brain for a moment longer, and as she hit the brakes at a red light, she turned to Wendy.

'Wend ... look, I hardly dare ask this, but ... do you think there's a chance, any tiny chance at all, that she *did* this? Sam? Could ... could she?'

Wendy glanced at Cora and then looked away again, fixing her gaze on the people scurrying across the road in front of the car.

'I ... I don't know, Cora.' Her voice was barely a whisper. 'It's something I'm not letting myself think. It's *Sam*. Our friend. She just *couldn't*, could she?'

Cora was silent for a long moment, then shook her head. 'No, she couldn't. There's an explanation somewhere, there has to be.'

'Yes. We *have* to think that, Cora, or it's all over. We have to believe she's innocent. She says she is, and that has to be that. Right?' Wendy sounded stronger now, decisive.

'Right. OK, let's do this.'

The traffic started moving again, and they sat in silence, Cora still dreading the visit that lay ahead. By the time she and Wendy were sitting in the prison's visits hall, she was actually feeling physically ill. The extensive security checks, involving metal detectors, a pat down and a thorough sniffing by drugs dogs, had left both of them feeling quite dehumanised, and wondering how on earth their friend was managing to cope in this place.

They sat in silence, waiting, squirming a little on the hard chairs, knowing that once Sam appeared they had just the allotted thirty minutes to talk. One by one, prisoners were entering the room, smiles breaking out on drawn faces as loved ones were spotted. All around them were babies being hugged, tears and laughter and low, urgent conversations. In one corner children played with coloured bricks and chased each other in and out of a plastic Wendy house in a cordoned-off area with bright Disney character stickers on the walls. One little boy crawled determinedly round and round on the floor, pushing a large red fire engine in front of him, oblivious to the stampeding feet of his companions and chanting 'Nee naw, nee naw' in a soft, childish monotone.

'Here she is!' Wendy nudged Cora in the ribs, and they both watched as Sam finally appeared, picking her way between the tables, eyes bright as she leaned across to peck them both on the cheek. She sank onto her own chair opposite them, and for a moment they all looked at each other and grinned, simply happy to be back together again.

Sam looked much better than she had in court, Cora thought with relief. Although still pale, her hair appeared to have been freshly washed and she even had a little make-up on – a touch of mascara and eyeliner. But it was the *look* in her eyes that had changed the most – a fiery, determined expression, so different from the fear and despair that had been evident when she was standing in the dock.

'So,' Sam said, leaning across the scratched plastic table and gripping Cora's left hand and Wendy's right in her own. 'How are we going to get me out of here then?'

They talked non-stop for a solid twenty minutes, Cora first telling the story about Adam and the forensic lab, then she and Wendy recounting their meeting with David Cash. Sam's disappointment that a lab mix-up was now highly unlikely, and that David couldn't have been involved in the murder, was clearly intense, but she took a deep breath and kept talking, running other ideas past them. If they were now working on the theory that she had somehow been framed by somebody, what about that former newsroom runner who had been so totally inept and lazy that she had insisted he be fired?

'Tristan? Nope. He moved to New York. Two of the other runners went out to visit him a few weeks ago. They were still there with him when Marcus was killed,' said Wendy. 'I remember that clearly, because they were so shocked when they came back and heard you'd been arrested that they both burst into tears in the morning meeting, bless them.'

They started brainstorming again, trying to think of anyone else who might hold even the slightest grudge against Sam. One of the unsavoury characters *Morning Live* had featured in recent times, maybe?

'I mean, there must be plenty of them who didn't like the publicity. That dad, the one whose son was running riot on that housing estate? What about him, for example?' Sam ran her fingers through her hair, and Cora nodded, remembering.

The man had indeed been frighteningly angry when a camera crew had turned up outside his home on the evening after a local newspaper report claimed residents were living in fear of his seven-year-old son. The child had been terrorising the run-down Derby estate on which the family lived, screaming abuse at elderly neighbours, posting dog dirt through letterboxes and throwing lit fireworks through open windows, and Sam had despatched a crew to try to get an interview with his family. The father had grabbed a baseball bat when the *Morning Live* team arrived, and threatened to smash up both their equipment and their heads, but the decision had been made to run the story anyway, using a few shots of the rampaging, bat-wielding father that the cameraman had managed to snatch from the safety of his locked car before making a speedy getaway. The dad had then bombarded the newsroom with barely literate emails for days, accusing the programme of harassment and making menacing promises of retaliation.

'I mean, I know he stopped the threats when we eventually called the police,' Sam said. 'But maybe he was still seething away? He could have been quietly plotting revenge for months.'

Cora considered for a moment, then shook her head.

'Unlikely. Why target you? I know you sent the crew to cover the story, but how would he know that? Much more likely that if he wanted revenge, he'd go for the reporter, or the cameraman. Same with all of the dodgy types we've filmed and run stories on. And anyway, how on earth would he have been able to get hold of anything with your DNA on it?'

Sam sighed. 'Suppose so.'

They all sat in silence for a minute, thinking. At the next table, a heavily tattooed inmate with blue hair, who'd been arguing with her girlfriend in a low, venomous voice for the past five minutes, suddenly stood up, shouted: 'Piss off home then, and don't bother coming back, you selfish bitch!' and stalked out of the room, two guards hastily following.

Wendy shuddered. 'Bloody hell, Sam. How do you cope?'

Both she and Cora had talked to Sam about conditions in the jail during their phone calls in recent days, but it was a totally different matter now they were here and seeing it for themselves.

Sam shrugged. 'You just have to. I've been lucky because I have a cell to myself at the moment, as I told you, and it's got a TV. I just keep myself to myself, read, watch telly, go to the gym when they let me. I just keep telling myself it's not for long, you know? That this is all a bad dream, and any minute now I'm going to wake up and I'll be back at my desk in the newsroom. I'm just so ... so sad though. I miss Marcus so much, so terribly, terribly much. That's the hardest thing to cope with. If he was alive ...'

She looked at them both in turn, and Cora felt a physical ache in her guts as she saw the anguish in her friend's eyes once more. Then she and Wendy both jumped as Sam suddenly pounded a fist on the table, sending tremors through the plastic.

'The hairdresser!' she said, her voice suddenly almost gleeful.

'What? Who?' Cora stared uncomprehendingly, and Wendy was looking equally blank.

'Marcus's ex-girlfriend! Don't you remember, I told you about her?'

Wendy frowned. 'Oh. Vaguely. She worked at the salon you go to, and was a bit funny with you when she realised you were dating him?'

'More than a *bit* funny. She used to glare at me across the room. My stylist asked her to make me tea a few times, and once I wouldn't drink it – it looked really odd. I was convinced she'd spat in it or something. Gosh, maybe ...'

'Hang on, I must have missed out on this story, I don't remember it at all. Start from the beginning, but hurry up.' Cora glanced at her watch. 'We only have about five minutes left.'

'OK, so Marcus was dating this girl – Katie, her name is – before me. It was quite a long relationship, they were together about two and a half years, but it was quite fiery, he said. She sounded a bit unstable to me, to be honest, from the stories he told. She was incredibly jealous, hated him going out on his own, that kind of thing. Used to fly into a rage and smash things. She's really beautiful, and he said they did have good times too, but eventually he'd had enough and he ended it. She went totally off the deep end then, turned up at his work and built a bonfire outside on the pavement with some shirts and things he'd left at her flat. Anyway, it all calmed down after a while, although it put him off dating for ages. He hadn't been with anyone in over a year when Betsy introduced him to me ...'

Her voice tailed off and her eyes suddenly brimmed with tears. Cora stretched across the table and clasped her arm.

'I'm so sorry, darling, I know how horrible it is to think about him, but just try to finish this story, it could be important. She ended up working in the hairdressers you use?'

Sam wiped her eyes fiercely with the backs of her hands.

'Yes. I'd seen her there, but I didn't realise she was the same Katie. Then one day I was showing my stylist, Megan, some photos on my phone, of me and Marcus.

And Katie was passing, and spotted his picture, and started asking all sorts of questions – how long we'd been together, how serious the relationship was and so on. I thought she was just being nosy – I just didn't twig, you know? – but then that night Marcus got a barrage of abusive texts from her. I asked to see a photo of her and of course it was the same girl. She seemed to think he'd dumped her for me, which was ludicrous seeing as we hadn't even met until nearly a year after they finished. After that, every time I went to get my hair done she'd be there, giving me all these sinister looks. I just ignored her, but ... well, she really seemed to hate me ...'

'And she wouldn't have been too keen on Marcus either, at that point,' Cora said slowly.

'And if we're still thinking that someone somehow framed you with your DNA, Sam, a hairdresser would have ample opportunity to nick some, wouldn't she?' Wendy was sounding excited.

'Yes! Hair cuttings of course – you can get DNA from those, can't you? Can you? I don't know. But I had endless glasses of water and cups of tea there, as you do in a hair salon. You can get DNA from cups, definitely – saliva and stuff. And used tissues, maybe ... I mean, I don't know how long DNA lasts on stuff like that, but, girls, it would have been easy, if she'd wanted to! What do you think?'

Cora hesitated. The idea that somebody had framed Sam by somehow stealing her DNA and planting it at the murder scene still seemed remarkably unlikely to her, but she couldn't tell Sam that. Or Wendy, really. And it certainly seemed that it might at least be worth having a chat to this Katie girl, if they could.

'Sounds like the best lead we have, right now,' she said. 'Leave it to us, Sam.'

16

Thursday 23rd May
36 days to the deadline

'Your ear? Your EAR? How in the name of sanity could you have got your *ear* stuck in your car door?'

Nathan, camera on one shoulder, shook his head in amazement as Cora snorted with laughter, then tried to turn her guffaw into a cough when Rodney glared at her. His right ear was bright red and slightly swollen, a little trickle of dried blood tracing its way down to his pink earlobe.

Nathan clicked his camera into place on top of its tripod and turned to Rodney again. 'How? Seriously?'

Rodney rubbed his ear gingerly, grimaced and sighed. He was wearing a green tweed jacket with brown suede lapels over a white T-shirt, which made him look pretty normal from the waist up, Cora thought. It was just the bright orange cargo pants and rainbow patterned trainers which spoiled the effect somewhat.

'And are they *girls'* shoes? Because I have never, *ever* seen shoes like that in a men's shop. *Ever.*'

Nathan pushed his floppy fringe out of his eyes and looked at his soundman with an expression that combined disbelief with amusement.

'I don't know. I got them in that big designer discount place. Everything's all mixed up together. And I don't really care, Nathan, because *I* like them.'

'They're cool, Rodney. Shut up, Nathan. Is your ear very sore, Rodders?' Cora made a valiant effort not to start giggling again as she looked at the right side of Rodney's head. She could almost see the ear throbbing.

'It's a bit painful, yes, thank you for asking, Cora.' Rodney stuck his tongue out at Nathan and bent to pick up his mixer, which had been sitting on the ground nearby.

'And I didn't actually get my ear *stuck* in the door. I just sort of started closing the door before my head was fully inside, and it got caught for a moment ...'

Rodney stopped talking and rolled his eyes as Cora and Nathan both exploded into cackles again, then grinned himself.

'OK, OK. I'm an idiot. I'm going to get some spare batteries from Scott. Back in a bit.'

He marched off towards the sweeping staircase to their right, following the cable Scott had laid earlier. Cora put her notebook down on the edge of a large tank inside which four or five large stingrays were swimming placidly back and forth, and picked up the mug of tea she'd put there a minute earlier. As she sipped, she gazed into the water, noticing that on the sandy bottom of their pool, several other rays were lying completely still, virtually invisible, their markings acting as almost perfect camouflage. It was just after 5 a.m., and the crew was setting up for a live broadcast from the tropical lagoon section of the Midlands Aquarium, after the RSPCA had released a report expressing concern about a growing trend for exotic sea life pets in the nation's homes. Next to the stingray tank, a second large pool housed dozens of clown fish, their bright orange and white bodies darting through the clear water, zooming past anemones and luminous corals.

'That coral's the same colour as Rodney's ear,' Nathan

remarked, pointing at a particularly vivid red specimen.

Cora spluttered into her tea. 'You do give him a hard time, Nath. Poor old Rodney.'

'He loves it really. And he knows I don't mean anything by it. I love the bones of the guy.'

It was true, Cora thought, as she clutched her warm mug and wandered over to look at a third tank which was surrounded by palm trees. In the blue depths, angel fish, red snappers and oriental sweetlips swooped and dived, creating an ever-changing kaleidoscope of colour. She watched them, enjoying the moment, grateful to be here doing a job she loved with a team she adored. They might bicker like children, but deep down she and the three boys were solid friends, and they were all in a good place at the moment, despite their collective devastation about what was happening to Sam.

Engineer Scott, who had been through some personal difficulties last year, had had counselling and was now back on track, enjoying his life again, thankful that his wife Elaine and two beloved daughters had stuck by him. Rodney was just Rodney, content with his tolerant girlfriend Jodie, who ran a children's nursery near their Bristol flat. And Nathan was ecstatically happy with his life in a Gloucestershire cottage with his partner Gareth and their ever-growing menagerie of chickens and ducks.

'And I have Adam,' Cora thought. 'Even if what's going on with Sam has put a bit of strain on us recently.'

She exhaled heavily. Since the visit to Sam at the weekend, she had really wanted to tell Adam about Katie, Marcus's ex-girlfriend. After his telling off from his boss though, his reaction over the past few days to her continued defence of Sam had been a little less tolerant than it had been previously, so she had decided to keep quiet. There was no point in telling him, really, unless there was actually some real evidence that the girl had been involved in the murder, she reasoned. No point in rocking the boat any more than she had to. She and Wendy had done some detective work, calling the salon Sam had given them details of to discreetly check whether Katie was still employed there, but they hadn't had a chance to actually visit her yet. That was planned for tomorrow afternoon, with Sam expecting a phone call with an update tomorrow night. With Sam's permission, Cora had also made contact with her friend's legal team, telling them that she was doing a little 'investigative reporting' on the case and would keep them in touch with any developments. Even though they were supposed to be on Sam's side, Cora had sensed their slight scepticism about what she was up to, which didn't really surprise her. In her heart of hearts, she couldn't help feeling that it would all be a waste of time, just like the visit to David Cash, but at least they were trying. At least they were doing *something* ...

'Cora? I'm Colin Stanford, aquarium director. Lovely to meet you.'

She turned to see a tall, smiling man approaching, hand held out in greeting. He was wearing a navy blue polo shirt, 'Midlands Aquarium' stitched in aqua thread on the left breast above a rainbow-coloured shark. She shook his hand, dragging her mind back to the job in hand. Sam would have to wait, but just until tomorrow.

'Colin. Thank you so much for opening up this early for us, we really appreciate it. Have you seen the RSPCA report?'

He shook his head. 'No, not yet. Do you have a copy?'

'I do. Is there somewhere we can sit? I'll talk you through it.'

116

Twelve hours later, Cora sank onto her living room sofa with a grateful sigh. She was shattered, desperate for sleep, and as yet unassigned for tomorrow's programme. This meant one of two things, the most likely of which would be an early morning call from the desk to go and cover a breaking news story. The alternative – remaining unassigned and thereby getting a morning off – happened so rarely that she didn't dare to hope for it, and so had already laid out a couple of outfit options for the morning, one for a potential indoor broadcast and one for an outdoor story.

She picked up the TV remote control and started idly flicking through the channels, pausing for a minute on *Come Dine with Me* to watch a red-faced woman with flour in her hair making an almighty mess of her homemade pastry before giving up, throwing it in the bin and announcing that she was 'going to give them bought stuff instead, and pretend'. Cora sympathised – *she'd* never even attempted to make anything with shop-bought pastry, never mind doing it all from scratch.

She had just switched channels and was trying to remember how many years it had been since she'd actually sat through an episode of *Neighbours* when her mobile rang, Wendy's number flashing up on the screen.

'Cora! Something SO weird has just happened. You're not going to believe this ...'

Fifteen minutes later, she ended the call with a small bubble of excitement slowly forming in her belly. Could what had just happened to Wendy mean something – mean hope for Sam?

She lay back on the soft cushions, TV forgotten, running through the conversation again in her mind. Wendy, on the early shift in the *Morning Live* graphics studio, had finished work at two o'clock, picked up a bouquet at a nearby florist's and hopped on a bus to Chiswick, making her way to Pope's Meadow, the park where Marcus's body had been found. The little clump of trees which had been the centre of the murder scene had been turned into something of a temporary shrine, flowers from friends and colleagues arranged on the grass, sympathy cards expressing shock and sorrow propped next to a teddy bear in an Arsenal shirt and a collection of candles. There was even a six-pack of beer, which Wendy said bore the poignant message: 'One last drink, mate. I'll miss you.'

She had added her own flowers to the pile and then lingered for a while, reading the messages, partly just out of interest and partly, she told Cora, to see if there was anything vaguely suspicious about any of them, anything that might imply a sense of guilt.

'Great idea, Wendy! I'm impressed,' Cora had said. It *was* a good idea – it certainly wasn't unheard of for a remorseful killer to return to the scene of the crime. But Wendy had spotted nothing untoward. Although Marcus's parents were both dead, and he had no siblings, there was a scattering of messages from other relatives, and many from friends and workmates, all seemingly genuinely distraught. She had been about to leave and head home when a young woman walking down the path towards the trees caught her eye.

'She was carrying flowers, which was why I waited,' Wendy told Cora.

Wendy, now standing at the far edge of the makeshift shrine, had watched the girl, who she described as tall and very pretty, with beautiful eyes which were noticeable even from a distance, despite heavy-handed make-up which gave her small face a painted doll look. Dressed in black ankle boots, leggings and an oversized grey top, she had choppy blonde hair, funkily streaked with pink. She had tenderly placed the large wreath she was carrying right in the very centre of the pile, moving several bouquets and cards out of the way to make room, 'as if she wanted hers to have prime position', Wendy remarked.

She had then knelt there in the grass for several minutes, staring first at the tributes in front of her, then gazing ahead into the clump of trees.

'She was sort of twisting her hands together in this really *anguished* way,' said Wendy. 'Just kneeling there, staring, but her face was all screwed up as if she was about to start bawling. And then she did. Start bawling, I mean. All of a sudden. She *howled*, Cora! It was horrible, like watching a wild animal caught in a trap or something. And it went on, and on. The park was pretty empty at the time, but there were a couple of mums and kids over at the swings, and they looked pretty freaked out when she didn't stop after two or three minutes – they gathered their children together and left. And there's me, hovering nearby, wondering what to do …'

'So? What *did* you do?'

'Well, I went over, of course. Somebody acting so oddly, at Marcus's murder scene? Had to, didn't I? I had a pack of tissues in my bag so I used that as an excuse, went over and offered her one. She took it – her mascara was all over her face by this point. Clearly not waterproof. Anyway, I sat down on the grass next to her, and once she'd calmed down a bit, I asked her who she was, and how long she'd known Marcus. She said her name was Katie Chamberlain – *Katie*, Cora! And – and this is where it got *really* peculiar – she said she was his girlfriend. His GIRLFRIEND!'

Wendy practically shouted the last word down the line.

'His *girlfriend*? What? Was Marcus two-timing Sam, then? With Katie, his mad ex?' Cora, who had still been lying back on her cushions as she listened, suddenly sat bolt upright. 'No way!'

'No, no he wasn't. I don't think so, anyway.' Wendy explained that she had quickly decided not to reveal that she was a friend of Sam's, but instead had casually remarked that she had thought that Marcus's girlfriend was currently in prison, awaiting trial for his murder.

'Oh, well, yes, of course,' Katie had said, a faint blush staining her heavily powdered cheeks. 'I mean, I *was* his girlfriend, until fairly recently. And I would have been again, if ... if ... that bitch hadn't stolen him from me, and then killed him. He still loved me, I know he did. It was only a matter of time, before he came back to me. I mean – have you seen her? That Sam person? What she looks like? Why would he want her instead of me?'

She had started to cry again then, and Wendy had waited patiently until the tears subsided once more, hoping to elicit a little more information.

'Did you know her well? This Sam, I mean?' she had asked tentatively, as Katie accepted another tissue and started scrubbing her face angrily, eyes now glued again to the little cluster of trees where Marcus's body had lain.

'I knew her well enough. I'm a hairdresser, and she came to the salon. And oh boy, did she love to taunt me. Always flashing pictures around of her and Marcus, even talking about how she was sure he was going to pop the question soon. Him, marry *her*? What a joke. Yes, I knew her well enough. Well enough to hate her, that's for sure. But it's OK. I made sure she got what she deserved.'

Katie had stopped rubbing her face now, and turned to look at Wendy properly for the first time, streaks of eyeliner and clumps of dark, damp mascara somehow emphasising the striking blue-grey of her eyes.

'Got what she deserved? What … what do you mean?'

Katie had sat quite still for a moment, looking at Wendy. Then, quite unexpectedly, she had stood up, her face twisting into a scowl, eyes flashing. She bent to scoop up her handbag from where it had been lying on the grass, and then turned to Wendy once more.

'Thanks for the tissues. I don't mean anything. But, well, its karma, isn't it? Look where she is now. Goodbye.'

'And then she just stalked off. Bloody hell, Cora – what do you make of that?'

Now Cora stared at the muted television, where a punch-up had just started between two tanned young men in surf shorts in the coffee shop on *Neighbours*. She didn't really know what to make of it at all, and she didn't want to jump to any crazy conclusions. After all, if Katie Chamberlain loved Marcus so much and wanted him back, it seemed highly unlikely that she would have murdered him just to get Sam in trouble. Or would she? If she was as unstable as Sam believed she was, could she possibly have thought a dead Marcus would be preferable to a Marcus married to someone else? That line, 'I made sure she got what she deserved.' That was very interesting, Cora thought. Very interesting indeed.

17

Friday 24th May
35 days until the deadline

'Katie Chamberlain? Yes, she's just gone on her tea break out the back. You're a reporter, did you say?'

Cora nodded and handed over her card. The receptionist, a young man with black, spiky hair, took it and disappeared through a purple velvet curtain that hung over an alcove behind his counter. Cora rested her handbag on the shelf at the front of the reception desk and waited, trying to calm her nerves. She'd been called out after all last night, and she and Wendy had chatted again on the phone this morning, as soon as Cora had finished her live broadcasts from the scene of a grim four-car pile-up on the M42. As she made her way back towards London, where she was looking forward to a weekend with Adam, Cora told Wendy it was probably better if she approached Katie Chamberlain alone, given what had happened yesterday.

'Agreed. Why don't you just say you're a reporter for *Morning Live*, gathering background information for after the court case, and you're trying to talk to as many people who knew Marcus as possible? She doesn't have to know you're a friend of Sam's. You can always lie, say you're just a colleague who doesn't know her very well, if she asks you.'

It was a good plan. But now, as Cora waited for Katie

to emerge, she was finding it hard to control the butterflies in her stomach. From what the hairdresser had said to Wendy – that menacing line about Sam getting what she deserved – there could be a real possibility that she'd had some role to play in the murder. Adam would *have* to act, surely, if Cora found out anything that implicated Katie today? She glanced around the salon. Unsurprisingly on a Friday afternoon, every chair was occupied, hairdryers buzzing, juniors rushing back and forth with sweeping brushes, trays of tea and glasses of white wine. The stylists all wore black, but colour was where the similarity of their outfits ended. One woman wore a skin-tight dress with towering, bejewelled shoes, while next to her a colleague had teamed leather leggings with a floaty, chiffon shirt and Converse trainers. Across the room, a male colourist in an aviator-style jumpsuit was applying highlights with remarkable speed, painting on the tint with his little brush before wrapping each section of hair in a square of foil so quickly Cora could barely see his fingers moving. It was a small but chic salon, tucked away on a side street off Fulham Road. The heavy velvet curtain behind reception matched the purple leather chairs in which clients were being primped, preened and gossiped to, and the elaborate frames around the enormous mirrors at each work station were crafted from twisted metal painted mulberry and silver.

'Hello? I'm Katie Chamberlain. Can I help?'

Cora, who'd been staring, mesmerised, at the super-quick colourist, turned to see a tall blonde woman, who looked to be in her late twenties or early thirties, smiling at her. She was indeed very pretty, the artfully streaked blonde and pink hair Wendy had described pulled back in a high ponytail, emphasising her fine bone structure and unusual eyes. Her black outfit was a simple pair of canvas jeans, wedge shoes and a plain tunic top, but she'd added a stunning statement necklace made from large, irregular black and white gemstones which gave her a striking, high-fashion look.

'Katie. So good of you to make the time, I know you're on your break. I'm Cora. Cora Baxter.'

She quickly gave the hairdresser the cover story she and Wendy had decided on, and then paused.

'So – would you be able to spend a little time with me? I know from my research – talking to Marcus's friends and so on – that you dated for quite a while, so it would be great to hear a little about the man himself, maybe some stories about your time together? It would really help with the piece I'm putting together for after the trial.'

Behind her back, Cora crossed her fingers. She didn't like lying, but needs must. In actual fact, she wasn't even covering the story for *Morning Live*, Betsy agreeing with her that she was far too close to this one to be able to report on it impartially. The job had been given to Hannah, a relatively new reporter who didn't know Sam very well and was thrilled to have been given such a big story to cut her teeth on.

'Well – yes, I suppose so.' Katie looked doubtful for a moment, then her face cleared. 'Actually, yes, it would be good to talk about Marcus. And my three o'clock client has cancelled, so unless there's a walk-in I'm free now for about forty minutes. Do you want to come through? It's a bit noisy out here, with all the dryers and everything.'

She pointed to the curtain and pulled it aside. Cora slipped behind the reception desk and made her way through the archway. A short corridor opened up into a small but pleasant staffroom, with a sofa, a scattering of comfortable-looking chairs and a few low tables piled high with hair and fashion magazines, a few empty coffee cups and some discarded chocolate and sandwich wrappers. Off to one side was a kitchen area. Katie gestured at Cora to sit down.

'Tea? Coffee?' she said, opening a cupboard above the sink and grabbing two tall white mugs.

'Tea would be lovely. Black, please. Er ... I don't suppose you have any Earl Grey?'

'We do, actually. Boss drinks nothing else.' Katie turned and smiled before busying herself with the drinks. When they were ready she put them both carefully on the nearest little table and sat down in the chair opposite Cora's.

'Right. What do you want to know?'

Cora picked up the notebook and pen she'd pulled from her bag while Katie was making the tea and smiled.

'Just a bit of background really. Let's start with how you met.'

Katie smiled back, and launched into a long, detailed story about how she'd met Marcus while they were both out running in Hyde Park, how they had instantly been attracted to each other and how he had taken her to the 'most romantic little Italian restaurant *ever*' on their first date. She seemed so pleasant and animated that Cora couldn't help but warm to her. There was certainly no sign here of the distraught, angry woman that Wendy had described.

'Did you know many of his friends, his family?'

Katie shook her head, and pushed an errant strand of pink hair back from her forehead. 'He didn't have much family – his parents both died quite soon after each other a few years back, mum from breast cancer and dad from a heart attack, I think. There were a few aunts and uncles and cousins but they all lived outside London and he didn't see them that often. His friends were OK though, the guys from his work.'

'What about female friends?' Cora asked the question tentatively.

'He didn't need female friends – he had me.' Katie's voice suddenly had a coolness to it.

'Oh yes, of course. It's just that my boss at *Morning Live* – Betsy Allan? – well, she was quite a good friend of his. I wondered if you'd ever met.' Cora smiled warmly at Katie, trying to appear as non-threatening as possible, and the hairdresser seemed to relax again.

'Ah yes, Betsy. I met her once or twice. They'd known each other for years, it was purely platonic, you know? She was OK. But as I said, once he was with me he didn't need other women in his life. I was enough.'

'Of course. Tell me more – what sort of things did you do with him?'

'Oh, we were so much alike, we just loved being together. It didn't really matter what we did. But there was this one time when …'

Katie plunged into another long story about a trip to Scotland when she and Marcus decided to camp all night on the shores of Loch Ness in an effort to catch sight of its legendary monster, and Cora nodded politely, scribbling on her pad, wondering how she was going to turn this conversation to Sam and the night of the murder. She'd just have to *do* it, she supposed, so when Katie paused to draw breath, Cora held up a hand.

'That all sounds wonderful. So what went wrong – why did you split up?'

'Oh.' Katie looked down at the table and was silent for a moment. When she raised her eyes again, her expression had changed from one of someone reliving joyful memories; now, she suddenly looked harder, older.

'He ...' She paused. 'He ... well, he had commitment issues. You know what men are like.' She gave a brittle little laugh. 'But he would have come back to me in the end. He still loved me, I know he did. If only that stupid bitch hadn't come along ...'

She looked back at Cora, narrowing her eyes. 'Hang on – you must know her. If you work with Betsy, at the breakfast show? She worked there too, as a producer. Is she a friend of yours or something? Is that why you're asking me all these questions?'

Katie stood up, smoothing her tunic with her hands, a large silver ring on one finger glinting, a suspicious frown creasing her smooth brow.

'No, no, not at all. I barely know her – I'm a reporter, so I'm out on the road most of the time. We don't really get to know the producers at all, they're just voices on the end of the phone.'

Cora tried to keep her voice calm and level, hating the lie. *Please don't ask me to leave now, just when we're getting to the good bit*, she thought.

'Oh, OK.' Katie sat down again, and took a deep breath. 'Well, you won't mind me saying what a horrible, arrogant cow she was then?'

Cora forced a grin. 'Not at all!'

Katie's lips curled into something halfway between a smile and a grimace. 'I couldn't stand her. She thought she was something special, you know? With her big TV job and everything. Every time she came in here she was flashing photos around, talking about where Marcus had taken her last night. She even said she thought he was on the verge of asking her to marry him. I mean, really!' She laughed a hollow laugh again.

Cora sat quietly, nodding, letting her talk. Tell me what happened the night of the murder, she urged silently.

Come on, Katie. Tell me you got your revenge on Sam. *Tell me.*

'She was an idiot. Marcus would never have married her. He loved me, you see?' Katie's eyes flashed for a moment, then, quite suddenly, she slumped back in her chair, her face crumpling.

'But we'll never be together now, will we? Because she ... because she ...' She started to sob, burying her face in her hands. Cora reached out a hand and patted her knee.

'Don't cry, Katie. I didn't mean for you to get upset. We're almost finished here. Can you ... can you just talk me through the night – the night Marcus died? If you can?'

Katie lifted her face from her fingers and stared at Cora, oblivious to the rivulets of eye makeup streaking down her cheeks.

'Well, I wasn't around on the actual night, of course. I didn't even know, until I got out of hospital, and then I only knew what was in the papers and on the TV. I just felt sick, I couldn't believe ...'

'Hang on – what?' Cora, who had been pretending to write more notes, looked up sharply. 'Hospital?'

'Yes – oh sorry, didn't I say? I was in hospital the day Marcus was ... the day Marcus died. My appendix burst on the Bank Holiday Monday afternoon. I'd been in pain all weekend but I'd ignored it, thought it was the after-effects of a dodgy Thai takeaway I'd had on the Friday night. Then I went shopping on Monday afternoon and collapsed in Topshop. They had to call an ambulance and everything, it was a bit of a drama.'

She smiled, as if pleased at the memory. 'Anyway, I had the operation that afternoon, and they kept me in until the Thursday. So as I said, I didn't know anything about the murder until I came out.'

'I see. Well, thank you.' Cora stood up slowly, a wave of depression sweeping over her. Marcus had been murdered late on that Monday night. If Katie was in hospital having surgery, there was simply no way she could have been involved. So what had she meant in her comment to Wendy yesterday, about making sure Sam got what she deserved? It didn't make sense, but it now seemed pretty unlikely that she could have been involved herself. Could she have got someone else to kill Marcus and plant Sam's DNA at the scene on her behalf? But if so, who? Or was that just too far-fetched? Was this just another ludicrous wild goose chase? Cora's head felt as if it was stuffed with cotton wool as she said her goodbyes to Katie and headed out of the salon. Now, the feeling she'd kept getting since the start of all this, if she was being honest, was getting even stronger – this whole 'somebody's stolen my DNA and framed me' scenario was just ridiculous. There had to be another explanation.

She exhaled heavily as she clambered into her car and slammed the door. She'd have to call Sam tonight as promised, to update her on what had happened with Katie, and she was *not* looking forward to that conversation.

Inside the salon, Katie Chamberlain stood by the floor to ceiling window that looked on to the street, slowly wiping her ruined makeup from her cheeks with a dampened cotton pad. She waited until she saw Cora's car pulling away from the kerb, then moved swiftly to the door, stepping out on to the pavement. She stood stock still, watching, until the BMW turned right on to Fulham Road and disappeared out of sight. Then she laughed, quietly, almost under her breath. Another stupid bitch, she thought to herself. They're all just so *stupid*. With a final glance down the street, she turned and headed back into the salon, smiling.

18

Saturday 25th May
34 days until the deadline

Cora stretched limbs that ached after a particularly long run the previous night and then, trying not to wake Adam who was still snoring gently beside her, plumped up her pillows and sank back into them. Her early bird body clock had woken her at 6 a.m., far too early for a day off, and while she didn't think she would manage to doze off again, she could at least indulge in a bit of a laze.

Lying on her back, she watched the gently waving patterns on the ceiling as the morning light danced through the branches of the tree outside the window, and her mind drifted back to last night and the conversation she'd had with Sam when she'd returned from her run. The news that Katie Chamberlain had been indisposed on the night of the murder had been yet another blow for her friend.

'But – but what about what she said to Wendy? About making sure I got what I deserved? She *must* be involved, Cora!' Sam had said, sounding suddenly desperate. 'Because if not her, then who? Who did this?'

'I'm so sorry. I just don't know. But Sam, we're not going to give up, OK? Something will come up eventually, it has to.' Cora hoped she was sounding more positive than she felt.

Sam sighed heavily at the other end of the phone. 'OK,

well – I just don't know any more, Cora. But – well, I did wonder if this might happen with Katie, so I've been wracking my brains, hitting it from every possible angle, like we would with a news story, you know? I don't have much else to do in here, after all. And I thought, well, what about the possibility of my DNA somehow matching someone else's, even though that's not supposed to be possible? What if it was some sort of fluke, a billion to one chance? These things do happen, Cora, we know that, we see stories all the time …'

Cora's heart sank. Come on, Sam, don't be ridiculous, she wanted to say. She took a deep breath.

'Sam, it's just so unlikely. But, well …' Cora paused. Sam was clearly once again desperately clutching at straws, to use a cliché that the producer had a long time ago banned the newsroom's journalists from using in their reports. But if it kept her spirits up …

'OK, I know who to talk to. Remember that doctor at the IVF clinic on Harley Street? We interviewed her when that woman had sextuplets? She was a bit of a DNA expert, I seem to remember, and she was friendly – I could pop in and run it by her, pretend I'm researching a story?'

'Oh, Cora, would you? That would be brilliant. Thank you. Thank you *so* much.' The relief in Sam's voice made Cora's throat tighten with emotion. This must be a total nightmare for her friend, she thought, and however unlikely and ludicrous-sounding her theories are, I'm just going to have to go along with them. She'd do the same for me.

'I'll do it on Monday, after work, OK?'

'OK. And then call me, straight away?'

'Of course.'

Now Cora shifted position, edging her leg closer to

Adam until it was touching his, the fine blond hairs on his thigh tickling her skin. He twitched slightly but didn't wake. She still hadn't mentioned her meeting with Katie Chamberlain to him, and she didn't intend to mention her trip to the IVF clinic either, not unless anything useful came of it. She'd ask the doctor there about how easy it would be to frame somebody with stolen DNA too, when she went. And about how long DNA could survive, if somebody *had* managed to steal Sam's. She rolled over and picked up her BlackBerry from the bedside table to check today's date. The twenty-fifth. Time was marching on. Less than five weeks now until Sam's next court appearance. Despite the warm duvet, Cora shivered.

In Richmond, David Cash had been awake and out of bed for over an hour. His girlfriend Sue hadn't stayed over last night, as her mother was visiting from Wales, so after showering, shaving, dressing carefully and downing two cups of coffee, he'd decided to take the opportunity to add the latest clippings to his scrapbook. Sue and her mother were going to be joining him in a local eatery for breakfast later, and he wanted to get it all done and tidied away again before he went out.

In his little home office, formerly the upstairs box-room, he slipped his fingers behind the heavy wooden frame of a large print on the wall and retrieved the small key that was resting there. Returning to sit behind the desk, he unlocked the left-hand drawer and pulled out a burgundy-coloured scrapbook, its pages still empty. Then he reached back into the drawer for the envelope. He lifted the flap and tipped the contents out onto the polished wooden desktop, then started gently smoothing out each piece of paper. Newsprint creased dreadfully, he thought, running his fingers across a photograph. You have a big line right across your face, Sam. Sorry about that. Once all the pieces of paper were lying flat, in orderly lines across the desk, he leaned forward, scanning each one, a half smile on his lips. She was still so beautiful. Sam's face looked back at him from the newspaper cuttings, the headlines above it varying according to the paper the article had been taken from. "TV producer charged with lover's murder", said *The Telegraph*, while *The Sun* screamed "BODY IN THE PARK – HOTSHOT TV BABE IN COURT".

David rearranged the cuttings, making sure they were in date order. Then he remembered the handkerchief. Should he put that in first? Yes, he could staple it on to the first page of the scrapbook. He lifted it carefully out of the drawer. It was one of his own, a blue and white plaid print cotton square. They'd been to the cinema, while they were together, to see a sad film, and she'd cried and he'd lent it to her to wipe the tears away. She'd used it, and then popped it in her jacket pocket and forgotten about it, remembering only a few days later when they were out together again and she'd stuck her hand into the same pocket. She'd offered to wash it, of course, but he'd insisted that he'd do it himself. It still smelled of her, he thought now, bending his head to sniff it delicately. It would make the book smell nice too. He reached for the stapler, carefully attached the fabric to page one, then reached for the glue. He'd stick all the cuttings in, nice and neatly, then he'd head off to meet Sue and get on with his day.

19

Monday 27th May
32 days until the deadline

Cora stared at the hand-drawn chart on the wall of the little cubby-hole round the corner from the studio. It was where presenters went to pick up their microphones and talk-back units before the show, but the wall above the equipment shelf was normally adorned with nothing more exciting than roster sheets and flyers advertising local bars. Today, though, a large grid of names, some with a row of blue stars against them, dominated the space. Cora's own name had just one star next to it.

'What on earth is this?' She jabbed a finger at the wall.

'A potty mouth chart. Far too much bad language in this place. And not enough spare cash for booze. So, we thought – we being the floor managers – we'd fine all the reporters and presenters every time they swear, and we get to drink the proceeds on a Friday afternoon.'

Cecily, one of the longest serving floor managers, grinned. 'So, everyone's a winner. You lot clean up your act and we have a fun Friday. Here you go, stick that up your top.' She handed Cora her microphone and then, grabbing her by the upper arms, firmly turned her around and started attaching the packs to the waistband of her wide-legged black trousers.

'Oh – and your star is for "knob", on that 3D printer, if you were wondering. I know that was more than two weeks ago, but none of us could remember you swearing since then, amazingly, and we had to put you on for *something*.' Cecily finished what she was doing and turned Cora round to face her again.

'Oh come on, a knob is an actual thing, you know! It was just everyone else's filthy minds that made that sound rude ...'

Cecily adjusted the microphone clipped to Cora's lapel and shook her head. 'Nope. A rude word is a rude word, even if unintentional. Come on, a quid in the box.'

'*So* unfair.' But Cora grinned as she fumbled in her bag for a pound coin and popped it through the slot in the money box under the wall chart. She studied the names for a moment.

'Blimey – what happened to Alice? *Seven* stars?'

'She broke a heel on the way down from the newsroom on Friday. Louboutins I think they were. Never heard so much swearing in my life. She ticked up all seven stars in about thirty seconds.'

Cecily giggled. 'She's a changed woman since last year, and I do love her now, but honestly, Cora, for a minute the old Alice was back. It was hilarious.'

Cora chuckled to herself as she headed into the studio to read the 6 a.m. news. Alice was indeed a totally different person nowadays to the nasty, insecure girl she'd been before Jeanette's murder. In those days, she had terrorised the younger staff and alienated herself from the older members of the crew. Now, with her transformation from girl about town to doting mother, she was slowly becoming a valued friend and colleague, her true and really quite sweet personality finally coming to the fore. But, thought Cora as she settled at the news desk, it was quite nice in a strange way to see that a little of the old Alice fire still burned somewhere deep inside.

It was nearly four o'clock by the time Cora finally managed to extricate herself from the newsroom and hail a cab to Harley Street. As they pulled up outside the Wellford Clinic, a tall Georgian building with a handsome, grey-painted door, she paid the driver and climbed out of the taxi, pausing for a moment to take in the splendour of the street. It had been London's most prestigious address for the medical profession since the late 1800s, its elegant sweep running northwards from Cavendish Square and on to Regent's Park. Now, the historic buildings housed state-of-the art-technology, but if Cora closed her eyes, she imagined she could still hear the clack of horses' hooves and the rumble of the wheels of hansom cabs whisking the wealthy down the street. She stood for a moment, letting her mind's eye take her back in time, then jumped as an irate female voice barged into her consciousness.

'Excuse me, *please*!' Cora opened her eyes to see a small, very round woman in a dark brown trench coat and slightly comical cat's-eye glasses attempting to manoeuvre what looked like a vintage Silvercross pram around her.

'Gosh, sorry, miles away.' Cora stepped back to allow the woman to pass, catching a glimpse of a small baby swaddled in a pale blue blanket under the navy hood. The woman glared at her, tutted loudly, and stomped off, the pram rolling smoothly in front of her on well-oiled wheels. Cora watched them go for a moment, gathering her thoughts, then turned and pushed the brass doorbell. She had rung the Wellford first thing this morning, and luck had been with her. Dr Ana Taylor could spare her twenty minutes if she could get to Harley Street anytime between four and six, as she had 'ring-fenced those two hours to catch up on some admin', according to the woman who'd taken the call. It had taken nearly half an hour to get there from the South Bank and was now just coming up to 4.30, which was perfect, Cora thought. She and Adam were planning to pop out for an early dinner at their favourite local Italian, and she was already salivating at the prospect. It would be a rare treat for a Monday night, but Adam had told her he realised how tough the whole Sam business was and that she needed a treat, and she wasn't going to argue.

A young woman with a broad smile and a smart tan-coloured dress opened the front door and ushered her into a large waiting room with a plush cream carpet, armchairs upholstered in soft green fabric and, on one wall, a widescreen television playing a film of a tropical coral reef – the modern equivalent of a waiting room aquarium, thought Cora wryly as she took a seat. On the wall to her left hung a large framed photograph, and she squinted to read the caption underneath it: 'Dr Humphrey Barden, our founder and friend', it said.

She had been waiting less than a minute when the door opened and another woman walked in, older but also dressed in tan. Unlike her smiling younger colleague, she looked ill at ease and frumpy in her slightly flared skirt and rumpled blouse, her greying brown hair clipped back severely from her plain face. She looked at Cora, and her eyes suddenly widened in recognition. Cora smiled, realising that this latest member of staff must be a *Morning Live* viewer, but her smile froze as the woman's expression suddenly changed to one more akin to fear. They started at each other for a moment, Cora unsure what to do, and then the woman's face cleared.

'Miss Baxter? I'm Eleanor Hawkins, one of the nurses here. If you come with me, Dr Taylor can see you now.'

Her voice was low and sullen, and now she didn't look at Cora at all, her eyes flitting around the room as she spoke, as if following the trajectory of a fly.

'Thank you.' Cora stood up and followed the woman out of the room and down a long corridor carpeted in the same plush cream. How on earth did they keep it so clean, especially in winter? Did they make everyone take their shoes off? Cora pondered as they made their way around a corner to the left and paused outside what looked like a freshly painted door with a small silver sign bearing the doctor's name.

'Knock and go in,' Eleanor Hawkins muttered abruptly, and then turned and scurried off in the direction they had come. Somewhat amused at the woman's slightly odd behaviour, although people did sometimes act oddly when confronted with someone they'd only ever seen before on the TV in their living room, Cora did as she'd been told, and pushed the door open. The room inside was warm and bright, walls covered with framed academic certificates and a few black and white lithographs, a light aroma of fresh coffee hanging in the air. At the far side of the office, a tall, elegant woman was already emerging from behind a huge mahogany desk, hand outstretched.

'Miss Baxter, how nice to see you again!' The voice was soft and melodious with a hint of a West Country accent. Dr Ana Taylor, chic in a tailored black suit and pearls, and with dark hair in an Audrey Hepburn-style pixie crop, smiled broadly.

Cora smiled back. 'Oh, please call me Cora. Thank you so much for seeing me at such short notice.'

She settled herself in the low-backed club chair in front of the desk and for a couple of minutes they made polite small talk. Then, aware of the time, Cora decided to get to the point.

'Dr Taylor ... I know you're a bit of an expert on DNA. I wanted to run something past you. It's for a ...' she paused, not wanting to say too much, 'a crime story I'm working on, a murder charge which hasn't come to trial yet so I can't really go into detail. But the case hangs on DNA evidence. I wanted to check a couple of things. First – and I think I already know the answer to this, but I just wanted to double check – is it possible, by the remotest of chances, for two unrelated people to have the same DNA profiles? Because, in this case, the police say they've found the accused's DNA on the murder weapon, and this person is absolutely, one hundred per cent adamant that they are innocent. So, *could* there be a tiny, tiny chance of it being somebody else's DNA, which happens to be the same?'

Dr Taylor shook her head. 'It's an argument that criminals often try and use – "there must be somebody with the same DNA as me, because I didn't do it". But ...'

She leaned forwards, hands on the desk, a large emerald ring sparkling on one middle finger. 'Look, we get our DNA from our parents. So people who are closely related, like siblings, will have similar DNA profiles, and identical twins will have, to all intents and purposes, the same profile, except on incredibly detailed analysis. But even when you get to first cousin level, the likelihood of a match is about one in a hundred million, and for unrelated people it's about one in a billion. Hence, if you look at the population of the whole world ... what are we at now, around seven billion? That's about six other people on the planet with *possibly* the same DNA profile as me or you, but in reality ... well, the chances of unrelated people having matching DNA is one in several trillion. It's like a personal barcode. There's very little room for error.'

'I see. So unless this person has an identical twin, then they probably ... they probably committed the crime themselves?'

'Yes.' Dr Taylor nodded.

'Right.' Cora ploughed on, not letting the crushing feeling that was creeping over her take hold. 'OK, so the other thing is – well, the person accused of this crime thinks that maybe somebody might have framed them, by stealing their DNA, then carrying out the murder themselves and planting the DNA at the scene. How easy would that be? And how long does DNA last, say for example on a water glass, or something else?'

Dr Taylor raised an eyebrow. 'Well, it's *possible*,' she said, sounding sceptical. 'But again, a little bit far-fetched. I mean, we can't go anywhere without leaving some trace of ourselves. This isn't really my area, but in theory somebody with access to us, our home, our belongings, could take something with our DNA on it and, I suppose, use it at a crime scene. It's as simple as swabbing a drinking glass, or a cigarette stub, and then wiping that swab on something at the scene. But they'd have to make damn sure they didn't leave any of their own DNA there too, otherwise it'd be a bit of a waste of time. As for how long it lasts, well, it depends on the conditions. A sample of human DNA found in Spain was found to be seven thousand years old, for example. It's impossible to say, really – I'm not an expert in forensics. But in the right environmental conditions, well looked after, it can certainly hang around for a while. Is that any use to you?'

'It is, yes. Thank you, Dr Taylor.'

'Is that it, then? Anything else I can help you with? That was too easy!' The doctor laughed and leaned back in her chair again, adjusting the pearls at her throat.

'No, that's it. Thanks so much for your time.'

143

Cora stood up, suddenly feeling deeply depressed. Dr Taylor's information about DNA possibly being used to frame somebody had been interesting, but Cora realised now that she had simply stopped believing in that possibility. And with the fact that nobody else could have the same genetic profile as Sam now confirmed, she faced the prospect of telling her friend that her last faint hope had been dashed. How on earth would she react? And what was left? If there was no lab mix-up, nobody who had framed Sam and nobody with the same DNA as her, that meant … as Cora left the clinic, she pushed the thought from her mind. *Sam is not a killer, Sam is not a killer, Sam is not a killer.* She chanted the words in her head like a mantra as she made her way back out on to the street and hailed a cab.

As she sat in her taxi, mind whirling, Cora suddenly decided to pay Sam's mother a visit. Ellen Tindall must be distraught, so it would be a nice thing to do anyway, but maybe, just possibly, she could help. Maybe Sam had some old enemy that none of them knew about, who might have come out of the woodwork now to get revenge and frame her for murder. And maybe I'll see a pig flying down the street in a minute, thought Cora, and leaned her forehead against the cool glass of the side window as the black cab lurched to a halt yet again in the evening rush hour traffic. On Marylebone Road, tourists were pouring through the doors of Madame Tussauds as it closed for the day. A harassed-looking woman in a floral dress was trying to shepherd a small flock of schoolchildren into a line, gesturing impatiently to two other adults, a man and a woman who both wore dark tracksuits, to help her. Normal people, trying to cope with the normal, small inconveniences of life, thought Cora, as the taxi jolted and moved off again. And then there's me, with one of my best friends facing life in prison for murder, and me facing an impossible deadline to save her from that fate, desperately scrabbling for any little bit of hope at all. She shut her eyes for a moment, sighed, then opened them again, reached into her bag for her phone, and called Ellen Tindall's number.

20

Tuesday 28th May
31 days until the deadline

'You know it's Sam's birthday on Thursday? Her thirty-first? Imagine spending your birthday in prison. I can't bear it, Cora, I really can't.'

Wendy slumped over her desk, a picture of despair. Cora, swinging disconsolately from side to side on the swivel chair next to her, felt as gloomy as Wendy looked. It really *was* a dreadful thought. Sam's response to Cora's findings at the Wellford Clinic had been predictably bad when Cora had called her last night, and now she was facing a birthday in jail to boot.

'I mean, can we even send her anything? A cake? We can't let her have *nothing* to celebrate with, we just can't, it's just too awful. She was so looking forward to the big night out we were all going to have, and now she's going to be all on her own, in that dreadful place …'

Wendy sat up abruptly, eyes glinting with tears, and turned to Cora with an anguished expression.

'We can't send much, I checked last week. No food or toiletries. But we can send DVDs, books, stuff like that.' Cora stopped swinging and leaned forward to squeeze Wendy's arm.

'Let's get some bits from the two of us this afternoon. And we can see if Ellen wants to send anything too, when we see her later. Put it all together in a nice package for

147

Sam. I'll drop it off at Henworthy tomorrow on my way home, OK?'

'OK. Thanks, Cora.' Wendy sniffed and ran a finger under each eye, checking for mascara runs. They were sitting in the *Morning Live* graphics suite, a big room which was always in semi-darkness to allow the graphic artists to see their screens more easily. It was a four-strong team, working round-the-clock shifts, so Cora had been relieved to find Wendy alone when she'd popped in after coming off air, wanting to recount her telephone conversation with Ellen Tindall. Sam's mother had been delighted at the prospect of a visit from Cora, and had begged her to bring Wendy too, a request to which Wendy had happily agreed. They'd been invited for afternoon tea, a prospect which had briefly cheered them both up – Ellen was well known for her baking skills. The gloom had soon descended again though, thoughts of Sam's birthday making both of them feel utterly miserable. They all loved birthdays, and celebrated them lustily – Cora's thirty-sixth birthday party in April had been an all-day affair that had taken three days to recover from. The prospect of Sam sitting alone in a jail cell without so much as a glass of bubbly to mark hers was hideous.

Cora sighed heavily. 'So ... your shift ends at two, right?' She stood up, smoothing down her navy suede skirt.

Wendy nodded. 'Come and get me. We can pop into Covent Garden quickly to pick up the presents and then head to Ellen's.'

'OK. I've got plenty of work to do in the newsroom before then, got a couple of big interviews in the bulletins tomorrow ...'

She turned as the door opened and Miranda walked in, casual today in an off-air outfit of pale denims and a loose

148

coral jumper, her dark hair pulled back in a ponytail.

'Oh – Cora, hello! I wanted to see Wendy about a graphic for this head lice piece they want next week, before I head off to the New Forest to do some filming later. Hi, Wendy – is this a bad time?'

'No, you're fine, I was just getting rid of this pain-in-the-ass reporter.'

Wendy glowered at Cora and then her face broke into a smile, and Cora, appreciating the effort her friend was making to appear normal, punched her gently on the arm.

'Rude!'

Miranda laughed. 'I love the banter between you lot. I bet you're missing Sam. How ... how is she, have you heard?'

Cora and Wendy exchanged brief glances. 'She's OK. Bearing up. She's tough, our Sam. It's her birthday on Thursday though, her thirty-first, which is going to be pretty grim for her.'

Miranda gasped, her hand flying to her mouth. 'Oh! That's just awful! It's mine in a couple of weeks, on the fourteenth of June – I'll be thirty-one too. I'm going away to Paris on the Eurostar with some of my medic friends, I'm so excited. Poor Sam. I can't even imagine ...'

She sat down heavily on Cora's recently vacated chair, looking stricken.

'I know. But we're going to put a little box together for her, some DVDs and books to keep her going. We can celebrate properly when she gets out,' Wendy said firmly.

Miranda nodded. 'That's nice. Look, give her my best wishes, won't you?'

'Of course. You could visit her too, you know, if you like? You don't need a visiting order, not while she's on remand,' said Cora.

Miranda looked unsure. 'I'm not sure I know her well

enough yet for that. But … maybe. I'll think about it.' She sat up straight, suddenly business-like again, and smiled at Wendy.

'So – how are you at drawing nits?'

'Ugh. You bring me all the best jobs, Miranda.' Wendy grimaced, and Cora headed for the door.

'Two o'clock!'

'Two o'clock,' echoed Wendy. 'See you then.'

Cora took a detour to the canteen to pick up an Earl Grey and a raisin flapjack, then wandered back to the newsroom. Chewing, she logged on to the internet and began to research the interest rate story that would feature in tomorrow's bulletins, and for which she'd be interviewing a leading economist during the 7 a.m. news. She was just getting stuck into an analytical article from one of the financial magazines, making notes on her pad, when she became aware of somebody hovering at her elbow. She turned to see Betsy standing there, elegant as always in a fitted grey dress, her shiny blonde curls framing her face.

'Oh, hi, boss … can I help you?'

Betsy smiled. 'No, no, just wandering, seeing what everyone's up to. You working on the William Freeman interview for tomorrow?'

'Yep. Think he'll tell us that rates are likely to rise sharply in the fourth quarter. All speculation of course, but I wanted to be prepared with some pertinent questions …'

Cora's voice tailed off as she realised Betsy was no longer looking at her, and instead was gazing across at the news desk, currently occupied by Sean, a freelance senior producer from Dublin. It was Sam's usual seat, and Cora felt a pang as she looked at it, knowing how desperately her friend was missing her job.

150

'Good, good. You're always well prepared.' Betsy's eyes flitted back to Cora, one hand fiddling with her hair. She suddenly looked uncomfortable, her cheeks flushing slightly. Cora watched her, puzzled. Betsy was normally so – well, so *together*.

'So, er ...' The programme editor cleared her throat. 'What's happening with our best producer then? Any chance of getting her out of that place and back here where she belongs any time soon?'

Ahh, that was it. She was just worried about Sam, like everybody else, thought Cora. She shook her head sadly.

'Not at the moment. But her lawyers are working on it. I'll let you know as soon as we know, Betsy. She's keeping her spirits up though, you know what she's like.'

Betsy nodded, patted Cora on the shoulder, then spun on her heels and strode off in the direction of her office. Cora stared after her for a moment, then shrugged and turned back to her computer screen.

21

It was just after 4.15 p.m. when Cora and Wendy clambered out of their taxi outside Ellen Tindall's mansion block home. The red brick Victorian building, of a kind seen across central London, had been built in the late nineteenth century, for the flourishing middle classes who wanted *pieds-a-terre* in the capital. It was in King's Cross, once an area of London very much to be avoided, so Ellen and her late husband had snapped up their two-bedroom flat for a song thirty-odd years ago. In recent times though, this area had changed dramatically, partly due to the transformation of the nearby St Pancras station into a Eurostar terminal. Now the haunt of city workers, arty types and students, it had become a desirable place to live, and Sam had often talked about how pleased her mother had been, after years of relative hardship, to see the value of her home rise so astronomically.

Clutching their bags of gifts hastily chosen in Covent Garden after work, Cora and Wendy waited for Ellen to buzz them in then climbed the stairs to the third floor. As they approached the door marked with a large silver number twenty-seven, they could see that it was already ajar, and moments later Sam's mother flung it open, beaming.

'Girls! It's so lovely to see you.'

She held out her arms and they hugged her in turn, before they were ushered inside and down the hallway into the lounge. Although rather dated in its décor, the room had a high ceiling and large sash windows which flooded it with light. A floral three-piece suite, what looked like the original fireplace (but with a vase of dried flowers currently in the hearth instead of a fire) and side-tables covered with framed photographs gave the room a homely feel, as did the small dining table in one corner, laden with plates of food.

'Make yourselves at home, take your jackets off, sit down! Kettle's just boiled so I'll make the tea and then we can have a proper catch-up. It's *so* nice to see you, I can't tell you.'

Ellen bustled out of the room, heading for the kitchen, and Cora and Wendy smiled at each other.

'Bless her.' Cora dumped her bags on the floor next to the sofa, slipped off her jacket and draped it over the back of a chair, then wandered across to a mahogany sideboard, eyes drawn to a photograph of a familiar face.

'Look, Wend. Sam's graduation. She hardly looks any older now.'

Wendy, shrugging off her own coat, grinned. 'She doesn't, does she? Gosh, she's in virtually every photo, isn't she? It's like a Sam-through-the-ages exhibition.'

Cora walked slowly around the room, taking in the pictures. It was true – Sam as a baby, asleep in a pram, smiling toothlessly on a sofa, clutching a teddy bear; Sam as a toddler, on a rocking horse, and on a beach next to a sandcastle bigger than herself; a slightly older-looking Sam, on a bicycle with stabilisers on the back, on a pony, in her first school uniform. Sam with her mother, and several with a man who was, presumably, her late father.

'He died when she was fourteen. Heart attack, I think. Must have been tough. From what she's said on the rare occasions she's mentioned him, they were pretty close.'

Wendy pointed at a photo of Sam, probably about nine

or ten years old, strapped into a fairground ride next to her grinning dad.

Cora nodded. 'Yes, I got that impression too. Her mum and her get on great, but I know losing her father was hard for her to come to terms with. He was a newspaper reporter, wasn't he, on the *Evening Standard*? And on some Scottish paper before that – that's why Sam has a Scottish accent. They rented this place out when he got the Scotland job and came back down to London years later when he landed a senior job on the *Standard*. I think he inspired her to think of journalism as a possible career when she was really quite young. He'd have been so proud of her today, she's done so well.'

'Yep.' Wendy sighed, then turned as Ellen reappeared, carrying a large white china teapot.

'Tea! Now, come and sit down and tuck in. You must be starving after your early start, Sam always is.'

They all sat, Ellen busying herself pouring tea, fussing over the milk and sugar and proffering plates of food. For a few minutes, they made small talk, Cora and Wendy oohing and aahing over the smoked salmon sandwiches and the selection of no fewer than five varieties of cake, from a moist lemon drizzle to a decadent chocolate fudge. But once they'd updated Ellen on their love lives, Cora filling her in about Adam, and Wendy about her now long-term relationship with Dan, one of the *Morning Live* video editors, Cora cleared her throat. Lovely as this was, they had come here for a reason.

'So – Sam's birthday on Thursday. Not the nicest place for her to be spending it, is it?'

Ellen shook her head, a grimace of pain suddenly crumpling her face. Her dark hair, thinning at the temples, was pulled back into a low bun at the nape of her neck, and despite her cheery demeanour today her cheeks were hollow and there were dark circles under her eyes.

'I was so hopeful she'd be out by now. I don't understand why she's in there, it's such a terrible mistake. I know they'll realise it soon, and she'll be freed, but why is it taking so long? Her lawyers don't seem to be much help …' Tears filled Ellen's eyes and she covered her face with her hands.

'Oh, Ellen, I'm so sorry, I didn't mean to upset you.' Cora reached out and touched the woman's arm.

'We're just as worried as you – that's one of the reasons we're here. We're trying to help get her out, and we just wondered if there was anything, anything at all, the police might have missed,' Wendy said gently.

Ellen raised her head, looking at them both in turn, tears streaking her pale, powdery cheeks.

'Something they might have missed? I don't really understand – like what?'

She sniffed, and reached into her trouser pocket for a tissue.

'Well …' Cora hesitated. When she'd spoken to Sam after the visit to Dr Taylor, Sam had admitted she still hadn't told her mother about the DNA evidence against her, not wanting to worry her unduly. Now though, in desperation, she'd told Cora to let her mother know the full extent of the police's findings.

'Mad as it may sound to my mother, if there's any chance at all that I have some long-lost enemy I don't know about, who might have killed Marcus and somehow planted my DNA at the scene, then now's the time to find out about it,' Sam had said morosely. 'And I'd rather you tell her about it all, Cora. I can't bear to.'

Now, Cora decided there was no easy way. She'd just have to say it. 'Well … look, I don't think you know this, but there's DNA evidence. Evidence that places Sam at

156

the scene. So, as we're all sure she didn't do it, what we were wondering ...'

'DNA? What do you mean? *Sam's* DNA? That's not possible, is it? Why didn't she tell me this, when I speak to her every other day?'

An expression of fear and horror on her face, Ellen stood up, pushing her chair backwards so sharply it tipped over.

'She just didn't want to worry you,' Wendy said. 'Because clearly, Ellen, it's either a forensics mix-up, or somebody put her DNA there deliberately, to make the police think she did it.'

'Her DNA? How ... how can that have happened?' Ellen didn't seem to be listening any more, her hands clawing at her hair.

Cora stood up, righted the fallen chair and gently guided the woman back into it.

'Ellen, please don't be distressed. Yes, the police, their forensic people, say it *was* her DNA. And they insist it wasn't a lab mix-up. So I've spoken to a DNA expert, and although we know it sounds unlikely, we're wondering if somebody might have framed her? It's possible, if you know what you're doing, you see, but we can't think of anyone who would have hated her enough to do that. Is there anyone you can think of, Ellen? Anyone Sam had a run-in with in the past?'

Ellen looked aghast. 'No, of course not! Sam didn't have any enemies at all, everyone loves her, you know that. That can't be what happened, it just can't ...'

Cora nodded, her heart sinking.

'I know, Ellen. It's unlikely. But the only other possibility is somebody else with the same DNA as Sam, which isn't possible – it would have to be an identical twin, and of course Sam is an only child so ...'

Ellen jolted upright. 'Of course she's an only child,' she said sharply.

'Er … yes, we know. Sorry, I wasn't doubting that.' Cora and Wendy exchanged glances.

Ellen sank backwards again, her face flushing. 'Sorry. I'm so on edge at the moment. I didn't mean to snap at you. I'm just so worried …'

'Don't worry, we understand.' Wendy patted Ellen's hand and the older woman smiled gratefully at her.

'We do, totally.' Cora smiled reassuringly. She glanced at Wendy again, and could see the question in her friend's eyes too. Was Ellen reacting a little oddly here?

'Thank you.' Ellen rubbed at her eyes with her tissue, crumpled it in a ball and placed it carefully on the edge of her plate, then looked back at both women in turn.

'I just don't think I can help. I even wondered …' She paused, the pain flashing across her face again. 'I even wondered – and I've hated myself for this – but I even wondered, just for a few minutes one day, if maybe she *did* do it, you know? Because everyone seems so sure. And that was before I knew about this DNA thing. I thought, could she? Could my Sam get *that* angry? I mean, she can be impatient, and a bit intolerant, can't she? But as soon as I thought it, I stopped thinking it, if you know what I mean. My Sam just couldn't hurt anyone, not like that. She hasn't got it in her. You know that, don't you? You must know that. DNA evidence or no DNA evidence.'

Cora nodded. 'We do. We believe she's innocent, Ellen. That's why there *must* be something. Something nobody's thought of. Somebody Sam has upset, someone with a grudge, who might have somehow accessed her DNA and framed her, or something else we don't know about. Ellen, we're trying so hard here, to help her, so if

158

you think of anything …'

She leaned forwards in her chair and gripped the older woman's hands. 'It's for Sam, Ellen. For her future. Please think. *Please*. Think really hard, and even if something strikes you and you don't think it could really be important, give us a ring anyway, is that OK?'

Ellen stared silently at Cora for a moment, motionless, an unidentifiable expression in her eyes. Fear? Confusion? Or something else? Cora couldn't work it out. Then Ellen slid her hands from Cora's and stood up.

'I will. Of course I will. Look – I'm a bit upset. Do you mind if we finish up now? It was lovely to see you both, but I think I just need to be on my own for a bit.'

'Of course. It was great to see you, Ellen. And the food was delicious – thank you.'

Minutes later, slightly awkward goodbye hugs exchanged and promises to speak soon made, Cora and Wendy were back out on the street. Neither had said a word as they walked down the corridor away from Ellen's flat and made their way to ground level, both aware that sound echoed easily through the tiled hallways of these mansion blocks. But the second the front door was closed behind them, they turned to each other simultaneously.

'Was it just me, or …?'

'No, that was definitely weird. Why such a strange reaction?'

'She's hiding something, Cora.'

'I think so too. But what?'

'No idea. And no idea how we find out, either.'

'Unless she tells us. Do you think she'll tell us, when she's had a chance to think about it?'

'Maybe. Now that she knows how serious things are looking for Sam.'

'Maybe. But what the hell is it?' Cora shook her

head. It was all very bizarre, but the sudden change in Ellen's behaviour when the DNA conversation had begun was definitely suspicious.

'I'll give it until tomorrow evening, then I'll give her a call. We haven't got much time, Wendy. Sam's back in court in a few weeks. If there *is* something the lawyers and police need to look into, we need to know what it is. And we need to know fast.'

The mystery was still playing on Cora's mind later that evening as she and Adam sprawled on the sofa, her feet on his knees, both half watching *New Tricks* on the television and half lost in their own thoughts. Once again, Cora had decided not to tell Adam about her ongoing attempts to prove Sam's innocence, telling herself there really was no point unless she unearthed anything concrete. But having secrets from each other was not normally how their relationship operated, and she didn't like it. Her gaze drifted from the TV screen to Adam's profile. His strong jaw, close-cropped blond hair and – although she couldn't see them now, in the flickering light from the television – striking green eyes still had the power to make her stomach flip. Much as she loved Sam, and wanted this all to work out for her, it couldn't be at the expense of her and Adam. It couldn't, and she wouldn't let it.

'I love you, Adam Bradberry,' she said softly. He turned and smiled.

'Love you too, Cora Baxter.' They held each other's gaze for a long moment, then Cora felt the hand which had been cradling her right foot begin to move gently up her calf and on to her thigh, caressing her bare skin. As Adam's fingers reached the hem of the short nightshirt she'd changed into after dinner, she put her hand on his, leaned forward and kissed him. He responded urgently, pushing her back on the sofa, her nightie riding up, his hands under it now, making her groan with pleasure.

'Bedroom, or here?' she gasped.

'Here seems fine to me,' said Adam, grinning down at her. She grinned back, reaching for his shirt buttons. Sam could wait, Ellen could wait, just until tomorrow.

22

Wednesday 29th May
30 days until the deadline

'Oh no, oh no, oh no, oh NO!'

Cora looked up from her desk, where she was simultaneously tweaking a script for the eight o'clock bulletin and gossiping with Alice who'd come in on her day off for an early meeting. She was feeling increasingly awkward about leaving poor Alice out of the ongoing Sam saga, although she knew it was the right decision, for now at least – much as Alice was now a valued friend, discretion wasn't her greatest quality. But Cora felt guilty every time Alice mentioned Sam, so whatever was happening now was a welcome distraction. The source of the anguished outburst was Miranda, a few desks away.

'Errr … everything OK, doc?' asked Cora.

'She doesn't seem very OK to me,' muttered Alice, pushing her sleek blonde mane back to get a better look. She was right. The doctor's face, which had appeared quite normal when Cora had greeted her a few minutes earlier, was now wearing an agonised expression, and slowly flushing to a bright pink.

'No. No, everything is not OK. Everyone's going to laugh, and I can't bear being laughed at, I just can't …'

She stood up, breathing heavily, jabbing at a mobile phone she was holding in her hand, then groaned loudly, oblivious to the heads turning her way. Just as Cora, growing increasingly concerned, was about to walk over and see what on earth was wrong, Miranda all of a sudden seemed to regain her composure, her face relaxing. She flopped back down into her chair, still prodding the phone, although slightly less frantically now.

'Oh, I give up. Flipping heck, girls. You won't believe what I've just done ... there's no way to retrieve an email you've just sent, is there, so the recipient doesn't see it?'

Alice shrugged, and Cora shook her head. 'Not as far as I know. Why would everyone laugh at you? What on earth have you said? And to who?'

'Aaargh.' Miranda stopped stabbing at the phone, dropped it onto the desk and sank her face into her hands. Cora watched, amused, then hit save on her computer and sent her updated script to the printer.

'Miranda? Come on, spill!'

Miranda looked up, and sighed. 'Oh well, it's done now. I'm just so tired, we had to get up at four this morning to get back for my slot on the sofa, I just can't concentrate ... OK, so I was emailing the hotel I stayed in last night, in the New Forest. I left my favourite silk shirt hanging in the bathroom – I was trying to get a few creases out of it with the steam from the shower, but then I decided to wear something else, and then we were in such a rush I forgot all about it and left it behind.'

Cora stood up, aware that her bulletin would be starting in just four minutes. 'OK, so?'

Miranda grimaced. 'So I just emailed the hotel to ask them if they'd mind sending the shirt on to me. Except I didn't type "shirt". Look.'

She picked up her phone and handed it to Cora.

Hi, Dr Evans here from Morning Live *– we stayed with you last night, and I wondered if you could do me a favour? I left a shit in the bathroom. It was a particularly* *nice one, one of my favourites in fact, so I'm hoping it's still there! I wondered if you might be able to retrieve it and send it on to me at my home address? Happy to cover postage and packing charges – it will need to be wrapped quite carefully. Thanks so much! Regards, Miranda Evans.*

'No! Oh, Miranda, that is BRILLIANT!' Cora snorted with laughter, and passed the phone to Alice, who let out a shriek.

'Miranda, that's hilarious! Don't worry, just email them back and tell them it was a typo, I'm sure they'll see the funny side.'

'I suppose so. But how excruciatingly embarrassing. As if I'd ask them to send … to send *that* on to me. I'd never have made a mistake like that before I worked here. These stupid early mornings are rotting my brain, I'm just so knackered all the time,' said Miranda morosely, then grinned suddenly as Cora and Alice continued to snigger.

'Oh, shush. Go to your meeting, Alice. And go and do your bulletin, Cora.'

'I will, but thank you. You've made my morning. See you later.' Cora, still smiling broadly, grabbed her script from the printer, waved to a still giggling Alice, and headed for the studio. Miranda really was quite funny, she thought, making a mental note to tell Sam the story when she spoke to her tomorrow on her birthday. It would make her laugh, and the poor girl had been a little short on laughter lately.

Two hours later Cora had just taken a large bite of her post-programme Danish pastry when her phone rang. Wendy, who had just joined her at her desk for a coffee break, glanced at the display.

'It's Ellen, Cora! Ellen Tindall. Want me to answer it?'

Cora shook her head, swallowed and grabbed the phone. 'Wonder what she wants? Hello – hello, Ellen?'

Ellen Tindall's voice sounded thin and shaky on the other end of the line.

'Cora, love. Cora, there's something ... something I need to tell you.'

She paused. Cora looked at Wendy, wide-eyed. Wendy slowly put her coffee cup down on the desk, and leaned forwards, a questioning expression on her face.

'OK, Ellen. Go ahead, I'm listening.' Cora felt her heartbeat speed up.

'It's ... it's very difficult for me, Cora. This is something I've never told anyone. Sam doesn't know, nobody knows. Just me and her dad knew, and he's gone.'

She paused again.

'OK, well, go on, please. Is it something that might help Sam, help get her out of her ... her predicament?' Cora could barely conceal her impatience, but tried to keep her voice level and quiet, although there were few people within earshot.

'I don't know. I don't see how it can, really. But you said to say, if there was anything ... and, well, there is someone. Someone who would have the same DNA as Sam, I think. I mean, I'm no expert, and even if we could find them I don't see how they could be involved in the murder. But, you said to say, if there was anything ...'

Her voice tailed off again. Cora clenched her spare hand into a tight fist, staring at Wendy who was practically jumping off her seat now with impatience.

'Ellen ... please, whatever it is, just tell me, please. It might be important. It might get Sam out of prison. Please, Ellen.'

There was a deep sigh on the other end of the line, then Ellen spoke again, her voice stronger this time, as if she'd made a decision and was announcing it.

'Right. The thing is … Sam, she's not our biological child. She was adopted, Cora. We got her when she was just a few weeks old, so we've always felt she was our child, right from the beginning. I couldn't have children, you see, and I wanted one so much, and there she was, this little mite of a thing, abandoned by her mother. I always planned to tell her, when she was older, maybe sixteen, but then when her dad died, I just couldn't. I thought, I've lost my husband, what if I lose my daughter too, what if she rejects me if she knows she's not really mine? I couldn't bear it, so I just didn't, I just didn't tell her.'

Her voice cracked, and the line went silent again. Cora reached out and gripped Wendy's hand.

'Oh. My. God.' She mouthed the words at Wendy.

'What? *What*?'

Cora shook her head. She needed all the information first, before Ellen cut the call.

'Ellen? Ellen, are you there?'

There was a sniff, and then Ellen spoke again.

'Yes, I'm here. Sorry, I'm just a bit upset.'

'I understand. You're doing brilliantly, Ellen, thank you so much for sharing this with us. So … are you thinking maybe her parents? Her biological parents? They would have similar DNA, but not the same …'

'No.' Ellen interrupted, her voice suddenly tremulous again. 'No, not her parents. She … she wasn't an only child Cora, not when she was born. She had a sister.'

'A sister?' Cora was hardly breathing. Wendy, eyes glued to her friend's face, let her mouth drop open.

'Yes, a sister. When she was born … when she was abandoned, she had a sister. Not just a sister, Cora. A twin. A twin sister.'

167

23

Thursday 30th May
29 days until the deadline

The boat rocked gently up and down and Cora leaned back in her seat and relaxed a little for the first time in nearly twenty-four hours. It was just after 5 a.m., a golden dawn was breaking off the Weymouth coast, and she and the boys were moored about half a mile out in the English Channel, on a small vessel called *The Molly Sue*. Her skipper, a rotund, ruddy-faced man with a beard to rival Father Christmas's, beamed at his passengers, showing a gap where one front tooth should be, then turned and gestured at the dark, slightly choppy water surrounding them.

'Give 'im 'alf an hour and we'll see 'im, I reckon. Usually makes an appearance around 'alf five. If you get your kit ready, should get some nice pictures. It's gonna be a beautiful mornin', by the looks of it.'

He turned away again, and Rodney and Nathan, neither of whom were great sailors, exchanged slightly pained looks. Rodney, in particular, appeared to be a little green in the face. Either that, or the vivid pea-green waterproof jacket he was wearing this morning was casting some sort of reflection on to his pale skin, Cora thought with some amusement, but managed to refrain from saying that out loud.

This morning's assignment was a relatively simple one

169

– or it would be, as long as the dolphin they were waiting for made an appearance. The creature, dubbed Dandy the Dolphin by the coastal town's local media, had been hitting the headlines in recent days, and Betsy had decided that some pretty pictures of the marine mammal frolicking in the waves would be just the thing to brighten up what was otherwise proving to be quite a dull week, news-wise. The dolphin had taken to following local boats for hours, frequently adorned with long strands of seaweed which he somehow managed to artfully arrange around his neck like an elegant scarf, and which flowed gracefully behind him as he leapt from the water. His show-off behaviour generally started not long after dawn, and Cora and her crew had duly been despatched to Dorset to try to capture his antics on camera.

It was just the three of them on the boat – Scott and his satellite truck were parked up back in the harbour, dish up and ready to transmit the pictures and Cora's piece to camera as soon as his colleagues could manage to do their filming and get the results back to dry land.

'Bet Scott's asleep back there,' muttered Nathan. He pulled the collar of his thick black fleece up around his ears and shivered. Although it did indeed seem that the skipper was correct, and a lovely morning was in the offing, the weak rays of the slowly rising sun had yet to bring any warmth to the little boat, and although they'd all dressed warmly, it was hard not to feel slightly envious of Scott in the cosy truck.

Cora shifted position on the rather uncomfortable bench seat and stretched her legs out in front of her, careful to avoid the camera and sound equipment stacked in the centre of the bow. Opposite her, Nathan and Rodney were scanning the horizon, on dolphin watch, both keen to get this job over with as soon as possible.

She was with them on that, and also hoping that their on-the-road schedule for the remainder of this week would allow her to keep the appointment she'd managed to arrange for tomorrow afternoon at the London adoption agency which had brought a baby Sam and her parents together.

'I can't believe it's still going ... how lucky is that?' she said out loud.

'The agency?' Nathan instantly understood. 'Yep, pretty incredible after thirty-odd years. Though I'm still not sure how useful it's going to be.'

Cora nodded. She was still feeling pretty shell-shocked after Ellen's revelations, but having thought about little else since yesterday morning, she knew that the chances of any of it actually helping to get Sam out of prison were very small. After admitting that Sam had a twin sister, Ellen had gone on to tell Cora the few details she knew. Baby Sam, just days old, had been abandoned on the steps of a London medical clinic. She'd been snugly wrapped in blankets, under which she was beautifully dressed in warm clothing, and tucked into her vest had been a note from her birth mother. The letter had explained that the woman had given birth to identical twins, but due to extremely difficult personal circumstances had felt herself unable to cope with two children, so in desperation had decided to leave one for somebody else to take care of. She had begged the clinic, and whoever ended up in charge of her baby's future, to make sure she went to a loving, caring home, and expressed her devastation about what she was being forced to do. The note concluded with the information that she had relatives in the USA, and was leaving the country with Sam's twin immediately, to live with them. As far as Ellen was aware, the woman, and her other child, had not been heard from since – Ellen had been told at the time that it had been decided it was in nobody's interest to prosecute her, and she had been allowed to simply vanish.

'Probably not something that would happen nowadays,' Cora had commented.

'So – you've made an appointment, at the agency which arranged the adoption? Do you really think they'll be able to give you any info? Or be allowed to? And what about Sam – when is somebody going to tell her?'

'Oh, Nathan, I don't know. Going to see the agency is a long shot, yes. And I think it's up to Ellen to tell Sam, I can't do that. I've told Ellen she must, but she was so upset ...'

Cora paused, remembering how distraught Sam's mother had been as they ended their phone call.

'She knows she has to, and she said she will. But it might take her a while, and that's going to make it really awkward for me to tell Sam what I'm up to. I'll just have to be vague, or maybe avoid calling her for a few days, until I see if I can get anywhere. Although it's her birthday today, so I'm going to *have* to call her ...'

Rodney, who was looking greener by the minute, suddenly groaned softly.

'Urgh. Cora, if this dolphin doesn't show up soon I am seriously going to puke. Anyone got a bucket?'

Nathan leapt from his seat. 'Vomit on me, Rodders, and you're going overboard. Go and sit by the side and hang your head over or something.'

Slowly, as if in pain, Rodney stood up and staggered to the starboard side of the boat, where he slumped to his knees, resting his chin on the gunwale. The skipper, who'd still been scanning the horizon, turned and gave another gap-toothed smile.

'Won't be long now lad, mark my words. 'Nother few

minutes. Try an' keep your breakfast down 'til then.'

Rodney moaned again, then nodded. Nathan, who was still looking less than chirpy himself, returned to his seat, leaned back and closed his eyes.

'Stick with it, Rodney mate, we'll be off here soon. Cora, it's down to you, I'm afraid. Looking at that water's making me too queasy. Shout when you see the bloody thing. Camera's ready to go.'

'OK. But you really are a pair of wimps.'

'Yeah, yeah, whatever.'

Cora grinned, then returned her gaze to the gently rising and falling water, her mind drifting back to last night. She had phoned Adam from Cheltenham when she'd got home ahead of her two days on the road, deciding that surely a discovery of such magnitude as a potential person with a DNA profile matching Sam's was worthy of police investigation. If they really were identical twins, of course. If not, then their DNA wouldn't be the same, and although Ellen seemed to be fairly sure, Cora didn't dare get her hopes up too much just yet. She'd been deeply disappointed, although in retrospect not entirely surprised, by Adam's reaction.

'Cora, darling, I love you so much and I admire your loyalty to Sam so much. But even if there is a twin sister, and even if she is identical, and can be found, why on earth would she suddenly turn up out of the blue after thirty years and murder her sister's boyfriend? It doesn't make any sense, does it?'

Cora had to admit that it didn't, really. 'Well, no, that would be a bit unlikely. But surely it's worth trying to find her anyway? Just in case ...'

'Just in case what? Just in case this alleged sister, who was taken abroad as a baby, and who nobody except Ellen knew existed until now, somehow tracked Sam down, but decided that instead of getting in touch she would have her twin jailed for murder? Cora, it makes zero sense. The forensics, Sam's relationship with the victim – it all points to her. I know you don't want to believe it – I mean, I sure as hell don't want to believe it. But my hands are tied. It's a cut and dried case, and we're releasing Marcus's body to the family this weekend so they can bury him. I'm sorry, Cora. If you feel the need to try and pursue this, and track this woman down, that's up to you. But as far as the police are concerned, it's a no-go.'

They'd ended the call on a slightly frosty note. Cora knew, if she was being really honest with herself, that Adam was probably right. But if there was a chance, even the tiniest chance, that there could be anything in this, then she simply had to follow it up.

'I can't give up. Not yet.' She whispered the words out loud, then jumped as there was a shout from the stern.

'There! Look!'

The skipper was pointing behind her, and she swivelled in her seat. Sure enough, just metres away from the boat she spotted a sleek grey shape moving through the water.

'Hooray! Nathan, Rodney, we're on!'

She stood up, and both of the boys did too, even Rodney suddenly looking bright and focused. Time to start work.

In London, Katie Chamberlain had just dragged herself out of bed for her daily session on the treadmill in her spare room, before getting ready for another long day in the salon. She had slept badly, her dreams full of Marcus. When she'd woken just after 5 a.m., her cheeks had been wet with tears. She ached for him, the pain suddenly overwhelming her, and for a few brief moments she'd wondered if there was any point in going on. That TV producer bitch stealing him from her had been bad enough, but now she couldn't even tell herself that one day he'd come back to her. Maybe she should just end it all, here and now. She had plenty of painkillers in the bathroom, and there was a bottle of whiskey in the living room cupboard – would that be enough?

But then she'd started thinking about Sam, rotting in prison, the thieving cow getting what she deserved, and the tears dried. Neither of them had Marcus, but at least Katie was free to get on with her life. It would be foolish to throw that away. And anyway, she wanted to see the bitch get her life sentence. Life in prison. Because she deserved it, for what she had done. Deserved every second of the miserable life she must now be leading. Steal from me, you get your come-uppance, Katie thought as she threw off the duvet and pulled on her workout gear. As she switched the treadmill on, she was smiling.

wondered if there was any point in going on. That TV
producer had, ebullibly, taken from her that lease had
turned. But now she couldn't. Even if herself that one
day he'd come back to her. And the time should, instead it
all, here and now. She and plenty of penalties in the
bathroom, and there was a light of a shimmer in the room,
non-chalance, would think enough.

But then she'd spilled thinking about rum rotting in
prison she allowing how getting what she deserved, and
the time she'd neither of them had Morton, but at last
Katie was freezing at sea with her lags, he would be looking
to follow and saing. And anyway, she wanted to see his
pitch get her life sentence. Life in prison. Brought she
deserved it, for that. He had come. Deserved every
second of the, miserable. The she must now be reading.
Sisal plan you you get some consequences, Kate, though
as she threw off machiver had put through her work out good.

As she switched off, accomplishing, she was smiling.

24

Friday 31st May
28 days until the deadline

The City Adoption Agency was on the ground floor of an early Victorian building in a sleepy side street not far from London's Euston Station. As she buzzed the door intercom, Cora glanced at her watch. Two o'clock. Miraculously, she and the boys had been unassigned for that morning's show and, wanting to take a break from her endless driving, she'd decided to catch a late morning train to the capital. If she was lucky, she'd be back at Paddington and on her way home to Cheltenham in a couple of hours – Adam was working all weekend, so she was seeing Rosie and Nicole tonight, and desperately hoped that there'd be some good news to share with them.

The door opened and a cheerful woman with very white teeth and an extremely dark tan welcomed her inside, ushering her into a small waiting area.

'Take a seat, and I'll see who's free. Would you like a cup of tea, or coffee?'

'No thanks, I'm fine.' Cora smiled at the woman, who smiled back and bustled out of the room. A minute later she was back, and Cora was being led down a hallway with shiny black and white floor tiles, and into a room at the rear of the building. A man and a woman, who'd been sitting in easy chairs around a low table, stood up to greet her.

'Miss Baxter, nice to meet you. I'm Lis Hoyle.' The woman was petite, with a soft blonde bob and a pleasant face, and dressed in a simple grey shirt and black jeans.

'Joel Anderson.' Her colleague, a tall, muscular man with close-cropped hair, held out a hand, and Cora shook it.

'Thanks so much for seeing me,' she said, as they all sat down. 'As I said to the lady I spoke to on the phone, this is a slightly unusual situation, and I'm not sure you're going to be able to help me, but I needed to try. Have you been told? What I'm here for, I mean?'

'A little, yes.' Lis picked up a notebook from the top of a pile of papers on the table in front of her and flicked through it, scanning the pages. 'Ah, here it is. So – your friend is in prison for a crime she says she didn't commit, despite DNA evidence. You've now discovered that she was adopted, and may have a living sister – a twin, possibly identical – and you want to find her, in case … in case it was actually her, the twin, who committed the crime, and not your friend? Is that right?' she said, doubtfully.

'Yes, it is. I know it sounds … well, a little far-fetched.'

'It does, a little,' smiled Lis.

'I wondered … well, if we could maybe find her birth mother, who I know a little about, then that would be the easiest way to go about it? I don't know her name, otherwise I could have done some online searching and so on myself. But I thought you might still have records, even though it was a long time ago …' Cora's voice tailed off, realising that Lis was slowly shaking her head.

'I worried that you might be going to ask us something like that. Even if we did have that information, we couldn't just hand it over to you. It's highly confidential.

178

We'd need to talk to your friend personally for a start, which I understand is not really possible right now due to her position. I'm sorry, but our hands are tied.'

Cora felt her mouth go dry. 'But – this could be her only hope. I know it's a long shot, I know it sounds crazy, but please. Please, I'm not asking you to hand over any records or anything. Even just a name would do, if there is one. Could you just look it up? It would have been thirty-one years ago, a baby abandoned on the steps of some clinic in London and ending up with your agency? With a letter, saying the mother had given birth to twins, but couldn't keep both, and was taking one abroad to relatives? I don't know if the mother signed her name, but she might have. Please, there can't have been any other case like that?'

Lis was still shaking her head. Opposite her, Joel had been jotting down notes on a foolscap pad. He turned to Cora, placing his pen carefully on the table before he spoke.

'It's unlikely we would have had another case like that, no. Sounds like a pretty unique set of circumstances.' His voice was deep, with a melodic West Indian lilt. 'But Lis is right, we can't just hand our files over to anyone who walks in off the street. I'm so sorry. Chances are there would be no name on them anyway – mothers who abandon babies mostly do it anonymously. If your friend wants to *attempt* to trace her birth mother, the easiest way would be to instruct her solicitor to get her records from the clerk of the court which granted the adoption. Those records will have any details that were available to the court at the time.'

'Right.' Cora ran her hands through her hair, thinking. If she really couldn't get any information here, then yes, the court records would be the next best thing, but that would mean Sam would need to be told immediately about her family history. And who knew how long it might take to get hold of the adoption records? It could take weeks, or months …

'Hang on …' Lis was speaking again. 'If it's a criminal trial these records are needed for, why don't the police get a warrant to seize them? That would be the quickest way. Why are *you* doing this research, and not the police?'

Her voice had a slightly suspicious ring to it now. Joel too was looking a little puzzled.

'Because … because the police, although they've been told that there may be an identical twin, don't think it's a valid line of enquiry.'

Cora could feel her throat getting tight, and willed herself not to start crying. 'They say that even if there's a twin somewhere, it makes no sense that she would turn up after thirty odd years and murder her long-lost sister's boyfriend, then vanish again. And it's not just the DNA evidence against my friend, there was other stuff … they'd had a row, she was seen on CCTV going into the park where he was murdered at the right time … I can kind of see their point, but even if it's a long-shot, I need to try to find her.'

She paused, aware that both Lis and Joel were now wearing slightly shocked expressions, and realised that that had been the first time she'd actually mentioned that the crime involved was murder.

'Err – yes, it's a murder case,' she said lamely.

'Gosh.' Lis stood up suddenly, tugging her shirt down. 'Well, I'm so sorry that you're going through this, but as I said, our hands are tied. If the police get a warrant …' She shrugged. 'And now, please excuse me, I have another appointment at half past. I hope everything works out for you though, and for your friend.'

She reached out to shake Cora's hand, giving her a sad little smile as she did so, then hurried out of the room. Joel, who was still sitting down, reading the notes he'd written, sighed heavily.

'She's right. I'm so sorry. We can't help you.'

Cora stood up slowly, tears suddenly springing to her eyes. She'd known she'd be unlikely to get much out of today's visit, but the futility of the mission suddenly felt overwhelming. Even if the court records could be obtained, what were the chances of the birth mother's name being on them? Joel had been right – Cora had covered numerous stories about abandoned babies over the years, and how many mothers had left a *signed* note with their unwanted child? None, that's how many. It was impossible.

'Tissue?' Cora suddenly realised that Joel was standing next to her, proffering a box of Kleenex. She took one gratefully, feeling embarrassed, and wiped her eyes.

'I'm so sorry, genuinely,' he said in his gentle sing-song voice.

Cora nodded and smiled a watery smile. 'Thank you. It was silly of me really, to think you could hand over stuff like that. I'm a journalist, I should know better. I'll get out of your way.'

'OK. I'll show you out.'

Joel led her down the hallway and opened the heavy front door, then turned to look at her.

'You have a little streak of mascara, on your cheek. Might want to clean that off before you go,' he said, smiling.

Cora dabbed at her cheek with the tissue, but he shook his head. 'No, here, look – may I?'

He reached out and touched her face lightly with his thumb, wiping the mark away, and she was struck by how big and yet how gentle his hand was, and by the warmth in his eyes as he scrutinised her face for a moment then nodded in satisfaction.

'Perfect. You can go now.' He grinned, showing white, even teeth, and she grinned back, despite herself. He was a good-looking man, and a nice man, she thought, even if he couldn't give her what she needed.

'Thank you, Joel. Bye.'

'Goodbye.'

Cora stepped out into the street and the door closed gently behind her. She took a deep breath and looked at her watch. She had plenty of time before her train home – maybe she'd pop to Covent Garden and do a little shopping before heading to Paddington. The thought cheered her a little, and she turned and started walking swiftly down the street, deciding it would be easier to hail a cab on the main road. She was almost at the junction when she heard pounding feet behind her, somebody obviously running and gaining on her quickly, and she shrank back against the wall to allow whoever it was to get past. To her astonishment, Joel skidded to a halt in front of her, panting.

'What – what is it?'

'Look – this could get me in a whole bunch of trouble.' He paused to catch his breath, wiping his hands on the front of his dark sweater. 'But you said you were a journalist, right? And a journalist can't reveal their source, if they're working on a certain kind of story?'

'That's … that's right, yes.' Cora's heart had begun to pound, hope suddenly bubbling up inside her.

'Right. Well, I know it's not what I should be doing, and if I'm caught, I'll lose my job. But I had a friend in trouble once, and I know I would have done anything to help him, and I couldn't. And you may not be able to either, but you deserve the chance to try, however unlikely it is that it'll lead to anything.'

Cora hardly dared to ask the question. 'Does that mean ... does that mean you'll help me?'

'I'll help you. I don't know if there'll be anything of any use in that file, or even if the file will still exist. But I'll look. I'll work late tonight, and I'll look.'

25

'So – she actually threw up? Live on air? Seriously?'

Rosie, who'd just finished pouring white wine into three large glasses, put the bottle down on the little side-table next to the sofa and stared at Cora, aghast.

Cora, who'd been regaling her friends with a story from earlier in the week, about an unfortunate, pregnant studio guest who'd been suffering from dreadful morning sickness, nodded.

'Well, almost. She leapt off the sofa the second her interview was over, and just managed to get to the side of the studio, out of camera range, before she really went for it. They'd put a bucket there, just in case, because she'd warned them beforehand that it might happen. The noise was dreadful though. Sound didn't cut her microphone early enough, so everyone watching at home heard a good five seconds of the most hideous retching. Ugh, it was awful. Made me feel sick too. I had to read my bulletin thirty seconds later, and I could smell it …'

Cora, who was quite squeamish when it came to anything to do with blood or vomit, shuddered at the memory, and gratefully held out her hand for the glass Rosie was now proffering.

'Poor woman. Morning sickness is vile. Luckily not something I'll ever have to experience again, unless something goes badly wrong,' said Nicole, who was sitting next to Cora. She accepted her wine glass too and took a deep slug. Her little boy Elliot was three now, and adorable, but she and her husband Will had decided to stop at one. Rosie, on the other hand, had three children, and still hadn't ruled out having another at some point.

'I had it bad with Ava and Alexander, but hardly at all with Amy,' she said, and plonked herself down on the other sofa with a weary sigh. She reached for her own glass and took a gulp, then put it carefully down on the table again and leaned back against her cushions, smiling at her friends.

Cora and Nicole had arrived just as Rosie was shepherding her brood to bed, and had helped her tuck them in and read them their stories. Cora had been assigned to Ava who, at six, was the oldest, and a mini-replica of her petite, red-haired mother. A sweet child, with a serious face but a sharp sense of humour, she had snuggled happily under her Disney print duvet as Cora read her current favourite book, which was about a fish called Neville who couldn't find his best friend, Comet the crab. With one arm looped around the sleepy little girl, Cora had lost herself in the story, and felt quite sad when Neville's day-long search of the seabed was successful and he and Comet were re-united, bringing the book to an end. For the ten minutes or so that she'd spent quietly reading aloud, she'd been able to stop dwelling on the ongoing Sam saga, and that had been a wonderful, if very temporary, relief. As she carefully manoeuvred her arm out from under the now soundly sleeping child, dropped a light kiss on her forehead and slipped out of the room, the worry had come crashing back again, twisting her stomach. Would Joel be able to track down the relevant file? It had been more than thirty years, after all. What if records weren't kept that long? If it *was* there, would he find anything of any use in it? And would he keep his word and call her?

Now, curled up on the sofa next to Nicole, she smiled back at Rosie and gazed around the room, trying to calm herself. It was a beautiful space, with almond white walls, deep red sofas and a shiny walnut floor. The fireplace, where Rosie always had a crackling fire in the winter months, was filled now with white candles, flickering hypnotically and emitting the soft scent of magnolias.

'So, what's the latest about Sam, Cora? Has her mum told her she's adopted yet?'

Cora sighed and turned back to look at Nicole.

'Not yet. She's promised she will though, and soon. I hope she does. I spoke to Sam last night, Wendy did too, because it was her birthday, but we just kept it short, and when she asked if we'd come up with any more ideas about who might have framed her, we just had to say no. I hate keeping things from her. Ellen really needs to come clean as soon as possible, for Sam's sake.'

'Suppose so.' Rosie sounded doubtful. 'But it won't be an easy thing to do. Or for Sam to hear. Imagine being her age and not knowing something as massive as that about yourself. It's horrible, isn't it? As if she isn't going through enough, now she's going to find out her parents aren't even her parents ...'

Her voice tailed off, and she picked up her glass again, a stricken expression on her face.

'Especially her dad,' said Cora. 'I mean, she loves her mum, of course she does, but she *adored* her father, hero-worshipped him. That's going to hit her hard. I just can't bear to think about it. I wish I could be there with her, when Ellen tells her, to give her a hug. How can so many bad things be happening to one person? It just isn't fair, poor Sam ...'

She stopped talking, a lump suddenly forming in her throat as the sheer awfulness of the whole situation hit her again. Could it really be less than a month since all this started? It seemed like for ever.

She took a breath and carried on. 'That's why I'm determined to keep trying to help her, even though I know you guys probably think it's a waste of time. If she *is* proven to be guilty of this crime, then at least I've tried my very, very hardest for her. And if I do find her sister, or her biological parents, or both, then at least that's some blood relatives she'll have, and that might be some small comfort to her, after everything she's going to find out from Ellen. So, however pointless it seems to everyone – and even to me, sometimes – I'm going to carry on with this, as far as I can.'

Cora held out her wine glass.

'So, shall we drink to that? To Sam?'

'Of course. To you and your mission, Cora. And to Sam.'

The three of them clinked. Then they all jumped as Cora's phone, which was lying on the cushion next to her, started ringing loudly.

'Is that … is that the theme tune from *Charlie's Angels*?' Nicole stared at the phone, an incredulous look on her face.

'Yep.' Cora grinned suddenly. 'Damn Charlie, never leaves me alone, always calling me …'

Nicole and Rosie smiled too, and the atmosphere in the room instantly lightened. Cora grabbed the phone, glancing at the number flashing on the screen. She didn't recognise it.

'Hello, Cora Baxter here.'

'Cora. It's Joel Anderson. From the City Adoption Agency? Can you talk?'

Cora stood up. 'Joel! Yes. Yes I can talk. Have you got anything for me?'

Rosie and Nicole exchanged glances, and Cora looked from one to the other, anxiety tightening her throat again. She put a finger to her lips, then hit the speaker button on the phone so they could all hear the conversation.

'I have, actually.'

She sank down onto the sofa again. 'Tell me, please. Quickly. *Quickly.*' Rosie and Nicole edged closer, eyes wide with anticipation.

'OK, OK.' His deep voice sounded amused. 'Right, well, I found the file. Took a while, as you can imagine. It was buried deep in a room we never even go into any more, down in the basement where all the old pre-computer stuff lives, although it was all fairly organised in there, just a bit dusty. I was amazed we still had it. It started off with the basic details, pretty much as you told us – the baby, your friend Sam, was left on the steps of a medical clinic, with a note from the mother saying she had had twins, and couldn't cope with two babies.'

'Do you know if the twins were identical?' Cora crossed her fingers.

'The note says identical, yes.'

'YES!' Cora punched the air, and Rosie and Nicole both started jigging in their seats, grinning.

Joel laughed. 'Well, that's the good news. The sad news is that the mother also wrote that she'd recently lost her husband. She said he'd died in an accident, which was why she felt she couldn't manage both children.'

'Oh no.' Cora gasped. So Sam's biological father was dead. Rosie clapped her hand to her mouth, and Nicole shook her head slowly, as Joel continued.

'Yes, pretty sad story. The clinic where she left the baby is still there too, by the way – the Wellford, on Harley Street. She chose a good one.'

'How weird, I know that clinic. I was there only a few

days ago.' Cora frowned at the coincidence, then said: 'Sorry, please go on. Was – was the mother's name on the note? Please, please tell me it was, Joel ...'

'It wasn't. The note wasn't signed.'

Cora's heart sank, and Rosie groaned audibly. Nicole grimaced at her. 'Shhh!' she hissed.

Cora swallowed. Her throat was so dry it felt as if it was cracking. 'But – but you said you had something for me? That isn't it, is it?'

'No, that isn't it. She said in the note that she was taking the second baby, the twin sister, to the US, to New York, where she had an aunt who was willing to put them up for a while. And yes, that note was unsigned. But further on in the file, among all the official adoption paperwork and court documents pertaining to Sam as she went through the system, there was one more letter. And that one *did* have the biological mother's name on it.'

'A – another letter? What sort of letter?'

'The mother got in touch again a few months down the line. She wanted to check that everything was all right – that the baby, Sam, was well and healthy and had been found a good home. And this time, she put her name on the letter. Well, I should say she put *a* name on the letter. We can't be sure it's her real name, of course. Although I think that in this case, it might be, because she gave an address too.'

Cora gasped. 'A name, and address? Seriously?' Rosie and Nicole looked at each other, wide-eyed, then back at Cora.

'Seriously. She gave her name as Clare, Clare Henderson. And a New York address. She said she wanted it to be kept on file, in case at some point in the future the child wanted to track her down. Nobody pursued it at the time – it was considered to be in the best

190

interests of the child to have her adopted, and a prosecution for abandonment was not sought. Of course, that was thirty-odd years ago, so the chances of Clare still being at that New York address are slim to none, I'd say. But I knew you'd want to take it further, so I've started the ball rolling. I hope that's OK?'

'OK? It's – it's amazing, thank you. What have you done?'

'Well, as luck would have it, I actually know a private investigator in New York. He's a friend from back in Jamaica – we went to school together. So I've asked him if he wouldn't mind just checking the address out, see what he can find. He'll do it as a favour, you don't need to pay him, not at this stage ...'

'I don't mind paying, honestly! Joel, this is fantastic, thank you so much. I don't know what to say ...' Cora held her left hand in the air and Nicole and Rosie high-fived her in turn, then hugged each other. They were all grinning widely.

'No worries. I'll keep you posted. He's going to see what he can do over the weekend, so I may have news for you very soon. I'll call as soon as I hear, OK?'

'OK. Very, very OK. You're wonderful. Bye for now, Joel. And *thank you*. Thank you so, so much.'

'A pleasure. Bye, Cora.'

26

Thursday 6th June
22 days until the deadline

'National Gardening Exercise Day? Are they serious? How much sodding exercise can you get from gardening? And look – the tagline says "get out and exercise with your plants". How? Take their little leafy hands and dance round the flower bed with them?'

Nathan snorted, rolled his eyes and stomped back to where his camera was all set up and ready for their live broadcast. Cora giggled, then took a final look at the poster in the greenhouse window and scribbled a few notes on her pad. They were at a council allotment near Norwich today, a site of around two acres with twenty-four plots, some well-kept and tidy with perfect rows of leafy vegetables and neat, freshly painted sheds, others a little scruffier, spades leaning against tumble-down shacks, the soil unweeded. National Gardening Exercise Day was, apparently, an annual American event which the allotment users here had decided to adopt. The idea was to promote the health benefits of gardening which, despite Nathan's obvious scepticism, were said to include getting aerobic exercise and strengthening all major muscle groups as you raked, hoed and dug. It was just after 6 a.m. now, and as yet the allotment was deserted, apart from one large satellite van and four weary breakfast news staff. But for the show's 7.40 a.m. slot, Cora had been promised at least a dozen keen gardeners, who would all be happy to show off their planting skills and tell her how gardening had improved their fitness. She finished her note-taking and turned to head back to where the boys had set up their kit and where, she noted with a grin, Nathan and Rodney were now doing some sort of strange Irish jig, the soundman waving what looked like a handful of asparagus spears in the air, and Nathan with a stick of rhubarb in his back pocket like a gardening version of Morrissey.

'Put those vegetables down, idiots! Where did you nick them from anyway? And be careful where you're dancing, I promised the allotment holders nothing would be damaged.'

'Spoilsport.' Rodney stopped prancing and Nathan, slightly pink of cheek, collapsed onto an upturned wheelbarrow, breathing heavily. Life on the road certainly wasn't very good for personal fitness, Cora thought as she scanned her notes one last time. She felt so much healthier now that she was in the studio three days a week and could actually squeeze regular runs into her schedule. When she'd been a roving reporter full time that simply hadn't been possible.

'Right – are we ready?'

'Think so.' Nathan stood up, groaning a little as he straightened his back, which like many cameramen he often had problems with. Television cameras, even the newer, more compact ones, were surprisingly heavy.

'Scott – do you know how long to us?' Cora checked the time on her phone, making sure it was on silent, and shoved it into her pocket. They were just doing a quick one-minute piece now, at the end of the six o'clock news, to outline the story and tell viewers to tune in later – what was known in television terminology as a 'tease'.

'They're coming to us in about a minute. Oh, and you've got a hole in your jeans, Cora. I saw it when you stepped up into the truck earlier, forgot to tell you because I got distracted by the damn dish sticking as usual ... bugger, hang on, that light shouldn't be flashing like that ...'

Scott's voice in Cora's earpiece faded as he moved away from his microphone inside the truck to tackle whatever this latest problem might be. She frowned and looked down at her grey jeans.

'A hole? Where?'

Nathan peered around his camera, and Rodney pushed his little, round glasses further up his nose and pointed.

'There. Couple of inches down from your crotch, on the left leg.'

'What? How did that happen?'

Cora bent over and peered at the spot Rodney was pointing out, tutting as her earpiece slipped out of her ear as she tipped her head to look. Her soundman was right, dammit – a hole, about the size of a fifty pence piece, had somehow appeared at the top of her left leg. How annoying, she thought. I love these jeans too ...

'Cora. CORA.'

Rodney suddenly hissed her name. She ignored him, poking the edges of the hole and muttering to herself.

'CORA. CORA.' Still bent over, she looked up, frowning. Rodney was waving frantically and mouthing something at her. Behind the camera, Nathan was grinning widely.

'What?' Irritated, she bent down again to glare at the hole once more, sighed and stood up.

'WE'RE ON AIR.' Rodney's hiss was a loud whisper now, and Cora's heart suddenly started to pound. What? On air? *Now*?

'SPEAK, CORA. JUST. START. TALKING.' Her soundman's whisper now had an anguished tone. With a sense of horror slowly creeping over her, Cora glanced at Nathan. Behind his camera, he was bright red in the face, one hand stuffed into his mouth, shoulders shaking.

Oh no. Please, no. I was on air, bending over, staring at my own crotch? Cora gulped, groping around her collar for her earpiece and shoving it back into her ear as she opened her mouth and began.

'Good morning, Alice. So sorry, errrr … earpiece problem. Well, I'm here at the lovely Cobsworth allotment just outside Norwich, where later this morning we'll be talking to a group of gardeners …'

As she talked, she tried desperately to ignore her crew, but it was impossible not to be aware of the state they were both in. Nathan was wiping tears of laughter from his cheeks with one hand while he operated the camera with the other, while Rodney was now lying on his back on the upturned wheelbarrow, sound mixer on his chest, feet kicking up and down as he shook with suppressed mirth.

As soon as Cora stopped talking the boys both exploded.

'HAHAHAHA! Oh Cora, that was priceless, I haven't laughed so much in ages. HAHAHA!' Nathan was bent double now, howling as he mimicked Cora scrutinising the hole in her jeans.

'Cora, why didn't you put your earpiece straight back in as soon as it fell out? You knew we were only a minute or so from on air, and that they often come to us early. You're such a *twit*.' Rodney, still lying on the wheelbarrow, rolled off it onto the ground and lay there instead, giggling like a schoolboy.

Cora groaned. 'Aaargh! How long was I in vision for?

Surely they can't have seen much – can they?'

'Good ten seconds.' Scott, beaming, suddenly appeared, brandishing a kettle. 'Alice tried to get your attention three times. She was grinning like a Chelsea cat. She's not going to let you forget that one in a hurry!'

'Cheshire, not Chelsea!' Cora, Nathan and Rodney all chorused.

Scott laughed. 'Whatever. I'm going to fill this up, there's an outside tap over there. Be OK to drink, won't it, if it's boiled?'

Not waiting for an answer, and still smirking, he headed off to fill his kettle.

'I don't know if it's safe, and right now I don't care. I've just been caught with my head between my legs on national television.' Head in her hands, Cora groaned again. Why did things like this always happen to *her*?

'Well, I did try to warn you. Several times, in fact.' Rodney was on his feet now, brushing mud off the red velvet jacket he had inexplicably selected from his vast, weird wardrobe for today's job.

'Don't worry, Cora. Made my day, that did, and they'll all forget about it soon enough.' A wide grin still on his face, Nathan draped an arm around her shoulders. She shook her head, then rested it on his shoulder and sighed.

'Oh, Nath. I am such a *numpty*. Time for tea?'

'Time for tea.'

'Thanks, Scott.' Cora took the steaming mug of Earl Grey from the engineer, sniffed it dubiously – *was* it OK to drink tea made from water from an outside tap? – and settled back in her seat in the satellite truck.

'It's fine. Looked it up on Google, don't worry. Safe as blouses,' said Scott, as Nathan and Rodney, both sprawled on the truck floor, looked suspiciously at their drinks too.

197

'Houses, Scott. Houses. Not safe as blouses. What's safe about a blouse? But OK. If we die, we die together,' pronounced Nathan, and gulped down a mouthful of black coffee. 'Tastes fine, actually.'

Cora took a tentative sip of her tea. It did taste fine. 'At least something's going right today,' she said with a sigh.

'Ahh, forget the crotch thing, Cora.' Rodney reached up from his position near her feet and patted her knee. 'What's the latest on the Sam saga?'

'Still waiting to hear from New York. It's driving me mad, Rodders. I just feel so *helpless*.'

It had been nearly a week now since Joel Anderson had asked his private detective friend in New York to try to find Sam's real mother, and so far there had been no news at all. Joel had phoned Cora again on Monday morning, telling her that, to nobody's surprise, the address in the adoption agency file had drawn a blank. But the detective, who was called Kymani Campbell, had told Joel he had a few leads, and was happy to continue the search, for a modest fee.

Cora had quickly agreed. She had no intention of asking Sam to pay for this, and she didn't have limitless resources herself – her job paid well, but not ridiculously so – but she had a few thousand in savings. She'd transferred some money to Kymani's account and told him to do what he could. But there were just over three weeks to go now until Sam's court appearance, she calculated as she sipped her tea. She was getting twitchy. Come on, Kymani, please, she urged silently. *Call me.*

'And what about telling Sam she's adopted? Has her mum done that yet?' Nathan arched his back and groaned. 'Urgh, I need a chiropractor appointment. This job is killing me.'

'Yes. Told her a couple of days ago, in person when she visited. Poor Sam. I spoke to her afterwards, and she was in shock. I don't think she'd quite taken it in yet, she was really upset. And then, when I told her I was on the trail of her real mum, and that there was an identical twin sister ...'

'Wow. Kind of mind-blowing for her.' Scott put his mug down on the little shelf next to his chair and rubbed at a stain on his sweatshirt.

'I know. She's not sure what to do right now, whether she wants to contact her real mum or not. But it's given her a bit of hope too, and I'm not sure if that's a good thing or not.' Cora took another mouthful of tea. Sam had swung from one intense emotion to another during their telephone call – despair and disbelief that her beloved parents were not her parents after all, anger that it had taken this long for her to be told about her past, but then excitement when Cora had confessed about her attempts to hunt down Sam's real family.

'A sister. An identical twin sister. It's just unbelievable. I've always, *always* wanted a sister.' There had been awe in Sam's voice, but as the implications of a twin had dawned on her, her wonderment had turned to something else.

'So it could have been her. Who killed Marcus. It *could* have been, Cora. Because she'll have the same DNA profile as me, won't she? And I didn't do it. So it must have been her. It MUST. You have to find her, Cora. You just have to.'

Cora had promised that she would do her best, but had also tried to reason with Sam, with the same arguments she'd heard so many times from different people in recent days – why would a sister, never heard of before, suddenly turn up in London and kill Sam's boyfriend? It

199

clearly made no sense, but Sam had refused to listen.

'Cora, I didn't kill Marcus, and yet my DNA was found on the murder weapon. If it wasn't a lab mix-up, and nobody stole my DNA and framed me, then the only other explanation is that somebody else has the same DNA as me. Which made no sense initially, because it wasn't possible – but it is now. Now, we know that somebody else *does* have the same DNA, because I have a twin sister out there somewhere. And if the police won't find her, because they think it's too far-fetched, then it's down to you. Please, Cora. Please, please find her.'

Now, Cora took a deep breath, trying to stop herself dwelling on the other, unthinkable explanation – that Sam *had* killed Marcus herself. Maybe what Nathan had suggested when they'd first discussed all of this was right – that their friend genuinely didn't remember doing it. Maybe it had all been so horrific that her brain had simply shut off all memory of the deed. That happened sometimes, didn't it, when people had gone through terrible experiences? But no, her friend couldn't, just couldn't have killed somebody, could she? And there had to be a chance, didn't there, that the mysterious twin sister could have done it? A tiny chance, but a chance nonetheless …

Cora jumped as her phone rang. She reached into her pocket and pulled it out, stabbing awkwardly at the answer button with her left hand, her tea mug still clutched in her right.

'Cora Baxter.'

'Cora, good morning. It's Joel Anderson. Sorry to call so early but I have news, and I thought that with your line of work you'd probably be up …'

'Joel! Yes, up for hours, on a job … so, tell me!' Cora carefully placed her mug on the floor next to her feet, nerves suddenly fluttering in her stomach. The boys had fallen silent, eyes fixed on her face, Rodney with his tea cup halfway to his mouth as if he'd been turned to stone.

'OK, well – it's good news. Ky – sorry, that's Kymani – has found her. Your friend's biological mum. Took a bit of tracking down, but he's confident it's her. She's still in New York, living in Brooklyn. Not the nicest of places, apparently, but …'

'He – he found her? Sam's real mother? I can't believe it. I just can't …' Cora paused, feeling slightly overwhelmed. Nathan was punching the air, and Scott and Rodney were repeatedly high-fiving each other with alternate hands.

'Shhh!' she said, but she was grinning. Could it be this easy?

'Joel – what about the sister though? Sam's twin? Is she there too?'

'Ah. Well, therein lies our problem.' Joel hesitated. 'The mother – Clare Henderson – is a little … well, a little unwell, would probably be the best way to put it. Ky believes she's had issues with drugs, although I'm not sure if that's still ongoing. Anyway, Ky can be pretty persuasive, and he managed to get into her apartment to talk to her, but she won't communicate any other way – just face to face. No telephone, and won't use email. Ky says she seems to think she's being bugged. No grounds for that, as far as he can tell … she's just a bit paranoid. He told her about you, and about Sam, and she listened but didn't say much, and then refused point blank to talk to him about her other daughter when he asked her about that. She said – and this is where the problem falls – she said that if you want to talk to her, you're going to have to go and see her yourself.'

'Go and see her? In *New York*?'

'Afraid so, yes.'

'Hang on.'

Cora took the phone from her ear and stared at it for a moment, then looked at the three sets of eyes glued to hers.

'If I want to talk to Sam's mum, I have to go to New York,' she said quietly.

The boys exchanged glances. 'Cora, it's only three weeks or so until our deadline. If you've got to go to New York, bloody go to New York.' Scott banged his fist on the desk, as if the matter was settled. Nathan and Rodney nodded in agreement.

'Go, Cora. You've started this now. You'll never forgive yourself if you don't see it through.'

'You're right, Nath.' Cora picked up the phone again. 'Joel? I'll do it. I'll go to New York. In fact, I'll go tomorrow. I need to do this as quickly as possible.'

'Great. This might sound a bit odd, but how would you feel about me coming with you? I'm due some leave and I'd love to link up with Ky again. And I want to see how this ends now, now that I've got involved this far.'

Cora raised her eyebrows, then shrugged. Why not – it would be good to have the company, she thought.

'Can't see any reason why not. Let me get back to you this afternoon with the details – I need to speak to my boss, I'm supposed to be filming a charity event on Sunday. And Joel – thanks so much.'

'A pleasure. Speak later.'

Cora ended the call, and sank back in her seat.

'Blimey,' she said. 'New York here I come.'

27

Friday 7th June
21 days until the deadline

'Thanks, Betsy. I'm so sorry about this. I should be back in on Monday.'

'Don't worry, Cora. Take it easy over the weekend and give me a call on Sunday night to let me know if you're feeling up to Monday's show.'

'I will. Bye, Betsy.'

'Bye, Cora.'

Betsy Allan put the phone receiver down and stared at it for a moment. Cora Baxter calling in sick for the shoot she was supposed to be doing on Sunday was slightly inconvenient, and more so if she was still out on Monday, but that was the least of the programme editor's current worries. She stood up, arched her back and sighed, then smoothed down her flower print chiffon shirt and wandered across to the window. She stood there for a moment, eyes fixed on the ground seven storeys below, then shuddered and turned away. That was the spot where her predecessor, Jeanette Kendrick, had been found dead. What a way to go, thought Betsy, and returned to her desk. She had so much work to do – it was June already, with the silly season approaching, and not nearly enough fillers planned for the show. "The silly season" was the term given by the media to the period of the summer from late July to early September, when schools were on

203

holiday, the House of Commons took its summer recess, and the High Court, Court of Appeal and Supreme Court did not sit – in fact, it was actually into October when the courts returned. Finding enough stories and features to fill a three-hour news programme was always a challenge during this period, and Betsy was normally buzzing with ideas. But in the past few weeks she'd struggled to concentrate, anxiety whirling through her brain and dulling her creativity.

She reached out and pulled her desk calendar towards her. It was one of the old-fashioned, tent-shaped ones, the days of the month on the right-hand side of each tear-off page and a motivational or amusing quote on the left. June's quote was: "Silence is powerful. Sometimes, the best thing you can do is say nothing at all."

Betsy ran her finger across the dates on the right. Three weeks. Exactly three weeks today, Sam would appear in court and the wheels of justice would start rolling. She swallowed hard. Silence, Betsy, she told herself. Silence. Say nothing, and all this will soon be over. She took a deep breath, pushed the calendar back into its correct position, straightened her keyboard and started to type.

Cora, who had been home for an hour after a morning broadcasting from Cardiff, and who was now stretched out in a deckchair on the terrace of her Cheltenham flat, closed her eyes as Alice let out another cackle on the other end of the phone.

'Cora, I nearly *died* laughing. I just couldn't work out what on earth you were *doing*. I mean, I throw to you, and you pop up on the split screen, and you're standing there with your head between your legs, muttering something incomprehensible about a hole …'

She exploded into giggles again, and Cora waited

patiently, enjoying the warm sunshine on her face and unable to suppress a grin herself. She really did get herself into the most ridiculous situations on live television, but if you didn't laugh, you'd cry, and she'd done enough of that recently. The hilarity her faux pas of yesterday had caused was actually quite therapeutic – there hadn't been nearly enough laughter among her group of friends since Marcus's murder, and this seemed to have tickled all of them.

'Yeah, yeah, all right, I'm a numpty, I know.'

'You are, Cora. But you're a lovely numpty.' Alice paused, and Cora could hear a sudden wailing in the background.

'Dammit, the princess is calling. Her afternoon naps aren't nearly long enough these days. Got to run. Get well soon, OK? See you next week. If you're still feeling ropey on Sunday night, let me know. I'm sure I can find a sitter for Monday morning if you need me to cover the news.'

'Thanks, Alice. Have a good weekend.'

Cora ended the call, feeling even guiltier than she had when she'd spoken to Betsy. She'd only ever faked being ill to get time off work a couple of times before, and always for very good reasons. Needing to urgently fly to New York tonight to speak to Sam's biological mother was probably the best reason ever, but Cora still felt deeply uncomfortable about lying to her boss about feeling dreadful with "some sort of summer flu bug". *That* wasn't a lie – she *did* feel dreadful, especially about deceiving Alice too.

Right, she'd better get moving. She sat for a moment longer, watching Oliver – the sleek black cat owned by a neighbour – on the adjoining balcony, stretched out in the sunshine with his newly acquired best friend, a small tabby called Pebbles. The two, who had become inseparable, lay with limbs entwined, pink noses touching. Cora sighed, wishing she and Adam were as content as that right now. As she reluctantly rolled off her deckchair and headed in to the bedroom to throw a few things into a bag for her trip, she recalled the amazement in his voice when she'd called him at home in London last night to tell him why she wouldn't be able to see him this weekend.

'You're going WHERE? To do WHAT? Cora, have you taken leave of your senses?'

'Adam, I knew you'd react like this. But …' Cora had hesitated, unsure how to explain her reasoning for going so far to pursue Sam's twin sister. It was something she was still struggling to justify even to herself.

'Look, I know you think there's no point in finding her, and that she couldn't possibly have been involved in Marcus's death. But I need to be sure, Adam. Sam's my friend. Not just a friend, one of my closest friends. And she's in terrible, awful trouble, and if I can do this one thing for her, and tie up what she's convinced is the final loose end, then I have to do it. Can you understand that, at all?'

On the other end of the phone, Adam had sighed heavily. 'Cora, as I keep telling you, I love you. I love your impetuousness, and your loyalty. But I think this time you've gone a step too far. Paying a private detective, and flying thousands of miles to talk to some woman who for some weird reason can't speak on the telephone or read an email? And for what? To find a sister who can't possibly have any connection with the case? It's madness, Cora. And to cap it off, you're going out there with some guy you've only met, what, once?'

'Yes.' Cora's voice had been small and subdued. She knew everything Adam was saying was probably right, but it didn't matter. She'd made up her mind. The tickets were booked, and she was going, and that was that. 'I'll be careful, I promise. Joel is OK, honestly. And I won't be on my own with him at any point, not really. It'll be fine.'

They'd been together long enough for Adam to know there was no point in trying to change his girlfriend's mind once she'd made a decision like this, and he didn't even attempt to, but the rest of their conversation had been terse and uncomfortable, and Cora had sat very still for a long time when the call was over, wondering yet again if what she was doing made any sense at all or if she'd gone completely mad. Finally, deciding that sleep deprivation would not help, she'd crawled into bed ahead of this morning's 3 a.m. alarm, and had woken up feeling more positive again. Adam loved her, and everything would be fine. Casting a final eye over her case, she zipped it shut, then checked that her passport was, as usual for a roving reporter, in her handbag. It was, of course – it was a sackable offence for her ever to be without it. She glanced at the clock on her bedside table. Just after midday. Her flight from Heathrow was at five, and she'd need to allow at least two and a half hours to do the drive and find a parking spot once she got there. Better get going.

She grabbed her jacket and car keys from the bed, picked up her suitcase and headed for the door.

In Central London, Adam pushed half a brie and bacon sandwich disconsolately around its paper plate with the end of his pen, then sighed heavily. He hadn't seen Cora last weekend because he'd had to work, and he'd been hugely looking forward to her arrival tonight, and to spending the weekend with her and Harry. Instead, she'd now be thousands of miles away. But it wasn't just that

207

which was unsettling him. He looked at the half-eaten sandwich, then picked it up, plate and all, and tossed it into the bin at the side of his desk. He really wasn't hungry, and the slight feeling of unease which had crept over him from the minute Cora had told him about the existence of Sam's identical twin sister was growing. The murder case was solid, he was sure of that, and the body had been released to the family, with the funeral scheduled to take place on Monday. This news, though, had definitely planted a seed of doubt in his mind. A tiny, weak seed, but a seed nonetheless. Although ... what possible motive would Sam's long-lost sister have for killing Marcus? It was nonsensical. And yet, this was another little loose end, just like the third dog-walker on the CCTV footage, the one they hadn't managed to trace. The sender of the mystery gifts too. That was another one. Adam detested loose ends, and although he still didn't believe that anyone other than Sam could be responsible, judging solely by the evidence, he felt uneasy. He hadn't mentioned this feeling to Cora, but it was nagging him. Should *he* be doing this, flying to New York to check out the whereabouts of this mysterious sister at the time of the murder? He'd referred it upwards earlier, mentioned it to his superior, Chief Superintendent Brian McKay, but the response had been predictable.

'Adam, we're not looking for anyone else. The case is solid, you know that. If the CPS are happy, then so are we. If it was just the DNA, I'd be with you – it might be worth having a chat to this twin sister. But Samantha Tindall had the motive, the opportunity, she was there at the park at the right time ... *and* her DNA is all over it. She did it, Adam. Please, let it go. Let the family bury him, and move on.'

Reluctantly, Adam had agreed. His boss was right, but

what if ...? He stood up suddenly, tired of thinking about it. Cora was on a wild goose chase. Let her find the sister, fine – it might be of some comfort to Sam, to know she had a twin out there. Maybe the girl would visit, and they could get to know each other. But could she be involved in the case? Adam shook his head. She couldn't. It was ludicrous to even think it. He was starting to feel guilty though now, about how he'd reacted to Cora's announcement that she was flying to New York. She was only trying to help her friend, and he knew he should have been more supportive. He'd make it up to her when she got back. He glanced down at his desk, where a mound of paperwork awaited. If he was going to be home in good time for Harry's arrival later, he needed to get a move on. He sat down again, then looked into the bin. Glancing around the room to make sure nobody was looking in his direction, he surreptitiously leaned over and fished the sandwich and its plate out again. He'd need some sort of sustenance to get through this lot. Grabbing a pen from the plastic holder next to his computer monitor, he set to work.

28

As the yellow cab sped along under the East River and then emerged from the Midtown Tunnel, Cora felt a little quiver of excitement, as she always did when she arrived in this city. She had been here many times – once for a three-day break with an ex-boyfriend, and on numerous occasions for work, covering *Morning Live*'s New York office when the regular correspondent was on holiday. And no matter how tired she was, she was always suddenly wide awake and raring to go as soon as she reached Manhattan, the energy and vibrancy of the noisy, bustling streets seeming to infiltrate her very bones. She could feel it happening now, even though it was two o'clock in the morning back home in London, a time when she would normally have been in bed hours ago. At 34th and Broadway she gazed out of the taxi window at the flashing lights and enormous video screens of Herald Square, Times Square's little brother, and then clapped her hands with glee as she spotted Macy's.

'Biggest department store in the world. Covers a whole block. One of my very favourite places to go shopping.'

She turned to Joel, sitting next to her in the back of the cab, and grinned. He smiled back, clearly as delighted to be there as she was.

'I flipping love New York,' she added.

'Me too.'

The plan for tonight was to head straight out for a late dinner with Kymani Campbell, who was due to meet them at their hotel. He would brief them fully about his encounter with Sam's biological mother, Clare Henderson, and then let them get some sleep. He had arranged the meeting with Clare for ten o'clock tomorrow morning. Cora and Joel's flight back to London was early on Sunday morning; what they would do for the rest of Saturday would very much depend on what they discovered when they spoke to Clare.

The flight to JFK had been a very pleasant one. Because they'd booked their trip at such short notice, only business class seats had been available. Joel, who told Cora he'd recently had a small inheritance from a relative who'd passed away, said he'd initially winced at the price but then decided life was short, and that maybe his windfall had been fate. Cora had checked the dwindling balance on her savings account, sighed and then shrugged. She could start saving again when all this was over. And, as they sat side by side in their comfortable, fully reclining seats, sipping chilled Sauvignon Blanc, they had both agreed that there were definitely worse ways to travel three and a half thousand miles.

They had passed the eight-hour flight watching movies, dozing a little and chatting. Cora had been surprised at how easily the conversation had flowed, and at how much they had in common, despite their very different jobs and lifestyles. As savoury snacks appeared in front of them to accompany their pre-dinner drinks, Joel had told her about how his family had moved to the UK from Jamaica when he was a child.

'It was a shock to the system at first, and I really missed the sunshine, and my friends at school. But I got used to it pretty quick. I'm London through and through now, I love it.'

'Good. I'm pleased. Erm … you not eating those?'

Cora gestured at the untouched bowl of nuts on Joel's tray, and he laughed and passed them to her, his forearm brushing hers. Just for a moment, she could feel the hardness of his muscles under the smooth skin and thought, not for the first time, how attractive he was. Not that she was interested, of course. But if she had to be cooped up in a plane for hours, it was certainly rather nice to spend it sitting next to someone pleasant on the eye.

'Here we are – this is our hotel. Cora – you awake?' Joel's voice interrupted her reflections, making her jump, as the taxi slowed and then stopped.

'Sorry! Miles away.'

They clambered out into the warm night and, once Cora had paid for the cab – she'd made him agree that she'd pick up the tab for all such expenses, this being *her* mission after all – they checked in, dumped their bags in their rooms, spent ten minutes quickly freshening up and then returned to the hotel reception area, where Kymani was waiting. As introductions were made and Cora shook his hand, she marvelled at the differences between the two men, who Joel had told her had been best friends at school in Kingston and had never lost touch. While Joel was at least six foot three inches tall, Kymani was barely five foot two; while Joel's dress sense was classic and stylish (tonight he was wearing a simple short-sleeved white shirt and grey chinos), Kymani was flamboyantly attired in a Hawaiian-style shirt and skin-tight leather jeans; and while Joel's body had the muscular, well developed look of a regular gym goer, Kymani was skinny – well, not skinny *exactly*, but certainly lean and sinewy; he had that spare, wiry look that she'd often seen in marathon runners. Marathon runners she'd observed while watching the London event from the comfort of her sofa, of course. She might now be a runner herself, of sorts, but she considered marathons to be for crazy people.

'My bum's about three times the size of his, dammit,' she thought to herself, pulling her short denim dress down self-consciously as she walked across the lobby behind the two men, who were chatting animatedly, slapping each other on the back, clearly thrilled to be back in each other's company.

New York was enjoying a sunny June, and it was still around twenty degrees even at this hour, so Kymani had thoughtfully booked them a table at a restaurant with outdoor seating. Just five minutes' walk from their hotel, the cobblestone patio, with mismatched wooden tables and chairs, was lit by old-fashioned lanterns slung along the wall, and candles stuck into the tops of wine bottles. It had a retro feel which Cora instantly loved, and as soon as she saw the menu she knew she'd love the food too.

'Wow, Kymani, you've chosen well. These arancini are to die for.' She swallowed another mouthful of the delicious risotto ball, flavoured with gorgonzola and bacon, then picked up her dark cherry Manhattan. She really needed to slow down after this, she told herself. She'd already had several glasses of wine on the flight, but the cocktail menu here had looked too good to resist.

'Glad you like it. But call me Ky, please. All my friends do.' He beamed at her, showing teeth as perfect as Joel's.

'Always did like his food, did Ky – not that you can tell from looking at his skinny ass,' said Joel, then ducked as his friend threw a breadstick at him.

'Can't fatten a thoroughbred. And you were a skinny ass too, until you discovered the gym. Used to call him Chicken Legs at school. They ain't no chicken legs now.'

They all laughed. Ky was just as easy to be around as Joel, and Cora, although already growing anxious about tomorrow's meeting with Clare Henderson, realised she was actually enjoying herself, despite being with two men she barely knew. Remembering this, and Adam's incredulity that she was crossing the Atlantic with someone she'd only met once, made her put her glass down again. She needed to keep her wits about her, she thought. She felt very safe and comfortable with Joel and Ky, but this wasn't a holiday. She was here for one reason, and one reason only – Sam.

'So, Ky – can we talk about Clare Henderson?'

'Sure.' He wiped a piece of focaccia around his plate, soaking up the last of the lemon aioli that had accompanied his calamari starter, and popped it in his mouth.

'It just seems so weird that she wouldn't talk to me on the phone, or even via email. What's she like?'

Ky swallowed his bread and wiped his slim hand delicately across his lips, checking for crumbs.

'She's … well, a bit *vacant* might be a good word. She's had addiction issues in the past – mainly prescription painkillers, from what I can gather. Maybe alcohol too. She's clean now … well I think so, anyway.'

His voice wasn't as deep as Joel's, but he had the same musical Jamaican lilt, thought Cora, although with an American twang.

'But whatever she was taking seems to have left her a bit paranoid.' Ky paused as a waiter appeared and started swiftly clearing their plates. They all sipped their drinks until he'd finished, then Joel spoke.

'Paranoid how? Just the phone and email thing or is it worse than that?'

'Paranoid about pretty much everything, really. Rarely goes out. She has some nice neighbours, they help her out, do her food shopping, stuff like that. But she's scared to open the door to anyone she doesn't know – I had a helluva job getting in, had to charm a lady friend of hers in the downstairs apartment to accompany me to her door to persuade her I was a nice guy, and even then she kept me standing outside for ages, peering at me through the crack and firing questions at me. She doesn't own a phone, or a computer, hence no calls or emails – told me they're too easy to bug. She's right, they are. Done quite a few myself over the years.'

He smiled again, and Cora and Joel smiled back.

'Bet you have.' Joel scratched his closely cropped head, then frowned. 'Poor woman. Sounds like a miserable existence.'

Ky nodded. 'I think, from talking to her, that it all actually goes back to the reason you're here. I think she's spent her whole life riddled with guilt that she left one of her children behind when she came to America, and has never stopped being afraid that one day the police would turn up on her doorstep and lock her up for it.'

'But it clearly says, in the adoption file, that it was decided that no prosecution would be made. She must have been told that?' Joel looked puzzled.

'Yes, yes, I mentioned that, and yes, she knew. She just kept saying she didn't believe it, that it was a trick, that one day they'd come for her. I honestly think it's the guilt, eating her up for all these years. It's tragic really.'

'And she asked you about Sam – the baby she abandoned?'

'Her eyes lit up. She wanted to know everything – what she'd been like as a child, what she did for a living, her hobbies. I didn't know much, of course, only the bare bones that you told me on the phone, Cora. I told her Sam was in trouble, and a little bit about the case, and that you'd fill her in on everything else. You being one of

216

Sam's best friends was the only reason she agreed to let you come, I think. She's desperate to hear more about her.'

Cora nodded slowly. The poor woman, it couldn't have been easy for her. What a terrible decision to have to make – to pick a child to leave behind, because she couldn't care for both.

'So what about Sam's twin – the one she took to New York with her? Would she talk about her?'

Kymani shook his head. 'Clammed up totally. I got the feeling there'd been some sort of falling out there. Certainly no sign of the daughter around the apartment – no pictures or anything. It's over to you on that one, Cora. I'm hoping she'll talk to you about her.'

Cora exhaled heavily, suddenly deeply apprehensive.

'Gosh, so do I. Otherwise I've … well, both of us, have come a very long way for nothing.'

She looked at Joel. He looked into her eyes for a moment, then reached across the table and covered her hand with his. It felt huge and surprisingly soft, and very comforting.

'Don't worry, Cora. It'll be OK.'

She gazed back at him for a moment, then dropped her eyes, suddenly feeling uncomfortable. Why did he have to be so damn good-looking, and so bloody nice with it?

'Thanks, Joel.' She gently slid her hand out from under his, and there was an awkward silence for a long moment, Kymani looking quickly from Cora to Joel and back again as they both looked anywhere but at each other. Fortunately, the waiter chose that moment to reappear at the table balancing main course plates, and soon they were tucking into fettucine with clams, chicken marsala and garlic-crusted salmon, and chatting happily about their favourite places in the city, the awkwardness forgotten.

They called it a night shortly after that, the combination of cocktails and jet lag suddenly hitting both Cora and Joel. Ky dropped them back at their hotel, promising to email them Clare Henderson's address as soon as he got home, so they could meet there just before 10 a.m.

As Cora slipped wearily between cool cotton sheets, and sank gratefully into the deliciously soft feather bed, she suddenly remembered that she hadn't called Adam to let him know she'd arrived safely.

'He would probably have been asleep anyway, by the time I landed,' she thought, a little guiltily, as she drifted off to sleep. 'I'll call tomorrow.'

29

Saturday 8th June
20 days until the deadline

Tomorrow began for Cora just after 7 a.m., when she was
woken by a shaft of bright sunshine streaming in through
curtains which in her worn-out state she'd failed to close
properly the night before. Squinting, she staggered across
to the window, intending to yank the heavy drapes shut
and go straight back to bed. Instead, she gasped, as her
eyes adjusted to the light and the view stretching out in
front of her came into focus.

She'd been in too much of a hurry to get ready for
dinner, and later too exhausted, to notice it last night.
Now, from her corner room on the thirty-first floor, she
drank in the spectacular skyline. All around her were
other, even taller skyscrapers, the morning sunbeams
bouncing off their shiny black windows, dazzling her.
Looking down, she saw cars moving slowly along the
criss-cross of streets and avenues, and tiny, scurrying
people, dizzyingly far below. Directly opposite her room,
a figure moved across a rooftop garden and, in the far
distance, she caught a glimpse of New York's biggest
green space, Central Park, a shimmering green blur in this
post-dawn sunlight. Sleep forgotten, Cora, suddenly
desperately wishing that Adam was here with her to
share it all, bounded back to the bed to grab her mobile
and dial his number. I love you, Adam. I wish you were

here, she thought, as the phone began to ring. Their conversation was brief – it was lunchtime back home, and Adam and Harry were about to order food in a local café – but when Cora put the phone down, she felt happier than she had in days. Adam had surprised her by telling her he was sorry about the way he'd reacted to her New York trip, and that what she was doing would mean so much to Sam.

'If I had a sister I'd never met, and was locked up in jail, I'd be thrilled to bits if a friend tried to track her down for me. It's a good thing you're doing, Cora. I hope you find her. If the worst happens, I'm sure it will be a great comfort to Sam to know she has a sister,' he said.

Cheered by his words, Cora pulled on her workout gear. Forty minutes on the treadmill would clear her fuzzy head, she thought. Taking one more long glance at the stunning view, she grabbed her room key and headed for the hotel gym.

'So this is it. Pretty … well, pretty grim, isn't it?'

Cora stuffed the change from the taxi fare into her purse, watched slightly uneasily as the cab drove off, then turned to where Joel was peering up at a tall, mud-coloured apartment block. Graffiti covered the dirty brown bricks at street level, and bags of rubbish leaned against the wall, flies buzzing around one from which a foul-smelling liquid was oozing. Many of the building's windows were covered with wooden or metal panels; some of those which still had glass were open, curtains flapping lazily in the breeze. Towels and pieces of clothing, presumably residents' laundry, hung from others. They were in a residential area of eastern Brooklyn, a neighbourhood which Ky had told them was dominated by public housing and which had significant levels of poverty and crime, and Cora had felt a tension in the air even before they'd left the safety of the taxi. Now, she nervously moved closer to Joel as they waited for Ky to arrive.

'Pretty grim, yes. And I'm not liking the look of those guys,' she answered quietly.

Across the street, three young men, baseball caps pulled down low over their eyes, leaned on a wheel-less car, watching them silently. Cora, taking a quick look back from behind her sunglasses, was sure she could see the tell-tale bulge of a gun at the waist of at least one of them and, despite the warm sunshine, she suddenly felt a shiver run down her spine.

An older man, wearing a filthy grey sweater and slippers, limped past, mumbling to himself. As he passed Cora and Joel, he stopped, turned and took a few steps back towards them. He looked from one to another for a moment with rheumy eyes, then spat viciously on the ground, causing Cora to leap backwards in alarm. The old man laughed, a guttural, rasping sound that chilled her, then shuffled off again, still muttering incoherently.

Cora was used to working in all sorts of dodgy areas as a news reporter, but this felt dodgier than most. Come on, Ky, she urged silently.

'Here he comes … thank goodness for that.'

Joel pointed down the street, and there indeed was Ky, walking briskly towards them, a black felt fedora perched at a jaunty angle on his head, and wearing dark green combat trousers rolled at the ankle, startlingly white trainers and a bright red T-shirt with jagged black lines across the front.

'He's an American version of Rodney, I swear he is.' Cora smiled, despite her anxiety.

'Who's Rodney?'

'My soundman at work. Has a slightly … unusual dress sense.'

'Ah. Yes, Ky definitely walks his own fashion path.' Joel winked at her, then held out his hand as his friend reached them. 'Good morning, Mr Campbell. About bloody time.'

'Sorry, sorry.' Ky grinned. 'Enjoying the neighbourhood? Come on, let's get inside.'

The apartment was tiny and claustrophobic, every available surface including the floor piled high with old newspapers, stacks of clothing, books and random household objects. One rickety wooden chair was home to several broken lamps, their shades torn, wires snaking from their cracked bases into a twisted pile on the ground below. The table by the lounge window was covered with tins of food – tomatoes, meatballs, sweetcorn, tuna, pears – but in stark contrast to the objects strewn across the rest of the room, these were neatly lined up, like with like. At one end of the table, a perfectly square space was empty, occupied by a raffia placemat with a faded picture of Big Ben and the Houses of Parliament. A knife and fork, perfectly aligned, sat either side of the mat. It was the only part of the entire place that looked clean and orderly, and Cora's eyes kept being drawn back to the spot. How, she asked herself, had Clare Henderson ended up living like this?

When the woman had finally allowed them into her fifth floor home, after some gentle persuasion from Ky at her battered front door, Cora had been almost open-mouthed with amazement. True, Clare had the haunted, prematurely aged look of a woman who had lived a tough life, and the pallor of one who had spent many years mostly indoors. But even so, Cora had instantly seen the resemblance to Sam – it was there in the pert nose, the intelligence in the dark eyes, even the way she moved. Cora could not take her eyes off Sam's biological mother as she gestured them into her oppressively warm lounge, all the windows tightly shut, and told them to sit on a sofa which had obviously been swiped clear of its usual occupants ahead of their arrival – all around it, cuddly toys, some with limbs missing, were piled on the floor in untidy heaps. Stepping over a panda, which had a miniature version of itself clasped to its chest, Cora marvelled at the similarities, the wonder of nature over nurture.

She looks like her. I kind of expected that. But she dresses like her too, Cora thought. That dress is faded and doesn't fit her properly, but the way she's wearing it with that scarf – it's how Sam might wear it. And she *acts* like her too … the way she moves her hands when she talks, the way she touches her hair. It's *weird*, she thought, unable to stop staring, as Ky gently made the introductions, then nodded at Cora to join the conversation.

She pulled herself together then, eased into it slowly, her reporter's training taking over, allowing an initially hesitant Clare to ask her questions about Sam first. The woman's eyes grew brighter with every answer, her pale, deeply lined face, which Cora could see must once have been very pretty, growing more and more animated as she learned about Sam's childhood, her television career, her friends and her life in London.

'So she grew up happy. She had good adoptive parents. I've always worried about that. You can't imagine how much I've worried, over the years, thinking I might have abandoned her to bad people, people who didn't treat her right. You can't imagine …'

She stopped talking, and her big, dark eyes, already bloodshot and red-rimmed, filled with tears. Cora fumbled in her handbag, which she was still clutching with both hands, and found a tissue, which she handed to Clare. Joel and Ky sat quietly on the sofa next to Cora, listening but not saying anything. Perched on the edge of an over-stuffed armchair opposite, Clare sniffed, wiped her eyes and then dropped the tissue onto the carpet with a shaky hand.

'She *did* grow up happy. You did the right thing, Clare, I'm sure of that. If you couldn't cope with more than one child, because of your circumstances at the time, then you did the right thing. You left Sam where she would be safe, and she grew up happy and secure.'

Cora reached across and patted Clare awkwardly on the knee. The woman recoiled slightly, looking nervously around the room, and Cora quickly drew her hand back. She didn't want to spook her, not now, not before they'd got to the important bit.

'So, Clare – Ky here told you, didn't he, that Sam is in trouble? That her DNA was found at a crime scene, but that it's a crime she says she didn't commit?'

Clare Henderson was staring at the carpet. She nodded.

'Yes.'

'So, we – her friends – have been trying to help. The police think the case is closed, and they're not looking elsewhere. It seemed impossible that we could do anything either, but when we heard that Sam had an identical twin sister, possibly in New York, we decided we needed to find her. Just in case ... just in case, by some crazy longshot, she might have some connection with the crime ...'

Cora paused as Clare's head shot up, her eyes flashing.

'You think Sally did it? Sally committed this crime?

Why would she? She's never even met Sam. I never even told her she had a sister, she doesn't know. That doesn't make sense.'

There was anger in her voice, but she was right, thought Cora. The woman might be odd, but she was still sharp. It didn't make sense, not really. But she'd come this far … she took a deep breath and carried on.

'Sally? Is that her name, Sam's twin, the child you brought to New York with you? Sally?'

'Yes.'

Clare stood up, and started to pace the room, weaving her way expertly among the piled belongings, wringing her hands, her mouth moving but no sound emerging. Watching her, Cora could see that there actually was some order here, carefully arranged paths between the stacked possessions. They all sat in silence, not sure what to say, waiting for her agitation to pass. When she'd completed four circuits of the lounge, Clare stopped at her armchair, looked nervously around again and sat down, breathing heavily.

Cora waited a moment, then said quietly: 'Can I talk to you about Sally? Just for a minute?'

Clare's eyes darted from side to side. 'OK.'

'Where is she? Where does she live? Because she'd be thirty-one now, wouldn't she, same as Sam? She obviously doesn't live here, with you?'

Clare shook her head. She was staring at the carpet again.

'She moved out. Years ago, when she was in college. She went to college, drama college, here in New York – always a bit of a drama queen, was Sally. And she could have stayed at home, but she didn't want to. We had a nice place then too, not this … this …'

She gestured at the room with both hands, then gripped

them tightly together. She bent forwards in her chair and started to rock slowly back and forth, and Cora could see that tears had filled her eyes again.

'Are you all right, Mrs Henderson?' Joel's deep voice, even though so gentle in tone, seemed to alarm her. She sat up abruptly.

'Fine. I'm fine.' She looked back at Cora. 'She moved out. I was on the painkillers back then, quite bad, and she couldn't handle it. So she went. I don't blame her. She kept in touch though, always sent cards at birthday and Christmas. Well, until recently anyway. Didn't hear from her this Christmas past. But she's a good girl, my Sally. I was just a bad mother. I didn't deserve her. I didn't ...'

Her voice tailed off. Cora was on the edge of her seat now, heart starting to pound.

'Do you – do you have her latest address? And maybe a photo? We'd really love to talk to her, if you could help us find her?'

Clare was already on her feet, heading for a chest of drawers in the corner. One of its feet was missing, a small heap of old telephone directories propping up the corner. She pulled the second drawer open, and the unit wobbled precariously, a vase which had been lying on its side on the top slipping to the ground but miraculously not breaking. It rolled a couple of feet, then stopped, halted in its tracks by a mound of pillows stacked by the wall. Clare didn't seem to notice, intent on rifling through the drawer, muttering again as she pulled out cards and pieces of paper, casting them aside onto the floor until she finally found what she was looking for.

'There!' she said triumphantly. She returned to her chair, sat down, then leaned across and handed an envelope to Cora.

'That's her. The most recent photo. Not very recent of

226

course, it was taken before she moved out. So it would be when she was about ... nineteen? Yes, nineteen. So it's twelve years old. But she never really changed, my Sally. Always looked the same. Same in that photo as when she was ten, really.'

Cora slid the picture out of the envelope, and gasped.

'Oh my goodness!'

'What?' Joel and Ky asked the question simultaneously.

Cora shook her head, momentarily speechless. It was like looking at a photo of a younger Sam. Sally was standing in a garden, or maybe a park, next to a rose bush, grinning at the camera, hand on hip, in an exaggerated catwalk model-type pose. It was just the sort of pose Sam would strike, if somebody turned a camera on her when she was in a silly mood. The hairstyle was different – Sally had long, curly hair, while Sam had a wavy bob – but the hair colour, the eyes, the smile, all were identical. And although this was clearly a much younger Sally, she looked just like the pictures Cora had seen of a younger Sam, and very similar to how Sam still looked now, right down to the little turned-up nose. Even their teeth looked similar. It was as if somebody had picked up an old photo of Sam from Ellen's London flat, and spirited it away to this New York apartment.

'They're identical. It's just so ... so *bizarre*,' whispered Cora, unable to tear her eyes away from the photograph. First the similarities between Sam and Clare, and now this ... it was almost too much to take in. These people would blow Sam's mind if she ever met them. *When* she met them, Cora corrected herself.

'Well, I suppose they would be. Being identical twins and all that.' There was amusement in Joel's voice, and she turned to look at him and smiled.

'I suppose so, yes.'

She turned back to Clare, who was rocking again, humming quietly to herself, seemingly back in her own little world.

'And the other piece of paper, Clare? In your hand? Is that Sally's address?'

Clare stopped rocking and looked at her right hand, an expression of surprise appearing on her face.

'Oh yes, sorry. I'm a bit forgetful, sometimes.' She smiled briefly, a smile which lit up her face, and Cora again saw a flash of the beauty she must have once been. Then the smile vanished. Clare held the folded scrap of paper out in a shaky hand, and Cora took it from her gently.

'That's the last address I had for her. Can't remember when she gave me that. But she sent me a card for my birthday in July. I didn't hear from her at Christmas, first time ever, and I've not heard anything since. It's my birthday again soon though. I'll probably hear from her then, won't I?'

She looked hopefully at Cora. The hand wringing had started again, and Cora's heart twisted with sympathy. If only Sam could have been part of this woman's life too, maybe she wouldn't be living like this, alone in this horrible place, obviously ill, with nobody to care for her except a few kind neighbours.

'I'm sure you will. Thank you for this.'

She carefully unfolded the piece of tatty paper and scanned the address, then looked up sharply.

'Clare? Are you sure this is *Sally's* address?'

She stood up and crossed to Clare's chair, thrusting the scrap of paper at her.

Clare looked at it, frowned, then squinted up at Cora.

'Yes, positive. That was the last one I had for her, I

told you that. She might still be there, she might not. She liked to move around, got bored easily ...'

'What's wrong, Cora?' Ky looked puzzled.

She stared back down at the address.

'But I don't understand. This address is in ...'

'It's in England. Didn't I say? She moved there, a while back. Can't remember when exactly. Wanted to pursue her acting there, be on the West End stage. Acting was all she ever cared about, and she always had a thing about England, even though she left it when she was so young. Cutest little baby, she was ...' Clare smiled dreamily, and resumed her rocking.

'In England? Sally is living in *England*?'

Joel was on his feet now, looking over Cora's shoulder, his breath warm on her neck, eyes wide as he read the address, written neatly and clearly in black ink.

'Not just in England,' said Cora. 'In London. We've come all the way to New York to find her, and she's living in bloody *London*.'

229

30

'Thanks for trying anyway, Wendy. I'll keep you updated, and I'll ring you when I get back tomorrow night.'

'OK. You take care out there, all right? And Cora – we *will* find her, OK?'

'OK. Bye, Wend.'

Cora ended the call and put her phone down on the table in front of her with a heavy sigh. It was now Saturday afternoon in New York, early evening back home, and she and Joel had been holed up in a coffee shop near their hotel for the last couple of hours, desperate to get a head start on the hunt for Sally Henderson back in London. Cora had called Wendy and filled her in on what they'd discovered, and Wendy had immediately offered to go straight to the address Clare had given them. She'd called Cora as soon as she'd left the place, to inform her that sadly, but not entirely unexpectedly, her trip had been a wasted one.

'No joy, I presume?' Joel looked up from his iPad and arched his back slightly to stretch it, his tight T-shirt clinging to his muscled chest. Cora glanced at it admiringly for a moment, then forced herself to look back at his face. For goodness' sake, Baxter, she thought. There were definitely more important things to be doing right now than ogling her companion's body, although a very fine body it certainly was.

'No joy. It was a B&B, and the woman there didn't really keep proper records, but Wendy showed her the photo we emailed of Sally and she remembered her. She said she stood out from her usual guests because she was American, and very pretty. She can't remember when she stayed, but she thinks she was there for three or four days at some point, and left no forwarding address. Well, you don't, do you, if you stay in a B&B? Not sure why she bothered sending that address to her mum though, if it was just somewhere she was staying temporarily? A bit weird.'

Joel shrugged. 'Probably just wanted to reassure her mother that she had somewhere to live?'

'Maybe.' Cora picked up the mug in front of her and swallowed the last of her tea, then shuddered slightly. It was almost cold. She sighed again, put the mug down and turned to her laptop.

'Where are we up to?'

'Nothing at all from the general Google search. Plenty of Sally Hendersons, but none that fit her profile. And she's definitely not on Twitter, not under that name anyway. I've looked at every Sally Henderson account and none sound or look right. Of course, she could use another name, a nickname or something. But as far as an initial search goes, nothing.'

'And we've already done Facebook and Instagram and LinkedIn and Pinterest … every social media site seems to be a big fat blank. She's thirty-one, everyone of that age is on social media, so why isn't she? Bloody hell, Joel, this is SO FRUSTRATING!'

Cora banged both fists on the table, making a passing waitress jump and almost drop the plate she was carrying. She turned and looked back, frowning.

'Please, no shouting.' Her accent was Eastern European.

'I'm sorry. Can we get the bill? I mean the … errr, the

232

check. When you have a minute?'

Cora suddenly felt an urgent need to get out into the warm afternoon sunshine, breathe some air, maybe have something cold to drink instead of the tepid tea. They were getting nowhere, and she was developing a stress headache.

The waitress nodded and turned away again.

'One moment, I bring,' she said tersely, over her shoulder.

'Sorry,' Cora said again, this time to Joel.

He smiled. 'That's OK.' He leaned across the table towards her, and rested his large right hand on her left one, running his thumb lightly across her skin. 'You're stressed, it's understandable. I kind of feel like yelling myself.'

Cora smiled, and gently slipped her hand out from under his, trying to ignore the little, not altogether unpleasant, shivery feeling his touch gave her. He's just being nice, Cora, she chided herself. There's nothing more to it. It's fine. She cleared her throat, and started busying herself packing her laptop and notebook back into her handbag. When she looked back up at Joel, he was staring at her, an amused smile playing around his lips, his eyes warm and affectionate.

'I know what we need,' he said. 'Fancy a drink? I mean a proper drink? I know a great little bar with a roof terrace, and they do good food too.'

'Sounds perfect.' Cora suddenly realised she was ravenous. They'd intended to have lunch with Kymani, but just as they'd left Clare Henderson's he'd received a phone call about an urgent job and had raced off, mouthing apologies and promises to meet them tonight for goodbye cocktails instead. Cora and Joel had ended up skipping lunch altogether as they tried to work out the best way to track Sally down, and the copious amounts of tea and coffee they'd downed as they worked had done little to fill Cora's stomach. Some bar food al fresco sounded like just what she needed.

Twenty minutes later she breathed a sigh of relief as she sank into her chair on the promised bar terrace. The building was only ten stories high, so it was dwarfed by the skyscrapers soaring above them, but it made for a dramatic drinking spot, and was still delightfully sunny. They ordered drinks – cold beer for Joel, and chilled white wine for Cora – plus some chicken wings and tacos, and sat for a while in companionable silence, chewing their food and enjoying the sunshine. It was a peaceful oasis in the heart of the city, Cora thought, making a mental note of the address for next time. The buzz of the packed streets below, with their teeming Saturday shoppers, tourists and horn-honking yellow cabs, was delightfully muffled by the height of their rooftop perch, and by the classical music streaming from speakers discreetly hidden among the foliage of huge plants in terracotta pots dotted among the few diners.

'Sally living in London – this is *huge*, Joel,' said Cora suddenly. She put her fork down and leaned across the table towards him. 'HUGE. Isn't it?'

He swallowed a mouthful of chicken and grinned. 'As you've said repeatedly for hours. And as I've replied each and every time, *potentially* huge, yes. But as I also keep saying, don't get your hopes up too much.'

'I know, I know.' Cora flopped back in her chair again. 'Sorry. I know I keep saying it, but I'm just so stunned by it, and what it could mean. I can't really take it in. We *have* to find her, Joel. We have to. Whether she's a suspect in the murder or not. I mean, she *could* be. She could be that third dog walker on the CCTV, the one who never came forward. Or she could have got into the park another way, over a wall or something, and killed Marcus without ever showing up on a camera. Yes, I know, I know, unlikely. But Joel, Sam has a sister, an identical twin sister, living in London. That is insane. It would mean so much to Sam to meet her, even if … even if she has to stay in prison.'

Cora paused and picked up her wine glass, her momentary elation suddenly subsiding. Every time she thought of Sam having to spend months, or even years, in that place – it was simply unbearable. She took a long drink, then put her glass down again and took a deep breath. Across the table, Joel was watching her, concern in his eyes.

'I know this is incredibly difficult for you. I'm so sorry – and I do understand, honestly. More than most.'

'What do you mean?' Curiosity piqued, Cora leaned towards him. 'You did mention, that day in London when you said you'd help me, something about a friend in a similar situation – is that what you're talking about?'

Joel nodded slowly. 'Yes. It was a guy called Joseph. He went to school with me and Ky, back in Jamaica. He was a good kid, you know? One of our best friends growing up. He moved to London too, with his family, and it was cool for a while – we hung out just the same as back home, and it was awesome for me having somebody with the same background, somebody who kind of got where I was coming from. But then, I dunno, we sort of drifted apart a bit as we got older, and he started hanging out with some other guys. Got into a bit of a bad crowd, basically.'

Joel reached for his glass and downed the last of his beer. Cora sat quietly, waiting.

'They were drug dealers, essentially. Into other stuff

too, but mostly drugs. And Joseph, he was impressed – they all had flash cars, and fancy clothes, and beautiful girlfriends. He was seduced by it all, wanted what they had. Even so, when they asked him to do a run for them, go back to Jamaica and bring some stuff back, he said no, at first. He was a good kid, like I said. He knew right from wrong. And then they got nasty. They knew where he lived, of course – he was still at home, with his mother. His dad had died a couple of years previously. And so they started to threaten him. Threaten him personally, at first. And then, when that didn't work, they moved on to his mother. One of them mugged her, outside her house, beat her up pretty badly. And then they told Joseph that had just been a warning. They said that next time, if he didn't do the Jamaica trip, they'd kill her.'

Cora gasped. 'Seriously?'

Joel sank his head into his hands and rubbed his eyes, then looked up again. 'They were bad people, Cora. What's an old Jamaican woman to them, when there's thousands, tens of thousands of pounds to be made? They didn't care. Of course they would have killed her, and Joseph knew that. So he did it. He went to Jamaica, got the drugs and tried to do as they'd told him to. Except of course he got caught, at Heathrow, on the way back in. Got ten years. He's still in prison.'

'That's … that's horrible.'

'It is, yes. And, like you, I tried to help. I didn't know what he was doing beforehand – he didn't tell me until after he was arrested, otherwise I would have done everything in my power to stop him going. But I tried, so hard, to get him out of there. I spoke to the police, to his lawyers, told them he'd been blackmailed, told them he'd never have done it if his mother hadn't been threatened. It didn't make any difference, in the end. He committed the crime, and he's doing the time, to use a cliché.'

Cora exhaled heavily. 'I know what you're saying, and I'm so sorry about your friend. And yes, there may come a point when I have to accept that Sam is going to stay in jail for this crime, and stop trying to help get her out of it. But I'm not there yet. I still believe her when she says she's innocent, and I'm not giving up on this. Not yet. Not until we find Sally Henderson, certainly. Can you understand that?'

She looked at him beseechingly, and he smiled a small, sad smile.

'I can. That's why I'm here, Cora, thousands of miles from home with someone I barely know. I couldn't help Joseph, but when you came along, it almost felt like a second chance, a chance to help someone who might be innocent, to succeed where I failed before. I don't even know Sam, but I trust your judgement for some reason, Cora, even though we've known each other for such a short time. And I'll keep on helping you as much as I can, or for as long as you ask me to.'

'Thank you. Thank you *so* much.' Feeling slightly overwhelmed, Cora picked up her wine glass and held it out towards him, and Joel picked up his empty beer glass. As they clinked, Cora suddenly made a decision.

'I'm going to ring Adam again, and ask him to help find Sally too. He'd be able to get so much further than we could, so much faster. I know he thinks she has nothing to do with the murder, but he's at least now being more supportive of me finding her for Sam. He might agree to help now, what do you think?'

Joel, who had heard all about Adam and his views on the case on the flight over, shrugged.

'Not sure, Cora. But maybe, yes, if it's just about Sam getting to meet her twin sister.'

Cora nodded. 'I'll ring him when we get back to the hotel, before we go and meet Ky.'

She picked up her drink again and drained the glass. She had a feeling she'd need the Dutch courage. Even though his attitude to her search for Sally had definitely softened, she had the distinct feeling that Adam's response to her asking him to spend more police time on this was going to be less than enthusiastic.

'Bye, Ky. It was so nice to meet you. And I can't thank you enough for all your help. You've been fantastic.'

Cora bent down to hug the diminutive private detective, and he grinned and hugged her back, his lean body surprisingly strong and brawny. He released her and turned to Joel, reaching out to shake his hand.

'Goodbye, Mr Anderson. Come back soon.'

Joel swiped the hand away and pulled Ky in to an embrace, the difference in their heights meaning Ky's face was suddenly buried in his friend's chest.

'You're suffocating me!' The muffled complaint made them all laugh, and Joel let Ky go, grinning.

'Sorry. I'll miss you. It's your turn now though – always a bed for you in my spare room in London.'

Ky saluted. 'Yes, boss. Maybe next year. Right – I'm off. You two get an early night – booked your cab to the airport?'

Cora nodded. 'All done. Thanks again, so much.'

Ky bowed his head, waved a hand and left, weaving his way niftily across the crowded bar terrace, neatly sidestepping a waiter who was coming in the other direction with a tray of glasses balanced on one hand over his head. Cora and Joel watched until Ky had disappeared into the throng, then turned to look at each other.

'It's been a lovely evening, thank you,' said Cora. It

really had been. Her conversation earlier with Adam had been easier than she expected, and he had agreed to do a quick check on Sally's possible whereabouts when he was back at the station on Monday morning. That had lifted Cora's spirits immeasurably, as had Ky's choice of venue for their last night in New York, a stylish rooftop bar in Midtown. The vast terrace had a retractable roof which, on this balmy June evening, was open to the skies. Ky had booked a corner table, which gave them a glorious view of both the city spread out beneath them and of the revellers around them, an eclectic mix of trendy New Yorkers, gaudily dressed tourists and one large group of elderly ladies in wonderfully eccentric outfits, who were knocking back the delicious offerings from the cocktail bar with gusto.

Cora, Joel and Ky had arrived just before dusk, in time to see the sun setting, its dying rays bouncing off the Art Deco curves and angles of the nearby Chrysler Building – Cora's favourite New York landmark – in spectacular style. They'd ordered Cosmopolitans, lobster sliders and a huge cheese board, and sat chatting, laughing and people watching until Ky had eventually called it a night, citing an early surveillance job the following morning. Cora and Joel should really have been doing the same – they needed to be at the airport for their flight home at 7 a.m. and it was already nearly midnight – but Joel seemed quite content to stay where he was and Cora too felt reluctant to leave, enjoying the warmth of the night, the vibrant atmosphere and, if she was honest, the company of the man sitting next to her.

I feel like I've known him for ages, and he has been so, so kind to me, she thought, admiring his strong jawline and the way his shoulder muscles rippled as he reached out to lift his glass from the table. Joel caught her glance and smiled.

'One for the road?'

'Oh, go on then. But wine, not another cocktail. And make it a small one. Nothing worse than travelling with a hangover.'

'True. OK, back in a moment. Don't talk to strangers while I'm gone.'

Joel slipped off his stool, winked and headed for the bar. Cora leaned back against the wall behind her, watching with amusement as one of the nearby group of elderly ladies – a woman who looked at least ninety, wearing a vivid floral tea dress, fishnet tights and bright white Nike trainers, and leaning on a wooden walking stick – slammed a Tequila shot glass on the table before downing the drink with a flourish, discarding the glass and grabbing a slice of lime from a plate held aloft by one of her friends. She shoved the lime into her mouth, sucked, shuddered visibly, then triumphantly tossed the peel back onto the plate, as the others in the group whooped and cheered their approval.

'Quite a gal, eh?' Joel was already back, bearing two small glasses of white wine.

'That was quick.' Cora took her glass and sipped. This would definitely have to be her last – she was starting to feel a little light-headed.

'Got lucky, gap at the bar.' Joel sat down, pulling his stool a little closer to the table, his knee resting lightly against hers as he picked up his own drink and took a gulp. Cora felt a little flicker in her stomach. Was that accidental, or was he doing it deliberately? He was so damn attractive, but she had a boyfriend, and he knew that. Surely he wasn't coming on to her – was he?

She moved her knee away from his, ever so slightly, but within seconds he had adjusted his position so his leg was against hers again. Then, as if to erase any final doubts she might have about his intentions, he reached out and gently touched her hand, thumb caressing her knuckles. Cora sat stock still, pleasure and guilt coursing through her in equal measure.

'Joel ... you're so lovely, but ...'

'Shhh.' He leaned towards her and before she had time to react, quickly and softly brushed his lips against hers. For a moment, Cora responded, her tongue flicking against his, his hands cupping her face now, drawing her towards him. Then, Adam's face flashed into her consciousness and she pulled back, breaking the kiss.

'I ... I can't. I just can't, Joel. I'm sorry.'

He let her go and sat back in his seat, looking crestfallen.

'No, no, *I'm* sorry. I know you're in a relationship, I should never have done that, it was wrong of me. I've had a little too much to drink, I think. Argh, I'm so embarrassed.'

He put his head in his hands and groaned theatrically, making Cora laugh.

'Don't be silly, it's fine, let's forget it ever happened,' she said, poking his arm. 'Come out from behind there and finish your drink.'

He peeped through his fingers like a child playing hide and seek. 'Are you sure? Not afraid I'm going to pounce on you again? That wasn't like me, honest. It's just that you looked so beautiful, in the moonlight ...'

Cora laughed again. 'Oh shut up. More like light pollution, not moonlight. It's fine, honestly. And I didn't exactly run away screaming, did I?'

'True. OK, I feel better now.' Joel lowered his hands and grinned cheekily. 'Let's not speak of it again. Ready to go?'

'Ready.'

As they made their way back to their hotel, both being careful not to sit too close to the other in the back of the yellow cab, Cora had a brief moment of regret. She loved Adam so much, but what harm would it have done? A proper kiss with Joel would have been *so* nice, and Adam would never have known … She gave herself a mental slap. Stop it, Cora. This is the best relationship you've ever had. Don't mess it up for the sake of a moment of passion with a handsome stranger. Because, in reality, she didn't actually know Joel that well at all, despite travelling the Atlantic with him. She decided then and there never to tell Adam what had just happened. He'd been uneasy enough about her trip with a relative stranger in the first place – no point in making it worse over something so inconsequential. The only thing that mattered now was finding Sally Henderson. Where on earth *was* the woman, Cora thought as the taxi finally pulled up outside their hotel. And, more importantly, how *quickly* could they find her? The deadline – Sam's next court date – was getting worryingly close. Sally Henderson needed to be tracked down, and the sooner the better.

31

Monday 10ᵗʰ June
18 days until the deadline

'Why can't people just order *coffee*? I've been standing down in that flipping canteen for ten minutes just to get a cup of ordinary tea, behind a queue of idiots ordering their decaf mocha-wocha twataccinos. It's COFFEE! *Just order coffee!*'

Wendy Heggerty plonked herself into a chair, scowling, then smiled as she spotted Cora Baxter sitting at the desk opposite.

'Twataccinos? Really?' Cora grinned.

'Yes. Twataccinos. Twats, ordering stupid complicated cappuccinos, equals twataccinos. Anyway, where's Miranda? She wanted me to do a graphic to show UVA and UVB and stuff for the Safe in the Sun feature next week, and I need to talk it through with her.'

'No idea. Haven't seen her. Or maybe I have. I don't know, I can't remember. I'm so tired I can barely see straight.'

After yesterday's flight back from New York, Cora had driven straight to Adam's, desperate for some rest ahead of her shift this morning. After a brief but passionate reunion with her boyfriend, Cora guiltily trying to wipe memories of *the kiss* (as she now thought of it) from her mind, she'd only managed a few hours' sleep before her alarm jolted her awake. Now, last bulletin of

243

the morning behind her, and no longer with her live TV adrenalin rush to keep her going, she was slumped in the newsroom, feeling utterly exhausted.

Thankfully, there had been no residual awkwardness with Joel when they'd met in the hotel reception yesterday morning to head to JFK, and the flight had been a pleasant one, with a return to the easy companionship they had enjoyed before *the kiss*. She'd decided not to mention it to any of her friends back home – it meant nothing, after all, and she knew she'd face endless ribbing from the boys and disapproval from Nicole, for one, if she admitted what she'd done. No, best not to say anything. She and Joel had parted with a friendly hug, more profuse thanks from Cora for all his help, and a promise from him to continue to help her in any way he could in the search for Sally Henderson back home.

'I'm not sure how much more I can do, to be honest. But if you need anything, just call,' he'd said, and Cora had gratefully said she would.

'Bet you could do without the funeral this afternoon, then. They're horrible enough at the best of times, but so much worse when you're knackered. Will you be OK?' Wendy was looking at Cora with concern. Cora groaned.

'Oh bugger. Yes, Adam did remind me last night, but I'd almost forgotten again. I was just fantasising about crawling back into that lovely bed this afternoon. But yes, of course, the funeral. Poor Marcus. Of course I'll be OK. Do you know who's going, from here?'

'Only a few. I spoke to Sam over the weekend and she's devastated that's she's not being allowed out of prison to go, although she totally understands why. She asked me to get as many people as possible to go along, but there haven't been that many takers – not many people here knew him, I suppose. I know your boys wanted to come, but they're on a story in Newcastle this morning so they won't be back in time. So it's you and me, and Betsy naturally, as they were old friends. And Alice is coming, she'll meet us there. And Miranda said she'd come too.'

Cora nodded sleepily. 'Great. Maybe we could all share a taxi then?'

'Good idea. I'll ask the runner to book it. Go and get yourself a coffee or something. A twataccino might help wake you up.'

'Maybe a strong tea. I don't drink coffee, Wend, as you well know. Wish I did sometimes.'

Wendy smiled, flicking her red curls back over her shoulders, then stood up and headed for the runner's desk.

'I know you don't. I just like saying the word twataccino.'

A few miles away, DCI Adam Bradberry sipped his own coffee and tapped at his keyboard, taking the odd surreptitious glance around the room to make sure none of his superiors were close enough to see what he was doing. After that latest discussion with the Chief Superintendent about Samantha Tindall's twin sister, when he'd been categorically told to move on from the case, it definitely wouldn't look good if he was caught *still* working on it, especially when he was currently supposed to be tracking down a particularly violent house burglar.

He tap-tapped a few more times. Nothing. She had no record, then. No Sally Henderson of the right age or appearance had ever come to the attention of any police force in the UK. He glanced at the clock on the bottom right of his screen. Three hours until the funeral. He'd spend that time on this, and that time only. Then he'd go and pay his respects, and get back to burglar-hunting.

'Nothing? Nothing at all? Not even a parking ticket?' Cora's voice was sharp with disappointment.

'Not a thing as far as a police record, no. So I did some further checks. She came into the UK a couple of years ago under her own name, and on a British passport. I was surprised at that, at first, but then I remembered she was actually born here, wasn't she? And went to the States as a small baby.'

Cora nodded, and Adam continued.

'But as soon as she passed through airport immigration, she seems to have vanished. No record of her applying for a National Insurance number or paying tax under the name of Sally Henderson. She doesn't appear on the electoral roll, and there's no marriage certificate for anyone of that name. No death certificate either, though. And no record of any Sally Henderson legally changing their name. So if she's still in the UK, she's using a false identity. Would she go that far, to distance herself from her mother?'

Cora shrugged, despair etched on her face. 'I don't know. Maybe. What on earth are we going to do now then? Sam is desperate for news, I can't let her down, I just can't.'

It was Adam's turn to shrug. 'I'm so sorry Cora, I really am. But there's really nothing more I can do.'

Aware that they were in a very public place, he patted Cora gently on the forearm for a moment, then withdrew his hand again. The small north London graveyard was full of people, around a hundred or so, Adam had counted, mostly friends and colleagues of Marcus's, plus the few aunts, uncles and cousins who made up his small family. The short funeral service itself had been private, for family only, but an open invitation had been extended for the burial, which was due to start any minute now. Little

246

clusters of sombrely dressed mourners chatted quietly, waiting, some with umbrellas up although it wasn't actually raining. It had been earlier though, the weather grey and dank for June, as if in tribute to the deceased.

'Cora – maybe, just maybe, it's time to give this up now?' Adam spoke quietly, not wanting to draw any negative attention to himself. He was here to represent the police force, and it wouldn't look good if he was seen rowing with his girlfriend in the churchyard.

'I mean, you've tried. You've tried so hard. You've travelled thousands of miles at your own expense. You're running yourself into the ground with exhaustion, and for what? Yes, it would be lovely for Sam to meet her twin sister, a sister she didn't know existed until recently, I can understand that. But ...' he hesitated, seeing something flash in his girlfriend's light green eyes, not wanting her to get upset and cause a scene, not here. But she said nothing, simply shaking her head, lips in a tight line.

'*But*, Cora,' he continued, 'even if you do somehow manage to find this woman, this Sally – it's not going to get Sam out of prison. It just isn't. You do know that now, deep down, don't you?' He touched her arm again, the fabric of her black linen jacket damp from the brief rain shower that had sent them both running for cover under a tree a few minutes earlier.

Cora swallowed, and he could see that the anger in her eyes had gone, and that she was now struggling to hold back tears.

'I know,' she whispered. 'I know. I know it's virtually pointless, But I still need to find her, Adam. I have to. Just let me do this, OK? I won't involve you again, I know it's difficult for you. I don't want to get you in trouble.'

A tear escaped and she wiped it away, checking her hand for traces of mascara. The anguish in her eyes was too much for Adam. Suddenly not caring who was looking, he reached out and pulled her close.

'I love you, Cora Baxter,' he whispered fiercely in her ear, pushing her soft brown hair back.

Her hands gripped his waist, and she moved her face to brush her lips against his cheek, already slightly rough despite his morning shave.

'I love you too, Adam Bradberry. Thank you for understanding.' She slipped out of his arms, composed again. 'Now, go and do your police thing. I'll go and join the others. I'll see you tonight.'

He smiled, relieved. 'See you later, beautiful.'

'Cora – look. It's David, David Cash,' hissed Wendy. 'That ex of Sam's that we went to see in Richmond. What's he doing here?'

'What? Where?' Cora edged closer to Wendy. They were standing a little way back from the graveside, along with Betsy, Miranda and Alice. The burial service was underway, the coffin sitting on a chrome stand next to the open grave, the packed cemetery silent apart from the vicar's monotone as he recited the opening prayers, and the occasional sob from an onlooker. Cora looked at the others, anxious that they'd heard what Wendy was saying, but all three seemed to be engrossed in the ceremony. Alice, tall and beautiful as always in a long black dress, her hair pulled tightly back into a ponytail and, for her, minimal make-up, looked sad but self-possessed. Betsy, on the other hand, was a mess, eye make-up streaked across her face, tears coursing steadily down her cheeks. She had started to cry long before the coffin arrived, the sobbing beginning when Adam, looking for Cora, had approached the *Morning Live* group earlier. Betsy had stared at him wide-eyed for a moment, then turned very pale and burst into tears. She'd apologised for her constant weeping, explaining that it was partly due to her long friendship with Marcus and partly that seeing a police officer had reminded her again of the horrific way her friend had died, but Cora, Alice and Wendy had exchanged bewildered glances as she snuffled and sniffed. Miranda had also shed a tear, but in a much more dignified manner. She stood now, grey eyes fixed on the vicar, white-faced, lips moving as she repeated the familiar funeral prayers under her breath.

Convinced that nobody was paying her and Wendy any attention, Cora asked again, keeping her voice low.

'Where? I can't see him.'

'There. Second row behind the vicar, next to that woman with the big hat. That's him, isn't it?'

Cora looked. Wendy was right. It was him. How very odd.

'Why on earth would he come to Marcus's funeral? He didn't know him, did he? He certainly didn't say he did, when we went round.'

'Dunno. Maybe to show support for Sam, as her ex? Although that would be pretty bad taste, seeing as everyone thinks she murdered the man in the coffin. Or maybe he's just one of those ghoulish people who likes funerals.'

'Maybe. Bit weird though. Should we say hello?'

Wendy frowned, then shook her head. 'Don't think so. No point. It was bad enough us turning up at his house unannounced. Probably shouldn't really accost him at a graveside too.'

'I suppose.' Cora was scanning the crowd, wondering if there was anyone else here she knew. Suddenly, a flash of pink caught her eye.

'Wendy!' She elbowed her friend in the ribs.

'Ouch! Don't *do* that. What?'

'Katie Chamberlain's here too. The hairdresser. Marcus's ex.'

Wendy looked in the direction Cora was indicating, and nodded. Katie Chamberlain was standing a little apart from the mourners crowded around the grave, seemingly alone. She was wearing black trousers and a black and white checked tunic, her pink and blonde hair flowing loosely around her shoulders. She was clutching a tissue, repeatedly dabbing her cheeks. Even from where Cora and Wendy were standing, it was obvious that her eyes were red and puffy.

'Not so surprised to see *her*. She was a bit obsessed with Marcus, after all. She looks terribly upset.'

As Cora watched the girl, Katie suddenly noticed her, and nodded, a smile briefly crossing her face before she turned her attention back to the vicar, who was now indicating to the funeral director that it was time to lower the coffin into the grave. The coffin bearers stepped forward, lifted it expertly from its stand and shuffled the few feet to the freshly dug hole, then began to gently lower it into position.

There was a sudden gasp from Cora's left. Miranda was swaying on her feet, her face deathly white now.

'Miranda! You look like you're going to faint … are you OK?'

Cora reached out and grabbed the young doctor's arm, and the swaying slowed, but Miranda's breathing sounded ragged. Then she took a big gulp of air and nodded.

'Yes … yes, I'm fine. Just feeling a bit dizzy.'

'Are you sure? You look awfully pale.' Cora let go of her colleague's arm cautiously. She didn't look well at all.

'Honestly, I'm fine. I just felt a bit faint. You know how tired I've been recently, and I haven't eaten much today so my blood sugar's probably quite low. I do sometimes get a bit faint if I've missed a meal and then have to stand up for a long time. Should know better, given my job, shouldn't I?'

She managed a small laugh. The colour was starting to come back into her cheeks, a slight rosy flush replacing the sickly pallor.

'OK, well go and eat something straight after this. That's an order, Dr Evans.' Betsy, who also seemed to have recovered her composure a little, patted Miranda on the arm.

'I'll come with you if you like. There's a nice little teashop just across the road. I'd kill for a slice of Victoria sponge,' offered Alice.

'Why don't we all go? It would be nice to do something a bit more cheerful after this.'

Wendy nodded across to the graveside, where the vicar now seemed to be wrapping up the service. Two elderly women, probably Marcus's aunts, stepped forward and dropped red roses into the grave. They stood there for a moment, clutching each other's arms, then turned away, one sobbing audibly.

'I can't. I need to get back to the newsroom, I have some work to finish up. I look a state, anyway. But you all go. I'll see you tomorrow.' Betsy scrubbed at her mascara-streaked cheeks with a dirty hanky, then seemed to give up and dropped the handkerchief into her handbag.

'OK. Bye, Betsy.'

The graveyard was slowly emptying now, little groups of people separating off and walking down the path that weaved its way between the headstones. Cora saw Adam trying to catch her eye as he too headed for the gate, and waved at him. He waved back. The grave diggers had begun to fill the grave now, the dull thud of the earth as it

251

landed on the oak coffin echoing eerily across the cemetery.

Cora shivered. Poor, poor Marcus. Could there even be the slightest chance that it *was* Sam who put him in that grave? Was that possible? It wasn't, was it? Then *who*? A slight wave of nausea suddenly washed over her and she swallowed hard, trying to ignore these hideous doubts that were increasingly creeping into her mind, then jumped as Alice grabbed her arm.

'Come on, Cora, tea and cake awaits!'

'OK. I'm coming.' Cora dragged her eyes from the cold, wet grave and allowed Alice to lead her towards the exit.

It was raining again. From under a tree at the rear of the graveyard, David Cash watched as Cora, Wendy and the other women headed down the path. There they were, the two who had appeared at his front door, making all sorts of accusations, going on about mystery gifts and the like. He'd recognised them straight away, when he'd arrived at the funeral. He thought they'd seen him too, sure they had in fact, even though he'd tried to keep in the background, not draw attention to himself. He was so glad now that he hadn't brought Sue along with him this afternoon. Imagine if he had, and those two had come up to them, started talking, asking him again about sending gifts to Sam. Sue wouldn't have liked that, she wouldn't have liked it one little bit. He'd only come out of curiosity, really, because he happened to have an afternoon off work. He'd thought it would be interesting to see who was there, who was mourning this man that Sam was accused of murdering. He was glad Sue didn't know how often he still thought about Sam, too. Because he did, quite often, even though he tried not to. He couldn't help it. He wondered how she was bearing up, in prison. He'd go mad in there, he knew he would. Imagine, somebody else tending his garden, walking his dog, while he rotted away inside a cell. He shuddered, and glanced towards the exit gate. The group of women were gone now. Time to go home.

With a last look towards the grave, where the cemetery staff were now carefully laying the flowers brought by the funeral-goers, he pulled his jacket collar up and strode across the grass towards the pathway. At the gate, he ducked to avoid a large black umbrella, held by a young woman who was blocking his path.

'Oh, I'm sorry. Horrible weather, isn't it?' She smiled, and he smiled back, struck by her beautiful eyes and interesting pink-streaked blonde hair. Then, as the rain began to get heavier, he turned and headed towards his car.

Katie Chamberlain watched the man go. He seemed to be the last, she thought. She reached out to unhook her dog's lead from the gatepost, and the miniature pinscher looked up at her eagerly, its entire damp little body quivering with excitement, tail wagging frantically.

'Come on, you,' Katie said softly. She'd felt bad about leaving the dog at the gate, but he had a tendency to yap, and she'd thought it would be inappropriate at a funeral. Holding her umbrella up against the now torrential downpour, she led the pup back in through the gate and followed the path towards the grave. There was nobody else there now, just the heaped soil, smoothed over, wreaths and bouquets arranged on top. She wanted to be on her own with him, with her Marcus, for the last time. Because he *was* her Marcus. He would always be *her* Marcus. Not that bitch's, the bitch who stole him from her.

I'm glad, so glad that she's locked up, that she's not here, that it's me here with him today, saying the final goodbye, she thought. It's how it should be. She'll never have him now. She didn't get to say goodbye, to stand at his grave, to touch the soil he's lying under. She'll stay in prison for years – maybe for ever – and that's what she deserves. She stole him from me, and that's her punishment.

Katie crouched down, reached out one manicured hand to stroke the cold, damp earth which covered Marcus's coffin and, clutching her dog with the other hand, started to cry.

Out on the street, Betsy had just climbed into the back of a black cab. She hesitated before she told the driver where she wanted to go, then gave him her home address. There was no way she could go back and work now, not after that. She wrapped her arms around herself, shivering. She felt sick. Had the police officer, Cora Baxter's boyfriend, noticed how nervous she was? She was sure he had been looking at her oddly. When would this be over, she thought desperately, tears welling in her eyes again. Surely it wasn't long now, until the trial? And then maybe, just maybe, she could breathe again.

Betsy leaned her head against the cold glass of the taxi's side window and shut her eyes. She normally took her little dog Toby for a walk when she got in from work, sometimes quite late at night if she was held up in the office, but she knew she wouldn't be able to face going out again this evening. He'd understand, just this once. He was a good dog, little Toby. She breathed deeply and mentally urged the driver to put his foot down. Home. She needed to go home.

32

Tuesday 11th June
17 days until the deadline

'Wine, or tea?' Wendy hovered uncertainly between fridge and kettle, looking at Cora for guidance.

'Tea for now I think. We need to keep our wits about us. Maybe wine later?'

'Good plan.' Wendy walked to the kettle and flicked the switch, and Cora busied herself with mugs and teabags. When their drinks were ready, they carried them into the lounge and settled themselves at the big dining table next to the window, where their laptops were already open and connected to Skype.

'Right. I'll get hold of the boys, you do Rosie and Nicole,' said Cora.

It was just after 8 p.m. and they were at Wendy's ground floor flat in Brixton. She had moved in with her boyfriend Dan a few months ago, and they were still doing the place up, but the "living slash dining room" had been one of the first rooms they had tackled. Huge abstract prints adorned the fresh white walls, and the table they were sitting at was a modern white melamine and steel affair, with surprisingly comfortable angular plastic chairs tucked in around it. The sash window next to the table was open, the smell of the honeysuckle in the flowerbed right underneath it drifting in on the warm evening air. The building was directly opposite a park,

255

from which every now and again the whoops of a group of lads engaged in an impromptu game of football could be heard. Cora had had many enjoyable evenings at this table, sharing a bottle of wine with Sam and Wendy and gazing out at the gently swaying trees until the sun went down, but tonight there was no time for pleasantries. They were here for a council of war, hastily arranged last night after Cora had shared the news of Adam's fruitless search for Sally Henderson. *He* might not be able to help any more, but that didn't mean Cora was giving up. She was a journalist, wasn't she? And journalists thought laterally, to get to the bottom of a story. So, here they all were, ready to take on the hunt themselves, Cora and Wendy chairing from the flat. Nathan, Rodney and Scott were joining them on Skype from the hotel they were staying in tonight in Aberdeen, while in Cheltenham Nicole was round at Rosie's.

'You look like the three wise monkeys.' Cora waved at the boys, who were lined up on a bed in one of their hotel rooms, and they waved back, grinning.

'Rosie and Nicole are here now too.' Wendy swivelled her laptop round to show Cora.

'Hey you two – thanks so much for doing this.'

'Of course.' Rosie and Nicole, sitting close together on one of the big sofas in Rosie's living room, looked serious. A wave of emotion suddenly swept over Cora. How lucky she was to know these people, these wonderful friends, all knowing it was probably pointless but still agreeing wholeheartedly to join this last ditch attempt to find Sam's sister, she thought.

She cleared her throat. 'Right, everyone, let's get started. Adam has gone down all the official channels as we know, and come up with nothing. And he can't take it any further than he already has, as the police don't think

Sally's relevant to the murder enquiry. So we need to think laterally. As it seems she may have changed her name, that makes it even trickier. I've been racking my brains and I'm struggling a bit, but if she's an actress, which we believe she is, my gut feeling is that if she's still in the UK, she'll be in London. There are way more opportunities here than there would be outside the capital, right?'

'Definitely.' Nathan's voice came clearly through the laptop speaker. 'If she's serious about acting, and from what her mother told you that seems to be her main passion, then I don't see why she'd move out of London.'

'She'd probably have an agent, wouldn't she, if she was looking for acting work?' said Rodney. 'So we should trawl through all the actors' agents. They always have photos of their clients on their websites, and as we know what she looks like, it doesn't really matter if she's using a different name. We just need to look out for someone who's the right sort of age and who looks like Sam.'

'Great idea, Rodney.' Cora smiled with relief. 'There must be hundreds and hundreds of agents in London though, it's going to take ages.'

'We'll do it between us,' said Scott. 'We can start tonight and carry on in the morning, in-between hits. We only sit around talking bollocks and drinking tea anyway, so we might as well have something constructive to do. There'll be a list online somewhere of all the London acting agencies – we can split it three ways alphabetically.'

'Brilliant. Which reporter are you with tomorrow though – Graham? Be careful he doesn't see what you're up to, won't you? We still need to keep all this among ourselves for now.'

257

'Yeah, Graham. He's a miserable sod though, always goes off and sits in his car on his own between hits. Won't be a problem,' pronounced Nathan.

Cora smiled. Graham Herrington, *Morning Live's* northern correspondent, was indeed a little dour and unsociable, but that would play in their favour this week.

'What can *we* do then, Cora?'

Rosie sounded anxious.

'Theatres?' said Cora. 'Unless she's got very lucky and has landed a film or TV part, in which case she'd almost definitely have an agent so would show up on the boys' agency search, she's probably doing theatre stuff. Can you two start trawling London theatres – big and small – and see what they've got on at the moment? See if you can spot any cast member who might be her?'

'OK.' Nicole sounded doubtful. 'Not sure they'll have cast photos though, particularly the smaller theatres, and certainly not if she's only got a bit part. But worth a try, I suppose.'

'I know. But I can't think what else to do. Anyone?' Cora picked up her tea, looking from laptop to laptop and then at Wendy, who was frowning in concentration.

'What if she doesn't have an agent yet?' she said. 'There are loads of websites where actors just put their bios and headshots, in the hope that they'll be spotted. You know, like *StarSearch*, websites like that? Casting directors for smaller productions – student films, corporate stuff and so on – go to those sites to hunt for actors who'll work for free, or for peanuts. We'll need to search those too.'

'Nice one, Wendy. Will you do that then?'

'I will.'

'Great. Anything else, anyone?'

There was silence for a moment as everyone sat

thinking. Then Nathan's voice suddenly boomed out from Cora's laptop.

'I'm forming a sort of idea. How about *we* do a casting call for an actress? In case we don't find her on any website. I'm thinking social media. We've got thousands of followers on Twitter and Facebook between us, and lots of them in the media world. If they all retweeted and shared, we'd reach tens of thousands of people really quickly. Any one of us could start it off – we could say we're working on a short film in our spare time, nobody would find that weird, loads of media types do it. We could say we need a very specific look, an actress in her early thirties, and then describe Sally Henderson. It might be another way to find her, if she's actively looking for work?'

There was another silence.

'Can't hurt, I suppose. I mean, Cora's already searched all the social media sites and not found her, but she probably *is* on one of them, just using a different name. Slim chance she'd pick up on it and get in touch, but worth a try,' said Rodney, and everyone murmured in agreement.

'OK, perfect. Well, I'll do that then. I'll get it out on social media tonight, and see what happens. Thanks Nathan, that's not a bad idea.' Cora sat back in her chair, smiling at the mini-Nathan on her screen, and he saluted in acknowledgment.

'Right. So unless anyone can think of anything else for now, sounds like we have a plan to get us started. We need to get on to it as soon as possible – starting tonight, whoever has time? We only have about two and a half weeks until Sam's court date, and yes, I know, I know, nobody needs to say it again, I know thinking that Sally could be the one who actually killed Marcus is probably ridiculous, but if we could just find her by then, just in case …'

Cora's voice tailed off.

''We'll get on to our bit straight away, Cora, soon as we end this call, don't worry,' said Nicole, from Wendy's laptop.

'Us too,' said Scott.

'I love you all. Goodnight, and let's speak tomorrow, see where we're at.'

Goodbyes were said and the two Skype calls ended. Closing their laptops simultaneously, Cora and Wendy looked at each other across the table.

'Cora, what do we do, if we actually find her? Because we haven't really discussed that at all. I mean, do we ask her straight out if she murdered her sister's boyfriend? The sister she's never actually met, and doesn't even know exists? Because I can't see that going very well …'

Cora exhaled heavily. 'Wend, I have absolutely no idea. Shall we cross that bridge when we come to it? Because this is a one-step-at-a-time kind of job, and something tells me we have a lot of steps to take before we get to that point.'

Wendy raised her eyebrows. 'Gosh, Sam would hate every word of that sentence. Any more clichés, before I go and get the wine?'

Cora smiled. 'No more. Go on, then. Pour me a small one, and let's get started.'

33

**Thursday 13th June
15 days until the deadline**

Thursday dawned bright and clear, the sun's early rays casting a golden glow over the Bristol Channel. On the long sandy beach at Weston-super-Mare, Cora and her crew were perched on the sea wall, enjoying their first cup of tea of the morning in companionable silence. The beach was beautiful at this hour, empty apart from the occasional walker, one or two of them with metal detectors, out hunting for spoils from yesterday's careless daytrippers. Although dogs were banned from this part of the shoreline between May and September, there would soon be plenty of four-legged creatures making their way along the sand – the famous donkey rides had been run by the Mager family on Weston beach since the 1880s, and even in these high-tech times seemed to be as popular as ever.

The beach had a darker side though, and one which unwary tourists could easily fall foul of. At low tide, treacherous mudflats were exposed, leading to those in the know dubbing the area 'Weston-super-Mud'. Those *not* in the know could find themselves in trouble, the thick grey-brown sludge occasionally trapping those attempting to cross it. It was the mud that had brought Cora and the boys here this morning, after coastguards were called out yesterday to rescue a man who'd been digging for fishing bait near the Grand Pier. Stuck up to his thighs, and gradually sinking, the terrified man had fortunately retained the presence of mind to use his mobile phone to call for help. Badly shaken but uninjured, he had agreed to join the *Morning Live* team on the beach at 7 a.m. to discuss his experience and warn others not to get into the same situation ahead of the busy summer season.

Now, at just after six, the crew was already set up and ready to go, savouring this quiet time before the buzz of the live broadcasts. They all sipped their hot drinks in silence, enjoying the gentle lapping of the waves on the shore, the peace marred only by the occasional screech of a seagull overhead, or the inevitable toot from a passing motorist entranced by the sight of a television crew.

'Wendy and I spoke to Sam on Tuesday night, after our Skype meeting,' Cora said suddenly, leaning forward to tip the last dregs of her now-cold tea out onto the sand below.

'How's she bearing up?' Sitting to her left, Nathan slugged the last of his coffee and set the mug down on the wall between them.

'She's OK. She's always OK, or so she tells us. Still grieving, and tearful occasionally, but generally holding it together. But I'm worried – even more worried than before now, to be honest. I'm starting to wonder if we should even have told her about her sister. She seems to be pinning all her hopes on us finding her, and it somehow being the key to getting her out of prison. And what if we can't find her at all? I'm going to feel like we've let Sam down, when she needs us the most ...'

Cora stopped talking, a lump suddenly forming in her throat. Nathan slipped his arm round her shoulders and pulled her in for a hug.

'She knows we're doing everything we can. It's Sam,

Cora. She knows we'd never intentionally let her down. We're doing our best. It's just so bloody frustrating that not one of us has come up with anything yet.'

'And we've been trying non-stop since Tuesday,' said Rodney from his spot further down the wall. He had taken off his small round glasses and was polishing them on his fleece, holding them up to the sun to check for marks before buffing them again against the fabric. The fleece was turquoise, a relatively restrained choice for Rodney, although he had teamed it with cobalt blue trousers, navy and peacock-coloured trainers and a teal baseball cap.

'Fifty Shades of Blue,' Scott had remarked dourly when they'd all arrived on site at 5 a.m.

'I know you have, thank you so much,' Cora said now, in response to Rodney's remark. All of them who'd been involved in the online meeting earlier in the week had indeed spent every spare minute frantically hunting for Sally Henderson in their allotted search category, but so far everyone had drawn a blank.

Cora had, as agreed, put out a social media call for an actress matching Sally's age and physical characteristics, and had actually had several replies during the day yesterday. Her heart had leapt each time, only to plummet into her shoes again when she had clicked on the applicant's headshots to see young, pretty women who fitted the general brief but who were clearly *not* Sally. She'd known this idea had been a bit of a long shot, but she was becoming more and more disheartened with each passing hour.

She sighed heavily and stood up.

'I had another idea last night,' she said. 'We didn't think about trying Equity, the acting union. I've had a quick look on their website – you can search their directory of members. I had a look for Sally Henderson, but there's nobody of that name on there, although of course we don't think she's using it so that's no surprise. But you can search by playing age, accent, hair colour, all sorts of things as well, so I'm going to do that later. Although some members apparently choose not to be listed, so it could be another dead end. Anything's worth a try though.'

The boys all nodded. Then Scott spoke, his voice tentative.

'Don't suppose we want to consider this really, but ...' He paused, and looked down at the sand for a moment, frowning, then continued.

'Well, what if she's given up acting? What if she's working in, I dunno, a restaurant or something? How we gonna find her then?'

Cora was silent for a moment. 'I know, Scott. I've thought of that too. But I just can't go there, not right now, it's just too depressing. Her mother said it was all about drama and acting for her, always had been. So we just have to assume that if she's come to London, she's still going to try to pursue that dream. I don't see any reason why she'd suddenly change her mind. Let's keep going on this track, for now at least, OK?'

'OK. You're right, it makes sense. Right – muddy man will be here shortly and London will be on the blower any minute. Let's get you miked up, Cora. Time waits for no flan.'

Cora, Nathan and Rodney exchanged looks.

'Er – time waits for no *man*, Scott. Why would you wait for a flan?' asked Nathan.

Scott shrugged. 'I would, if I was hungry. Is it really man? Are you sure?'

'Positive!' They all laughed. You could always rely on Scott and his malapropisms to lighten the mood.

264

Two hours later, as the crew de-rigged and discussed which of Weston's seafront teashops did the best full English breakfast, Cora's phone buzzed with a message alert. It was another actress responding to the casting call. Cora scanned the details quickly, her heartbeat quickening. The woman said she was a thirty-one-year-old brunette, five feet six inches tall and 133 pounds, with brown eyes. But it was the last line of the message which made Cora gasp.

'Oh wow. Please, please, please …'

Nathan and Rodney, who were both within earshot, stopped packing their kit away and turned to stare at her.

'What is it?'

'This actress – her name is Sarah Healey. Totally different name, but still with the initials S.H. That means nothing, on its own, but … everything sounds right description-wise, and look … I didn't even think to mention accent in the casting call, but look what she says here. *"I was brought up in New York, so can do various American accents, but my mom is British and I've been told my English accent is pretty convincing too. Not sure what accent this part calls for but I'm sure I can pull it off."* "I was brought up in New York, and my mom is British"! Bloody hell, do you think? Could it be? I can't breathe – I'm too scared to click on the photo …'

Cora's legs were actually starting to feel weak. The sliding side door of the truck was open, so she sank down onto the floor, hands shaking slightly as her finger hovered over the link to the photograph attached to the message.

'Here, let me.' Nathan took the BlackBerry gently from her and tapped the screen, then waited as the picture loaded. He looked at it intently for a few seconds, then looked from Cora to Rodney.

'It's not the best photo, to be honest. Full length, and not super-clear. But – I don't know. It could be. It bloody could be. Look.'

He passed the phone to Rodney, who scrutinised the picture and nodded slowly.

'Maybe,' he agreed.

Unable to wait a second longer, Cora leapt from the truck and grabbed the phone from the soundman. Nathan was right – it wasn't a great picture. The woman was leaning against the wall of a building on a busy city street, the photographer clearly attempting to pull off an arty shot with passing pedestrians blurred and his subject in sharp focus in the centre of the picture. He'd only been partially successful, and Sarah Healey was a little blurred too, but …

'Oh my goodness. It could be, couldn't it?' Cora's heart was pounding again, her mouth dry. Fingers still trembling, she zoomed in on the woman's face, comparing it in her mind with the photo of Sally that Clare Henderson had given her. The hair looked right, and the curve of the jawline …

Cora looked up, unexpected tears suddenly springing to her eyes.

'Guys, I think it is. I think we've found Sally Henderson.'

34

Friday 14th June
14 days until the deadline

The meeting had originally been fixed for 4 p.m., Cora gambling that wherever in the country she was sent that morning, it should still be possible to be back in London by late afternoon. As it happened, she and the boys were assigned to a story in Newbury, just sixty miles or so from the capital, so Cora had quickly contacted the actress again, telling her she would be able to meet her late morning instead of afternoon, if that would work for her. Sarah had readily agreed, and so it was just after 11.30 a.m. when Cora nervously settled herself at a window table in a small coffee shop in Covent Garden. The café was busy, customers packed closely together, a fraught-looking mother with a whimpering toddler occupying the other window seat just in front of Cora. The little girl, cute with auburn curls and wearing a denim dress, was refusing to eat the salad sandwich her mother had set in front of her.

'Cake, Mummy. I want cake,' she was insisting. Cora, normally a big cake fan herself, didn't blame her, although today she wasn't in a cake mood. She had bought an Earl Grey but, very unusually, ignored the excellent selection of muffins, fruit pies and huge double chocolate chip cookies arranged temptingly on the counter. Her stomach was churning, her apprehension about meeting this woman who could be so hugely important to Sam stealing her appetite. Remembering that today was Miranda's birthday, she passed a few moments texting the doctor with her best wishes, then sat fiddling with her teaspoon, twisting it between her fingers, eyes glued to the door, desperately hoping that Sarah wouldn't change her mind. Once more, she ran through in her mind the story she and Nathan had concocted about the short film they were allegedly making. They had agreed that Cora would tell any likely candidates who emailed that they would like to have a quick meeting, but had a few other people to see too, keeping possible filming dates and other details vague, until they were positive that they had found the right woman. But as she waited, tea untouched, Cora wondered for the hundredth time what she would actually *do* if Sarah Healey really was Sally Henderson.

If I'm sure it's her, do I tell her immediately that the film thing is all a big lie, and that she has a twin sister, an identical twin sister who's in prison ahead of a murder trial? How can you just land something like that on somebody in a crowded coffee shop? Cora put the teaspoon down and picked up her cup, then put it back on the saucer again. She was too edgy to even drink now, her throat feeling like it was closing up. She coughed and took a deep breath, trying to quell her anxiety. And do I then ask her where she was on the day of the murder, tell her we're all hoping it was for some totally unknown reason *her* who killed Marcus, and not Sam? No, of course I can't do that. But what *do* I do then? Why didn't we make a plan for this? What …

'Cora? I'm Sarah. *Are* you Cora?' The accent was American, the voice soft, but Cora was so lost in thought that she jumped violently, nearly knocking her little white china teapot over. She reached out a hand to steady it,

268

then looked up to see a slim, dark woman standing next to her table, an uncertain expression on her face.

'Yes – Sarah, hello. I'm Cora Baxter. Thanks so much for coming, have a seat.'

'Thanks.' A relieved smile on her face, Sarah slid into the chair opposite, dumping her large brown canvas bag on the table. 'I wasn't sure. Glad to meet you.'

She held out a manicured hand with neat, French-polished nails, and Cora shook it, unable to tear her eyes away from the woman's face, a sinking feeling suddenly replacing her earlier nervousness. Although Sarah had a vague resemblance to Sam, and to the picture of Sally, Cora knew instantly that she wasn't the right person. She was the right age and build, and her hair was right too; there was even a similarity in the shape of her face. But now that Cora was sitting in front of her, she could see that nothing else matched. Sarah's nose was long and slightly pointed, the complete opposite of Sam's little snub one, and although her eyes were the same dark brown as Sam's, they were bigger and rounder, giving her a very different appearance. Trying to hide her crushing disappointment but feeling unable to simply get up and leave, Cora went through the motions, asking Sarah about her background. The actress told her she'd moved to London from New York a year ago, leaving behind her lawyer father and university lecturer mother who disapproved of her choice of career.

'I thought I'd try my luck in London instead. I was doing OK in New York, got a few off-Broadway roles and even a small part in a TV commercial, but they never stopped nagging me, telling me I was too old to be messing around with acting and it was time to get a proper job. I got sick of it. Thought I'd come over here, make it big, win a Bafta and then go back. That'll show 'em.'

269

She grinned, and Cora forced a smile back, wondering how long she would have to keep up this pretence. It was clearly a waste of time sitting here, and she needed to get back to Cheltenham where she was meeting up with Rosie and Nicole later, before returning to London tomorrow afternoon to spend the rest of the weekend with Adam.

She cleared her throat, ready to make her excuses, then had a sudden thought. Why not show Sarah a photo of Sally Henderson, just in case? They were both actresses from New York, after all. OK, it was a big place, as was London, but Cora knew the TV world was a small one. Maybe the acting world was the same.

'Sarah – can I just show you something? A photo?'

Sarah shrugged. 'Sure.'

Cora reached into her bag and pulled out the file in which she'd been keeping all her notes about the hunt for Sally. Keeping it angled away from Sarah, she flicked through it, located the photograph and pulled it out.

'Here it is.' She pushed the picture across the table. 'I don't suppose you've ever met this woman? She's an actress too, from New York. I ... err, I lost her number, and I'm trying to trace her, for ... for the film.'

She stopped, not wanting to compound the lie. Sarah was looking closely at the photo, frowning. Then her face cleared and she looked up at Cora and smiled.

'You know, I think I *did* meet her. I mean, it's not a great photo, and she looks younger there, but I'm fairly sure it's the same girl. I'm talking ages ago – maybe September, October last year, I can't remember exactly ...'

She looked down at the photograph again. Cora suddenly felt as if her heart rate had doubled.

'Really? You met her? Here in London? Can you tell me anything else, anything at all about her?'

Sarah pushed the photo back across the table and grinned. 'Wow, you really are keen on her for your film, aren't you? Look, I'm sorry but I don't remember much. It was in London, yes. At a casting for an online ad campaign. They wanted native New Yorkers, and we ended up sitting together in the waiting room so we got chatting. September or October as I said, definitely autumn, because we were both griping about the weather in London versus New York. But we only talked for a few minutes, then she got called in, and as she came out they called me, so I didn't see her after that. We didn't exchange numbers or anything, and I never ran into her again.'

Cora clenched her fists. So close, and yet so far. 'I don't suppose you remember her name, anything else about her?'

'You don't even remember her name? What, you lost *all* her details, not just her number? Tough break!' Sarah laughed, then screwed up her face, thinking. 'I'm not a hundred per cent sure,' she said, slowly. 'But I *think* she said her name was Sally. I didn't get a surname, sorry. Is that any help?'

Sally, thought Cora. *Sally*. She smiled.

'It is, yes. Thank you. Well, Sarah, it's been really nice meeting you. You've definitely got the right look for the part, but we are obviously looking at a few other people too. If we decide to take it further, I'll drop you a line early next week, OK?'

Sarah looked a little crestfallen, but nodded. 'Sure. Thanks.'

Cora stood up. 'Right, I'll be off then. Bye, Sarah. Thanks again for coming. And thanks for your help.'

'Sure,' said Sarah again. 'Have a great Friday.'

Friday. As Cora weaved her way between the tables

271

and headed for the door, a slight sense of panic began to replace the excitement she'd felt about Sarah having met Sally Henderson. Two Fridays from now, Sam would be in the dock. *Two weeks*. OK, so the good news was that it seemed Sally had definitely been in London looking for acting work in the past year, and indeed that she was obviously still using her first name, so maybe it was just her surname that had changed. But many months had passed since the casting Sarah had mentioned. Sally could easily have moved on by now. And even if she hadn't, the time they had left to find her was running out, and running out quickly. How on earth were they going to track her down?

35

'Oh, Cora, I would have DIED! Why do these things always happen to *you*?'

Rosie, cheeks flushing at the very thought of the event Cora had just recounted, collapsed onto the sofa in a fit of giggles. Cora, who always swung between tearfulness and hysteria on Friday afternoons, joined her, unable to stop giggling herself. Adam always told her she was "a bit bonkers" on Fridays, and she knew he was right – lots of her *Morning Live* colleagues experienced the same phenomenon, the slightly manic feeling that resulted from a combination of extreme tiredness after a week of little sleep, and the joyful prospect of a day off tomorrow before it all started again on Sunday, when the assignments for Monday's show were handed out.

Nicole, who was setting up her laptop on the dining table, shook her head in despair.

'Honestly, you two. We're here to work, remember, seeing as Sarah Healey turned out to be yet another dead end. Well, apart from her nugget about Sally being in London, of course.'

'Oh come on, Nicole, it's FUNNY!' Rosie sat up, wiping her eyes, then let out another little snort of laughter.

'I suppose so. You're such a twit, Cora.' Nicole grinned, then headed for the door. 'I'm going to make tea, seeing as you both seem incapable. Think you can pull yourselves together by the time I get back?'

Rosie and Cora looked at each other, and exploded into guffaws of laughter again. It really wasn't even that funny, Cora thought, but it felt so good to laugh after the tension of the past few days. It was just after four o'clock and they were in her flat in Cheltenham, Cora having raced home from London after her meeting with Sarah Healey. The plan, seeing as they all had this afternoon off, was to carry on with their online search for Sally Henderson for a couple of hours, hoping that doing it together might spark some new ideas on how to find her. They all had separate plans for the evening: Cora intended to catch up on some sleep before heading back to London in the morning to spend the weekend with Adam and Harry; Nicole had bagged a babysitter and was having a rare date night with Will; and Rosie and her husband Alastair were hosting a barbecue for some of their school parent friends. It was nice, therefore, to spend a couple of hours together this afternoon. Nicole always closed her veterinary surgery at 1 p.m. on a Friday, although she remained on call for emergencies, while business was going so well at Rosie's florist shop that she had now hired an assistant, who'd been left to close up today. The girls had arrived bearing, as was traditional for their afternoon get-togethers, a box of cakes, today jam-filled doughnuts and sticky chocolate éclairs oozing cream. Cora had grabbed an éclair so enthusiastically that it had immediately slipped out of her fumbling fingers and slid along the polished wood floor, reminding her of a somewhat embarrassing incident in a courtroom a few weeks ago, and it was this which had rendered Rosie helpless with laughter.

Cora had been covering a day-long court case, listening to closing arguments in a protracted hearing which saw a well-known judge in the dock, accused of taking bribes from several defendants and allowing them to walk free. She had returned to court slightly late from lunch, rushing in after everyone else had just taken their seats, and had frantically pulled notebook and pen from her bag, anxious not to miss anything. Unfortunately, along with the notebook and pen had also come a tampon, which had been rolling around loose in the bottom of the handbag. Dislodged by the removal of the notebook, it flew into the air and, watched by a horrified Cora, sailed merrily across the press bench to land right in front of the lawyers' table.

Aghast, cheeks burning, Cora had cringed in her seat as, amid sniggers from around the court room, the elderly male usher had retrieved the offending object, holding it delicately out in front of him between thumb and forefinger as he carried it back to its mortified owner.

'I believe this is yours, miss,' he had said solemnly, eliciting further titters of laughter from a couple of tabloid newspaper journalists sitting alongside Cora.

'Yes. Thank you. I'm so sorry,' she had whispered, squirming with embarrassment and shoving the tampon firmly back into her bag.

Now, she punched a still-sniggering Rosie in the arm. 'Right, come on, enough silliness, we need to get some work done. Let's be all serious at the table when Nicole comes back.'

'Oh, go on then.' Rosie hauled herself off the sofa and they both settled themselves at the table, booting up their own laptops. When Nicole returned two minutes later with a tray laden with steaming mugs, a milk jug and some plates and napkins, they were tapping away, engrossed in their screens.

'Blimey.' Nicole dumped the tray on the table. 'I'm impressed.'

Rosie and Cora both looked up and smiled.

'Just a few moments of madness. I needed that after the week I've had,' said Cora.

'I know, I get it. Let's do this.' Mugs and plates distributed, Nicole sank down onto her chair, selected a doughnut from the box, took a large bite and then started work.

For twenty minutes or so there was, apart from the occasional tut or sigh of frustration, mostly silence, as Rosie and Nicole worked their way through endless lists of theatres, now extending their search to Greater London and the Home Counties after drawing a blank with the more central venues. Cora's Equity search had proved fruitless too, and after staring into space for a full minute as she chomped her éclair, she decided to hit Google again, now that she was fairly sure Sally was still using her real first name. She began trying search after search with multiple word combinations – Sally, actor, actress, drama, New York, USA, London, play, film, casting. It was when she tried "Sally + actor + American" and started scrolling half-heartedly through the page after page of search results, that a photograph caught her eye. Sally? *Was that Sally?*

Startled, she clicked on the image and a newspaper article appeared on the screen. As Cora read the headline, she gasped, staring at the words.

'Oh no. Please, no. This can't be happening. This *can't be happening* ...' The words came out in a strangled whisper.

'What? What is it?' Rosie's voice was sharp with alarm. Nicole, who had put headphones on to listen to music as she worked, pulled them off, spooked by the expressions on her friends' faces even though she hadn't heard a word of what they had said.

'It's … it's Sally. Here, in this local newspaper piece. I … can't …'

'What? Hang on, let's see.'

As Rosie and Nicole leapt from their chairs, Cora spotted the date on the newspaper article. November. November last year. Months before the murder. Months before Sam went to prison. That's it then. It's over, she thought. It's all over. As her friends leaned over her shoulder, impatient to see what had caused such a reaction, she pushed the laptop aside, sank her head onto the table, and started to cry.

36

They sat in stunned silence, lined up together on one sofa, wine glasses in hand now instead of tea mugs. Cora was still shaking slightly, her glass clinking against her teeth as she tried to take a drink. The implications of what they had just read in the article from the *Islington Gazette* were still sinking in, but all three of them were fully aware that no good was going to come out of what they had discovered.

'I need to look at it again.' Cora staggered across the room to retrieve her laptop from the table, her legs feeling wobbly and alien. Maybe this was all a bad dream? She often had trouble with her legs in dreams, dreams in which she needed to escape from somebody or something, but felt she was running through quicksand, each step requiring superhuman effort. Maybe that was what this was? But as she sank back onto the sofa, she knew that this was all too real. Real, and horrible.

She tapped the space-bar to wake up the screen, and read the article again, slowly this time. *Woman killed in High Street collision* read the headline, the photograph next to it a smiling Sally, leaning on a red London telephone box, her longer hair blowing in the breeze but her face Sam's face. There was no doubt, no doubt at all. She was Sam's identical twin sister; the likeness was uncanny. And then, the details, not many, but enough. Enough for them all to know that the searching they'd been doing for days had been in vain. This *was* Sally

Henderson, *their* Sally Henderson, and she was dead.

A 30-year-old woman died today after a driver lost control of his car on Islington High Street and mounted the pavement. A 47-year-old man and a 3-year-old girl were taken to hospital with minor injuries. The woman who died was later identified as Sally Derson, an American actress who had been working in the UK for some time. The 86-year-old driver of the car is believed to have suffered a stroke at the wheel ...

'Derson. Sally Derson. She just dropped the "Hen",' said Nicole softly.

'Yes.' Cora's throat felt tight. She picked up her wine glass and tried to drink, but she could barely swallow. She put the glass down, and checked the date of the article once again, running her finger over the words on the screen. Maybe she'd read it wrongly? But no. The sixth of November, last year. It made sense now that Clare Henderson hadn't heard from her daughter this past Christmas. Sally had been dead since before Christmas, dead for months, dead long before Marcus was murdered. And that meant ... that meant ...

'She couldn't have been involved then. In Marcus's murder. She was already dead. She'd been dead for ages. So ... what does that mean?' Rosie was pale, her scattering of freckles more pronounced than usual against the whiteness of her skin.

Cora shook her head, a wave of nausea suddenly robbing her of her ability to speak, and Nicole sighed a deep, shuddering sigh, eyes closed, head pressed back into the sofa cushion.

'It just means ... it just means that we've lost a possibility.'

'What?' Rosie frowned.

Nicole opened her eyes and turned to her friends.

'Remember, Cora, you told us that right back at the start of all this, Nathan listed four possibilities? Even though some sounded pretty unlikely? One, that Sam was framed by a person or persons unknown who somehow nicked her DNA and planted it at the scene, although we have absolutely no idea who or why. Still possible, I suppose, but we've failed to come up with anyone who might have done that. Two, a forensics mix-up. Three, that someone else's DNA matched Sam's, which we dismissed of course until we found out about Sally's existence. And four – the one none of us want to consider, but a possibility nonetheless – that the police are right, and Sam did it after all.'

Cora took a deep breath, willing the nausea to pass.

'So we're down to three. Or two, really. Adam is convinced there was no forensics mix up, and I believe him. He nearly got himself in big trouble going down that road, but he checked it out thoroughly. So ...'

She took another deep breath. 'So what we have left is that somebody, somehow, framed Sam. Or ... or that ...'

Tears sprang to her eyes again. This was ridiculous. Why couldn't she say it? Why couldn't she stop crying?

'Or that Sam is a murderer.' Cora and Nicole turned to look at Rosie. She was staring straight ahead, eyes wide, as if unable to believe what she had just said.

'Yes,' said Cora quietly.

'Liane, thank you so much for that. I really appreciate it. And again, I'm so sorry.'

'Thank you, Cora. Nice to talk to you. Bye.'

Later that night, alone now after saying a subdued goodbye to Rosie and Nicole, and calling Wendy and the boys to update them on the dreadful news and call off the search for Sally, Cora had done a little more detective work. The newspaper article about Sally's death had quoted two friends, Liane Jermyn and Rachel Larsson, described as "Sally's devastated flatmates". Both women had been easy to track down: both, it quickly emerged, were also actors, with profiles on several casting websites. Liane also had a Twitter account under her real name, and when Cora sent a brief message asking the woman to contact her about Sally Derson, the reply came swiftly. A couple of direct messages later, and Liane was on the phone. Cora, crossing her fingers as she told the lie, explained to Liane that Sally's mother Clare was a friend of a friend in New York, and had expressed concern about not hearing from her daughter for some time. Cora had promised that she'd keep an eye out for Sally in London, and had been browsing the internet when she had come across the shocking newspaper article. Liane seemed happy with the explanation, and chatted openly to Cora about her late flatmate.

'We met at a casting, hit it off straight away,' she said. 'Rachel and I were looking for a new flatmate and when Sal said she needed somewhere to live, we didn't think twice. She was great. We really miss her.'

'Did you know that she'd changed her name?'

'Yes, she told us a few weeks after she moved in. She'd come in to the UK on her real passport, but once she got here she started calling herself Derson instead of Henderson. She destroyed all her old ID, passport, the lot. She had another passport, under the new surname. She admitted it was a fake, but it was a good one – she'd got it before she came, through some dodgy contact in New York. It must have been good, because she had no problem using it as ID here, opening a bank account, getting a national insurance number and so on.'

'And why – why bother with the name change? Did

she tell you?' Cora crossed her fingers again, hoping Liane wouldn't get suspicious about the continued questioning, but the woman didn't seem to mind.

'It was all about her mum. She loved her, and said she dropped her the odd card or note so she knew she was OK, but she had no plans to ever go home again. Her upbringing had been pretty tough, by the sounds of things. Her mum had lots of issues, was on and off drink and drugs, and Sally had to grow up fast, and look after herself most of the time as a kid. She was sad about it really, rather than angry as a lot of people would be ... but that was Sally, she was just such a lovely person.'

Liane paused as her voice cracked with emotion. Such a lovely person – just like her twin sister Sam, thought Cora. If only they could have met, if only ...

'She just said that although she would always love her, she needed to sever ties with her mother, for her own sanity.' Liane continued, her voice even again.

'Even so, after she died Rachel and I tried for a bit to find her mum to let her know, but we couldn't find her address in Sally's things, or find her online anywhere, or even track down a phone number for her, so we gave up. The police helped briefly too, but they didn't have that much interest. It was just another road accident to them I suppose. They left it to us, and if I'm honest, we didn't try too hard, because of how Sally was about her. She didn't have a will, at least we couldn't find one, so we just asked a solicitor to see if he could sort it out – we told him as far as we knew, her mother was her only living relative. She didn't have much to leave, to be honest, just a few clothes and bits of jewellery, so we boxed it all up and handed it to the solicitor. He said he'd keep us posted, but we haven't heard anything. Not high priority, I suppose. Then we closed down all her social media accounts and took her profile off the acting sites and so on. We did our best for her, because we were all she had. We gave her a nice funeral too, small but nice. And ... well, that's really all I can tell you. Will you let her mum know what's happened now, if you have a way of contacting her?'

'I will, yes. Where – where is Sally buried, Liane? I might pop along and put some flowers on her grave, on her mum's behalf, if that would be OK?'

'Oh, Cora, that would be lovely, thank you. We try to put fresh flowers on it when we can, but it's hard to find the time, you know ... she's in Highgate Cemetery. She visited it once and really loved it, so we thought that would be nice for her. There are lots of famous people buried there, you know? Karl Marx, Jean Simmons, Malcolm McLaren – even Catherine Dickens, Charles Dickens' wife. Sally thought that was pretty cool.'

Cora smiled down the phone. 'It is pretty cool. I'll go there, this weekend if I can. Is her grave easy to find?'

'Fairly – the staff there are very good, they'll direct you to where the newer graves are. We put up the headstone a couple of weeks ago too, so that makes it easier. You have to wait a few months, you see, for the ground to settle? It's not a posh one, we kept it simple, mainly because of cost – we don't have lots of money. It just has her name, and the years, and a quote we liked that we found online. I hope it's OK.'

'I'm sure it will be. And I'm sure her mum will be incredibly grateful for how well you've looked after Sally, Liane.'

Now, Cora looked at the wall clock. It was only nine o'clock, but she suddenly felt overwhelmed with sadness and weariness. Sleep, then. Sleep, and then tomorrow work out how on earth she was going to tell Sam. And, even more importantly, what the hell she was going to do next. Were they now back to trying to work out who could have framed Sam? Was it just too late, too impossible a task? Too exhausted to think about it any more tonight, Cora turned the television off, and headed for the bedroom.

In his London flat, Adam was sitting in front of the television too, although he had no idea what he was watching – some American legal drama, he thought, but he hadn't taken in a word since Cora had rung earlier. His girlfriend had sounded, for the first time in weeks, utterly defeated. Sam's twin sister, the woman Cora and her friends had been searching for, was dead and had been for some time.

Adam had been overwhelmed by relief when he'd heard the news, that tiny seed of doubt he'd had about the case suddenly being swept away, but now he felt dreadfully guilty about being so pleased about it. Cora was devastated, and he could tell that she was struggling to cope with what this might now mean – that the chances that Sam was a murderer had suddenly, in Cora's eyes, increased dramatically. To be fair, despite the solid evidence against her, Adam was still finding it hard to come to terms with himself – Samantha Tindall, this clever, sweet, fun friend of Cora's, with whom they had spent so many great evenings and weekends over the past year, was a cold-blooded killer? The case spoke for itself, but even so. And if *he* was finding it hard to handle, he could totally understand how difficult it was for Cora, and why she was finding it so impossible to believe. Maybe now, though, she'd start to accept it. She was due in London at around 11 a.m. tomorrow. I'll take her out for lunch, somewhere nice, thought Adam, try to cheer her up, take her mind off it. She'll be OK. It'll just take a bit of time, that's all. And maybe I'll get Harry to make her a card or something in the morning, before she gets here.

At the thought of his son, he eased himself off the sofa and headed for the little boy's bedroom. Harry had developed a tendency to ignore instructions to go to sleep and instead spend an extra sneaky hour playing games on his iPad under the duvet after lights out, and Adam wanted to make sure he'd be fresh for the weekend – Cora adored Harry, but even so she might struggle to cope with a cranky six-year-old in her current frame of mind. A peek around the bedroom door, however, proved that tonight Harry had obeyed orders. Feet on the pillow, tousled dark blond hair just visible at the bottom of the bed, Harry was snoring softly. He had started sleeping the wrong way round in bed a couple of years ago, and it seemed to be a hard habit to break, but Adam didn't suppose it really mattered. His son was safe, happy and asleep. He hoped Cora was safe and asleep too. The happiness bit, he decided sadly as he returned to the sofa, might be a little way off yet.

37

Saturday 15th June
13 days until the deadline

Cora, bouquet of white lilies in hand, was waiting outside
Highgate Cemetery when its gates opened at 10 a.m. She
had been there just once before, many years ago, and as
she walked through the newer East Cemetery she was
again struck by the peacefulness of the place. It was vast –
over a hundred and seventy thousand people in over fifty-
three thousand graves – and yet there was still an intimacy
and serenity about its shady paths, winding through a
Gothic maze of ivy-covered tombs overlooked by silent
stone angels, elaborate mausoleums and carved vaults and
arches. Here and there, overgrown graves with
indecipherable inscriptions sat alongside shiny marble
headstones, the names of those resting below picked out
in gold lettering: the long-dead and the recently deceased
lying shoulder to shoulder.

Checking the map she'd been given at the entrance,
Cora took a detour to stand for a moment by the memorial
to the cemetery's most famous resident, Karl Marx,
immortalised in the form of a bronze bust atop a vast
granite plinth. Then, aware that she was running late, she
quickly located the row where Sally was buried. She
spotted the grave immediately, its simple white headstone
in stark contrast to the crumbling stone edifices either
side. Cora stood still for a moment, taking in the

inscription, then bent to gently lay her flowers on Sally's final resting place, a lump forming in her throat. As she walked away, the line carved on the white marble danced before her eyes.

"Step softly, a dream lies buried here."

Sally's dream of an acting career. Sam's dream of a sister, and what that could have meant. Cora's dream of saving Sam. Dead, gone, buried. For a minute, Cora stopped walking, her legs suddenly leaden. Then, slowly and with great effort, she headed for the exit.

'I love this card. It was so sweet of him. Thank you, again, for getting him to do this. I'll treasure it. Although if this is what he thinks my hair looks like, I need a salon appointment pronto.'

From his position sprawled on the sofa, Adam laughed. 'You look great, as always. Come here, Baxter.'

'Coming.' Cora ran her finger over the handmade card that Harry had proudly presented her with this morning, a drawing of herself on the front, brown hair sticking out in all directions from her head like wavy wires, and the words *"HAPPY WEEKEND!!!"* scrawled in bright red marker pen across her crooked legs. Inside, in Harry's neat, childish script, *"Hope you have a lovely weekend with me and Daddy, love Harry your favourite child ever ever ever"*, followed by three rows of kisses.

'Thirty of them. That means I don't have to *actually* kiss you for a whole month, because you've got them all in advance,' the little boy had said with a cheeky grin as Cora had studied the card, and then shrieked with joy as she had chased him around the room, finally catching him and smothering him with kisses which, in reality, he didn't mind at all.

Cora had arrived slightly later than planned after

288

getting stuck in traffic after her cemetery visit, and the card had lifted her spirits a little. She was feeling horribly low after a phone conversation she'd had with Sam during the drive, in which she'd filled her in on the news about Sally. Unsurprisingly, Sam had not taken it well. Her sobs had been heart-wrenching, reverberating around Cora's car through her hands-free speakers.

'Well, that's it then. I'm screwed, aren't I? It's all over. I'm going to spend the rest of my life in this stinking prison, for something I didn't do. I can't do it, Cora. I just can't, I can't …'

'I know, I know, darling, but please, don't give up.' Cora felt like bawling herself. She was running out of words of comfort and reassurance for her friend, with no idea what, if anything, she could now do to help her.

'Maybe – maybe there are other possibilities for someone who could have set you up.' Cora couldn't think of any, but she needed to give Sam even the tiniest sliver of hope.

'But how do we find them? We've tried … I don't know who else …' Sam's voice was choked with tears.

'I know. I know. But I'm not giving up, Sam. Not yet.'

There was silence on the line for a moment. Then Sam spoke again.

'No, Cora. I think that's it. You've done all you can, and I'll be forever grateful, but it's time to get real. I'll be pleading not guilty, of course. And then I'll just have to put my fate in the hands of the jury at my trial, hope they believe me … they have to. They *have to*. The alternative doesn't bear thinking about, does it? Mum's coming in this afternoon, so I'll update her on the latest. At least that's something to look forward to today. I'll be fine, don't worry.'

Matter-of-fact Sam was suddenly back, but Cora knew

289

it was just an act. As they said goodbye, her heart was breaking for her friend. None of this seemed real, and yet in less than two weeks' time Sam would be back in the dock, and the wheels of justice would continue their slow turn. And although there were still some days to go, the realisation that she was now bound to fail suddenly swept over Cora. Because she *had* failed, hadn't she? She'd told Sam she wasn't giving up, but she didn't know what else she could do, not now. She had failed. Failed, for the first time in her life, to meet a deadline. The thought made her feel sick, and when she'd finally got to the Shepherds Bush flat, it had been a struggle for her to act normally in front of Adam and Harry. Despite its grim start, though, it had ended up being a nice day. Vowing to push the case out of her mind, for a few hours at least, Cora had gone along with Adam's plans for an afternoon pottering a little further afield than usual in east London. A wander around the quirky little shops and vintage boutiques around Cheshire Street was followed by a delicious lunch at Cora's favourite Brick Lane eaterie, a Bangladeshi restaurant where they shared fish bhuna, fried okra, dal and egg and onion roti. Harry tucked in with gusto, and Cora admired, not for the first time, the way Adam and Laura had brought the little boy up to try everything – no children's menu of chips and chicken nuggets for Harry, ever.

As she watched the two of them across the table, banter flying back and forth between them as always as they ate, and so alike with their blond hair and green eyes, she felt a small, unexpected, wave of happiness wash over her, followed by a shiver of sadness. It was the little things that were important, she thought. Being with people you love, good food, walking in the sunshine. Will Sam ever have any of these things in her life again? I don't know how I can bear it, if she's locked up for ever, never sharing any of this with us again. How do I bear it? How does *she* bear it?

She had reached for Adam's hand and he had offered it immediately, squeezing hers gently, instantly understanding. Now, back home and with Harry tucked up in bed, she slid the card carefully into the side pocket of her handbag and went to join Adam on the sofa, where he had been watching a repeat of *Celebrity Squares* on the TV.

Still full from their large lunch, they had snacked on cheese, crackers and olives for dinner, the remnants of the meal still strewn across the coffee table. Cora briefly considered clearing it away, then decided it could wait. Cuddled up with Adam, her head on his chest, his arms wrapped around her, she tried to let the television gameshow distract her from her thoughts, but after five minutes she realised it wasn't working. Once more, she thought. I need to ask Adam, just once more. She stretched her arm out to grab the remote control from the table and pressed the mute button.

'Oi! I was enjoying that. Perfect Saturday night escapism nonsense. What are you doing?'

'Sorry, Adam – can we talk, just for a few minutes?' Cora sat up, moving away from him slightly so she could tuck her bare feet underneath her.

He frowned. 'That sounds ominous. Not dumping me, are you?'

He smiled, and she smiled back.

'Of course not, idiot, as if. No, it's … well, it's about Sam.'

Adam groaned. 'Cora, really? I know how upset you are, but could we not just forget about it for one night? It will do you good, I promise …'

She was shaking her head. 'I can't, Adam. Please. Look, I spoke to her this morning, and this Sally thing has totally wiped her out. She was devastated. I know she's got us, and her mum's supporting her through it like we're all trying to, but she's on the edge now. She still insists she didn't kill Marcus, she's going to plead not guilty and put her life in the hands of the jury, hope they believe her. And ... and I still believe her, Adam. Doubts creep in sometimes, but in my heart I do. I know you think I'm deluding myself, but I *know* Sam. I know her, and I know she couldn't have done this.'

Cora paused. Did she still know that, really, truly? Yes, she had to stick with Sam, she *had* to. Otherwise, what hope would her friend have, if she really was innocent? She swallowed and carried on talking.

'It's only a fortnight now, less than a fortnight in fact, until her court appearance. Adam, please, I know this is driving you mad, but is there anything, *anything* else that can be done?'

Adam had covered his face with his hands while she spoke. Now, he looked up, his expression a mixture of frustration and tenderness.

'No, there isn't,' he said simply. 'I wish, so much, that I could say something different to you, but there isn't. Most murders are carried out by someone the victim knows, not by strangers, Cora. Look at the facts. Sam was the victim's girlfriend. They'd had a row. She was in the park around the time he died – we have her on CCTV, and she's admitted that anyway. Her DNA is on the murder weapon. Hers, and nobody else's. There is no evidence whatsoever that that DNA was planted there by somebody else, or that there was any sort of a laboratory mix-up. Even if there had been an identical twin sister, which we now sadly know there isn't, the evidence against Sam is

292

too strong. She did it, Cora, and we all have to accept that. I'm sorry, sorrier than you can imagine, but that's the way it is.'

Cora was staring at her hands, her mind racing.

'But ... but you still haven't traced that third person you saw going into the park that night, with the dog, have you? Or the person who was sending her those gifts? Maybe ... maybe ...'

Adam reached over and took both of her hands in his. 'We haven't, no. But Cora, the DNA evidence, and everything else I've just said ... it's too strong. The dog-walker is irrelevant, I'm sure of it. The gifts too. Please, please let this go. Please. It's going to drive you mad if you don't.'

Cora nodded, slipping back into his arms, and Adam un-muted the television, relieved that the conversation was over. He hugged her close, kissing her hair, and she nestled into his arms, trying to relax. Inside though, she was a churning mess of emotions; frustration, sadness, anger and desperation making it impossible to concentrate on anything else, even when Adam flicked over to a re-run of an early episode of *Friends*, a show Cora could normally happily watch all day long.

As Monica, Phoebe and Rachel chatted on screen, Cora remembered that she still hadn't informed Clare Henderson about her daughter's death, and wondered how best to go about it. It seemed too cold and impersonal to inform the New York police department and ask them to call round with the news. Maybe Kymani Campbell could do it? At least Clare now knew him a little. Cora vowed to phone Joel at the adoption agency in the morning, and ask him if that would be all right. Poor Clare. Poor Sally. Poor Sam. What a bloody mess this was.

38

Monday 17th June
11 days until the deadline

The girl, who was fifteen and skeletally thin, was huddled in the make-up room chair, shivering despite the warmth of the morning and the thick, black and white striped poncho she was wrapped in. As Sherry the make-up artist gently applied blusher to the teenager's jutting cheekbones, the girl's mother flicked anxious glances at her daughter from the seat to her left. Finally, the teenager turned to her with a small smile.

'I'm fine, Mum. Stop worrying.'

'I know you are, darling. Sorry.'

'It's OK. I love you, Mum.'

'I love you too, Alex.'

Across the room, Cora grabbed a lip gloss from the counter, touched by the scene. Alexandra Young was suffering from anorexia, and she and her mother were appearing on *Morning Live* to talk about the devastating effects of the disease and to beg other parents to look out for the warning signs. Alexandra had been shaking and crying with nerves when she'd arrived at the studios a couple of hours earlier, but now, despite the shivering, she was composed and focussed, and had spoken calmly and eloquently about her condition during the seven o'clock hour of the show, resulting in hundreds of supportive emails and tweets. Her second appearance of the morning was coming up in ten minutes' time, guests often doing more than one slot on the same show due to the unique nature of a breakfast programme – few viewers watched the entire thing, most dipping in for a few minutes here and there as they rushed to get ready for work or the school run.

The girl's transformation from terrified to relatively tranquil had, Cora had been impressed to note, been almost entirely down to Miranda Evans, who had spent at least an hour chatting to her, making her laugh, putting her at her ease and gently urging her to be as frank as possible on air.

'You can help so many other girls, and boys, by what you say today. And you'll have your mum, and me of course, sitting there with you, so there's honestly nothing to worry about, I promise. It's hugely, massively, important that this subject is talked about more openly, and I can't tell you how much it means to us that you've agreed to do this, Alex,' the doctor had said, and the teenager had nodded, then grinned widely as Miranda added:

'Plus, Olly Murs is on after you and I've asked him if he'll come and do some photos with you when he's done ...'

Once Alex and her mother had been taken to the green room, Cora had pulled Miranda aside.

'That was brilliant. You handled her so well. I honestly thought we'd have to pull the interview when I saw the state she was in. You were fab.'

Miranda had flushed. 'Thanks, that means a lot. It's a subject I ... well, sort of specialised in really, a few years back. Nearly three-quarters of a million people in the UK suffer from an eating disorder, did you know that? That's a lot of people hating themselves and their bodies,

296

obsessing about their weight and their shape. And not just those with eating disorders, other conditions too. Some even have unnecessary plastic surgery, and ...'

She paused, a stricken look in her eyes, then took a deep breath and continued.

'It's the most horrendous thing ... I'm so glad she went on air, she was great, wasn't she?'

'She really was. I hope she recovers, poor girl.'

'She will. She wants to now, and that's half the battle. I said I'll stay in touch, help her out if I can. I know ... I know people, young girls, who didn't get the help they needed soon enough, with awful consequences ...'

Her voice shook a little, and Cora suddenly wondered if Miranda was speaking from personal experience.

'Did ... did you ...?' she started to ask tentatively, but they were interrupted by Cecily the floor manager marching into the room to drag Miranda off.

'One minute, Miranda, one minute, come on!'

Cora watched as Alex and her mother were led out of the make-up room once more, the teenager striding confidently on her painfully thin legs, a glow on her face that was not solely down to Sherry's skill with a blusher brush.

Miranda made a real difference to that girl today, Cora thought. She turned back to the mirror to finish patting down some flyaway strands of hair with a little styling cream, then frowned as her mobile buzzed in her handbag. Who was calling her before 9 a.m.? None of her friends or family would ever do that on a weekday, knowing the chances of her answering while the show was on air were minimal.

Tempted to ignore it, with her last bulletin of the morning just minutes away, Cora nonetheless opened her bag and peered at the phone's display. Then, startled to see a New York number flashing on the screen, she grabbed it and hit the green button.

'Hello? Cora speaking.'

There was silence on the line for a moment, then a woman's voice, small and distant.

'Cora? Is that you? It's Clare, Cora. Clare Henderson? In New York. Sally's mum.'

'*Clare*?' Cora was stunned for a moment. She did a quick calculation. Just after 8 a.m. in London meant it would be just after 3 a.m. in New York. What was Clare doing calling her in the middle of the night? She didn't even have a phone, did she? Cora had rung Joel Anderson yesterday afternoon, apologising profusely about calling him on a Sunday, but he'd sounded delighted to hear from her, and genuinely upset to hear the news about Sally's death. He'd readily agreed that Kymani was best placed to break the news to Clare, and had promised to call him immediately. That would have been at around 10 a.m. New York time yesterday, so Cora now assumed that Clare had probably been told about her daughter's demise some hours ago. Even so, why the phone call?

'Clare?' she said again. 'Are – are you OK? It's so late there.'

There was another moment of silence, then Clare's voice again.

'It's the early hours of the morning, yes. My neighbour, downstairs, she left her cell phone with me, in case I needed her during the night. She was with me when I heard the news ... the news about Sally ...'

Even on this crackly line, Cora could hear the emotion in Clare's voice.

'She has a real phone too, in her apartment, you see? She left me the cell phone and told me to use it to call her, if I needed anything in the middle of the night. But that detective guy, he gave me your number, in case I had any questions, he said. So I thought I'd call you, instead. Is that … is that OK?'

'Of course. Of course it's OK. Oh, Clare, I'm so sorry about Sally. We all are – all Sam's friends, I mean. We were so hoping we might find her. It's tragic, and I'm so sorry you had to hear about it like that.'

'Thank you. Was she … was she happy, when she died? Do you know?'

'She was, Clare, yes. She was working on her acting, doing really well. And she lived in a lovely flat and had lots of friends, really nice friends. I've chatted to one of them on the phone, and she said what a wonderful person Sally was, and how much everyone liked her.'

Cora crossed her fingers as she spoke, knowing she was embellishing the truth somewhat but hoping that her words would be enough to bring Clare some comfort. She decided to omit what she'd learned about Sally wanting to cut Clare out of her life. There was no point in revealing that – the woman was clearly suffering enough as it was.

'That's good. That's good.' There was another long pause, the phone line gently hissing. Then Clare's voice again, even smaller and more distant now.

'So … so I've lost two daughters now. Two gone. It's not fair, is it? Life isn't fair, Cora.'

'Life can be tough, yes.' Cora agreed. 'But – well, you haven't *lost* two daughters, not exactly. Sam is still alive and well. Maybe you could, I don't know, write to her in prison or something?'

She stopped, suddenly remembering that Sam still hadn't decided whether she wanted contact with her birth mother or not, but she'd said it now. Damn. Then she realised that Clare was speaking again.

299

'No, no, I don't mean Sam. I mean the other one. The baby.'

'The – baby? The other one? I'm sorry, Clare, I don't understand?' The woman was obviously getting confused, and Cora looked at the clock anxiously, aware that she should be heading into the studio in the next minute or so.

'I mean the other one. There were three, you see. Didn't I say? It was identical triplets I had. Sally, Sam and another one. She died, though. Died at birth. Stillborn, they call it. So I was left with twins. And now I've lost two. Sam's the only one left.'

It was nearly eleven o'clock before Cora had time to sit down and properly process the conversation she'd had with Clare. She sat at her desk in the newsroom, half-heartedly nibbling a cold cheese and ham croissant, and ran through it again in her head. Three babies. Triplets. Seriously? Was Clare's memory to be trusted, addled as it must be by her years of drug abuse, and now further by grief? She had sounded definite enough about it though, on the phone.

Cora pushed her plate aside. If it *was* true, this was a tragedy that kept on growing. So Sam was one not just of twins, but of triplets. And now both of her sisters were dead. And Sam was in prison, and possibly staying there. A sudden, sick, sinking feeling washed over Cora. Yet more bad news to break to Sam. I can't do it, thought Cora. I can't phone her, yet again, with nothing but doom and gloom, and tell her she actually had *two* sisters, once. Somebody else will have to do it. I'll tell Ellen, her mum. She can break it to her.

She stood up, intending to go straight down to graphics and tell Wendy the latest, then remembered her friend was on a day off, treating her own mother to a birthday spa day. Bugger, she thought, and sat down again. I'll ring her later. Instead, she grabbed her phone and dialled Nathan's number. She needed to speak to him anyway, about a story they were working on later in the week, but when he answered she filled him in on her conversation with Clare first.

'TRIPLETS? Are you serious? Do you believe her?'

'I think so. I mean, she's definitely a bit odd, and vague, but she sounded pretty convincing. Said the third baby had been stillborn. It's just so bloody sad ...'

'Sad, but odd too. Was there a funeral? Is there a grave or anything?'

'I – I don't know. I didn't really ask her much about it. Why? So Sam can visit it, if she ever gets out?'

'No ... well maybe that, yes. But I'm thinking it's just a bit weird that we haven't heard about this before. I mean, wouldn't there be documentation, if there was a third baby? In the adoption file? There was no mention of it, was there? It just had stuff about Sally, the baby who was taken to America, and Sam, the baby who was abandoned. No mention of a third sibling. Why would that be?'

Cora thought for a moment. 'I don't know. I suppose it just wouldn't be relevant for the agency to have that information, would it? If the baby had been still-born, I mean. They were just concerned with the living baby.'

'I suppose so. Only – this fact that there was a third child. A third identical child, who would have had the same DNA as Sam and Sally. What if – and this is a huge what if, Cora, but we *are* clutching at straws here, let's face it – what if ...'

Nathan paused.

'What if WHAT?' said Cora.

'Well – I have no idea how we'd go about checking up on this, but … what if she's still alive? What if the third baby *didn't* die?'

302

39

Cora had waited until she was back at Adam's flat later that afternoon before she called Joel. Nathan's suggestion that the third baby might actually still be alive, grown up and walking around out there killing people seemed unlikely, if not downright bonkers, but a phone call to check couldn't hurt, she supposed.

Joel had sounded extremely surprised at her request, saying he'd seen nothing in the file to indicate that Clare had had triplets, but that he'd go and check anyway. An hour later he was back on the phone, sounding sheepish.

'Clare was telling the truth. I've found a death certificate, tucked into an envelope in a pocket at the back of the file. Sorry, Cora, I didn't notice it before – although, to be fair, we were only really looking for information about the mother and the abandoned baby and I stopped going through everything once we had that.'

'That's OK. Thanks for finding it though. We just wanted to confirm it really, that Clare was telling the truth about the third one dying and there wasn't by some miracle another sister out there. Is there any more information about this baby?' Cora sat, pen poised, ready to take notes. She could pass it all on to Ellen Tindall, she thought, when she asked her to ring Sam.

'Let me see, hang on.' There was a shuffling of papers at the other end of the line. 'Hmmm, not much. Unnamed baby girl, stillborn. A few scribbled notes here from the doctor who delivered the triplets – the handwriting is terrible, but I think it says something about her being very tiny and having underdeveloped lungs, heart and brain, incompatible with life. Very sad. But at least Clare had two healthy girls. Triplets must have been a bit of a rarity, at the time. Well, still are I suppose.'

'Thanks, Joel. I'm so sorry to bother you yet again. I'm sure this will be it now – would you mind just emailing me a copy of those notes and the death certificate though, just in case Sam wants to see them at some stage? They'll be all she has of that poor little girl – her other sister.'

'Of course, no problem. I'll do it straight away. You take care, Cora.'

'Thanks, Joel. You too.'

She ended the call, and clambered off the sofa to make a cup of tea. Joel was true to his word – by the time she returned, the email icon was flashing on her screen. She put her steaming mug down on the coffee table and clicked on the message, scanning it with little interest as a sudden weariness with the whole business overcame her. There was nothing positive in any of this, she thought, just misery upon misery for Sam. But then she paused as a familiar name caught her eye. Dr Humphrey Barden. Where had she seen that name before? She picked up her drink and sipped slowly, trying to remember. Humphrey Barden. Humphrey Barden. It was such an unusual name, and she was sure she had seen it recently. She could even see a face in her mind's eye, attached to the name …

Then it came to her. The framed photograph, on the wall in the waiting room at the Wellford clinic.

"Dr Humphrey Barden, our founder and friend …"

She'd seen it that day when she'd visited Dr Ana Taylor to pick her brains about DNA. That was it, definitely. It said here that he had delivered Clare's babies. It would explain why Clare had picked the steps of the Wellford clinic to abandon Sam, Cora thought – if the man who had delivered her babies worked there, Clare must have thought it was a safe place to leave her child. But why was there no mention of this prior relationship when the clinic reported finding a baby on the steps? It certainly wasn't in any of the paperwork about Sam and Sally. All the documentation made it sound as if clinic staff had simply found this poor child and called the police. There was nothing about one of their staff having delivered the baby himself.

Puzzled, Cora rang Nathan. He listened while she updated him, expressing disappointment that the third baby was definitely dead. But when she explained what she had just found out about Dr Barden and the clinic, and her concerns about it, he didn't sound convinced.

'Well, there's probably quite a simple explanation for that. I mean, babies all look the same, don't they? And he probably delivered loads of them all the time. What are the chances he'd recognise one if it turned up on his doorstep, even if he *had* delivered it fairly recently?'

Cora felt a bit silly. 'You're right, yes. And there was no name or anything, on the note Clare left with Sam. Although the note did say she'd had two babies, and was taking one with her to America, didn't it? That should have raised his suspicions – I mean, how many multiple births would there have been around that time? You would have thought he might have made the connection ...'

'Yes, but he might not have found baby Sam on the steps himself, or seen that note or anything. We don't know who found her, do we? I don't think there's anything in that, Cora. He's a baby doctor, he delivered Clare's babies, so when she decided to leave one behind, she picked his clinic. Makes sense to me.'

'Yes, I suppose so. OK, thanks.'

But after they had finished their conversation and ended the call, Cora sat thinking. Most of it made sense, yes. But Dr Barden was an IVF doctor, founder of the clinic if the portrait there was to be believed. It wasn't a hospital, not as such, so why was he delivering babies, unless that was something he did on the side? Or maybe he delivered the babies he helped create. Did that mean that Clare's babies were IVF babies? Multiple births were definitely more common if the mother had IVF, she knew that. Clare had never mentioned having IVF, but that didn't surprise Cora, knowing the woman as she did. But wouldn't such a successful IVF treatment have been quite rare back in the mid-eighties, and hit the headlines? And even if they were IVF babies, was that relevant in any way? Probably not, she thought. But something about this was niggling at her, and she couldn't work out what it was. It was all immaterial now, as far as Sam was concerned, but Cora was curious. And if the very least she could do for her friend now was to get her family history straight for her, then she wanted to do it. Maybe she should go back to the clinic and have another chat with Dr Taylor. She picked up her phone again, and dialled the number.

40

Tuesday 18th June
10 days until the deadline

Cora sat in the Wellford's waiting room, weary after her morning news-reading shift and another night of disturbed sleep, and gazed at the picture of Dr Humphrey Barden. He was a distinguished-looking man in a pin-striped suit, with dark hair greying at the temples and kind eyes. Weird, Cora thought, how I came here before just to do some research, not knowing that you had a part to play in Sam's story. You delivered her, brought her in to the world. Where are *you* now – retired, I presume? There had been no mention of Dr Barden on the current staff list on the company website, although his name was there as founder in the section about the Wellford clinic's history. It had opened thirty-five years ago, Dr Ana Taylor one of the first to join the practice.

'You can come through now.' The voice was low and surly, and Cora turned to see Eleanor Hawkins, the nurse she had met on her last visit, standing by the door, eyes cast downwards. Strange woman, Cora thought, as she followed her silent escort, dressed in the same frumpy tan uniform as before, along the cream-carpeted corridor to Dr Taylor's office. It was just after 3 p.m., and as Cora entered the room and the doctor rose from her seat with a smile and offered a hand, the afternoon sunlight streamed in through the large windows, highlighting the millions of dust motes dancing in the air between the two women.

'Thanks so much for seeing me again. I'm researching another story, as I think you were told when I rang? I won't take up too much of your time.'

Dr Taylor smiled. 'Always a welcome change from the daily grind to chat to a journalist. What is it this time – more information on DNA?' She adjusted the long strand of pearls which had strayed off-centre over her black sleeveless sweater as she stood up, and settled back in her chair. Her arms were tanned and toned, noted Cora. She must have been in her late fifties, even early sixties, but looked a decade younger.

'No – actually, I was hoping that you might be able to point me in the direction of your founder, Dr Humphrey Barden? His name has come up in a story I'm working on, but I didn't see his name on your website. Has he retired?'

Dr Taylor frowned slightly, then her face relaxed again. 'His name has come up in a story? Do you mind me asking what sort of story?'

Cora hesitated, then decided a few facts wouldn't hurt. She didn't have to mention Sam and the murder trial.

'Err … well, it was a case of an abandoned baby. Just over thirty years ago. The baby was left on the steps of the clinic, but it seems he also delivered the child. And it's now emerged the baby was one of identical triplets, one of whom was stillborn. I can't really say any more than that, I'm sorry … look, I have a death certificate here, with Dr Barden's name on it.'

'Triplets?' The doctor's tone was strangely sharp. She cleared her throat and reached for the document. Cora, watching her face, was surprised to see it suddenly flush red. When Dr Taylor looked up again, her open, smiling expression had changed to one of guarded coolness.

'I don't know anything about this case, I'm sorry.'

308

'But – you would have been working here, when it happened? You don't remember an abandoned baby, or Dr Barden being involved in the birth of triplets? Surely that would have been quite an event, in those days?'

'I don't remember, no. Do you know how many women we've seen here over the past three decades? Thousands. Thousands, Cora.'

'I understand. But ...' Cora thought for a moment, then made up her mind. What did she have to lose?

'Look – I haven't been entirely honest with you. My friend, Sam, she was one of the two surviving triplets. The one abandoned on your steps. She was later adopted. She's in prison now, on a murder charge. She says she didn't do it, and I believe her, but her DNA was on the murder weapon. That's why I've been asking about DNA, and that's why I've been trying to track down her family, her sisters. We – my friends and I – have been trying to help her, and when we discovered there were sisters, identical sisters who would have the same DNA, we just thought we needed to find them, just in case ...'

Dr Taylor was staring at Cora, an astounded look on her face.

'What ... in case they had committed the murder, and not her? Really?'

'I know, I know, it was a stupid idea. But we were desperate, Dr Taylor. We even went to New York, and tracked down Sam's birth mother, who moved there with her other baby. And then we found out that the triplet who'd been taken to America, Sally, was killed in an accident long before the murder took place, so that ruled her out. And the third child was stillborn, as you can see on the death certificate. But when I saw Dr Barden's name, and realised that not only did he deliver the triplets but that Sam was also left here on your steps, I just wanted to talk to him. I know it won't help Sam's case, but I thought the least I could do was try to get her family history documented for her, now she knows she's adopted. I don't really know what I thought Dr Barden could do, really, to be honest, but there were just a few things that seemed a bit odd, like why he delivered the babies ...'

'Stop, enough.'

The doctor suddenly lifted her hands to her face, covering her eyes. She sat there like that for a long moment, then brought her hands down onto the desk with a thump, leaned forward and looked straight into Cora's eyes.

'I understand why you're so concerned about this, but you won't find the answers here. As I said, I don't remember these triplets, but if two are dead, they clearly cannot be implicated in this murder, and I can't help you with your quest to establish a family history. I'm sorry you've had a wasted journey.'

She pushed the copy of the death certificate back across the shiny mahogany and stood up.

'Well ... can you give me a contact number for Dr Barden, then? Maybe he would talk to me?'

Dr Taylor shook her head.

'Maybe he would, if he was still alive. But Humphrey died from pancreatic cancer five years ago. I'm sorry, Cora, but I need to get on and you need to leave. Nobody can help you here.'

41

Wednesday 19th June
9 days until the deadline

'Cora, what on *earth* is this on your latest expenses claim? Am I seeing things?'

Cora looked up from her computer screen, where she was tweaking the script of a late breaking news story in her eight o'clock bulletin, and frowned. She was sure she hadn't claimed for anything particularly large, or unusual, had she?

Betsy Allan was at her shoulder now, waving the blue form at her.

'Errrmm … what's the problem, Betsy?'

'This, Cora. *This* is the problem.'

She dropped the piece of paper onto the desk and, with a perfectly manicured index finger, stabbed at a line about halfway down the page. Cora peered at it, then smiled, realising what the programme editor's issue was. There, just above *"£4.99, batteries for microphone"* and just below *"£38, crew breakfast"*, Cora had neatly written *"£20 to prostitute, Birmingham"*.

'I mean, I know your job is stressful and busy, and I know you don't have much time at home with that gorgeous policeman of yours, but I think maybe hooking up with prostitutes while on *Morning Live* business in the Midlands is going a little far, Cora.'

There was a sudden creaking of chairs and cessation of

311

conversation at all the nearby desks as producers and researchers turned to listen properly to the suddenly very interesting discussion between reporter and editor. Cora turned to see Betsy grinning, her eyes twinkling.

'Oh, *that* expense claim.' Cora smiled back, realising that Betsy knew exactly what the expenses entry was about and was just in a mischievous mood. It had been a few weeks back, and she and the boys had been sent on a story in Birmingham, where there'd been a recent spate of serious assaults on prostitutes. Cora had tried for hours to persuade one of the sex workers to talk to her on camera about the attacks, and had finally found one who had agreed, albeit with her back to the lens and for a fee. Cora had happily handed over twenty pounds, hence her expense claim.

'Well, what can I say? Desperate times call for desperate measures. Good value though, wasn't it, at twenty quid?' she said, arching her eyebrows at her boss.

'I suppose so. OK, I'll let it through this time, but don't go making a habit of it.' Betsy winked at Cora, retrieved the blue form and marched back to her office.

'Show's over, nothing to see here,' she announced over her shoulder to the agog eavesdroppers, and they all quickly turned back to their monitors, some wide-eyed, others smiling, realising it had been some sort of in-joke between Cora and the boss.

Cora chuckled quietly to herself as she hit "save" on her keyboard. Betsy was such a refreshing change after Jeanette. She was tough but fair, and could be really good fun when she was in the mood. Programme ratings had climbed steadily too, since her arrival. The show was much, much better now than it had been before, and Cora was enjoying her job more than ever. If only Sam was there ... She sighed, stood up and headed to the printer to collect her scripts.

Back in her office, Betsy grinned and filed the expenses form. That had been fun, especially when Cora had played along. She liked Cora Baxter, liked all of her staff really. They were a good team, and the show was going from strength to strength. She had high hopes of awards in the coming months, something the programme had missed out on in recent years. A *Best Daytime News Show* trophy would look rather good on that shelf over there, Betsy thought, leaning back in her chair. She'd been feeling better over the past few days, her mood lifting after the trauma of Marcus's funeral had eased, and she was now starting to feel she could finally relax a little. There had been no further visits from the police, their case seemingly sewn up, and Sam was due to appear in court to enter her plea at the end of next week. Despite her sense of relief about this, something inside Betsy twisted as she thought about Sam, her star producer. It was such a waste of talent, and she'd liked Sam too, liked her a lot as a person, not just as a member of staff. It was horrible, really horrible, that things had turned out like this for the girl. Betsy shuddered, then pushed the thought away and grabbed her desk phone as it started to ring.

'Editor,' she said.

'I know it isn't going to help Sam, not with her trial. But I just want to get her background straight for her now, and there's just something ... I don't know, something odd about it all. The way Ana Taylor reacted. She was definitely hiding something.'

'Like what?' Wendy speared a cherry tomato with her fork and popped it into her mouth. They were sitting in the *Morning Live* canteen on the third floor, eating salads at a window table. Below them, lunchtime joggers and

313

office workers streamed past on the riverside walkway, enjoying the warm sunshine.

'I don't know. But she definitely remembered the triplets, I'm sure she did. I just don't really understand why she was so weird about it. Why lie?'

Cora pushed a radish across her plate with her knife. She wasn't very hungry, and suddenly realised she hadn't been for a couple of days. Stress usually made her reach for the cake tin, but now it seemed to be having the opposite effect.

'Cora, please eat something. You'll pass out.' Wendy jabbed her fork in the air in Cora's direction. 'Go on. For me.'

'Oh, all right.' Cora was half-heartedly chewing on a piece of chorizo when her mobile rang. She glanced at the screen and her eyes widened. It was the Wellford clinic's number.

'Hang on.' She dropped her fork and grabbed the phone. 'Hello, Cora Baxter speaking.'

'Miss Baxter. Cora. It's Dr Ana Taylor. Can you speak?'

'Yes. Yes, I can. What is it, Dr Taylor?'

Across the table, Wendy slowly put her cutlery down too, and leaned forward in her chair, eyes on Cora's.

'I've been thinking about what you said. Thinking a lot, actually. About the ... the triplets that you were asking about. I think you need to come back in, for another chat.'

'Of ... of course. But why? You said you didn't remember anything, and Dr Barden is dead, right?'

'He is, sadly, yes. But – look, I'm really sorry about this, but I wasn't honest with you. It was just such a shock, after all this time ...'

Her voice tailed off, and Cora waited a moment, then

said: 'So you *do* remember?'

'I do, yes. Is she all right, Clare Henderson? It's been so many years.'

'What? You know Clare Henderson? Seriously? Yes, she's fine – well, sort of. But how on earth …? Were you involved in delivering her babies too?'

'No. No, I wasn't. But I was there when …'

She stopped talking again.

'There when *what*?'

Cora could hear the doctor swallowing on the other end of the line.

'There when … look, we can't do this over the phone. Can you come back in to see me, this afternoon?'

'I suppose so, yes. Yes, OK.' Cora looked at her watch. 'If I leave immediately after my shift I could be there by about three again, if that suits?'

'Fine. I'm going to tell you everything, Cora, because you know a lot, but you don't know it all. And if there's a chance that something good can come out of it, after all this time, something that could help your friend … I'll see you at three.'

The line went dead. Cora stared at her phone for a moment, then put it slowly down on the table and met Wendy's eyes.

'What the hell's going on? You're going back to the clinic? Why?'

Cora shrugged, but there was suddenly a little bubble of hope and excitement fizzing deep inside her.

'I don't know, Wend. I really don't know. But it seems that the good doctor has something to tell me.'

42

Dr Ana Taylor was standing in front of her desk, waiting, when Cora knocked on her door. There was a silver tea tray ready on a side table, and Cora accepted a cup of black Assam and settled in her chair. Her stomach was suddenly churning, and Dr Taylor's appearance wasn't helping. The doctor, normally impeccably groomed, looked as if she hadn't slept much the previous night. There were dark shadows under her eyes and, as she sat down behind her desk, she repeatedly twisted the large emerald ring she always wore, drawing Cora's attention to her red nail varnish, which was chipped in several places. What was wrong with her, and what was she about to reveal?

Cora took a sip of tea, carefully placed her cup down on its saucer and waited. Dr Taylor took a deep breath, as if to steady herself, and began.

'It was in the eighties, of course, when IVF was really just taking off. They were heady times for doctors in our field, Cora. Louise Brown, the first test tube baby, had been born in 1978, and over the years that followed techniques were improving and developing at such a rate … it was so exciting, and there were so many people who wanted help, so much hope suddenly for couples who desperately wanted babies.'

The doctor's eyes shone as she spoke, and Cora could see the passion in them.

'Clare Henderson … she was a friend of a friend of

Humphrey's – Dr Barden, our founder, I mean. He had met her a few times, at parties and so on. She was a party animal, that girl, and she had had issues with drugs and alcohol. But then she met this man, George. He was a nice guy, steady job, and he loved Clare. They got married, and she cleaned up her act a bit. They tried for ages, to have a child, and nothing happened, and she started to get very depressed about it, so she came in to see us here at the clinic, and begged us to help. But the thing was, Humphrey knew that she was still dabbling in drugs, and so ethically he couldn't do anything for her. He couldn't risk it, he was scared she'd get pregnant and then damage the babies. So, initially, he said no, and sent her away. God, I wish he'd stuck to that decision.'

She breathed out heavily, clasping and unclasping her hands in front of her.

'So – he didn't, then? He changed his mind, and gave her IVF treatment? Why?'

'He did, yes. Why? Because he was a nice man, too nice in many ways. Kind. So he made her promise, faithfully, that she'd kick the drugs. We all knew she probably wouldn't, not really, but he gave her the benefit of the doubt, and the treatment went ahead. And then, something remarkable happened.'

She sat forward in her chair, eyes bright again.

'Humphrey only implanted two embryos, pretty cautious for the time. When he did the first tests, he was really expecting it to have failed, but it hadn't. Well, one embryo did fail – but the other split into four.'

Cora was trying to keep up. 'I'm sorry – what? One embryo failed, and one split into four? But that makes …'

'It wasn't triplets, Cora. It was quads. Quadruplets. Four identical babies. Clare Henderson was pregnant with *four* babies.'

318

43

'Oh, come on, this is getting ridiculous!'

Cora stood up and started pacing the room, trying to process what Dr Taylor had just told her. *Four* babies now? This was crazy. How could the number of babies Clare Henderson had produced be increasing by the week? Quads? Seriously? And why hadn't Clare mentioned that? She'd told Cora she'd had triplets – the stillborn baby, plus Sam and Sally.

She turned to look at the doctor.

'Are you sure about this? It sounds pretty far-fetched. Wouldn't that have made the newspapers and everything? It would have been a press sensation at the time. Quads are so rare.'

Ana Taylor nodded slowly. 'Yes, incredibly rare. Four identical girls. Quadruplets, from one embryo. The odds of one embryo resulting in four babies … but we knew Clare couldn't take it, you see. There would have been a media storm, and she wouldn't have been able to handle it. She was too fragile. There were just a few of us here who knew about it, so the decision was made to keep it a secret. We thought that maybe after the birth, if her mental state was strong enough, then maybe she could choose to tell the papers herself, if she wanted to. It seemed like the right decision. But … well, that was the only right decision that was made, as it turned out. Because after that, Humphrey – well, all of us, really – made a few more decisions. And they weren't good, Cora.

They weren't good at all.'

Cora, who was back in her chair now, felt her stomach flip. She was struggling to process all this.

'OK, I'm still struggling with the fourth baby thing, and desperate to know what happened to her. Go on, Dr Taylor, please. And hurry.'

The doctor nodded. 'OK, I'm trying. There's just so much to tell. The first decision – first mistake, in retrospect, was that we didn't even tell Clare she was carrying four babies. We thought it would freak her out, stress her out too much. We were concerned about the babies, you know? It was such a major coup, to produce four like that. We wanted to protect them, as far as we could. So Humphrey just told her she was pregnant, that the IVF had been a success, and left it at that. She assumed, therefore, that it was just one baby, a normal pregnancy. She was ecstatic, they both were, she and George. And for the first few months, everything was great. She was well, and healthy, and the babies were small, so she didn't look enormous, and nobody guessed. But as time went on, she started asking questions – there were a lot of feet in there kicking her, not just the two, and she could obviously feel that, and wondered what was going on.'

She smiled for a moment at the memory, then the smile faded. Cora's eyes were fixed on Ana Taylor's face. She couldn't quite believe what she was hearing.

'And she was getting big too. People would have started asking questions. So we decided to move her into a private clinic, for the last couple of months, at our expense. We told her we wanted to monitor her, as it was an IVF baby, and she was so happy that she just went along with it, didn't really question it. It was such a nice place too, she loved it. She had a big sunny room, TV, en

320

suite bathroom, sitting area, all mod cons. It was nicer than their marital flat, to be honest, and she was waited on hand and foot, and George could stay over whenever he liked. She was really happy there.'

'So when? When did you tell her she was expecting quadruplets?'

Cora was heartily wishing she had brought some kind of recording device along with her. Nobody was going to believe this. She was hardly able to believe it herself, although something told her Ana Taylor was telling the truth. What would she have to gain by making up such an incredible story?

'Well ... well, that was the second bad decision. Not just bad ... terrible. Awful. But at the time ... well, we were on such a high, you see, Cora. We were creating *life*. Can you imagine, how amazing that was? We had the power to change lives, to make people so happy. And so ... and so, we did something dreadful.'

She swallowed hard. Cora sat motionless, a shiver running up her spine. This was all starting to freak her out a little.

'We did a scan, made sure the picture was quite confusing – and it was, as you can imagine, a tangle of arms and legs – and then showed it to Clare. But we lied to her. We told her she was having triplets. Three babies, not four. Again, she didn't even question it, didn't ask how it had taken this long for us to realise that. Humphrey just muttered something about the other two being hidden behind the biggest one on previous scans, and she was so thrilled that she just accepted it. She was having triplets, and she was over the moon.'

'But why? Why lie to her at that point? Three, four, what's the difference? I don't understand.' Cora rubbed her forehead hard to try to shift the headache she could feel coming on. This was getting more and more confusing every second.

Ana Taylor was staring at her desk. When she spoke again, she kept staring at it, not lifting her eyes to Cora's.

'We told her there were three, and not four, because we needed a baby, Cora. We needed a baby for somebody else.'

44

'You ... you *what*? You needed a baby for somebody else? So ... let me get this right ... you told Clare Henderson she was only having three, and then you stole the fourth one and GAVE IT TO SOMEBODY ELSE?'

Cora was wide-eyed, horrified. She suddenly realised she was standing up, and shouting. Ana Taylor stood up too, gesturing wildly with her hands.

'Please, please, sit down, be quiet. Nobody else can hear this, please. Please, let me finish. It's ... it's not as bad as it sounds ...'

'Well, it sounds pretty damn bad to me. How can it not be as bad as it sounds? This is *insane*.'

Cora sat down again, her heart pounding. This was like some stupid movie. In fact, if it were a movie, she'd have turned it off by now – the storyline was just too ridiculous. Could this really be true? And why was Ana telling her all this, if this was really what had happened? Didn't she realise she was incriminating herself, that stealing babies was a crime?

The doctor sat down too, breathing heavily.

'I'll tell you about the fourth baby in a minute. But before that ... before the birth, something terrible happened. Clare's husband George had been coming and going as I said, staying over at the clinic some nights and going home others. He worked shifts at a factory, erratic hours. Then one night, he didn't turn up to stay over as planned. By the next morning Clare was distraught, and then we heard the dreadful news. He'd been killed in a car crash the night before, on his way to see her.'

Cora swallowed hard. She already knew that Sam's natural father was dead of course, from the adoption file, but it was still horrible to hear the details. Poor, poor Clare. How many bad things could happen to one person? Drug addiction, a dead husband, two dead daughters, another daughter in prison facing a murder charge. And a stolen baby too, if Ana Taylor was to be believed.

The doctor was still talking, twisting her ring back and forth.

'It went downhill from there. Clare was beside herself with grief. She got hold of some booze from somewhere, and drank herself into a coma, then refused to eat. In the end, she went into premature labour at thirty-one weeks. There were just three of us there for the birth – myself, Humphrey and a nurse, who'd been in on it all from the beginning. Not nearly enough people to deliver four babies, but we couldn't risk anyone else finding out that it was quads, because of what we were about to do …'

She took another deep breath.

'We managed though. The first two were beautiful, healthy little things. The third was stillborn, and that was devastating. We'd known one was a lot smaller, but the scan hadn't shown the extent of the underdevelopment of her organs. And then, number four, again perfect. It was one of the most emotional days of my life, I'll never forget it.'

There were tears in her eyes now, and she wiped them away with the backs of her hands. Cora sat waiting, feeling almost faint with anticipation. The fourth baby, what happened to that fourth baby? She wanted to scream the question, but she bit her lip and remained silent.

'So, we told Clare one child was stillborn, but that she

324

still had two perfect, gorgeous little girls. She didn't seem to care much at that stage, she was still grieving for her husband so badly, and anyway the babies needed to be rushed straight to incubators, being so small and premature. She just didn't want to see them at that point, and never knew we'd delivered four, not three. The little girl who was stillborn was cremated – Clare didn't want a funeral. Her ashes are still here, in this building, in a cupboard in the basement.'

She stopped talking, her eyes focused on some distant memory. Cora couldn't bear it any longer.

'So, tell me, Dr Taylor. Two of the surviving babies were obviously my friend Sam, the one Clare left behind, and Sally, the one she took to New York, right? And one died at birth. So the fourth one – the one you *stole* – where did she go? And where is she now?'

She couldn't disguise the shock and disgust she was feeling, and she saw Ana Taylor flinch at the venom in her voice. The doctor dragged her eyes back to Cora's face.

'She went … she went to the nurse. The nurse who had helped deliver the babies. She had wanted a baby so badly, for such a long time, but she was infertile, and single. She'd been married once, for a while, but he dumped her when he found out she couldn't have children. And she had been with us from the beginning, was so loyal, so hard-working. And that's why Humphrey – well that's why all of us – decided. Clare could never have coped with four babies, even if her husband hadn't died – she couldn't even cope with two, as we soon found out when she abandoned one on our steps a few days after she was discharged. And we had *created* these babies – without us, Clare would never have got pregnant. Nobody else would have helped her like we did.

325

And I know it seems like a dreadful decision now, but at the time it seemed to make sense. Clare didn't need all those babies, didn't want them. Our nurse could have one, and we knew she would love and cherish it. And we were right. She did.'

Cora's heart was pounding again. Could you actually have a heart attack from listening to a story, she wondered?

'I need to find her, Dr Taylor. I need to know where she is, quickly. Do you still have the nurse's details, do you know where they live, where the daughter is now?'

The doctor had slumped back into her chair, looking smaller somehow than she had half an hour ago, as if finally telling her story after so many years had drained her of more than just energy.

'I do, yes. But first, Cora ... I need to know. What are you going to do, with the information I've just given you? Are you going to go to the police? It will ruin me, Cora. Ruin this clinic. And we've done so much good work, over the years, made so many people so happy. We still do, every day. It was one mistake, Cora. One huge, terrible, unforgiveable mistake, but it was so long ago, and it worked out for everyone in the end, didn't it?'

There was desperation in her eyes. Cora stared at her, her mind whirling. She had no idea what she was going to do, or who she was going to tell. She just knew that she needed to find this other baby, this other sister of Sam's, and tie up the final loose end. And then, after that, she would decide.

'I don't know, Dr Taylor. I just don't know. But I won't do anything yet, I promise. I'll think about it, carefully. But in return I *need* those contact details, OK?'

The doctor leaned forwards in her chair, gingerly as if she was in pain, and opened her desk drawer. She pulled out a leather-bound diary and turned the pages slowly, then tapped one of the neatly written entries.

'Here it is. She's off for a few days, gone to France for a mini-break with a friend. But I know she's due back late Friday night. I'll write her address down for you. You'll probably be able to catch her at home …'

Cora was frowning. 'What do you mean, off for a few days? She actually still works here?'

Dr Taylor looked up, a surprised expression on her face. 'Oh, sorry, I thought I'd said. Yes, she still works here. It's Eleanor. Our nurse, Eleanor Hawkins. You've met her once or twice, she generally shows people in when they have appointments with me. She's the one we gave the fourth baby to.'

45

**Saturday 22nd June
6 days until the deadline**

It had been, Cora had decided, the longest three days in the history of the world. Since Ana Taylor's revelations at the clinic on Wednesday afternoon, everyday life had, on the face of it, continued as normal, but Cora's every waking – and indeed dreaming – thought had been about Eleanor Hawkins and the baby she'd been given, the fourth quadruplet, Sam's only living sister.

Ellen Tindall had now told Sam about her stillborn sister, news she had stoically accepted. Hence, after some debate, it had been decided to tell her about the latest development too. Cora had discussed it with Ellen, with Wendy and the boys at work and with Rosie and Nicole on the phone, worrying about getting Sam's hopes up once more, but they had all concluded that as she'd been kept fully informed about everything they'd discovered so far, it was only fair to tell her this latest piece of news. It had been hard for Cora to convince the others that what she was telling them was true – she could still hardly believe it herself, Ana's story being just too outlandish – but Sam had, once again, been surprisingly accepting of the astonishing disclosures.

'The man I loved and wanted to marry has been battered to death. I'm in prison for a murder I didn't commit. My mother isn't my mother, and my father wasn't my father. I'm not an only child, as I've believed my whole life. My world hasn't just been turned upside down, it's been kicked to Timbuktu and back, and I have no idea which way is up any more. Being one of quads instead of one of twins or triplets is just another minor detail in the insanity that has become my life,' she told Cora on the phone.

'Nothing you can tell me can shock me now. I just want this to be over, either way. Whether the jury ultimately believes me and I'm freed, or whether I'm in here for years, I just need to get on with it, Cora. You've done your best, and if you find this girl, this latest sister, and you think by some miracle it could be her DNA and not mine on that murder weapon, then that will be the best thing that's ever happened to me and I will love you for ever. But I'm not holding my breath, not any more. I don't know why I'm in here, but I am and that's that. And I'm not being defeatist or giving up, just finally getting real. Just keep me posted, OK? Your calls are one of the few bright spots in my tedious, ever-lasting days in this shithole.'

Cora had promised to call again at the weekend, as soon as she had seen Eleanor Hawkins. And now, finally, the weekend was here. Deeply anxious about the impending encounter, Cora had spent Friday night at Adam's flat, eating takeaway Thai food and pretending to watch *Silent Witness*, her mind elsewhere. She had told him about the stillborn baby sister, and he'd been sympathetic, but she'd decided to keep the latest twist quiet for now, and he had put her distraction down to her usual Friday night weariness after a long working week and tried to look after her, topping up her wine glass and offering a foot massage. She'd accepted both wine and massage willingly, but neither had really helped. She was still wrestling with whether to tell him, or somebody else in authority, about Ana Taylor's confession. The gang had had mixed views on that, Nicole adamant that the doctor would have to be prosecuted ('She stole a *baby*, Cora! Lied to a mother about how many babies she was carrying, stole her child and gave it to another woman! I don't care what her motive was, or how long ago it was, come to that. Her colleague might be dead and has got away with it, but she can still pay for the crime, come on!'). Nathan, though, had been more circumspect.

'I know it was a pretty shocking thing to do, but in the end, what real harm was done? Clare clearly couldn't have coped with more than one baby anyway, so she would just have dumped two instead of one, wouldn't she? The baby would have gone up for adoption like Sam did. At least we know she went to that nurse, someone who really wanted her. Is that so terrible now, after so many years?'

Cora really didn't know what to think; the whole thing was making her brain hurt, and she resolved not to do anything until she had tracked down Sam's surviving sister. Clare Henderson would have to be told too, of course. Told that she had another daughter, one who was still alive and well, one she never even knew about. Cora didn't know how that would best be done either, but she'd decided that that too could wait, just for a little while.

Now, after telling Adam she had a few errands to run and arranging to meet him later for lunch, she was sitting in her car just a few doors down from the address Ana Taylor had given her. She glanced at the scribbled details on the yellow sticky note again, checking that she had the right place. Number 68. Yes, that was it. The house, a small semi-detached with a neat front garden, was midway along a quiet residential street in Colliers Wood in south-west London. Cora wasn't familiar with the area, but it seemed pleasant enough – a couple of big out-of-town retail centres, a busy local high street, a few large parks and the River Wandle wending its way past eighteen-century mills, well-tended allotments and a nature reserve before joining the Thames at Wandsworth.

Cora took a deep breath, got out of her car and walked the few metres to the nurse's house, nodding at a man who was washing his van outside number 62. He smiled and waved a soapy sponge at her, then returned to his task, whistling tunelessly. Nervous now, she made her way up the short pathway from the front gate and stood in front of the black-painted door of number 68 for a moment, composing herself. Then she pushed the doorbell. Just seconds later, she heard movement in the hallway beyond, and a security lock being unlatched. The door opened, and Eleanor Hawkins' face, looking tired and free of make-up, her short grey-brown hair uncombed, peered around it.

'Hello? Can I help you?' She looked blankly at Cora, but then her eyes suddenly widened in recognition.

'Oh! It's you! What … what are you doing here? What do you want?' Her voice was sharp, and she looked startled, frightened almost. Cora instantly realised she needed to tread very carefully.

'Eleanor – Miss Hawkins – I'm Cora. Cora Baxter. I'm a news reporter, and I've been talking to Dr Taylor, at the clinic, about a story I've been working on – you remember we met briefly a couple of times? Anyway, she suggested I talk to you. I know you've been away, and I'm sorry to bother you first thing on a Saturday morning, but it's fairly urgent. Do you mind if I come in? It won't take long.'

The woman was still peering round the door, half-hidden behind it, but some of the wariness had gone from her eyes.

'Ana suggested you talk to me?'

'Yes. If that's OK? She said you might be able to help me.'

Eleanor hesitated for a moment, then stepped back and pulled the door open.

'Well, if Ana sent you, I suppose ... come in. Sorry about the state of me, I had a lie-in. Got back very late last night.'

She was wearing a long, pink, fleecy dressing gown, pulled tightly in at the waist with a tie belt. As she led Cora down the narrow hallway into a living room at the rear of the house, bare feet with un-painted nails slapped on the laminate floor. She gestured to Cora to sit, and Cora obliged, perching on the edge of the seat of a small armchair covered in seventies-style green and brown floral fabric. Eleanor sat down on a matching sofa directly opposite.

'Do you want tea?' she said abruptly.

'No, no thank you. I'm fine. I don't want to take up too much of your time. So – well, as I said, I'm a reporter. For *Morning Live*, the breakfast show?'

'I know. I recognised you first time I saw you at the clinic. I watch it nearly every day. Well, when my shifts allow.' A half-smile played on Eleanor's lips for a moment, then vanished again.

'Oh, do you?' Cora was surprised for a second, then remembered how the nurse had stared at her the first time she'd met her. 'Well, that's nice. Errr, so ... I'm working on a story. It's actually about my friend Sam. It's emerged she was abandoned as a baby on the steps of the Wellford clinic more than thirty years ago. She was adopted, and I've been trying to find out more, about her real family and what happened, why she was abandoned. And I spoke to Dr Taylor earlier this week, and ... well, she told me, Eleanor. She told me everything. The truth about what happened all those years ago.'

Cora had been watching Eleanor Hawkins carefully as she spoke, gauging the woman's reactions. At first she had simply frowned, but as Cora mentioned Dr Taylor, the little colour there had been in the nurse's face drained away.

'What?' Her voice was croaky now. 'What do you mean, she told you everything?' Her hands were gripping the belt of her dressing gown, knuckles turning white.

Cora took a breath. 'She told me about Clare Henderson, and the IVF, and the quadruplets. And how the fourth baby was taken, without Clare's knowledge, and given away. Given to you, Eleanor.'

The woman's eyes were wide now, horrified, her hands twisting frantically at the pink fabric at her waist.

'Why would she tell you? She wouldn't. Why would she? Why now?' She was breathing in sharp little gasps, face deathly white.

'Eleanor, please, it's OK.' Cora stood up, weaved her away around the coffee table and sat down on the sofa next to Eleanor. The woman looked on the verge of collapse.

'Calm down, it's OK. She told me because ... because ...'

Cora paused. She really had no idea why Ana had confessed all, not really.

'She told me because ... well, she said she hoped that some good might be able to come out of it all, after so many years. And my friend Sam – well, she's an only child. She's always wanted a brother or sister. How amazing it would be if I could re-unite her with her only surviving sister, Eleanor – your daughter. Wouldn't that be incredible?'

She mentally crossed her fingers. It would serve no purpose right now to tell Eleanor any more about Sam, or that she was in prison. Keep it simple, Cora, she thought.

Eleanor's breathing had steadied a little, but her eyes were fixed on the carpet in front of her. 'I can't … I can't believe she told you. Why would she tell you? I don't understand …'

'She did, Eleanor. And now that I know, I want to meet her, if I can. Your daughter? It would be so wonderful, if she could meet Sam, her sister, wouldn't it? After so many years?'

'Yes … yes, I suppose so. But …'

Eleanor lifted her head and looked straight at Cora.

'… well, that's not going to be possible. I never told her, you see. She doesn't know how … how she came to me. I always just told her that she was the result of a brief relationship, and that her dad had died – that was true of course, poor George. You know, about George, Clare's husband?'

'I do, yes.'

'I mean, how could I tell her the truth? What we did … what we all did … it was so wrong … but I wanted a baby so much, and I would never have been able to have one, not without Ana and Humphrey. It was all done out of love, you know?'

Cora nodded, not sure how to respond.

'And I've loved her so much, all these years, and I'm so proud of all she's achieved. She had some problems, you see, growing up, but she's turned her life around, she's done so well. So how could I tell her, now? How could I tell her that I'm not her real mother, that I stole her from another woman? I can't, can I? I just can't. And I

335

won't. She's never going to find out, OK?'

Cora's heart was sinking. How was she going to find this woman, if Eleanor wouldn't co-operate? Would Ana Taylor know where the daughter lived? She tried another tack.

'But aren't there adoption papers, legal documents? She'll find out one day, won't she? Maybe not until you've passed away, but one day? Wouldn't that be worse, her finding out you lied to her her whole life?'

Eleanor smiled, a small, sad smile.

'No. I never even officially adopted her, you see. There was no need. I just went and registered her birth, as if she was my own. Nobody ever questioned it – why would they? Nobody knew a child was missing, because nobody except the three of us knew that child had been born. It was so easy.'

Eleanor sniffed, tears suddenly filling her eyes, and she fumbled in the pocket of her robe and pulled out a tissue, then dabbed her face furiously. Cora stood up and returned to her armchair, thinking hard. There had to be a way of finding this girl, there *had* to be.

'OK, well – can you just tell me a bit about her? She would be thirty-one now of course, the same as Sam. What does she do, for a living? Or can you tell me anything else about her? I understand why you don't want me to talk to her, I do, really. But if I could just tell my friend Sam a few little bits and pieces about her long lost sister, that would be so nice. Even if she can't meet her.'

Eleanor was shaking her head, her eyes filled with fear again. 'No. I can't have you talking to her. I can't tell you anything, I'm sorry. She's a very private person. Please don't ask me any more questions.'

As she spoke, her eyes flitted behind Cora, then back again.

'Please, I can't talk about this any more. I'm just too upset. But I need to know … are you planning to go to the police about this? Please don't. *Please*. I worried so much at first, worried myself sick, I was so scared that someone would find out what we did. But we made a pact, the three of us, never to tell, and as the years passed I started to feel safer. I don't understand why Ana has told you, told anybody, after so long. I mean, she often talked to me about it, about the guilt she felt, but I never thought … and if my daughter finds out now, after all this time …'

Her eyes darted to something behind Cora again, then back to Cora's face.

'So – are you?'

Cora swallowed. If she told Eleanor she still hadn't decided about whether to tell the police or not, she'd get no more out of her.

'No, Eleanor, I'm not going to the police,' she said quietly. 'I just wanted to find her, Sam's sister, that's all.'

'Thank you. And I'm sorry I can't put you in touch with … with my girl. I just can't risk it. You understand?'

Cora nodded, and Eleanor stood up abruptly.

'I'll make tea then, before you go,' she said, and headed for the door, swinging it shut behind her. Cora waited until she heard the clatter of cups, then turned quickly in her chair, scanning the room. What had Eleanor been looking at, behind her? There was nothing there but an antique desk, a green leather chair tucked under it. Was it something in the desk? Some clue to her daughter's identity, maybe?

Cora leapt off her chair. There was nothing on the desk top but a mug of pens – some shiny and new, others with tooth-marked caps – and an A4 pad of paper. Cora picked up the pad and flicked through it. Nothing. It was empty, unused. The drawers then. She wrenched open the right-hand drawer and rifled through it. More pens, envelopes, a roll of sticky tape, some notebooks, a calculator, a few highlighter pens. Damn it. Why had Eleanor kept looking back here, then? Cora slammed the drawer shut and pulled on the other one. For a moment it stuck, but she tugged harder and it opened suddenly, a few bits of paper which had been inside fluttering out onto the floor. Cora bent to pick them up, then paused to listen. There were still noises coming from down the hallway, pans clanking now, Eleanor maybe putting some dishes away while she waited for the kettle to boil.

Cora glanced at the pieces of paper in her hand, then shoved them back into the drawer. Just receipts, for books and stationery. This drawer was fuller than the other – a few chargers, probably for mobile phones and cameras, user manuals for household appliances, more receipts, takeaway menus, batteries. And then, Cora saw something that made her freeze. It was a photograph, a graduation photograph. She pulled it slowly out of the drawer, staring at it. Eleanor in a smart blue suit, a string of beads, coral lipstick, smiling at the camera, glowing with pride. And next to her, linking arms with her, smiling happily too, wearing a new graduate's cap and gown, a young woman. A woman Cora recognised, immediately.

Incredulity creased Cora's brow. She peered back into the drawer, and took out some more photographs. The same young woman, the woman Cora recognised so clearly, in photo after photo, alone and with Eleanor. One taken here, in this room, the two of them raising glasses to the camera, clearly at some sort of party. The two of them, sitting at a restaurant table, outside in the sunshine. Abroad? And the two of them, posing with a birthday cake, blue icing spelling out the words "Happy Birthday

Mum". What? Why was that woman in these pictures? Why was she in these pictures with Eleanor Hawkins? She couldn't be her daughter. She couldn't be Sam's sister. Could she? No, of course she couldn't. It made no sense. No sense whatsoever.

46

Wendy, fresh from the gym in black sweatpants and top, pushed a red curl out of her eyes and stared at the graduation photograph, her smooth forehead crinkled in a frown.

'I don't understand. This can't be the fourth quadruplet. How can *she* be Eleanor's daughter? There must be some mistake, Cora.'

'I know. I don't understand either. But there were loads of photos, Wendy. Her on her own, her with Eleanor. A picture of a birthday cake with "Happy Birthday Mum" on it. Why would there be photos like that if she *wasn't* her daughter?'

Cora was pacing Wendy's lounge, her mind racing. She'd never felt so confused in her life. None of this made sense. When she'd heard Eleanor Hawkins' footsteps coming back down the hall, she'd had just enough time to stuff all but one photograph back into the drawer, shut it, and return to her seat, tucking the graduation picture into the waistband of her jeans, before the living room door opened. She hadn't stayed for the tea, instead telling Eleanor she'd had an urgent phone call and had to leave, and promising the woman she wouldn't tell anybody else about their conversation. Then she'd run to her car and headed for Wendy's, phoning her on the way to make sure she was in and telling her about the seemingly absurd discovery she'd just made. An incredulous Wendy, on her way back from a yoga class, had been waiting at the door when Cora arrived, and had practically snatched the photograph from her hands.

'But I just don't get it Cora. How can it be? For a start, they were *identical* quadruplets, right? And we know Sally was Sam's double, they were really, really alike. But her?'

She jabbed the photo with a finger. 'Her? She looks nothing like Sam and Sally. So she can't be their sister, can she?'

Cora sat down heavily on the sofa next to Wendy. No, Miranda Evans didn't look anything like Sam and Sally. The TV doctor didn't look like Sam and Sally at all. So why was she there, in so many photographs, with Eleanor Hawkins?

47

'OK, let's think about this logically.'

Cora and Wendy were both still staring at the photograph, trying to make sense of it.

'The facts. Dr Taylor says the nurse, Eleanor Hawkins, was given the fourth quadruplet. Eleanor has admitted that. And they were identical quads. Therefore, Eleanor's daughter should look like Sam, just like Sally did. And yet Miranda doesn't look anything like them. Similar height and build, roughly, I suppose. But different eye colour – Sam's are very dark brown, and Miranda has those lovely grey eyes. Their noses are completely different, their chins, everything … identical siblings they are NOT.'

Cora picked up her mug and took a sip of tea, then shuddered. It was some sort of berry tea, red and bitter.

'Wendy, this is vile. What's wrong with Earl Grey?'

'You drink too much caffeine, I'm thinking about your health. Now shut up and concentrate. OK, so they don't look alike. And Cora, they don't have the same birthday either. Don't you remember, when we were talking to Miranda in the graphics studio and telling her it was Sam's birthday in a couple of days' time, and she told us hers was in a couple of *weeks'* time and she was off to Paris?'

Cora nodded slowly. 'Yes, I do remember. Her birthday was mid-June, I texted her to say happy birthday while I was waiting for that actress, Sarah Healey. And Sam's is the thirtieth of May. So Miranda *can't* be the fourth quadruplet then, can she? Ana Taylor clearly said that all four were delivered at the same time. So why are there so many photos of Miranda with Eleanor Hawkins, in all those mother-daughter poses? And they don't even have the same surname, do they? Eleanor Hawkins and Miranda Evans. Neither of them is married, so why would that be? Aarrgh, Wendy, I think my head is going to EXPLODE!'

She put the mug of foul-smelling tea down on the table and sank her head into her hands, massaging her temples. Then she sat up straight again and turned to her friend.

'We can't take this any further on our own, Wendy. It's getting too complicated, and too confusing. I'm going to have to tell Adam, and see if he can check it out, get to the bottom of it.'

'I think that's a good idea. Do it.'

Cora stood up and strode purposefully towards the door. 'I'll call you as soon as there's any more news, OK?' she called over her shoulder.

'OK. Later.' Wendy watched Cora go, then spotted the undrunk tea and rolled her eyes. Then she got up too, and headed for the shower.

48

'Afternoon, boss. Wasn't expecting you today.'

'Just popping in to check a couple of things, Gary. I won't be here for long.'

It was four o'clock and Adam had just arrived in the incident room. As planned, he'd met Cora for lunch, and the conversation had been a rather surprising one, to say the least. Adam didn't know whether he was feeling irritated or impressed. Definitely a little irritated that Cora had ignored all his advice to accept Sam's guilt and assurances that the evidence didn't lie, he thought, as he sat down at his desk and switched his computer on. But, he had to admit, a little impressed by her unswaying loyalty and belief in her friend's innocence. She'd clearly been continuing to do rather a lot of her own detective work behind his back, and now she'd come up with something that he finally felt he couldn't dismiss – a possible living sibling of Samantha Tindall's, allegedly an identical sibling, although there seemed to be a lot of confusion over that particular part of the story.

Cora had refused to tell him how she'd made this discovery, saying a journalist couldn't reveal her source, and despite Adam's best efforts to pry the details out of her, she remained adamant. But she had given him some details and begged him to check it out, and he'd agreed, despite it being, on the face of it, a very strange story. Cora was now claiming that she'd discovered Sam had actually been one of four identical quadruplets, and that one other of the four was still alive. Most remarkable of all, Cora had told him it appeared that the *Morning Live* doctor, Miranda Evans, might be that sibling – this, despite the fact that the two women had different birthdays and little physical resemblance. But if there *was* something in it, it meant that there actually was someone with the same DNA profile as Sam, working alongside her in London, and known to the murder victim. And yet, what possible reason would Miranda have for killing Marcus? Adam couldn't help feeling he was yet again wasting his time, but he was here now. If Cora was right, something weird was definitely going on, and an hour or so checking the details wouldn't hurt.

A search for Miranda on the police national computer quickly confirmed that the date of birth Cora had given him for her was correct. Her record was clean, apart from one speeding fine several years ago, and the details of her driving licence showed her birthday as the fourteenth of June, two weeks after Sam Tindall's, who was born on the thirtieth of May.

'Different birthdays confirmed, then. Not really making much sense so far, then,' Adam thought.

He surfed the net, looking for more information about Miranda, and stopped when he came to an article on the *Daily Mail*'s website, a familiar name catching his eye. The doctor had been interviewed by the newspaper when she'd first joined the breakfast show, and the piece contained a few details about her medical training. She'd studied at University College London, which as a major research centre was considered to be one of the best medical schools in the country, and it was the UCL reference which had grabbed Adam's attention – he knew one of the Clinical Teaching Fellows there. Dr Iain Gainley was an affable Scot who had helped Adam with a

346

case a few years back, when a suspect was claiming he couldn't have been involved in the serious assault he was charged with due to a complicated medical condition. In the end, the man was exposed as a fraud and was now serving time.

Adam and the doctor had hit it off during the investigation, comparing notes over a few pints on a number of occasions, but it had been a while since they'd spoken. Adam went to his contacts file and found Iain's number. He answered on the second ring, and after they had exchanged pleasantries and Adam had apologised profusely for phoning on a Saturday afternoon, he turned the conversation to Miranda Evans.

'I do remember her, yes. She was an interesting character.' His accent was strong Glaswegian. 'She's done all right for herself now though – on the telly, isn't she?'

'She is, yes. But why do you say "done all right for herself *now*", Iain? Did she have problems when you knew her? What do you mean by "interesting character"?'

Adam picked up the coffee mug next to his keyboard, realised it had probably been there since yesterday, and put it down again.

'She had a few issues, yes. Have you ever heard of body dysmorphic disorder, Adam?'

'Hmmm. Maybe. Is that when people think they're ugly, when they're not?'

'Well, sort of. It's a psychiatric disorder – BDD for short. It manifests itself in different ways, but very commonly the patient becomes obsessed with a perceived physical defect, which nobody else can see.'

'So – they think there's something wrong with their appearance, even though they look fine to everyone else?'

'Exactly. And Miranda Evans … well, she was a pretty

girl. Very pretty. But in her first year with us she began exhibiting symptoms. Her medical history showed she'd had a few issues with an eating disorder in her teens, although she seemed to be over that. But the BDD … well, it became pretty bad. In her case, she had a very distorted view of her face, particularly her nose and chin, and her eyes. She thought her eyes were frighteningly dark – in reality they were a perfectly nice brown colour. And she thought her nose and chin were enormous and deformed, which they clearly weren't – as I said, she was a very pretty girl. We started to have grave concerns about her choice of career, to be honest – we thought we might have to ask her to leave UCL, to seek treatment. And then, amazingly, she turned it around.'

'How?'

'She went for plastic surgery. Now, this happens quite often with BDD sufferers, and for many, it makes no difference. They're still as distressed by their appearance afterwards as they were before. But for Miranda, it actually worked. She had her nose and chin altered, and got herself some coloured contact lenses, and came back to us a few weeks later looking like a different person. And, more importantly, *feeling* like a different person. She was finally happy with how she looked. We did some psych evaluations, and she was considered cured, if there is such a thing in BDD. Certainly, it was felt that we could allow her to proceed with her medical training. And we made the right decision. She turned out to be an excellent doctor. I saw her last year at a medical conference, and she looked stunning, and seemed very happy. It was a pretty good outcome. So tell me – what's your interest in Dr Evans?'

'Her name has come up in a pretty unusual case – that's all I can say for now, Iain, sorry. Listen, I don't suppose you have any photos of her, do you? I mean, before the surgery. I'm interested to see what she looked like.'

'Maybe. Hold on.' There was a clunk as the doctor put his phone down, and then the sound of tapping on a keyboard. After a minute or so, he was back on the line.

'Yes, I have a photo here. We opened a new laboratory during Miranda's first year here, and we took some shots of a few students at work in it for the UCL brochure. I remember it because Miranda kicked up a bit of a fuss about being in the photos – she was already obsessing about her looks by then. It was a different story after her surgery, she loved having her picture taken then. I can email this to you, if you like? It's a shot with two of our female students in it – she's the one on the right.'

'That would be great, Iain. Really appreciate it. I owe you a pint.'

'Make it two. And make it soon, it's been too long.'

'It has. Cheers, Iain, speak soon.'

Adam ended the call, and logged on to his email, refreshing it impatiently every twenty seconds or so until Gainley's message finally popped into his inbox. Adam clicked on it, and then on the photo attachment. It showed a laboratory bench, various pieces of equipment and two white-coated young women. The one on the left was thin and blonde, peering intently down a microscope. But the one on the right …

Adam zoomed in on the woman's face, astounded. If he didn't know that this was a pre-surgery photograph of Miranda Evans, he would have been absolutely convinced that he was looking at a picture of Sam Tindall.

49

At eleven o'clock on Sunday morning, Adam was sitting on Eleanor Hawkins' floral sofa. Cora had given him her address, telling him simply that she was Miranda Evans' adoptive mother and might be able to help him. In return, he had told her precisely nothing about his discoveries of yesterday, informing her that enquiries were now underway and that she would have to be patient. She had seemed to accept that, telling him she was relieved that he was now finally looking into things, and they had spent a pleasant enough evening cuddled up in front of the TV, with a few glasses of wine, some pasta and a sticky toffee pudding for dessert. This morning, Adam had urged Cora to go out for a long run, telling her he'd cook lunch after popping into the station for an hour or so. Instead, he'd headed for Eleanor's. It now seemed pretty certain that Miranda and Sam were related – surely two people couldn't look that alike if they weren't? But there were still too many unanswered questions and Adam – feeling slightly uneasy as he was no longer supposed to be investigating this case, so was doing this unofficially – needed those answers.

Eleanor Hawkins had looked absolutely terrified when he'd flashed his police ID card, for some reason thinking he was there to arrest her. When, puzzled, he'd assured her that wasn't the case, and that he simply wanted to ask her a few questions about her daughter, she'd reluctantly opened the door and shown him through to the living room. Now, she sat opposite him in a large armchair, nervously wringing her hands.

'What … what do you need to know, officer?'

Adam smiled, hoping to calm her nerves. 'Just a couple of quick questions, Miss Hawkins. You had a visit from a television reporter, who was researching the family of her friend, a young woman abandoned by her mother at birth?'

Cora had told him that this was what she had told Eleanor Hawkins, and he decided to stick to the story too, just for now.

'Yes … yes, she was here. Why, what does that have to do with the police?'

The woman's hands were visibly shaking now. Why was she so nervous? Adam kept his voice calm and quiet.

'It's just something that's come up during another investigation … nothing for you to worry about. But I just wondered if you could clear a couple of things up for me. Can I show you a photograph, Miss Hawkins?'

He pulled a copy of the photograph emailed by Dr Gainley from the foolscap folder on his knees and placed it on the coffee table in front of him, angled so Eleanor could see it, then tapped the picture with his finger.

'Is this your daughter, Miss Hawkins? Your adopted daughter?'

Eleanor gasped, the colour draining from her face.

'Where did you get …? I mean …'

She squeezed her eyes tightly shut for a moment, then opened them again, and reached out to pick up the photograph. She looked questioningly at Adam, then back at the picture, pain crumpling her features. Finally, she put

352

the piece of paper back on the table, and slumped back in her chair, as if exhausted.

'Well, it's obviously all out there now, isn't it? That reporter ... but how did she know ... I never told her who ...'

She sighed heavily, then sat up a little straighter, and looked directly at Adam.

'Did the reporter tell you that my daughter was ... was ... *adopted*?'

Adam looked at her for a moment, confused by her emphasis on the word "adopted". But that's what Cora had told him, wasn't it? He nodded.

'Yes, she did. Is that not right?'

Eleanor was silent for a moment, Adam noting an unexpected expression on her face. Relief? Then she nodded.

'Alright. I'll answer your questions. Yes, that's my daughter. My *adopted* daughter. That was taken quite a while ago though. She looks ... a little different now.'

Now we're getting somewhere, thought Adam.

'Can you confirm that your daughter is Miranda Evans, the television doctor?' he said.

Eleanor nodded, a sudden flash of pride brightening her features.

'I don't know how that reporter figured that out, but yes, she is. And I'm the happiest mum in the world, watching her doing her thing on the TV. After all she went through ...'

'I understand that she had a condition – BDD? And underwent surgery, to alter her appearance? Can you confirm that too?'

Eleanor raised her eyebrows, a bemused look on her face, then nodded. 'Again, how the heck ... but yes, that's true too. She was very ill for a while, but after the operation, she was a new woman. Happy again. It was the making of her. But, officer, please, I don't understand. Why does any of this matter now?'

'I can't explain, not just yet, I'm sorry. But I just have a couple more questions, if that's OK?'

The nurse shrugged. 'Whatever.'

'OK. Miranda's birthday. We have it as the fourteenth of June – is that correct?'

Eleanor hesitated. 'It is, yes.'

Adam frowned. 'It's just that it seems very odd that her birth sister has a birthday two weeks earlier. Can you explain that at all?'

Eleanor was staring at the carpet.

'Miss Hawkins? Can you explain that discrepancy?'

She looked up. 'Yes, I can. Look, I know this sounds a bit weird. But I didn't ... I didn't adopt her until two weeks after she was born. I knew her real birthday, of course I did. But to me, it was the day she arrived in my life that mattered. So I changed her birthday, to the day I took her home. I changed it on the birth certificate myself ... I did it quite well, and nobody ever seemed to notice. And I thought, it's only two weeks' difference, what does that matter over a lifetime? I wanted her so badly, you see. And I couldn't have children of my own. So when I got Miranda ... that was the first day of my new life, and hers. We had to commemorate it in some way, didn't we? So that became her birthday. I'd almost forgotten it wasn't actually the day she was born. But what does it matter, now, really?'

Adam shrugged. 'It probably makes no difference at all, Miss Hawkins.'

And just like that, the biggest oddity cleared up, he thought.

'One final question – you and Miranda have different

354

surnames. Why is that?'

Eleanor's eyes were on the carpet again. 'Hawkins was my married name. Yes, I was married once. Not for long though. He went off with somebody else, when he found out I couldn't give him any children. I kept his name, but when Miranda came along ... well, she was just mine, wasn't she? Not his. So I gave her my maiden name, Evans. She doesn't know, officer, that she's ... adopted. I told her, when she was old enough to ask, why our names were different, that she was such a special girl to me that I wanted her to have the same name as I did when *I* was a girl. She didn't seem to mind. She seemed to really like that story, actually. And she never really asked about her father much – I told her in her teens that it was a short relationship and that he had since died and she accepted that, never seemed too interested.'

'OK. Simple enough explanation then.'

Adam consulted his notes. 'One final thing. Miranda and Sam, her birth sister, somehow ended up working together, on *Morning Live*. Did you know that?'

A genuine look of astonishment crossed Eleanor's face.

'What? No! Really? Her birth sister works there too? Are you sure?'

'Yes, I'm sure. She's a producer though, not on screen, so you wouldn't have seen her on TV.'

Eleanor was shaking her head. 'Well, blow me down. What are the chances? And I've heard Miranda talking about a Sam too. They get on really well. She's her *sister*? I can't believe that ...'

Eleanor clearly hadn't made the connection between the Sam they were talking about and the Sam from *Morning Live* who'd been in all the papers after being arrested for murder, thought Adam. He frowned.

'And Sam is now in prison, charged with murder. Did you not see her photo in the papers, or on the news? She looks exactly like Miranda used to look, before her surgery. Did you not see her, and notice that?'

Eleanor's mouth had dropped open. 'She's in prison? Why didn't Miranda tell me? I don't really read the papers or watch the news, apart from *Morning Live* sometimes, but I often record it and just fast forward to Miranda's bits. I didn't know about that at all. How ... how awful.'

She paused, and took a deep breath. 'This is a lot to take in, sorry. I still can't believe they were working together.'

Adam nodded. 'Well, it's true. It seems neither knew they were adopted until recently – well, Miranda still doesn't know, does she? So was it just a bizarre coincidence, as far as I know. You do hear about it happening though, don't you – siblings separated at birth who've lived in adjoining streets all their lives and never realised it, stories like that.'

'You do. But still ...'

Adam smiled, then asked the other question he'd been leading up to.

'But what puzzles me is this. Obviously, Sam wouldn't have recognised Miranda in any way, when they first met. But Sam looks exactly like Miranda used to look, before she had surgery. I mean, *exactly* like her. So how come Miranda didn't think, "wow, this woman looks just like me, the pre-surgery me"? How come Miranda didn't question that?'

Eleanor's brow was creased into a frown. 'I don't know,' she said. 'I really don't. She never said anything to me ...'

There was a sudden noise from the hallway, a scraping of a key in a lock, a sound of scampering feet on laminate flooring. Then, a cheery female voice called 'Hi, Mum! Only me!'

Wide-eyed, Eleanor leapt from her chair.

'It's Miranda,' she hissed. 'Please, she doesn't know ... does she have to know?'

Adam didn't have time to reply. The living room door burst open, and in walked the familiar figure of Miranda Evans, smiling broadly, dressed in jeans and a sunshine yellow T-shirt and clutching a bouquet of sweet peas and pink roses. Running excitedly ahead of her, yapping now and almost tumbling over tiny feet in its efforts to greet Eleanor, was a small, brown dog.

50

Adam waited, fingers tapping impatiently on the glass-topped coffee table in front of him. When Miranda had entered the room, Eleanor had turned to him and begged him for five minutes alone with her daughter.

'I still don't understand your interest in Miranda, but this … this secret is all going to come out now, I know it is. Please, let me tell my daughter what she needs to know. *Please.*'

Reluctantly, Adam had agreed, and a deeply confused-looking Miranda had been whisked off to the kitchen by her mother. Minutes later, there was a shriek, followed by loud sobbing. Now, things seemed to have calmed down. Adam looked at the time on his mobile phone. Seven minutes had passed. That was long enough. He stood up, but before he'd taken a step the door opened and Eleanor and Miranda re-entered the room, both red-eyed. Even the dog seemed to have lost its jauntiness. It slunk across the carpet, flung itself onto the hearth rug and started licking its paws, ignoring them all.

'Everything OK?' Adam knew it was a foolish question. He sat down again, this time choosing the armchair so the two women could take the sofa. They sat too, Miranda positioning herself as far away from her mother as she could on the small two-seater.

'Miranda … I'm so sorry.' Eleanor's voice was barely a whisper.

Miranda was staring into space, her face drained of

colour, grey eyes fixed on nothing.

'I'm Sam's sister,' she said quietly. 'I'm Sam's *sister*. How can that be?'

'Miranda – I'm DCI Adam Bradberry. Can I just ask you …'

Miranda's head snapped round to face him. 'Why are you here? What has me being adopted, and not finding out about it until today, got to do with the police?'

As Adam tried to compose an answer, she looked at him more intently, and then gasped.

'Oh my God. You're Cora's boyfriend. It's you … you're the one who put Sam in prison, aren't you? It is you, isn't it? And Sam … she's my sister. My *sister*. I didn't know, I didn't know, I promise you I didn't. And now … and now …'

She broke down then, loud gasping sobs wracking her slim body, tears coursing down her carefully made-up face, her whole torso shaking.

Her mother, looking utterly bemused and horrified at the same time, attempted to put an arm around her distraught daughter, but Miranda pushed her away.

'No! You're not my mother. Leave me alone!'

Eleanor's face crumpled, and she retreated to her end of the sofa, tears running down her cheeks now too. Adam looked from one to the other, then fixed his eyes on Miranda, as her sobbing reached hysterical levels. She *was* Sam's sister. Her identical sibling. Which meant their DNA would match. There were still unanswered questions, like why she hadn't questioned Sam's physical appearance when they first met, but that could wait. He had enough to bring her in. He looked across to the rug, where the dog was now sitting up, staring at Miranda, an anxious expression on its small, pointed face. A dog. A small dog. He thought about the CCTV footage from the night of the murder, and the dog walker who had never come forward. Then, saying nothing, he stood up and left the room, closing the door quietly on the two crying women and their four-legged friend. Standing in the hallway, he dialled the station, requesting back-up and a marked car. Miranda Evans had some questions to answer.

51

Monday 24ᵗʰ June
4 days until the deadline

'I'm going mad with anxiety, Wendy. Adam's been looking into this Miranda thing since Saturday afternoon, and he still won't tell me anything. Not a bloody thing. Totally refuses to talk about it, but has insisted I don't contact Miranda. It's driving me *insane*.'

Cora ran her hands through her hair and groaned.

'Well, I'm not far behind you in insanity terms. Sam's back in court *this week*, Cora. On Friday. If Miranda could possibly have had anything to do with Marcus's death, time is running out for us to discover what. But I think we need to trust Adam. He's on to it now, and if there's anything to find out, he'll find it out, won't he? Come on, eat your muffin.'

Wendy pointed at the untouched lemon muffin on Cora's plate. The programme had just finished and they'd retired to the third floor cafeteria for a cup of tea and a snack, but Cora's appetite had deserted her once again. She sighed and poked the muffin.

'Don't want it now. Bloody good diet, this "friend in prison for murder" thing.'

'Well, at least drink your tea. Come on, Cora. It's going to be OK, I know it is.'

Their eyes met and Cora nodded slowly, wishing she could feel as confident about that as Wendy was. If only

Adam would tell her what was going on. She picked up her tea and took a sip, then put it down again.

'I hope so, Wendy,' she said. 'But I just have this horrible feeling that it's too late. We've let her down. *I've* let her down …'

Tears sprang to her eyes, and Wendy reached across the table to grab her hand.

'No,' she hissed fiercely. 'Never say that. You've done your best, more than your best. We've *all* done our best. And now it's up to Adam, and the police and the courts. And it *will* be OK, Cora. It will. We have to hold on to that thought, OK?'

Cora wiped her eyes with her free hand and nodded again. Please, Adam. Please let it be OK, she thought. *Please.*

'She's in interview room three now, Adam.'

'Thanks, Glenn. I'm on my way.'

Adam swallowed the dregs of his third coffee of the morning, gathered his notes into a neat pile and headed down to the interview room floor. It had been tough having to wait until this morning to interview Miranda, particularly with Cora ringing him every hour, begging him to tell her something, *anything* of what was happening, and him having to point blank refuse. But there had been no way of speeding up the process. By the time he'd managed to get a still-hysterical Miranda into the police car yesterday, and persuade her almost equally upset mother that it was best if she stayed at home, it had already been mid-afternoon. Then, realising Miranda was in no fit state to be questioned, he'd had to arrange for her to be seen by a medic, who had advised that she should be allowed to calm down overnight. That meant booking her into a cell, and lots of paperwork, followed by a long telephone chat with Chief Superintendent McKay, the outcome of which was that yes, Adam could formally return to the Sam Tindall case to question this suspect, as long as he never went behind his superior's back again and kept him fully informed about all future developments in the investigation. By the time all that was sorted out, it was nearly 10 p.m., and when Adam finally got back to Shepherd's Bush, Cora was grumpily heading to bed ahead of her 3 a.m. alarm.

Now, as he entered interview room three, where Miranda Evans, a duty solicitor and DC Karen Lloyd were already sitting at the table, he wondered if he'd have any news to tell his impatient girlfriend today. He'd thought about nothing but this case all night, snatching only an hour or two of sleep as the facts whirled around his brain. It was motive that eluded him. True, that had been the slightly weak part of the case against Sam Tindall too, but she was the victim's partner and she'd admitted they had argued not long before the murder. But Miranda? If she was involved in this case, something he had yet to establish, what possible motive could she have? How many times had she even met Marcus? And yet, the dog ...

He eased himself into his chair, nodded at Karen and the solicitor and looked across the table to Miranda, who was sitting directly opposite him. She raised her grey eyes, still swollen and puffy from last night's tears, and dipped her head slightly.

'Good morning, DCI Bradberry.'

'Miranda. I hope you're feeling a little better?'

She nodded. She was obviously much more composed today, he observed, but he sensed a brittleness about her, a fragility. Her long hair hung unbrushed around her pale face, and there was a tiny nerve twitching in her left eyebrow.

Adam started the recording, formally introducing everyone in the room for the benefit of the tape. Then he turned to Miranda, but before he could ask his first question, she raised a hand.

'Please. To save you any more time and trouble, can I just say something? It was me. I did it. I killed Marcus Williams.'

52

'I want to tell you what happened. All of it. I can't hide from it any more. Not now that I know Sam is ... is my sister.'

Miranda shut her eyes for a few seconds, then opened them again and looked first at her solicitor and then at Adam.

'OK,' said Adam. 'If you want to talk, talk. I'll ask questions later.'

He looked at Miranda's solicitor for approval. He shrugged and nodded.

'Go ahead, Miranda. Slowly, and from the beginning.'

'OK.' Miranda took a deep breath and pushed a strand of hair back off her face. Then, in a low, steady voice, she began.

'When I first started working at *Morning Live*, I was instantly drawn to Sam. Looking back now, what a bizarre twist of fate, for me to end up working with her, right?'

All three of the others nodded.

'Really bizarre,' said Karen. 'But I guess these things happen.'

Miranda smiled.

'We hit it off straight away, Sam and I. We seemed to have the same sense of humour, the same work ethic. I loved chatting to her, and she seemed to really like me too. There was just that connection, you know? And I know you're going to ask me the obvious question, so I'll answer it now. Why didn't I immediately see that she looked just like me, I mean just like I did before my surgery? I assume you know about my medical history, my BDD and operation?'

'We do, yes. And yes, I would have been asking you that question,' said Adam.

'Since I've discovered she's my identical sibling I've been asking myself that too. I think it must be something to do with my BDD. I couldn't see myself clearly when I was ill ... I would look in the mirror and see this monster, this hideously ugly girl with a deformed-looking nose and chin and spooky eyes. I know it sounds ridiculous, but that's what that disorder does to you. So I'm not sure I ever really knew what I looked like, to other people. And then, after my operations, when I was finally happy, I destroyed all the old photos, all the pictures of the old me that I could find. I just didn't want to see that girl any more. Mum went mad ...'

She paused. 'I was horrible to her yesterday, wasn't I? It was just the shock, of finding out I was adopted. She's still my mum, I shouldn't have reacted like that, I was awful.'

Her eyes filled with tears and she looked around the room.

'Here.' Karen leaned back to lift a box of tissues from a shelf behind her, and offered it to Miranda. She took one, sniffed and wiped her eyes, then took another big gulp of air.

'Sorry. OK, so I guess that's why I didn't think, "Wow, this woman looks exactly like I used to look" when I first met Sam. I felt a familiarity about her, yes. But I didn't see a physical resemblance. The really strange thing was that I was struck by how pretty she was, isn't that ironic? When I used to look just like her, and thought I was hideous?'

She smiled, and Adam smiled back. The poor girl must have been pretty screwed up, he thought.

'Let's move on. How well did you know Marcus Williams?'

'Well, that was the thing. I didn't, and to be honest, I didn't really want to. It's a bit embarrassing ...'

She shifted uncomfortably in her chair.

'My feelings for Sam ... they had started to become a bit more than just friendly. I started to feel ... well, I started to think it was more than that, that I was a bit in love with her. It was really weird, because I'm not gay, not even bisexual. Well, at least I never was before. This sounds mad, doesn't it?'

'No, you're doing great. Don't worry.' Adam smiled encouragingly.

'Now that I know she's my sister, well, this sounds even more awful. And it probably wasn't really a physical thing, as such ... it was just a really intense feeling. I think now that I confused that intense feeling with love. Every time I saw her in the newsroom, I wanted to be near her, to go and sit with her. She was lovely to me, but of course she was always really busy at work. We did go out a few times though, for a drink or for lunch, and they were just some of the happiest times of my life. I felt complete, somehow, when I was with her. Again, that sort of makes more sense now, knowing what I know, but at the time I just felt I'd met my soulmate, who just happened to be a woman.'

She sighed. 'But then Sam started getting more and more serious with Marcus. She invited me round to her flat once, for a drinks party, and I met him there. He was lovely, just like her, but I just felt so jealous ... it was horrible. I made an excuse and left early, because I couldn't bear to see them together. He kept putting his

369

arms round her, kissing her, and the way she looked at him … I just wanted her to look at me like that.'

A thought struck Adam. 'Was it you, Miranda, who was sending Sam those mystery gifts?'

A pink blush spread across her face and she groaned. 'Oh dear. Yes. Excruciating, isn't it? To my *sister*. When she started talking about how she thought Marcus was about to propose, I got a bit desperate. I thought that maybe if I dropped a few hints about how I felt about her, she might see me in a different way. But I wasn't brave enough to talk to her about it, so I sent gifts instead. Chocolates, after she mentioned that she liked a certain brand but hadn't been able to find them in the shops for ages. The giant cuddly bear, because we'd been talking over lunch about this amazing polar bear documentary we'd both watched. I thought she'd make the connection, realise it was me sending the presents, but she didn't twig. It was so frustrating at the time. I'm glad now though. Could you imagine, your own sister sending you lovey-dovey gifts like that? I'm mortified.'

She covered her face, bright red now, with her hands.

'You didn't know, Miranda. Nobody knew. Don't dwell on it. Would you like some water?' Adam gestured towards a jug and a tower of plastic beakers on a side table. Miranda looked up and shook her head.

'I'm OK. I just want to get this over with as soon as possible.'

Adam nodded. 'Fine. Shall we jump on then, to the night of the sixth of May? The night Marcus was murdered?'

Miranda swallowed. 'Yes. So … the gifts I sent hadn't done the trick. She'd taken the polar bear home, but had told everyone in the newsroom she had no idea who'd sent it. So I thought, right, grow some balls, Miranda. So I decided to go round to her place, tell her how I felt. Of course, when I got near, I started to chicken out. I'd taken Rupert with me – that's my dog – so I just wandered around the streets near Sam's flat, trying to pluck up the courage. We ended up in the park, Pope's Meadow. And that's when I saw him.'

'Saw who?' said Adam.

'Marcus. I saw Marcus, sitting on a bench. I'd only met him once before, as I said, but I recognised him straight away. So I went over, and sat down next to him, and we started chatting. And ... well, I told him. I couldn't help myself, it all came out. I told him that I had been on my way to see Sam, and that I thought I might be in love with her, and that it had been me sending her the gifts. And ... and he laughed. He laughed at me. I think he was partly laughing out of relief, because he had thought it was some *man* sending her presents, and that might have been a threat. But because it was me ... he didn't see me as a threat at all. He just thought it was funny.'

Miranda was flushing again, but this time there was a flash of anger in her eyes. Adam said nothing, watching her closely, waiting.

'He got up, and said he needed to go back to Sam's, to tell her. I begged him not to ... I thought, if *he's* laughing at me, she will too, and I couldn't bear that. But he was distracted, pulling out his phone, about to call her, and he started heading the wrong way in the dark, towards the trees instead of the other way towards the exit. I was following him, begging him all the way, asking him to forget what I'd said, not to tell Sam. When he got to the wooded bit and realised he'd gone the wrong way, he turned around, and I grabbed his arm, made him stop and look at me, tried to make him listen. He just shrugged me off, said he needed to get home, Sam would be worried.

And that's when I lost it. I admit it … I just lost it. This massive wave of … of rage, anger, just swept over me. I'd nearly tripped over something in the grass when I was following Marcus, and I bent down and picked it up. It was a bit of metal, like a pole or something, and I just swung it at him. I didn't intend to hurt him, not seriously … I was just so *angry*, so scared, and so tired, the job makes me so tired, and everything just got on top of me and … anyway, it caught him on the side of head, hard, and he just went down. And then … it's all a blur, I don't really remember what happened after that. I didn't know he was dead, but I knew he didn't look good, and I knew I had to get out of there, before somebody came. So I just went. I went home. There was blood, lots of blood, on my coat and shoes and … but I was wearing black, and nobody seemed to notice …'

She was crying again now, silently, tears coursing down her pale cheeks.

'What did you do with your clothing, Miranda?' Karen asked.

'Put it all in the bin,' said Miranda softly. 'Coat, shoes, the lot. The bin men were coming the next morning. It was all taken away. Gone.'

There was silence in the room, Adam, Karen and the solicitor exchanging glances. Then Miranda spoke again.

'And then Sam was arrested. And I couldn't understand it … how could anybody think it was her, when I knew it was me? I'd seen myself and Rupert on the CCTV footage, when you released it, and I was sure that you'd be knocking at my door, but nobody came. And as time went on, and there was apparently enough evidence to charge Sam, I got even more confused. It actually got to the point where I thought I might have imagined it, imagined that I did it. Was it just an awful

372

dream? Was I mentally ill again? I didn't understand, and I didn't know what to do, so I did nothing. I didn't even go to visit her in prison, I couldn't bear to. I just tried to carry on as normal, but it's been exhausting, I'm just so shattered, all the time. And then yesterday, when Mum told me ... well, everything changed. I mean, Sam's my sister, isn't she? And I did this. Well, I think I did. No, I'm sure I did. And I can't let my sister take the blame. So it was me. I did it. I killed him.'

'What do you think?'

Adam took a bite of his Mars bar. He and Karen had retired to the police canteen, Miranda having been returned to her cell for a break before they questioned her further this afternoon. Karen took a sip of her black coffee and winced. Foul, as usual.

'Not sure. It's a kind of weird explanation. She killed someone for laughing at her basically, and for threatening to tell his girlfriend she had a crush on her. Bit drastic. But that does look like her and her dog on the CCTV footage, now that we've viewed it again. I mean, it's not that clear, but it definitely *could* be her. And more significantly, she knew the murder weapon was a bit of park railing, didn't she? Well, she described it as a metal pole lying in the grass, but that's close enough. We never made details of the murder weapon public, did we?'

Adam shook his head. 'No. But all of the other things she mentioned ... the trees, the head injury ... all of that information is out in the public domain. If she's walked her dog in that park before, she may have noticed bits of railing lying in the grass. It could have been a lucky guess. I agree it probably was her in the CCTV footage, the third dog-walker, the one we never tracked down. So that part of her story is probably true – that she was headed for Sam's flat and ended up in the park. I'm still not a hundred per cent convinced she's the killer though. Sam was in that park too, remember, not long after that third dog-walker left. Our TV doctor has obviously got mental health issues ... maybe she's just covering for Sam, now that she knows they're related? Maybe she's lying, saying she did it, to save her sister? A noble gesture?'

Karen looked dubious. 'Maybe. But how will we ever know? They'll have the same DNA won't they, if they're identical siblings? How do we prove which of them did it?'

Adam opened the file that was lying on the table in front of him and flicked through it until he found the page he was looking for.

'Listen to this,' he said. 'I did some reading up on DNA last night. There've been cases like this in the past, identical twins both suspected of the same crime. I know our suspects are technically part of quads, but they're identical, so it's the same thing. This case in France, look.'

He tapped the paragraph he was referring to, and Karen craned her neck, trying to read it upside down.

'Twin brothers in Marseille. Their genetic codes were so similar that normal DNA tests couldn't tell them apart. Both ended up in court on a rape charge.'

'Doesn't really help us, then.'

'No, but look ... in recent years there've been a couple of breakthroughs. Scientists have found very, very subtle differences between the DNA even of identical twins, differences that the standard DNA test can't detect. The problem is that the tests aren't widely available, take a long time, and they're expensive. Very expensive. I don't know if the budget will run to it here.'

'So what do we do?

'Keep that as a last resort. In the meantime, look for more evidence. Search her home. If she did it, she may have dripped some of Marcus's blood somewhere when she was changing her clothes. Even a minute amount, that's all we need. She might not have noticed it. Our evidence against Sam Tindall is pretty solid, but if Miranda is claiming *she* did it, and her DNA matches, we're still going to need more if the CPS is going to drop charges against Sam and charge Miranda instead.'

'Sounds good. When's the search taking place?'

'They started an hour ago,' said Adam.

53

Wednesday 26th June
2 days until the deadline

'I just can't bear this waiting. It's killing me. Why is it taking so *long*?' hissed Cora.

She looked up at Wendy, who was perched on the edge of her desk, nibbling an apple.

'I know. It's doing my head in too. And when can we tell everyone that Miranda and Sam are definitely sisters?'

'Shhh. Not yet. Adam's asked me to try to make sure it doesn't get out, for now. Well, not outside our gang anyway – he's resigned himself to the fact I had to tell you lot. They're waiting for forensics to get back to them with results from the sweep of her flat on Monday. They're not releasing any details about anything until after that. But it should be soon, hopefully. It had better be. I'm going to explode if it isn't, and as for poor Sam ... well, she's shell-shocked enough from finding out Miranda is the fourth quadruplet. She's still trying to get her head round that little fact, never mind the added bonus of her saying *she* killed Marcus.'

Cora was still reeling herself – they all were. Phone lines between Cora and all her friends who were in the "save Sam" group had been buzzing non-stop since Adam had finally filled Cora in on the Miranda situation, and nobody had quite managed to process it yet. It was all a little bit too surreal.

'I know. And the gossip mongers here are going wild too. Nobody can understand why Miranda is being questioned about killing Sam's boyfriend. There are all sorts of rumours going round.' Wendy took another tiny bite of her apple, and grimaced.

'Like what?' Cora reached for her own apple, which had been sitting next to her keyboard for the past hour, then put it down again, wishing she'd bought some chocolate fudge cake instead. Since she'd heard about Miranda's claim to have carried out the murder, her appetite had suddenly come back. She was now ravenous all the time, food suddenly becoming a comfort despite the anxiety which continued to grip her.

'Oh, stuff like they were having a ménage-a-trois, and one of them killed him because they weren't getting enough attention. Silly stuff. You know what people are like.'

'Mmmm. Although the reason Miranda gave Adam is pretty weak too. She must be pretty unstable, to beat someone to death for threatening to reveal her secret crush.'

'Now who's being indiscreet … shhh! Adam probably shouldn't have told you that, and I don't think he'd want it broadcast in a newsroom,' said Wendy.

Cora, feeling guilty, quickly looked around, but most of the nearby desks were empty. 'It's OK, I don't think anyone heard,' she said, then lowered her voice to a whisper. 'Hey, I didn't even know she had a dog, did you? Seems likely it was her in the CCTV footage though, that person with a dog, the one the police never traced.'

Wendy shook her head. 'I didn't know either.'

'I remembered something though, when Adam said

378

she told him Marcus had laughed at her, and that's when she flipped. Remember I told you about the email she sent to that hotel, when she left her silk shirt in the bathroom, and she accidentally typed "shit" instead of "shirt"?'

Wendy sniggered. 'That was hysterical.'

'It was, but she did totally freak out at the prospect of people laughing at her about it. Just for a minute, then she pulled herself together. But it was clearly a big deal for her. Definitely a bit unstable. And remember her funny turn at Marcus's funeral? She said she felt faint because she hadn't eaten, but that looks a bit different now, in retrospect, doesn't it?'

Wendy nodded. 'Yep. Guilt probably, as she watched Marcus's coffin go into the ground.'

Cora was silent for a moment, thinking. 'Also, something else makes more sense now in retrospect – the way Eleanor Hawkins looked at me, when I first visited the Wellford Clinic.'

Wendy screwed up her face. 'Ah yes, I remember. You said she looked quite shocked to see you there, almost frightened?'

'She did. She clearly recognised me – she watches the programme of course, to see Miranda – but I'm now wondering if she looked scared because she knew I was a reporter, and thought maybe I'd worked out something dodgy about her and Miranda. Which of course I hadn't, not at that point.'

Wendy nodded, her face growing serious. 'Probably. It's all just so horrible, isn't it?'

Cora sighed. 'It is, so let's stop talking about it. Adam promised to let me know what's happening as soon as he can. Until then, we've just got to play this waiting game. Want to go down and get some proper food?'

She gestured towards Wendy's apple. Wendy looked

at it, then took aim and threw it towards the bin a few feet away, where it landed with a satisfying thud.

'Yes,' she said.

54

Thursday 27th June
1 day until the deadline

'Rodney, are you feeling all right?'

Nathan was looking at his soundman with an expression of great concern on his face. Cora, who had just got out of her car at today's location, an animal rescue centre in Wiltshire which had been threatened with closure due to lack of funding, turned to see what was wrong. Rodney was standing on the other side of a low wall, on which he had rested his mixer while he put fresh batteries in Cora's mic pack.

'Huh? I'm fine mate, what you on about?'

Cora studied Rodney. He looked fine to her too.

'Why do you think he's ill, Nath?' she asked, puzzled.

'Well, I can't say for definite, as I've only just arrived too, but ... well, look at him, Cora.'

Cora stared at Rodney, who looked mystified. Then, as her eyes travelled up and down the soundman, she realised what Nathan was getting at.

'Blimey, Nathan. I see what you mean. Poor Rodney ... is it serious?' She giggled.

'WHAT?' Rodney was completely bewildered now. 'What are you two ON ABOUT?'

Cora and Nathan both laughed uproariously, the noise causing Scott to poke his head out of the truck, which was parked next to Rodney's car.

'Wassup, guys?'

'It's Rodney's outfit, Scott,' Nathan explained. 'We think he must be unwell. Look at him. It's ... well, it's so *normal*. Brown jacket, tan jeans. You look co-ordinated, Rodders. You look, dare I say it, quite stylish. This is not the Rodney we know and love. Therefore, we conclude that you are ill, and unaware of what you were doing when you got dressed this morning, dear friend.'

Scott cast his eyes down Rodney's body, then snorted.

'Nothing to worry about, let me assure you. Wait 'til you get over this wall. He's fine, trust me.' He disappeared back inside the truck, and Nathan and Cora looked at each other, then walked across and peered over the wall.

'Ah. Phew. Normality has been restored.' Nathan wiped his brow dramatically.

'Ah,' repeated Cora, and grinned. Rodney grinned back, and did a few pretend Irish dance steps.

'Lime green, faux croc, lace-up brogues. I don't even want to *know* ...' said Cora. She shook her head and, still smiling, walked off to find the rescue centre manager.

Three and a half hours later they were packing up, Cora leaning one arm on the roof of Nathan's car as she tried to wipe fox poo off her shoe.

'This place does great work, and I really hope it isn't closed down, but bloody hell, it absolutely *stinks*.'

Cora scrutinised her shoes, decided that would have to do and straightened up.

'Where are we going for breakfast? I'm starving, amazingly.'

She was already fantasising about an enormous fry up, something she hadn't fancied in years. If this Sam thing wasn't sorted soon, this comfort eating was definitely going to become a problem, she thought, the fear rising again. Sam was due in court tomorrow. Please, Adam, *hurry*, she thought.

'Spotted a little place down in the village as I drove through this morning,' said Nathan, who was packing his camera away in its padded box. 'Should be open by now, hopefully. By the way, I meant to ask … is somebody going to tell Clare Henderson in New York that she has another daughter? A daughter she never knew existed? That's going to be one tricky conversation, isn't it?'

'It's going to be a massive shock to her, yes. But yes, I've sorted it. Joel from the adoption agency is asking his detective friend Kymani to go round to Clare's yet again, and break the news. We thought we should wait until we see if Miranda's going to be charged first though. Don't want to get her hopes up about a new daughter if that new daughter's going straight to jail. And I'll try to call her myself too, at some point over the next few days. I still have her neighbour's phone number.'

'But isn't Clare going to go to the police as soon as she finds out? I would, if I was told somebody had stolen my baby thirty odd years ago. Isn't it all going to come out?'

Scott, rolling cable back onto a drum, wiped a film of sweat off his brow with the sleeve of his striped shirt. It was shaping up to be a glorious day. Behind their parked vehicles, a field of linseed glowed blue in the morning sunshine, and the sky was clear and cloudless.

'I've thought about that, yes. But maybe that's what should happen, Scott. I never made Ana Taylor any promises. But I haven't gone to the police with the story myself, or mentioned it to Adam, not yet. It's just us, our little group, who know, and I know there are mixed views about what should be done, but I'm grateful you've all agreed to let me make the decision. And for now, I've decided that I personally am not going to report her. Yes, what they did back then was shocking, unethical, illegal, wrong in every possible way. But it's true, if Clare Henderson had been presented with an extra baby she would probably have just abandoned two instead of one. Miranda would have ended up being adopted anyway. Would it have made that much difference, in the end? If Clare decides to report Ana and the clinic, once she knows what happened, that's up to her.'

'Fair enough. Wish the cops would hurry up now though. Sam or Miranda? One of them's going down by the sound of it. Bloody hope they get the right one.'

Scott stomped off back to the truck, and Cora, Rodney and Nathan exchanged glances. It was such a dreadful situation, Cora thought. Sam, their dear, dear friend. And Miranda, the new girl at work who everyone had liked so much and who had shown so much promise as both a TV personality and as a medic. How was it possible that one of them was a murderer?

Lost in thought, Cora jumped as a phone started ringing.

'It's yours, numpty. There, look, you left it on the roof of my car.'

'Oh.' Cora reached for the phone, not looking at the display, and hit the button.

'Hi – Cora speaking.'

'Hello? Cora. Cora, it's me.' The voice was achingly familiar, and slightly shaky, as if the speaker was on the verge of tears.

'SAM? Sam, darling, what's wrong? Are you OK?'

'I am OK, yes. I've been released, Cora. All charges have been dropped. I'm coming home.'

55

In her corner office, Betsy Allan put her phone down with a trembling hand. She could almost feel the relief flooding through her veins, like an actual physical sensation. The phone call from DCI Bradberry had horrified her in one way – her new star, Miranda Evans, had been charged with Marcus's murder, and there would be a lot to deal with in the coming months, a wave of press interest, damaging stories in the papers. But she could handle that. She could handle anything, now. Oh, the liberation, the massive weight that had been lifted from her shoulders in the space of a single minute. Sam, her top producer, was coming back too, exonerated. What a day. What a bloody amazing day.

From the day that Marcus had been murdered, Betsy's anxiety levels had gone through the roof. She was a friend of his, and the police had looked at everyone he knew, in those first few days. And she'd been scared, so scared, that she would be implicated. It had been so many years ago now since Betsy had had her own run-in with the police, been arrested, locked up, questioned and ultimately charged with serious assault. So many years, but still so fresh in her mind, so painful. And she'd been guilty too. She'd attacked him with her own stiletto shoe, the man who'd tried to rape her. Attacked him with the sharp, pointed heel, stabbed him in the chest and neck, hurt him badly. And then, because it had been her word against his, because she'd had no injuries, and he was in a bad way, hospitalised, it was her who was charged. Not him. He got away scot-free, walked out of court laughing as she was handed a suspended sentence. He didn't laugh for long though. The idiot went and tried it again, didn't he? Tried to rape another woman, in exactly the same way as Betsy had described to the police. And this time, there was a CCTV camera in the alleyway he'd followed his victim down, and so this time it wasn't just her word against his, and he finally got what he deserved. Betsy's lawyers tried to appeal then, appeal against her assault conviction, but the judge decided he still wasn't sure about what had happened in Betsy's case, so the conviction should stand. But Betsy's boss believed her, let her stay in her job, gave her a glowing reference when she moved on, even helped her explain her criminal conviction to her new employer. And so it had continued, from job to job, Betsy's talent and drive taking her upwards, overshadowing her crime. She'd almost been able to forget it, until then. Until that dreadful day in May, when her friend Marcus died.

When Marcus was killed, Betsy didn't know that her background had never been looked into by the police investigating the murder … she was never a suspect, so why would they have done that? But she didn't know, so she worried, worried herself sick, worried that now, as she had just settled in to the best and most high profile job of her career, that it was all going to come out, that her past would be splashed all over the papers, that she'd lose the respect of her staff and peers, that it would all come to an end. And now it was all over. She was safe, she was fine, and Sam was free.

Betsy threw back her head, and laughed out loud.

It had been on the lunchtime news. Samantha Tindall, the

bitch TV producer who had stolen Marcus from her, had been released, and somebody else had been charged with his murder. Katie Chamberlain sat in a chair in the staff room at the rear of the salon and stared blankly at the screen. She'd switched the television off five minutes ago, but still she sat, remote control in hand, staring. Staring, and thinking. She had thought the bitch had got what she deserved, and now she was out and free. It wasn't fair, wasn't fair at all. Although, of course, Katie had punished her anyway, more than once. It's just that prison had been a better, much better punishment than anything Katie could have done.

It had been fun, though. There'd been many times that she had spat in Sam's tea before getting an innocent junior to carry it out to her. Many times. And how she'd enjoyed standing on the other side of the salon, watching, as an oblivious Sam happily swallowed the tainted drink. Once, she even slipped a slice of mouldy meat into the salad sandwich the bitch had ordered. The taste must have been disguised by the tomatoes and mayo she'd layered on top of it, because the stupid cow swallowed that too, every last bite. Katie prayed that she'd be violently ill later, imagined her throwing up, clutching her stomach in agony. Oh yes, she got punished all right. Remember that deep scratch down the side of your car, when you parked it down the road while you had your hair done, little miss TV producer? The one you blamed on those kids on skateboards? That was me. Remember when somebody accidentally spilled bleach on your new leather jacket, when you left it draped over the back of a chair in the salon when you went off for a shampoo? That was me too, not the Saturday girl who got the blame. And then, when you were arrested for his murder? Well, you certainly got what you deserved then, didn't you? Bitch. Stuck-up,

387

murdering bitch. Except …

Katie put the remote control down on the table. Except you didn't do it, then. Somebody else did. I really, really thought you'd done it. I think your friend thought you'd done it too, you know, when she came to see me. She didn't tell me she was your friend, of course, but I knew. You'd talked about her in here, hadn't you, Cora this and Cora that? So I knew. I enjoyed slagging you off to her, and she just had to sit there and listen. It was fun. She was stupid, and you were stupid too. You might have fancy pants jobs, and I'm just a hairdresser, but I'm cleverer than both of you. But you didn't kill Marcus. While I was in hospital, unable to save him, somebody killed him. Not you though, in the end. Well, fine. But you'd better not come back here again, wanting a haircut. Stay away from me. You still stole Marcus from me. You're still a bitch. Maybe not a murdering bitch, but still a bitch …

'Katie! Your two o'clock's here!' A cheerful voice interrupted her thoughts.

'Coming!' She stood up, cast a final, baleful look at the TV screen, and went to greet her client.

David Cash had seen the lunchtime news too. He was working from home today, but had stopped for a cup of coffee and a sandwich, which he'd enjoyed in the garden with his dog. The sun was shining, and Doug was being particularly entertaining today, racing up and down like a crazy thing, and all in all it was a very pleasant lunch break. He'd gone back inside though, to watch the headlines, and had been shocked to hear that somebody new was now in the frame for the murder of the man in the park, and that Samantha Tindall had been released without charge. He turned the TV off and went back upstairs to his office, but his mind was no longer on his

388

work. He eased the little key out of its hiding place, opened the desk drawer and pulled out his newest scrapbook, the one filled with cuttings about Sam. He'd have to buy a newspaper tomorrow, make sure he added the new cutting, because this was bound to make the papers. Maybe there'd be a new photo of her too. That would be nice.

He wondered, not for the first time, if he should try to stop this – try to stop collecting, try to stop stalking them on the web. Because this wasn't his only scrapbook, of course. There were lots, in this nice deep drawer that Sue never looked in, because he'd told her he'd lost the key years ago, and it didn't matter because it was empty anyway. There were lots in there. Fourteen, fifteen? He'd lost count. One for every ex-girlfriend he'd ever had though. Because he didn't like to let them go, not really. So he kept hold of them. They didn't know of course. Didn't know he was Googling them, stalking their Facebook, Twitter and LinkedIn pages, printing off photos they put online, pasting them into his books. Keeping an eye on them, for months, years, after they had long forgotten *him*. Sometimes, when they were stupid enough to say on social media that they were going to a certain bar or restaurant that night, he'd even turn up, watch them from a distance, see how they looked, who they were with. He never approached them though. Well, not any more. Not after the restraining order. That had scared him a bit. He didn't want Sue finding out about it. She'd caught him with some newspaper cuttings once, when one of his exes was in the papers after winning a decent sum on the Lottery, and he'd had to make up some silly excuse, say the woman was related to a workmate and the cuttings were for him. She'd been suspicious, though. That's why he'd been so relieved that she hadn't been there when those two TV women came round here, asking questions. He liked Sue, really liked her. He'd loved the holiday they'd had together, the holiday they were on when Marcus was murdered and Sam was arrested. It had been wonderful, so romantic, and when he'd returned he'd considered burning all the scrapbooks. Did he really need them any more? Then he'd changed his mind. He'd hang on to them, just for a little while longer. And he mustn't forget to buy that newspaper tomorrow.

David took a last, lingering look at Sam's photograph on the most recent cutting then gently shut the book, slid it into the drawer and turned the key.

56

Friday 28th June
The deadline

'The dog. The frigging dog. Who would have thought it was the dog that would solve the case for us? You always did say you felt uneasy about not tracking down that third dog walker. You were right, eh?'

Glenn Arnold slapped Adam on the shoulder, and Adam punched him in the arm in return, then tried not to visibly wince as his knuckles encountered what felt like a steel barrel. Bloody hell, the man had muscles.

'I was, although to be fair I never expected Miranda's dog to come up trumps like that. Blood, Marcus Williams' blood, on its collar!'

Adam sank down into his chair and stretched luxuriously. The relief was immense. He knew, knew for certain now, that they had the right killer in custody. Cora had been right about Sam's innocence all along, and he now wondered if he should have taken her arguments more seriously over the past couple of months, trusted her instincts. And yet, the evidence against Sam had been so compelling. He smiled. He knew Cora understood, and their relationship was as strong as ever, her joy that the truth was finally out as overwhelming as his own.

Miranda Evans had admitted everything, and although he'd been sceptical initially, it turned out she hadn't been lying. Hadn't been overly observant either, luckily for us,

391

thought Adam. Tiny splashes of Marcus's blood had spattered onto Rupert the dog's black leather collar as she had carried out the assault, and while that had gone unnoticed by Miranda, it had quickly been spotted by the police forensic team which had carried out an inch by inch search of her flat on Monday afternoon. Minute traces of blood had been found on her dark grey hall carpet too, and even on her nail brush. That, along with all the other evidence, plus her confession, had been more than enough for the CPS. Now, Miranda Evans had been charged with murder and Sam Tindall was home. And, to his immense relief, she wasn't bearing a grudge either. When he'd seen her earlier, she had hugged him, tears in her eyes, and thanked him for all he'd done.

'I don't blame you, Adam, for thinking I'd done it. You were only doing your job, and going where the evidence took you. Hell, *I'd* have thought I'd done it too, faced with what you were faced with,' she had said.

Adam leaned back in his chair and breathed a long, contented sigh. He had the weekend off, he had an extremely happy girlfriend, and tonight – well tonight, there would be one hell of a party. Just a final bit of paperwork to finish, and then he was out of here. Adam gave a little whoop, grinned at the amused glances from everyone around him, and got busy.

They'd taken over a large, private room at the rear of one of Cora's favourite bars in Notting Hill. The manager had even managed to cobble some food together, despite the short notice, and a long table along one wall was covered with delicious-looking delicacies – salt and pepper squid, crispy fried anchovies, hummus and tortillas, lamb tikka and a huge bowl of strawberries with a chocolate fondue.

Above the table hung a long banner, decorated with

images of fireworks, party poppers and smiley faces, and the words 'Welcome Home Sam'.

'Great job with the banner, Wendy,' Cora said, admiring it.

'Loads of people in the newsroom helped. But yes, it's a nice one!'

'Nicest banner I've ever seen.'

Cora and Wendy turned to see Sam standing behind them, clutching a glass of something pink and bubbly. She was glowing, hair freshly trimmed and blow-dried, make-up perfect, but there was still a hint of sadness in her eyes. Cora reached out and pulled her into a hug, and they stood there for a long moment. Then Sam wriggled out of her friend's arms.

'Enough soppiness. We've done all that. Let's party!'

'Are you OK though, really?'

Sam nodded. 'I am. I mean, Marcus is still dead, and that's going to take me a long time to get over. And prison … well, that's going to leave scars too. The fear, that awful, hopeless feeling, that dread that I was going to be locked up for ever for something I didn't do … I don't know if I can ever explain how that felt. It was like living in a nightmare. And now, this is a bit like a dream. I can't really believe it's over.'

'It is, though,' said Wendy, delicately wiping a blob of hummus off her chin with the corner of a napkin. 'And it's all down to Cora.'

'No, it was down to all of us. Everyone played a part. It wasn't just me.' Cora picked up her wine glass and took a sip. Gosh, it tasted so good tonight.

'No, but you kept going, kept everyone at it, never gave up hope, and always believed in me, even when all the evidence pointed at me having done it. And it was you who found out about Miranda, in the end. I can't thank you enough, Cora. I'll never be able to thank you enough, all of you, but especially you. I'll be grateful for this my whole life. I'll never, ever forget what you've done for me.'

There were tears in Sam's eyes now, and she reached for Cora's hand, then put her glass down and held her other hand out to Wendy.

'Love you both so much,' she whispered.

'Love you too,' whispered Cora and Wendy in unison, and they all laughed.

'Oi, what's this love-in all about? Room for another one?' Alice suddenly appeared at Sam's shoulder, looking ridiculously glamorous as always in a white cat-suit and silver sandals, large platinum hoops swinging from her earlobes, her long blonde hair shimmering, glass-smooth.

They broke their little circle and pulled her in. She'd been a little hurt when they'd finally filled her in on what had been going on over the past few weeks, upset that she'd been left out, but she'd quickly recovered, declaring that as long as Sam was free, what did it matter? Everyone now knew the astounding truth, and while there were so many bizarre twists and turns in the story, the fact that Sam and Miranda were sisters was the one that most were still trying to get their heads around. When she'd arrived at the party earlier, and once the whoops and cheers of delight at her appearance had died down, Sam had made a little speech, partly to thank everyone for their role in freeing her, but also – as she wryly put it – 'to stop me having to repeat myself a million times during the course of the evening.'

She was, she said, still feeling very fragile about the whole Miranda situation, and would find it hard to forgive her for what she had done to Marcus.

'I still find it difficult to think about, knowing now that

when I went into Pope's Meadow that night, Marcus was already dead, lying hidden in the trees. I'm so grateful that I didn't stumble across his body, so glad I can remember him the way he was before Miranda did what she did that awful night.'

She paused and took a deep breath, as everyone in the room stood silently, hearts aching for her and the anguish she must be feeling.

'But, at the end of the day, it seems we are sisters, Miranda and I,' she said. 'And I never had a sister, and I always longed for one, growing up. It's been a little odd, hearing about these feelings she had for me, but I know she was just confused. The weird thing is that I definitely felt something for her too – we had a connection, right from the start. I know she'll be locked up for a long time, but maybe one day in the not too distant future I'll feel ready to go and see her, make some sort of peace with her. That's all I can say about that for now.'

She had also announced that she and her mum – Ellen standing proudly by, grinning widely and nursing a sweet sherry – had decided that they would at some point make the trip to New York, to meet Clare Henderson, her birth mother.

'Mum will always be my mum, my wonderful, supportive, always-there-for-me mum, but maybe Clare can be a small part of my life too, now,' she said, and Ellen had nodded vigorously, wiping away a tear.

Now, as chatter and laughter filled the room, Sam suddenly waved her arm in the air, a slim silver bangle with a heart charm dangling from it encircling her wrist.

'I forgot to mention this, when I made my little speech.'

'It's nice,' said Cora. 'Where did that come from?'

'It was Sally's. My other sister. How weird, to be able

to say that. The solicitor sent her stuff round earlier. Thanks so much, Cora, for passing on my details to him. There wasn't much, and I'm going to take the rest over to Clare in New York when we eventually visit. But I didn't think she'd mind if I kept this. I'm going to collect my stillborn sister's ashes from the Wellford Clinic at some point too, if I can. And I want to visit Sally's grave – will you come with me, one of you?'

'We all will, Sam.' Alice put her arm round Sam, and squeezed. 'I'm so happy to have you back. When are you coming back to work?'

'Monday, I hope. Need my ace producer back in the hot seat.' Betsy suddenly joined the group, resplendent in a tight red dress and matching lipstick.

'You bet,' said Sam. 'Just try and stop me.' She held her glass out to Betsy's, and they clinked.

'Fabulous,' Betsy said. 'I need you to help keep this lot in line – did you know Cora's been claiming for sessions with hookers on her expenses forms?'

'WHAT?'

The expression on Sam's face was so astounded that Cora nearly spat out her mouthful of wine. Across the room, there was an explosion of laughter as Nathan, Scott and Rodney, who'd been regaling a group of producers and runners with tales of life on the road, reached the climax of their latest story. Rosie and Nicole, fresh off the train from Cheltenham with husbands in tow, hovered by the buffet table, piling their plates high.

In another corner, Adam was deep in conversation with Joel Anderson. Cora fervently hoped there'd be no mention of *the kiss*, but was pretty sure Joel would never tell. That darned kiss would just have to remain her guilty little secret. Joel was a good man, but Adam was the one for her. She watched him across the room as he threw back his head and laughed, his handsome face relaxed and happy. She loved him so much, and although the past few weeks had been tough at times, he had finally listened to her, trusted her, taken action even though it could have led to him getting into real trouble. She had thanked him last night, thanked him quite passionately and for rather a long time. She blushed slightly at the memory, just as he turned to catch her eye, and winked. She winked back.

'I love you,' she mouthed.

'Love you too,' he mouthed back, and blew her a kiss.

Cora mimed catching it, and pressed her fingers to her lips, then turned back to her friends, smiling. All the dramas in my life seem to end with a party, she thought, remembering a similar event last year, after Jeanette Kendrick's murder investigation had been wrapped up. She stood quietly for a moment, enjoying the happy scenes around her, and her mind drifted to Dr Ana Taylor, without whom none of this would be happening. If she hadn't decided to tell Cora the truth, the truth she'd kept hidden for so many years, Sam would still be in prison, there was no doubt about that. When Kymani Campbell had gone round to Clare Henderson's New York apartment to break the news about Miranda, he had asked Clare if she was intending to take any action. The woman had apparently sat very quietly for a full five minutes, thinking, before turning to the private detective and announcing her decision.

'She said no,' Kymani had told Cora on the phone, just an hour before the party started. 'She said that although it was a terrible thing to do, she knew that Ana had done the right thing. She said she could never have coped with more than one child, that yes, she would almost certainly have abandoned that one too, along with Sam. And that therefore, it had all worked out, in the end. So it seems

397

your Dr Ana is off the hook, Cora.'

I'll go and see her again, next week, tell her I'm not going to report her to the police and that she can stop worrying, Cora thought. She deserves that. Maybe I'll pick up those ashes for Sam while I'm there. And I hope Eleanor is OK. I'll stop by and see her too. All she ever did was want a child, and she loves Miranda so much. This must all be so hard for her too, but maybe a reassurance that the police won't be getting involved with the whole baby-stealing thing might ease her distress, just a little.

'Hey you, what's on your mind? Come and join the party.' Sam looped her arm through Cora's. Somebody had turned the music up, and people were starting to dance, Rodney boogying past wearing what could only be described as a red and white-striped nightshirt over black leather jeans. Behind him, Scott tried to copy his moves, a bright red lipstick kiss mark on his shiny, shaved head. He winked at Cora as he passed, and mouthed something.

'What did he say? I didn't get that,' said Cora, frowning.

'He said "made the deadline after all", I think,' said Sam. She looked at Cora, eyes shining. 'And you did, didn't you? The biggest, most important deadline you ever tried to make, and you did it. You bloody did it, girl. I thought for a while you might miss this one, but you didn't let me down.'

Cora grinned. 'I thought I might miss it too, for a while. But I never have, have I? And while I have breath in my body, I never will.'

Then she grabbed Sam's hand, and dragged her into the dancing crowd.

THE END

398

Gripping Crime Fiction from

Áccent Press

'Compelling, sharp, original – and very very funny' *Caroline Smailes*

Sex, SPOOKS & Sauvignon

ADVENTURES OF AN ACCIDENTAL MEDIUM

TRACY WHITWELL

SUNDAYS ARE SO ROTTEN

So I open my eyes and it's Sunday morning. Well, it's ten a.m. My mam would say that was nearly lunchtime. I'm still tired. I didn't go out last night, but I had three buckets of Merlot, talked rubbish at Milo over the phone, then watched *The Hairdresser's Husband* again. I love that film. Right now I have a jet black cat wrapped around my head. Inka has been licking my hair; it's streaked with damp, and I'm seeping tears the way my washing machine leaks wet foam if a sock gets stuck in the seal. I'm not sobbing. Tears are simply brimming and cascading steadily into my pillow, soaking it, and me, in brine.

Seconds ago I was in a field. The grass was warm and there were daisies. I was in Saltwell Park, a big, sprawling, beautiful place with a lake, ducks, rowing boats, greenery, swings and a fairy castle in the middle of it. I spent my childhood playing there and, just moments ago, I'd been back there with my friend Frank. Repeating his name in my head is enough to wrack a sob. We were eating egg sandwiches by the octopus tree. We were sitting on a red tartan picnic rug and he was laughing at me, smiling his goofy smile, because I was singing a song by The Smiths. He was joining in. It was 'What Difference Does It Make?' All we did was make the jangling sounds of the Johnny Marr guitar riff together.

'Dang-a-dang-a-dang-a-dang-danga-danga-dang-dang…'

Then he grabbed my hand, said, 'You're mental' and I woke up.

Frank died in a stupid car crash three years ago, and he was only thirty-two, so I still get a bit messed up when I see him in a dream. It happens every couple of months. They seem to be getting less frequent, but I always wake up wishing I'd given him the biggest squeezy hug in the world. Sometimes I think he's fooling with me. I never went out with him when he was alive; he was far too fickle, so now he plays hard to get with the whole cuddle thing. Sometimes I hear him talking to me in my head. I know I'm making it up, but it's still nice to hear his voice. I don't want to forget him.

I get up and mooch, then sob on my blood red velvet chair for a good ten minutes, filter coffee in hand, sunshine piercing through the mucky brown slats. I wonder if I should run a feather duster over them as I hiccough. I can multi-task when I weep – it's a talent. I miss Frank a lot, especially when I dream about him, but I am also a neurotic bitch and those blinds need a wipe.

Once I've mopped my face and my frog's eyes have un-swelled, I pull myself out of the misery chair and let in some light. My sitting room's bay window opens on to a teensy front garden and privet hedge two feet away. After that is my street, East View Road, a narrow row of terraced maisonettes, pretty and quaint with walls like paper (I can hear my next door neighbours breathe) and tiny back yards opening out on to each other with low, lichen-covered fences separating one from the next.

I rent it on my own, since the complete bastard I used to love moved out and left me to cover the huge rent, but ended the snide comments about my 'funny shape' and 'awful taste in mirrors'. He was actually much more nasty than that, but that's how petty it got before I eventually told him to get lost. Now I'm wandering about in leggings and a vest top, what passes for jim-jams these days, and pretty much deciding that the best way to cheer myself is to call Elsa. Elsa is my buddy, of sorts, and she's a character. She is so pathetically trend-conscious that she never wears a flat shoe, never gets bigger than a British size eight and always has sunglasses worth more than my car. (Bearing in mind I've owned spoons worth more than my old, but perfectly serviceable, car.)

I call her and she answers on the third ring. Funnily enough, she's another borderline alcoholic but still, most days, gets up to go to the gym before seven a.m. Almost all of my friends are nut-jobs of one kind or another, but she makes me laugh when she's not having life-sapping nervous breakdowns. She sounds groggy.

'Hi, Tanz.'

I hate my name. My mam called me Tania, barely a millimetre behind Annie as the blandest name she could have landed me with. Plus, no middle name. My dad I've forgiven, men are shit with names, but my mam could have had more imagination. Tanz is the only permutation I can stand.

'Hiya. Wild night? You sound tired…'

'Work. A stupid article for *Woman and Home* about housework. I hate housework. And women.'

I laugh.

'You want to meet me for lunch? I'm feeling rotten.'

'What's wrong?'

'Nowt. I just fancy some chips and wine.'

'Well, if you put it that way. Half twelve at Minnie's?'

'Yay! See you then.'

I feel better already. Warm day, and Sunday lunch

covered. I will endeavour not to think about Frank being so sweet in my dream. If I don't think, I won't cry.

One good thing is that I can be summery today. It's June and it's lovely out there. As soon as it's not cold I have flip flops welded to my feet. My latest faves are decorated with tarnished silver sequins and butterflies. I slip on my white hippy skirt with a little top. I'm addicted to comfort which is why I refuse to walk down to Minnie's in my best wedges, which will bring me out in blisters in 2.3 seconds. Elsa always looks glam, so I slick on a bit of gloss and layer on the mascara. What I can't do is make myself look tanned. Elsa has olive skin. Naturally, I resemble a bottle of slightly pink milk. Only false tan changes this, but I'm rubbish at applying it. My legs often sport the 'giraffe effect'. Not that I like showing my legs, anyway. I hate my knees.

When I open my front door I'm hit with an unexpected wave of gratitude. The warm air is only part of it. I'm grateful I'm alive and I'm grateful my ex doesn't live here any more. I always throw up some thanks to the gods when I get this feeling. When you moan as much as I do you have to balance the books a bit when you have a moment of clarity.

Fast, funny, spooky and disturbing: meet Tanz, Geordie actress turned accidental psychic, as she tries to cope with the voices in her head, especially when they lead her to a crime and into danger...

Tracy Whitwell is an actress who has worked in British film and television, including hit shows Playing the Field, Soldier Soldier and Peep Show. She has written for radio, stage and television and loves directing music videos. She lives in London with partner Don Gilet and their son.

For more information about
Jackie Kabler

and other **Accent Press** titles

please visit

www.accentpress.co.uk